"There are some things best left alone."

What could Ruby have meant? What could there be in a nursery that required that it be kept locked up?

Anne reached for the ring of keys that hung inside the door. The soft clink as it came free from the hook seemed to echo loudly through the kitchen, and she quickly silenced the sound with her hand, then hurried back toward the stairs.

She could sense something different as soon as she reached the second floor landing. She paused once more, listening, but the house was quiet, and outside the insects had begun softly chirping once again. And yet, as she started along the corridor toward the door to the nursery, a sense of unease—stronger than the vague guilt she had felt earlier—pervaded her mind.

Perhaps she should give it up, and simply put the nursery out of her mind. But she knew she couldn't.

Steeling herself for whatever she might find, she walked quickly to the locked nursery door. The eighth key fit. She twisted it in the lock, then turned the knob and pushed the door open a crack.

Inside, the room was pitch black, and Anne felt along the wall for a light switch. A moment later the room filled with a brilliant white light, and Anne pushed the door wide.

And screamed.

By John Saul

THE
UNLOVED

JOHN SAUL

BANTAM BOOKS
NEW YORK · TORONTO · LONDON · SYDNEY · AUCKLAND

THE UNLOVED
A Bantam Book / July 1988

ISBN 0-553-27261-6

Published simultaneously in the United States and Canada

Bantam Books are published by Bantam Books, a division of Bantam Doubleday Dell Publishing Group, Inc. Its trademark, consisting of the words "Bantam Books" and the portrayal of a rooster, is Registered in U.S. Patent and Trademark Office and in other countries. Marca Registrada. Bantam Books, 666 Fifth Avenue, New York, New York 10103.

PRINTED IN THE UNITED STATES OF AMERICA

O   0 9 8 7

**For Michael, Jane,
and Linda**

**May the second decade
be as wonderful
as the first**

CHAPTER 1

She was in the darkness somewhere, moving slowly toward him. Though he couldn't see her—he never saw her, never until the last minute—he could feel her coming. It was almost as if he could smell her, but that wasn't it either, for the smell—the strange musky odor that filled his nostrils—was his own fear, not the scent of *her*.

He wanted to hide from her, but knew that he couldn't. He'd tried that before and it had never worked. And yet now, as he felt her presence creeping ever closer, he tried to remember why he'd never been able to hide.

Nothing came into his mind. No memories; no images. Just the certain knowledge that he'd tried to hide before, and failed.

But maybe this time . . .

He tried to think, tried to remember where he was. But again there was no memory, no feeling of place. Only the blackness curling around him, making him want to shrink into himself and disappear.

Suddenly a streak of light cut through the darkness, and he shaded his eyes with a hand, trying to shield himself from the stabbing glare. Then, through the blinding light, he saw the angry visage, the woman's hate-twisted face as she stared down at him.

The door was pulled wider, and the light surrounded him, washing away the shadows that had failed to hide him. The woman stood before him, and though she didn't speak, his hands dropped away from his face and he looked directly up at her.

"Why are you here?" he heard her demand. "You know I don't want you here!"

He tried to think, tried to remember where he was. He looked around furtively, hoping the woman wouldn't see his eyes flickering about as if he might be searching for a means to escape.

The room around him looked strange—unfinished—the rough wood of its framing exposed under the tattered remains of crumbling tarpaper. He'd been in this place before—he knew that now. Still, he didn't know where the room was, or what it might be.

But he knew the woman was angry with him again, and in the deepest recesses of his mind, he knew what was going to happen next.

The woman was going to kill him.

He wanted to cry out for help, but when he opened his mouth, no scream emerged. His throat constricted, cutting off his breath, and he knew if he couldn't fight the panic growing within him, he would strangle on his own fear.

The woman took a step toward him, and he cowered, huddling back against the wall. A slick sheen of icy sweat chilled his back, then he felt cold droplets creeping down his arms. A shiver passed over him, and a small whimper escaped his lips.

His sister.

Maybe his sister would come and rescue him.

But she was gone—something had happened to her, and he was alone now.

Alone with his mother.

He looked fearfully up.

She seemed to tower above him, her skirt held back as if she were afraid it might brush against him and be soiled. Her hands were hidden in the folds of the skirt, but he knew what they held.

The axe. The axe she would kill him with.

He could see it then—its curved blades glinting in the light from the doorway, its long wooden handle clutched in his mother's hands. She wasn't speaking to him now, only staring at him. But she didn't need to speak, for he knew what she wanted, knew what she'd always wanted.

"Love me," he whispered, his voice so tremulous that he could hear the words wither away as quickly as they left his lips. "Please love me. . . ."

His mother didn't hear. She never heard, no matter how many times he begged her, no matter how often he tried to tell her he was sorry for what he'd done. He would apologize for anything—he knew that. If only she would hear him, he'd tell her whatever she wanted to hear. But even as he tried once more, he knew she wasn't hearing, didn't want to hear.

She only wanted to be rid of him.

The axe began to move now, rising above him, quivering slightly, as if the blade itself could anticipate the splitting of his skull, the crushing of his bones as they gave way beneath the weapon's weight. He could see the steel begin its slow descent, and time seemed to stand still.

He had to do something—had to move away, had to ward off the blow. He tried to raise his arms, but even the air around him seemed thick and unyielding now, and the blade was moving much faster than he was.

Then the axe crashed into his skull, and suddenly nothing made sense anymore. Everything had turned upside down.

It was his mother who cowered on the floor, gazing fearfully up at him as he brought the blade slashing down upon her.

It was he who felt the small jar of resistance as the axe struck her skull, then moved on, splitting her head like a melon. A haze of red rose up before him, and he felt fragments of her brains splatter against his face.

He opened his mouth and, finally, screamed—

He was sitting straight up in bed, the sheets tangled around him, his body clammy with the same icy sweat he'd felt in the dream. Before him the image of his mother's shattered skull still hung in the darkness, then was washed away as the room filled with light.

"Kevin?" he heard his wife ask, then felt her hand on his arm. "Kevin, what is it? Are you all right?"

Kevin Devereaux shook off the last vestiges of the dream and got out of bed. Though the mid-July night was hot, he was shivering. He wrapped himself in a robe before he answered Anne, his voice hoarse. "It was a dream. I thought my mother was trying to kill me, but in the end, I killed her." He turned to face her. "I killed her," he repeated, his voice echoing oddly. "I killed my mother."

"But it was only a dream," Anne replied. She reached over and fluffed up his crumpled pillow, then tugged the sheets straight. "Come back to bed and forget it. We all have strange dreams, but they don't mean anything. Besides," she added, "the way you feel about your mother, I'm amazed you don't have that dream every night."

Kevin tried to force a smile he didn't feel. "I did, for a while," he said. "When I was a kid I used to wake up with it all the time. They finally had to give me a private room at school, because my roommate said I screamed so loud he couldn't sleep. But I haven't had it since I was sixteen or seventeen. I thought it was over with."

Anne patted the spot next to her on the bed. "Now, come on. Whatever brought it on, it's all over with now, and you've got to get some sleep."

But Kevin only shook his head and knotted the belt of the robe around his waist. "It was different this time," he said. "When I was little I always dreamed Mother was trying to kill me, and I always woke up just before it happened. But this time it all changed. This time, right at the end, I was killing her, and I didn't wake up until she was dead."

Anne's eyes met his, and the smile that had been playing tentatively at the corners of her mouth disappeared. "You're serious, aren't you?" she asked. "You really think it means something."

Kevin spread his hands helplessly. "I wish I knew," he said. "I just have this feeling that maybe something's happened to her." He glanced at the clock, wondering if he ought to call his sister, then dismissed the idea. At three-thirty in the morning all he would do was give her a good scare.

But he knew he couldn't go back to sleep. Not yet.

Not until he had thought about the dream, thought about what it might mean, figured out why, after all these years, it had come back to him. He leaned down and brushed Anne's lips with his. "Go back to sleep, honey. I'm going to go down and raid the refrigerator."

Anne gazed at him for a moment, her eyes reflecting her concern. "If you're going to sit down there and brood, you'd tell me, wouldn't you?"

Kevin chuckled in spite of himself, and kissed her again. "All right, so maybe I'm going to brood a little bit. I'm forty years old, and I have a right to brood, don't I? Now go back to sleep, and don't worry about me. I'll be fine."

He switched off the lamp on Anne's bed table, slipped out the door and moved silently down the hall past his children's rooms, then down the stairs. But instead of going to the kitchen, he went into the living room and settled himself into his favorite chair—a big leather wing chair just like the one in the library, when he was growing up.

Just like the one his mother had never let him sit in.

But he was forty years old now, and his mother was nearly eighty, and he should have forgotten about that chair—and everything else—a long time ago.

And he thought he had, until tonight.

Now he realized that he hadn't forgotten anything, and that the dream had, indeed, meant something.

It meant that he still hated his mother as much as he ever had. He still wished she were dead.

Lucinda Willoughby jerked awake and instinctively glanced at the large man's watch on her wrist. Three-thirty, which meant she'd been asleep for more than two hours. Not that it mattered, really, for the old woman in the bed across the room usually slept straight through the night, and Lucinda didn't see what difference it could make if she herself dozed off for a few minutes. And she certainly had a right to, considering the way Helena Devereaux treated her. After all, she was a nurse, not a servant.

Her nap properly rationalized, Lucinda was just reopening the book that had fallen closed in her lap when the sound that had roused her from her catnap was repeated.

"Don't you hear me, missy?" Helena's querulous voice demanded. "I don't pay you to sleep all night, you know!"

The book snapped shut, and Lucinda heaved herself to her feet. "I wasn't sleeping, ma'am," she began, but then fell silent at the wrath she saw in Mrs. Devereaux's eyes.

"Don't tell me what you were doing," the old woman snapped. "I'm not dead yet, and I'm not blind!" Helena Devereaux was sitting bolt upright now, and Lucinda could see her reaching for the glass of water on the table next to the bed. Moving more quickly than her bulk should have allowed, the nurse snatched up the glass just before the old woman's fingers could close around it.

"How dare you?" Helena hissed. "You give me that this instant, do you hear?"

Taking a deep breath and counting silently to ten, Lucinda reluctantly handed the water glass to her patient.

Instantly, Helena hurled the contents of the glass into the nurse's face, then flung the glass across the room, where it shattered against the wall. "Now where is he?" Helena demanded. "Where is Kevin?"

Lucinda gasped, staring in shock at the old woman. She knew who Kevin was—there wasn't anyone in Devereaux, South Carolina, who didn't. But he hadn't been there in years, and how could Lucinda Willoughby be expected to know where he was?

"I want him," Helena rasped, her voice trembling. "I'm dying, and I want to see my son before it's too late. I want to see him!"

Suddenly Lucinda thought she understood, and reached out to take the old woman's shriveled hand in her own. "Now, Miss Helena, you just calm down," she said in her best professional voice. "You're not going to die, not while I'm taking care of you. I've never lost a patient yet, and I sure don't intend to start with you." As she talked, she took the old woman's pulse. It was slightly erratic, but Lucinda knew that was only a symptom of the old woman's anger, not an imminent heart attack.

"I won't calm down," Helena snapped, jerking her hand away. "I'm dying, and you know it! I want to see Kevin before I die!" Her voice rose to a high-pitched screech, and her eyes searched the table for something else to throw. "You get him for me, do you hear? It's your job, you lazy, good-for-nothing—"

"Mother! Mother, what's wrong?"

Helena's eyes snapped away from the nurse and fixed on her daughter, who stood at the open door to the room, clutching a robe to her bosom. "Kevin!" she said once more. "I want Kevin. I want to see him, and I want to talk to him!"

Marguerite Devereaux frowned, and glanced inquiringly at Lucinda, who could only shrug helplessly. Helena Devereaux did not miss the silent exchange, and her eyes blazed with renewed fury. "Don't either of you understand plain English?" she demanded. "I'm dying, and I want to see my son!" She fell back against the pillows, her angry outburst having drained her energies. Her frail bosom heaved erratically and her breathing took on the labored raling of approaching death. Instantly Lucinda Willoughby grasped her wrist, her strong fingers feeling once more for the old woman's pulse. A second later she found it, fluttering wildly as the pumping of her heart raged out of control.

"A glass of water, Miss Marguerite," she ordered. "Quickly." Her anger forgotten, she gently lifted the old lady into a slightly raised position, plumping up the pillows behind her. By the time Marguerite returned from the bathroom, Lucinda had Helena's medicine ready. She deftly slid the pills between her patient's thin lips, then held the glass as the old woman sucked in enough water to wash the pills down. A moment later Helena Devereaux's breathing returned to normal and her pulse evened out. Only when Lucinda was certain the immediate danger had passed did she signal Marguerite into the hall with her eyes.

"What happened?" Marguerite asked anxiously when Lucinda had pulled the door shut.

"I don't know. I'd fallen asleep, and when I woke up, she was screaming at me."

"But why?" Marguerite pressed. Then, remembering her

mother's words, she reached out to grasp the nurse by the arm. "Is it true?" she asked, her voice trembling. "Is she dying?"

Lucinda Willoughby hesitated only a moment, then nodded. "She could have died just now," she said. She paused, then decided there was no reason not to go on. "It's her temper, Miss Marguerite. If she'd just learn to stay calm, she could go on for years yet. But she won't. She'll keep flyin' off the handle at folks, and every time she does, she'll just make herself worse. Since we all know she isn't going to change, we better face up to the fact that she's going to die."

Marguerite stood perfectly still for a moment, letting the nurse's words sink in. She knew, of course, that it was true—had known it for years now. Her mother couldn't live forever. But there had always been something about the old woman that seemed eternal; Marguerite couldn't quite imagine the house she'd lived in all her life without her mother's presence. And yet, a few minutes before, she'd seen mortality in her mother's face, seen death stroking the old woman's sunken cheeks.

And her mother had been demanding to see Kevin.

It was the first time Helena Devereaux had spoken her son's name in more than twenty years.

Marguerite turned away from the nurse and started slowly along the wide second-floor corridor toward her own room. Almost unconsciously her right hand went to her hip, her fingers pressing at the pain. The sharp stabbing, like a hot knife driven deep into the bone, had been part of her life for so many years that she rarely noticed it anymore. Except that tonight it seemed even sharper than usual, and she could feel the lameness in her right leg shooting all the way down into her ankle.

Resolutely she put the pain out of her mind and tried to straighten her gait. At the door to her room she felt a touch on her shoulder and turned to see Ruby, the woman who had been in the house even before Marguerite was born, looking anxiously at her, her large, dark eyes reflecting her worry.

"What is it, Miss Marguerite?" Ruby asked softly. "Is it Miss Helena?"

Marguerite nodded and managed a sympathetic smile. "I'm afraid so, Ruby. I think—I think I'm going to have to call Kevin in the morning and ask him to come."

A slight gasp escaped Ruby's lips. "She asked for him? She spoke his name?"

Once again Marguerite nodded. "I wonder," she breathed, more to herself than to the old housekeeper. "I wonder if he'll come."

Ruby's lips pursed and her eyes narrowed. "He'll come," she replied. "And you won't need to call him, Miss Marguerite. He already knows Miss Helena's bad off."

Marguerite tipped her head slightly, examining Ruby's dark face in the soft glow of the tarnished brass sconces that lined the hallway. What was she talking about? "But he can't know," she said. "Ruby, none of us have even talked to Kevin for years."

"Don't matter," Ruby replied, her voice stolid. "He knows what's happening with his mother. He's a Devereaux, and that's the end of it. You see if I'm not right, Miss Marguerite. You see if he doesn't call himself, come morning." Without waiting for a reply, Ruby turned away and a moment later disappeared down the back stairs to her room, next to the kitchen.

When she was gone, Marguerite retreated into her own bedroom, closing the door behind her. She took off the robe and slid back into her bed, pulling only a sheet over her body. Even the worn cotton felt heavy in the humid warmth of the summer night, but she left it where it was, taking a faint reassurance from its closeness. Outside, the droning of insects and tree frogs all but screened out the soft murmuring of the sea a few hundred yards away, and the sweet perfume of honeysuckle drifted around her.

She thought about Kevin then. It would be good to see him again, good to meet his family. He'd been gone far too long, and though she'd never told her mother, she'd missed him terribly.

But did it have to be her mother's death that brought him home?

It wasn't fair. She shouldn't have to lose her mother to regain her brother.

Still, she had to come to grips with the fact that her mother was going to die, whether Kevin came home or not.

It was a fact of life, and life was to be dealt with.

And whatever happened, Marguerite had always dealt with life as best she could, and never complained.

She would not begin complaining now.

She would accept whatever happened, and deal with it.

With the perfume of the honeysuckle and the sounds of the night lulling her senses, she drifted into sleep.

In her own room, Helena Devereaux did not sleep. Instead, she lay still in her bed, willing her heart to keep beating smoothly, just as she had willed most things in her life to happen according to her own choices. Until the last few months her will had been sufficient. But she was nearing the end now. She could feel her strength slipping away from her, feel her grip on Ruby and Marguerite loosening, just as her grip on life was loosening too. Now, as she lay in the darkness of her room, she wondered which she hated most— the fact of dying, or the fact of losing her control over events around her. Not that it mattered, of course, for in the end it added up to the same thing: death was the ultimate loss of control.

Memories drifted through her mind.

Her first meeting with Rafe Devereaux, when she'd been only sixteen. Rafe had been ten years older than she, darkly handsome and dashing, and he'd promised her the world. But all he'd been able to give her were the remnants of a worn-out plantation and a family heritage that had been meaningless to her. What did she care for Rafe's Huguenot ancestors and their long-faded antebellum glory? She'd assumed, during the first months after she'd married him, that after a year or so he'd take her to New York and use his influence on behalf of her career. But it turned out that he had no influence beyond Charleston, and even there the Devereauxes weren't on the best social lists. Then Marguerite was born, followed eight years later by Kevin, and her dreams had slowly faded away until all that was left of her dancing was the lessons she gave to her daughter.

Then, when Kevin was seven, Rafe had given up on life completely and killed himself. She'd covered it up, of course, cutting his hanged body down from the rafters in the barn and shoving it off the edge of the hayloft herself. The doctor, as she'd intended, had called his broken neck an accident, and never even noticed the traces of rope burns on his throat.

It wasn't until the next week that she'd discovered that even in death Rafe Devereaux had done nothing for her. The entire estate was left to her only in trust. She could keep it until she died, but then must pass it on, intact.

And so, in the fury that had sustained her from that day forward, she'd banished her son to boarding school and devoted her energies to Marguerite.

Marguerite, too, had failed her, and in the end— and she knew now that the end was very near—she had been left with nothing. Nothing but a weakening body that kept her confined to bed most of the time now, and a weakening spirit that was losing its ability to dominate. She could even see it in their eyes. They weren't afraid of her anymore, not really. They were only humoring her in her last days.

Well, she wasn't through yet.

She might not be able to control Marguerite much longer, but there was still Kevin.

She chuckled silently to herself as she realized that now, in the end, her long-dead husband was finally going to help her. In his own will he'd given her the tool she needed to maintain her power, even after her body submitted to its final failure.

The chuckle still echoing in her mind, she at last let herself give in to sleep.

The first light of dawn was just beginning to turn the eastern sky a silvery gray when Kevin heard the creaking of floorboards in the foyer. A moment later his daughter came into the room, rubbing the last vestiges of sleep from her eyes. Kevin watched her for a moment, marveling as he always did at how much she looked like his sister.

Julie was fifteen now, and her light brown eyes had taken on the same slant as Marguerite's. Her dark, slightly wavy hair framed her heart-shaped face in the same flattering manner that Marguerite's had, and her body was even molding into the same lithely muscular proportions that Marguerite had had at the same age—the result of endless hours at the barre. But Marguerite had practiced her ballet with a deep intensity that Julie had never felt, and that neither Kevin nor Anne had ever encouraged. Privately, though, Kevin thought his daughter was already a better dancer than his sister had ever been.

He smiled fondly at her in the brightening light. "Shall I mark this day on the calendar? The day Julie got up without anybody having to yell at her?"

Julie grinned self-consciously and plumped herself onto the sofa. "I had a nightmare," she admitted, blushing slightly at the confession. "I know it's dumb, but I was afraid to go back to sleep."

"Join the club," Kevin offered. "I've been sitting here since four o'clock, for exactly the same reason, and I was just thinking of going back to bed." He winked conspiratorially at his daughter. "On the other hand, there's the possibility that the two of us could whip up a truly fabulous breakfast and surprise your mother and brother."

Julie grinned her reply and followed her father into the kitchen, where she perched on a stool while he began expertly preparing eggs Benedict. "How come you never opened a restaurant? You cook better than anybody else."

Kevin shrugged. "Economics. The restaurant business is the fastest way to go broke ever invented by man, and it always struck me that I'd rather feed you and your brother off a steady income than wind up broke feeding a bunch of strangers. Of course, when you two grow up and your mother and I have thrown you both out of here, I might change my mind."

Julie took the whisk her father handed her and began stirring the Hollandaise sauce. "By then you'll be too old, won't you?" she asked with carefully studied innocence.

Kevin scowled deeply and did his best to sound offended.

"I beg your pardon. In ten years I'll be fifty. Fifty, in case you didn't know it, is now considered the bare beginnings of middle age, and—"

Julie giggled, her eyes rolling. "And old age doesn't start until eighty," she finished. Then her voice suddenly turned serious. "But don't you get tired of working for someone else?"

Once again Kevin shrugged. "The Shannon is a good hotel, and I run it pretty well."

"But you wish you owned it," Julie stated flatly, her eyes meeting his. "Jeff and I hear you and Mom talking sometimes, you know."

"Children are snoopy creatures, and shouldn't listen to things they're not supposed to hear," Kevin observed mildly. "Besides, if the opportunity ever came up, I'd open a restaurant—or, even better, an inn—in a minute. But so far the opportunity hasn't come up."

Julie grinned mischievously. "Maybe Grandma will die and leave you a lot of money," she suggested, then her eyes widened as she saw the blood drain from her father's face.

Kevin turned to her, his voice tight and the muscles in his jaw knotting. "That's a terrible thing to say."

"I—I'm sorry," Julie stammered. "I didn't mean it. It was just a joke, Dad."

"Not a funny one," he told her, angry now. "You should never joke about things like that—"

Suddenly Julie felt herself getting angry too. "Why not?" she demanded. "You don't even *like* Grandma! You're always talking about what a mean person she is and how she makes Aunt Marguerite take care of her. What's the big deal if I make a joke about her?" She slid off the stool and ran out of the kitchen.

For a long moment Kevin stayed where he was. He should go after Julie and apologize to her, for he knew what she'd said was the truth. If it hadn't been for the dream, he wouldn't have reacted to her words as he had.

So the dream was still bothering him.

He glanced at the clock. It was almost six-thirty.

Ruby would be up, fixing breakfast for Marguerite and his mother. If anything had happened, she would know.

Making up his mind, he reached for the phone. . . .

Ten minutes later he went slowly up the stairs and woke Anne. As soon as she saw his face, she knew something was terribly wrong.

"We have to go down there," Kevin said, his voice flat. "I just talked to Marguerite. She says Mother is dying and is asking for me. I can't put it off any longer. I have to go home."

Anne looked at her husband in silence for a moment, then pushed the covers aside and got out of bed.

So it was finally going to happen.

For the first time in the eighteen years of her marriage, she was going to meet her husband's family.

CHAPTER 2

"How much farther?" Jeff Devereaux demanded from the back seat of the Dodge station wagon. Outside, what seemed to him to be an endless expanse of flat land dotted with mossy pine trees rolled past. For the last two hours even looking at the wide sandy beach between the left side of the road and the sea beyond had bored him.

"You just asked that five minutes ago," Julie told him. "So if it was fifteen minutes then, how long is it now?"

"I wasn't asking you," Jeff retorted. "I was asking Mom."

"It doesn't matter who you asked. It's still ten minutes. Why can't you just be quiet and watch the scenery like everyone else?"

Jeff glared at his older sister, wishing for the millionth time that it were possible for an eight-year-old boy to beat up a fifteen-year-old girl. But whenever he'd tried, Julie just held him away from her and started laughing, which only made him madder. Well, maybe he couldn't pound her, but he didn't have to let her boss him around. "I don't have to do what you say," he grumbled. "You don't know everything."

"And you don't know *any*thing!" Julie shot back, then realized that was probably exactly the response Jeff had been hoping for. Before she could say any more, Anne twisted around in the front seat to give both her children a warning look.

"Ten more minutes," she said. "And we can do without any quarrels for the rest of the trip. All right?"

"I didn't start it," Jeff piped. "All I did was ask a question. How am I supposed to learn anything if I can't ask questions? Dad always says—"

In spite of herself, Anne began laughing. "All right, all right! I don't care who started it, I just don't want it to go any further. And if you want to ask questions, go ahead."

Jeff's response was instantaneous. "How come we've never been here before?"

Once again Julie answered her brother's question before her mother had a chance to say anything. "Because Dad doesn't like Grandmother," she said.

"Why not?" Jeff pressed. "What's wrong with her?"

Out of the corner of her eye Anne saw Kevin's jaw tighten, and his knuckles whiten as he squeezed the steering wheel. "It's not that," she said quickly, hoping to distract Jeff's attention. "It's just that it's a long way from Connecticut, and we've never really had the time."

"But we go on a vacation every year," Jeff argued. "Why couldn't we have come down here? It's a better beach than the one on Cape Cod."

"I thought you liked False Harbor," Anne replied, welcoming the chance to change the subject.

"It's okay," Jeff reluctantly agreed. Then he spotted a sign as they passed it: DEVEREAUX—10 MILES. "Wow," he breathed. "Is there really a whole town named after Dad?"

For the first time in more than an hour, Kevin spoke. "It's not named after me," he said, his voice tight and his words clipped. "It's named after my family, and it's been there for a couple of hundred years. And it's not much of a town."

The tone of his father's voice made Jeff glance uneasily at his sister, but Julie didn't seem to know what was wrong with their father either. "What's wrong with it?" he finally ventured.

"In a few minutes you'll see," Kevin replied. Then he lapsed back into the heavy silence he had maintained all morning. For the next ten miles no one in the car spoke.

And then, abruptly, Kevin pulled the car off the road and stopped. "There it is," he said. "That's Devereaux. That's where I grew up."

Jeff opened the back door and scrambled out, then climbed to the top of a low bank that separated the road from the beach.

Ahead, another half mile down the road, was a worn-looking collection of buildings, some of them almost hidden in a tangle of vines. He could see a church steeple, an Exxon sign, and what looked like a row of shabby stores. There was also a scattering of houses, most of them fairly run-down, a few of them clearly abandoned. He looked up at his father, who was standing beside him now, Jeff's disappointment clear on his face. "Is that all there is?" he asked.

"It goes on for about half a mile," Kevin told him. "But it all looks pretty much the same. I suppose there are still a few nice places, but it just keeps getting worse." He smiled wryly. "Still want to spend your vacation here?"

"But what happened to it?" Anne asked. "It looks like it must have been a nice town once."

"It was," Kevin agreed. "A long time ago, before I was born. Probably before my father was born. It used to be cotton plantations, until the land wore out."

"But which house is yours?" Julie asked. "Where do Grandmother and Aunt Marguerite live?"

"Out there," Kevin said quietly, turning away from the town and pointing to a low island two hundred yards off shore, connected to the mainland by a narrow causeway built up from the shallow seabed. "That's Sea Oaks, where I grew up."

Julie's eyes widened as she stared at the immense white house that dominated the north end of the island. From where they stood, only the chimneys and a few gables were visible, for the building was surrounded by enormous live oak trees, their branches heavily laden with streamers of Spanish moss. Dotted among the oaks were a few white-blooming magnolias and some pines, but it was the wide, spreading branches of the ancient oaks themselves that caught Julie's eye. They seemed to cradle the house, as if trying to protect it from something.

"It—It's a mansion," she breathed.

"It's a white elephant," Kevin replied. "In its day it served a purpose. Now it's just a huge house that's outlived its usefulness, and unless something's changed since last time I was here, it's getting just as run-down as the rest of the town."

Julie cocked her head and looked up at her father curiously. "But if Grandmother lives there, she must be rich, isn't she?"

Kevin's lips twisted into a smile that was both wry and bitter. "There hasn't been a rich Devereaux in three generations," he replied. "My grandfather and my father hung onto the island by selling off the rest of the property bit by bit. A hundred years ago the family owned most of the county, and before the Civil War, a lot more. By now there can't be much left except the island."

"Grandmother owns the whole island?" Jeff asked, his voice reflecting his awe. "All of it?"

For the first time that day Kevin grinned, for he suddenly remembered when he was Jeff's age and spent endless days exploring the hundred fifty acres of the island—discovering the ruined remains of the slave quarters which were all but lost in the overgrown tangle of vines that had long since been allowed to reclaim the once cultivated tracts; combing the beaches after storms, in search of lost treasures that might have washed up; hunting the marshes and patches of forest for rabbits, squirrels, and an occasional deer. For the first time since he had grown up, he saw the island through the eyes of a boy, and reached down to tousle Jeff's blond hair. "Every acre of it," he said. "And if you can't find anything to do out there, then you're going to be condemned to a life of boredom." His mood suddenly lighter, he winked at Anne. "Come on. Let's go see just how bad things have gotten in the decadent South."

A moment later the family was back in the car, moving slowly toward Devereaux. As they came into the town, it was apparent to Kevin that nothing had changed. The main street was just as he remembered it, slowly rotting away in the heat and humidity. There was a somnolence about the place; even the people seemed to move in slow motion. A dog slept in the middle of the road, flies buzzing around its head, but even when Kevin tooted the horn, the animal refused to bestir itself, and finally Kevin had to maneuver the station wagon around it.

It didn't occur to him until he had passed the animal that it might be dead.

Just like the town, he reflected silently to himself. The whole place is dead, but nobody's noticed.

The scratchy sounds of the final moments of *Swan Lake* emerged from the speaker of the old phonograph in the corner of the ballroom on the third floor of Sea Oaks, and Marguerite Devereaux glanced quickly at the clock. For the first time in her memory, the hour-long ballet class seemed to drag on interminably and she was actually looking forward to her girls going home. Of course, she'd had to leave them twice already, going down to the second floor to explain to her mother that they couldn't expect Kevin to arrive much before eleven, and she knew that in letting her excitement about Kevin's arrival distract her from the lesson, she wasn't being fair to the girls.

The girls—only five of them this year—were the center of Marguerite's life. Only when she was with them, carefully passing on to them all the dancing technique she herself had learned in her youth, was she able to forget the pain in her hip. Indeed, sometimes when she was teaching her girls, she would forget her ruined hip completely and once more find herself dancing as she had when she was young. Of course, it wasn't the same—her movements weren't nearly as smooth as they once had been—but the girls always watched her carefully, seeing what she was trying to show them, rather than what she was actually doing. And somehow, despite the clumsiness her lame leg inflicted upon her, they were able to understand what she wanted from them.

Often, after the class was over, the girls would stay at Sea Oaks for a while, listening as Marguerite talked to them about what a career in ballet could offer them.

"It can be the key to the world," she would often say. "The dance can take you anywhere you want to go. It can open a world of music and art and beauty that no one else ever sees."

And it was true, even for Marguerite, whose life as a dancer had been cut short before it truly began. For even here, in the faded elegance of the ballroom, where no ball had been held for more than thirty years, Marguerite could still escape into the music, transporting herself to the great theatres of the world.

Sometimes she would imagine herself in the Royal Ballet of Copenhagen, whirling across the stage of that small jewel box of a theatre in the heart of a city she had never seen but could clearly imagine. And it was her dreams, as well as her knowledge, that she was passing on to her students. They didn't have to stay in Devereaux, didn't have to give up their futures to the enervating torpor of the dying town.

And some of them hadn't. Three of her students had gone on from her tiny classes on the third floor of the ancient plantation house to study in New York, Paris, and London. One of her girls was a prima ballerina now, and in her room, hidden away in the bottom drawer of her bureau, Marguerite kept a scrapbook full of clippings.

Once in a while, when she found a girl of particular promise, she would take the scrapbook out and share the treasured clippings. "This can be you," she would say. "All it takes is work, my dear, and you can have everything."

With the work, Marguerite offered the girls endless patience, giving them as many hours of her time as they wanted, never too busy—or too tired—to rehearse them one more time, until every movement of every step was as perfect as she could make it.

Except today.

Today Kevin was coming, and though she was doing her best not to let her impatience show, she knew the girls could sense that something was taking her concentration from their lesson. And so, as the last notes of *Swan Lake* faded away, she smiled, and clapped her hands once in the gesture she always used to gain their attention. "I think that will be all for today," she said. "And I want to apologize to you. I know I haven't been quite myself this morning, and I know it hasn't been fair to you. But my brother is coming today, and

I haven't seen him for nearly twenty years. I'm afraid I'm a little excited. I—"

The harsh sound of the buzzer over the door sliced through her words, the buzzer her mother could use to summon her in an emergency. She smiled apologetically once again. "I guess I'm talking too much, aren't I? Well, thank you all for coming, and I'll try to be better focused next week. All right?"

She started toward the door, pausing to speak to each of the girls as they said good-bye to her. Jenny Mayhew— Marguerite's favorite, though she tried never to show it— hung back, pacing herself automatically to match her teacher's slow step as they made their way down the stairs.

"Does your brother have children?" Jenny asked when they were halfway down.

Marguerite smiled at the girl. "As a matter of fact, he does. A girl just your age, and an eight-year-old boy." A hint of a smile played around the corners of her mouth. "I suppose you were hoping it might be a boy about your age, weren't you?"

Jenny flushed, but Marguerite chuckled softly. "Don't try to fool me, Jenny. It wasn't all that long ago that I was your age, and I can tell you I'd a lot rather have had a new boy coming to town than a new girl. It always seemed we had entirely too many girls, and not enough boys to go around."

Jenny's flush gave way to a grin. "I bet you could have had any boy you wanted, Miss Marguerite."

"Well, I won't say I didn't," Marguerite replied. "Of course, after my hip went, so did the boys. It's amazing how unpopular a limp can make you."

Jenny gasped in embarrassment, but Marguerite only laughed again. "Oh, come on, it wasn't the end of the world, even if it seemed like it at the time. And if I hadn't had the accident, I wouldn't be teaching, would I? And then I never would have gotten to know all of you."

"But you would have had a career—" Jenny started to protest, but Marguerite shook her head.

"It doesn't matter. I haven't had a bad life, and whatever I might have done couldn't have been as much fun as having you girls around.''

They were on the second floor now. A thin, high-pitched voice pierced through the door at the far end. ''Marguerite? Where are you? I want you!''

''Oh, dear,'' Marguerite whispered. ''Now I'm in trouble, aren't I? Well, you run along, Jenny, and I'll see you on Thursday.'' Giving the girl's hand an affectionate squeeze, Marguerite waited until Jenny had started down toward the first floor, then hurried up the hall to try to calm her mother once more.

She found Helena sitting up in bed, glaring angrily at Lucinda Willoughby, whose face was a mask of controlled indignation. On the floor at the nurse's feet were the remains of the breakfast the old woman hadn't touched all morning.

''She's fired,'' Helena snapped as soon as Marguerite came into the room. ''I won't have her in my house another moment!''

''Now, Mother,'' Marguerite began, but Helena cut her off.

''Don't you patronize me, Marguerite! This is my house, and I will have what I want.''

Marguerite opened her mouth, but for a moment no words came out. Finally she turned to Lucinda. ''What happened?'' she asked, though she was almost certain she already knew.

''I came in to ask her if her breakfast was all right, and found it on the floor.''

Helena's eyes sparkled with anger, and she drew herself up in the bed. ''I told her it was cold, and she took it upon herself to tell me I should have eaten it when it was hot! I won't have a—''

''All right, Mother,'' Marguerite broke in, struggling to control her own voice. ''I'll have Ruby take care of the mess, and we'll start looking for someone else this afternoon.'' With her eyes she signaled Lucinda into the hallway, then joined her a moment later, after listening to Helena's demands as to the sort of person who must replace ''the incompetent trash you hired.''

''I'm sorry, Lucinda,'' she said as she accompanied the

nurse down the main stairs. "I know it wasn't your fault, but I don't see what I can do—"

"It's all right, Marguerite," Lucinda replied. "If she hadn't fired me, I would have quit anyway. And not for the reasons you're thinking," she added quickly, seeing the concern in Marguerite's eyes. "I've dealt with a lot of patients and been called a lot of names. It doesn't bother me—sick people get that way, and I don't blame them. It's tiring being ill, and you have to make allowances for that. But for her, having me around isn't going to help." Lucinda sighed, and shook her head sadly. "She's just been getting madder and madder, and that's not good for her. With some people a little good, honest temper can help. But not for someone like her, with a heart that could go any minute. I'll think on it and see if I can come up with someone who can deal with her."

They were on the wide veranda that ran the length of the front of the house now, and Lucinda started down the front steps. Marguerite watched her as she got into her car, and waved to her as she began driving away. She was just about to go back into the house when she saw the station wagon coming along the road from the causeway, and knew immediately who it was.

She hurried down the steps, unwilling to wait even an extra few seconds to greet her brother.

"Well, I hope you're proud of yourself, Miss Helena," Ruby said as she carefully picked the last scraps of the ruined breakfast out of the threadbare carpet that covered the oak floor of the bedroom. "Now you got rid of Lucinda, so me and Miss Marguerite can do even more than we's doing already."

"Which is little enough," the old woman observed, lowering herself back onto her pillows. "And Lucinda isn't the only person who can be fired."

Ruby carefully got to her feet and glanced scornfully at the woman for whom she had worked for more than fifty years.

"Don't rightly see how you can fire Miss Marguerite, and there ain't anybody else left in the place."

"There's you, Ruby," Helena snapped. "I'll thank you to keep a civil tongue in your head when you speak to me."

"And I'll thank you for the same courtesy, though I know perfectly well I won't get it," Ruby replied. "Only thing that keeps me from quitting is that there ain't no other jobs around here. And I don't see how I can leave Miss Marguerite alone with the likes of you."

A vein in Helena's forehead began throbbing, and she pushed herself once more into a sitting position. "Don't you dare speak to me that way," she raged. "Don't you forget your place in this house—"

"And don't you either," the old servant snapped, her own eyes glinting with anger now. "You can't fire me, and you know it. And since I ain't going to quit, the best thing you can do is relax and try to enjoy whatever life you got left in you!" She moved closer to the bed, and Helena shrank back, pressing herself into the pillows. "Now, I'm willing to go on about my business and go on taking care of you and Miss Marguerite just like I've always done, but I won't have you throwing no more food around and driving no more nurses away! You think you're such a high and mighty aristocrat, seems to me you better start acting like one!"

She was about to say more when a car horn honked outside, and then the sound of voices floated in through the open window. Ruby smiled thinly. "Sounds like Mr. Kevin's finally come home," she said softly, her eyes fixing once more on the old woman in the bed.

Her words seemed to galvanize Helena Devereaux. She threw back the bed covers and swung herself around so her legs hung over the bed, though her feet didn't quite touch the floor. "Help me," she demanded. "Help me get dressed!"

Ruby's eyes widened. "Get dressed? Miss Helena, you ain't been dressed in five years! What are you thinking of?"

"He's my son," Helena insisted, her eyes burning feverishly now. "I am not going to greet my son wrapped in this rag and sitting in this bed. Help me!"

She tried to get to her feet but staggered, nearly falling,

until Ruby moved forward and grasped her under the arms. Moving slowly, the old housekeeper guided Helena across the room and lowered her to the chair in front of the vanity. Immediately Helena's hands began searching the top drawer for her comb and brush and the box of makeup she hadn't touched for years. A minute later she began brushing the thin wisps of hair that only partially concealed her pink scalp. "The black dress," she said. "Find the black silk, and the shoes that go with it. And my jet beads. I'll wear them, with the garnet brooch." She glanced into the mirror and saw Ruby still standing behind her. "Do as I say!" she commanded, her voice rising shrilly. "Now, damn you!"

As she began applying her makeup, Ruby went to the closet and searched for the dress.

Fifteen minutes later Helena examined herself in the mirror. "Nothing's really changed, has it?" she asked, her voice so soft that Ruby wasn't certain she meant to speak aloud at all. "I haven't changed, and the house hasn't changed. It will be almost as if he never left. We'll all go on again, just as if he'd never been gone!"

"But he's only here for a visit," the old servant replied. "He ain't going to stay."

Helena's eyes flickered in the mirror, then fixed on the servant. "Yes, he will," she whispered darkly. "He's a Devereaux, and no Devereaux has ever left Sea Oaks."

"Mr. Kevin did," Ruby reminded her. "And you can believe he'll leave again."

"He won't," Helena insisted. "I want him to stay here, and I'll see to it he stays." She turned and struggled to her feet. "How do I look?"

Ruby stared at her mistress, wondering what to say. Helena's hair—once luxurious, but now thin and limp—hung down around her shoulders, framing a face that had been turned into a garish parody of the beauty she had once been. The skin that years ago had glowed with a deep clarity was now covered with a mask of white powder. Thick blotches of rouge were dabbed on each cheek and a bright red slash of lipstick was smeared across the thin line of her mouth. Whatever remnants of dignified beauty might have remained to her had been completely lost in her vain attempt to turn back the ravages of time.

"Fine," Ruby breathed at last, knowing that what Helena saw in the mirror bore no resemblance to reality. "You look just fine."

Helena smiled at her. "Then I'm ready to go downstairs, aren't I?"

Once again Ruby's mouth opened in surprise. "Downstairs?" she repeated. "But Miss Helena—"

"Don't argue with me," Helena commanded. "If I wish to greet my son downstairs, I shall. Now give me your arm."

Almost against her own will, Ruby allowed the old woman to grasp her arm, then walked her slowly out of the bedroom and down the hall to the main stairs. Supporting Helena as best she could, she helped her into the seat of the ancient chair lift that had been installed in the house years earlier. She fastened the safety strap around the old woman's waist and waited as Helena arranged the flowing skirt of the old black silk dress. Finally, when Helena nodded her readiness, Ruby pushed the brass button at the top of the stairs.

Instantly the machinery rattled to life and the chair began its slow descent, carrying the frail body of Helena Devereaux down from the second floor of her house for the first time in nearly a decade.

At the bottom of the stairs Kevin and Anne Devereaux and their two children watched the slow approach of the strange apparition.

We should never have come here.

The thought flashed unbidden through Anne's mind, and she took an involuntary step backward before she caught herself. She forced a smile onto her face, feeling its falseness even as she made herself step forward once more to greet the mother-in-law she'd never met. At her side she felt Jeff's hand tighten in her own, and then, a second later, Julie took her other hand. Though neither of the children spoke a word,

Anne knew that both of them were feeling exactly the same thing she was.

Fear.

And yet despite this sense of fear Helena immediately induced in Anne, the old woman was tiny. She seemed almost to disappear within the folds of the rusty black dress she wore, and her face, all but obscured by the layers and layers of makeup, was strangely expressionless. But her eyes—two brightly glowing embers—seemed to reach out to Anne, grasping her in their grip, drawing her forward. She reached the bottom of the stairs just as the chair lift clanged to a stop, but said nothing. Whatever was to be said, she instinctively knew, would be initiated by Helena Devereaux.

The silence seemed to drag into eternity.

"So you are the woman my son married," Helena rasped at last, her eyes narrowing to appraising slits as her nostrils flared slightly. "Well, I suppose there's nothing to be done about that, is there?" Then her eyes flicked away from Anne, taking in each of the children in turn. Her head bobbed in a barely perceptible nod. "The girl is a Devereaux," she pronounced. "As for the boy, I don't—"

"His name is Jeff," Anne said, her voice emerging from her throat in a strangled squeak, forced out only to prevent her son from hearing whatever his grandmother had been about to say. "And he's every bit as much a Devereaux as Julie."

Helena's eyes—cold as a snake's now—fixed on Anne again, and once more Anne felt the strange power of the old woman. No wonder Kevin has nightmares about her, she thought. And no wonder he never wanted to come back.

And then, once again, another unbidden thought formed in her mind.

She doesn't intend for us to leave. Not ever.

Helena's eyes abruptly released Anne and moved to her son. "Kevin," she said, her tongue caressing his name. And then, though his mother said nothing else, Kevin stepped forward and offered the old woman his arm. Taking it, Helena struggled to her feet and started across the entry hall toward the open doors to the living room, her son on one side of her, her daughter on the other.

It's not just the island she owns, Anne reflected as she reluctantly followed the three Devereauxes into the gloomy depths of the parlor beyond the double doors. She owns Marguerite, and now she owns Kevin again too. And she wants to own my children.

As Anne settled herself on the sofa a moment later, her children flanking her and sitting unnaturally close as they warily watched their grandmother, Anne wondered if there was anything she—or anyone else—could do to thwart Helena Devereaux's wishes.

An hour later, when Helena finally returned to her room, Anne felt exhausted, as if from the old woman's very presence—her piercing eyes smoldering with the power of an indomitable spirit, belying the obvious weaknesses of her body. It wasn't until then that Anne realized the meaning of the makeup Helena had used to cover the ravages of age.

It was theatrical makeup, intended to cover up the person behind it, exposing only a carefully constructed façade to the world. Though the façade Helena Devereaux had created was truly frightening, Anne had the certain feeling that the terrifying mask, and the woman behind it, were one and the same.

CHAPTER 3

It was nearly two o'clock when Jeff and Julie finally escaped the cavernous gloom of their grandmother's house, emerging out into the brightness of the summer afternoon only to have the oppressively tropical heat close around them like shrouds of wet sheets. They stayed in the protective shade of the oaks for a while, gazing out at the shimmering air that lay over the island.

"It's weird, isn't it?" Jeff finally ventured. "Aunt Marguerite hardly said a word, and Grandmother looks like she already died."

Almost against her will, Julie snickered at the remembered image of the strangely painted old lady who had sat perched on a wing chair by the fireplace, ignoring the peeling wallpaper and mildewed plaster of the ceiling while she rambled on about how privileged the children should feel to be there. "It's like she doesn't even know the place is falling down around her," she said finally. "And she hardly even spoke to Mom."

Jeff rolled his eyes scornfully in a vain attempt to rid himself of the strange fear he had felt in the presence of his grandmother. "And did you hear her talking about how I look exactly like Mom? Everybody knows I look just like Dad."

Julie giggled. "I bet she tells Aunt Marguerite that Mom's just a carpetbagger and they should just pretend she doesn't exist."

"What's a carpetbagger?" Jeff asked.

Instead of answering his question, Julie got to her feet and started down the gentle slope that led to a group of ram-

shackle outbuildings a hundred yards from the house. "Let's
go see what's here," she suggested.

A moment later Jeff had darted ahead of her, disappearing
through the half-open door of a vine-covered barn whose roof
was almost barren of shingles. A few minutes later she
stepped through the door herself. The barn had apparently
once housed a stable of horses, but most of the stalls had long
since collapsed. Sunshine filtered down through the slats of
the roof, providing a soft, cool light which was tinged with
green by the profusion of foliage that had penetrated the
siding over the years. Perched on a loft at the rear, Jeff was
grinning down at her. "Isn't this neat?" he called. "If there
were any hay, I could jump down into it!"

"You be careful," Julie warned. "It looks like the whole
place could fall down any minute."

Jeff's grin only widened. "The stairs already have. Is there
a ladder in here?"

Julie searched the barn, finally finding a splintery wooden
ladder in the tack room at the rear. She propped it up against
the loft, and Jeff scrambled down. "What were you going to
do if I hadn't been here?" Julie asked.

"Jump," Jeff replied with the self-assurance of his eight
years. "I've jumped from the roof at home, and it's a lot
higher than that."

"And if Mom had caught you, she'd have cut you off TV
for a week."

"But she didn't," Jeff reminded her. "Come on."

They left the barn and made their way farther down the
slope to the row of collapsing cabins that had once served as
slave quarters. Pushing his way through the tangled vines,
Jeff found himself in a tiny room with only a single window
and door. There was a rickety shelf on one wall and a couple
of pegs still hanging precariously from the doorframe. Most
of the floor space was taken up by four rusty iron beds, long
since stripped of springs or mattresses. Just looking at it made
him shudder, and he looked up at his sister in awe. "Did they
really make people live here?" he asked, his voice dropping
to a whisper.

Julie shrugged. "I guess so," she ventured. "Sometimes
whole families had to live in rooms like this."

Jeff's brows furrowed seriously. "How come Dad never told us about this?"

"Because he's probably ashamed of it," Julie replied. "I mean, I certainly wouldn't want anyone to know my family had made people live like this."

"M-Maybe they didn't," Jeff suggested. "Maybe these were just storerooms or something."

"And maybe elephants can fly," Julie shot back. "Let's go—this place gives me the creeps."

They pushed through the vines once more, glanced into a garage that contained an aging Buick and a rusty hulk that neither of them could identify, then started toward what had once been cultivated fields. As they approached a marshy area, a figure suddenly stepped out of a patch of bushes and stood in the path, staring at them curiously.

It was a boy, about Jeff's age, with an unruly mop of tangled black hair curling over his forehead. He was wearing a pair of torn blue jeans and a T-shirt that must once have been white but was now a dingy gray.

"Who are you?" he demanded, his brown eyes fixing belligerently on Jeff.

Jeff stared back at the boy. "Jeff Devereaux," he replied. "Who are you?"

The boy took an uncertain step backward. "Toby Martin. How come I never saw you before?"

" 'Cause I just got here," Jeff replied. "How come you're here? Nobody but my grandmother and my aunt's 'sposed to live here."

Toby glanced furtively at the house. "I just come out here sometimes. I don't hurt nothin'. I just look around. You won't tell, will you? The old lady doesn't want anybody here."

Jeff glanced at Julie, who was studying Toby carefully. Finally she smiled conspiratorially at the worried little boy. "We won't tell anybody you were here, if you'll show us around. Okay?"

The look of uncertainty disappeared from Toby's eyes and he grinned crookedly, exposing a gap in his upper teeth. "I'll show you everything," he promised. "It's neat—there's marshes and ponds, and a neat beach. But you have to watch out, 'cause there's all kinds of snakes and stuff too.''

"Snakes?" Julie repeated, her voice trembling slightly. "Poisonous ones?"

Toby nodded solemnly. "Water moccasins, and rattlers, and all kinds of other ones. But if you watch out, they won't hurt you."

"Maybe we better not," Julie said uncertainly. "Maybe we better go back to the house."

"What's the matter, you scared?" Jeff taunted his sister.

Julie glared at her brother. "Why shouldn't I be?" she demanded. "If you had any brains, you'd be scared too!"

"Toby comes out here all the time," Jeff countered, and turned to the boy. "Nothing's happened to you, has it?"

Toby shook his head vigorously. "All's you have to do is watch out," he said. "My daddy says the snakes are more scared of you than you are of them." As if the issue had been decided, he turned and began picking his way along the path, Jeff instantly following him. A moment later, deciding she'd better watch out for Jeff rather than leave him alone, Julie followed.

They worked their way slowly toward the far side of the island, skirting the marshy areas and giving a wide berth to a pond in which an alligator lay basking, only his snout and eyes showing above the surface of the water. "Are—Are there a lot of them?" Julie asked, unable to keep her voice from trembling as she stared at the malevolent-looking reptile.

"Some," Toby replied. "You don't want to mess with 'em, but they won't hurt you. Unless they're hungry," he added, glancing at Jeff out of the corner of his eye and giggling at the sudden paleness of Julie's face. "Come on, let's go to the beach."

A hundred yards farther, the thick vegetation gave way to a wide expanse of glitteringly white powdery sand. Line after line of low surf swept in from the shallow sea beyond.

Julie stared at it in wonder, dropping down to sit on the sand in the shade of a small grove of smoky pines. It was by far the most beautiful beach she'd ever seen.

It was completely deserted.

"But—But where is everybody?" she asked. "You'd think everyone would be out here!"

"It's the old lady," Toby replied, his small face scowling deeply. "She's so mean she won't let anybody use it, even though it's the best beach around here. She makes everybody swim in the channel. We all hate her!" Then, suddenly abashed as he realized he'd been talking about Jeff's and Julie's grandmother, he tried to apologize.

"We don't care what you say about Grandmother," Jeff told Toby. "We think she's weird too. And our dad hates her!"

"Jeff!" Marguerite Devereaux's voice cut through the brightness of the day, and all three youngsters jumped slightly as she stepped out of the grove of trees and onto the beach. "Even if that were true, which I hope it isn't, it's not a nice thing to say. Keep in mind that although you grew up in Connecticut, you're still a southern gentleman."

Jeff's eyes widened and he swallowed nervously as his aunt turned her attention to Toby Martin. Her eyes fixed on him sternly.

"And as for you, young man, just what do you think you're doing out here?"

Julie glanced at Toby, fully expecting him to be on the verge of terrified tears. Instead, he was grinning up at Marguerite, his eyes dancing merrily.

"I was fixin' to steal a swim, Miss Marguerite," he said. "You won't tell on me, will you?"

The sternness left Marguerite's eyes, and she reached down to run her fingers through Toby's hair. "If I got you in as much trouble with your mother as you get me into with mine, you'd never speak to me again, would you?" Toby shook his head wildly, looking for all the world like a happy puppy. "Well, you got off lucky this time," Marguerite went on. "She's taking a nap, and she didn't see you. So scoot along home, but next time you come, you march right up to the door and knock. If Jeff invites you, she can't tell me to order you off the island, can she?"

Toby looked eagerly at Jeff. "Will you?" he asked. "I mean, invite me?"

"Okay," Jeff agreed. "But you have to invite me to your house too."

The eagerness faded from Toby's eyes and he looked uncertainly up at Marguerite. "We'll see," she promised him. "But as long as Jeff's here, you come out here any time you want to."

A few minutes later, as Toby started threading his way back along the path across the island and toward the causeway, Marguerite led Julie and Jeff up the beach toward the old mansion. They walked in silence for a few minutes, then Julie spoke shyly.

"Aunt Marguerite? Why won't Grandmother let anyone use the beach? It's so beautiful, it seems like everybody should get to use it."

Marguerite said nothing for a while, then put her arm around Julie's shoulders. "It's just the way Mother is," she said at last. "There isn't any reason, really. It's just that it's *our* beach, and Mother always worries about what's *ours*." She fell silent for a moment, then: "But it won't always be that way."

Jeff looked up curiously. "Why not?"

Marguerite smiled sadly. "Because she's dying, Jeff. And when she dies, things will be different."

For several minutes the trio walked in silence, then Julie spoke again. "Aunt Marguerite, don't you care if Grandmother dies? I mean, she's your mother."

Marguerite stopped walking and stared up at the weathered mansion surrounded by its protective grove of oaks, then her gaze drifted out to scan the sea. Finally her eyes came to rest on Julie. "Oh, yes," she said. "I care that Mother is going to die. I care very much." Taking Julie by the hand, she turned and started up the slope toward the great house.

That evening five people gathered around the huge table in the dining room of Sea Oaks. Kevin sat at the head of the table, with Anne and Marguerite to his right. Opposite their mother and aunt sat Julie and Jeff, and far down the table, empty and somehow removed from the group while still dominating it, sat the chair that Helena Devereaux would have occupied had she been well enough to come downstairs. But she had not come down. Instead, upon waking from her nap she had summoned Marguerite and told her that she would take dinner, as usual, in her room.

Five minutes after Ruby served the soup, the angry sound of the buzzer rent the conversation. Without a word Marguerite folded her linen napkin and moved stiffly out of the dining room. The family listened to her limping up the stairs.

A few minutes later she was back. Slipping into her chair, she resumed eating her soup as if nothing had happened.

The buzzer sounded again as Ruby was serving the entrée, and yet again before Marguerite had finished her salad.

When the buzzer sounded once more as Ruby was putting bowls of ice cream on the table, Marguerite again folded her napkin, but before she could leave the table, Anne spoke, smiling uncertainly at her sister-in-law. "Why don't you eat your ice cream before it melts? Whatever it is this time, surely it can wait a few minutes?"

Marguerite shook her head apologetically. "She hates to be kept waiting, and I don't mind, really. I've been doing it so long, I don't think I'd know what to do if I got through a meal without her calling me." Setting her napkin down, she hurried once more out of the dining room to laboriously climb the stairs.

Only when she was certain that Marguerite was out of earshot did Anne face her husband, no longer attempting to keep the anger out of her eyes or her voice. "Why didn't you say something, Kevin? Your mother treats her like a slave! Shouldn't she at least be allowed to finish her dinner?"

"You heard her," Kevin said mildly. "I really don't think she minds. And she's used to it."

"But her leg!" Anne exclaimed. "You can see that it hurts her. And for that awful old woman to make her run up and down the stairs all the time—well, frankly, I don't see why she puts up with it! If I were Marguerite, I'd have put her in a home years ago!" And yet, despite her brave words, Anne wondered if she were speaking the truth. Wasn't it more likely, given the strength she'd seen in Helena earlier, that she, too, would have given in to the woman's demands rather than face her wrath? She suspected she would have.

Kevin shrugged. "I don't disagree with you. In fact, I think you're right—I wouldn't tolerate it, and I wouldn't expect anyone else to either. That's why I got out—it was either that or knuckle under to her. But Marguerite's not like me—she deals with things, and she doesn't complain. She never even complained about her leg."

Julie put down her spoon and faced her father. "What happened to her?" she asked.

"An accident," Kevin replied. "I was just a little boy, and she was in her teens. I don't remember much about it, really, but she fell down the stairs and broke her hip. She was in the hospital for a while, and in a cast for a long time. But it never healed properly, and she's had that limp ever since." His lips tightened into a grim line. "She was going to be a dancer, and I guess she was damned good at it. The accident put an end to that, but I can't ever remember hearing her complain about that either. In a lot of ways," he added, "your aunt is a remarkable woman." He smiled. "And in a lot of ways, you're very much like her. You look like her, and you dance like her, and sometimes when I hear you talk, I'd swear I was listening to Marguerite when she was your age."

Julie's brows arched. "Well, I like her, but if Mom ever treated me the way Grandmother treats Aunt Marguerite, I sure wouldn't be around very long."

Kevin chuckled. "All right, so you're not exactly like her. Which is fine with me. I like you just the way you are." Then his voice turned serious again. "And as for your mother treating you the way my mother treats Marguerite, you needn't worry about it. If your mother were anything like mine, you can believe I wouldn't have married her."

Anne drew herself up in mock indignation. "That, Kevin, has to be the weakest compliment I've ever received. From what I've seen today, nobody in the world is like—"

But before she could finish, there was a sudden shrieking from upstairs, followed by a loud thump. Instantly Kevin and Anne rose to their feet and hurried up the stairs, followed by

Julie and Jeff. Behind them, moving her bulk more slowly, Ruby, too, started up the stairs.

Kevin opened the door to his mother's bedroom to find the old woman propped against her pillows, her eyes fixed furiously on Marguerite, who was sprawled on the floor by the bed, her lame leg twisted beneath her, her face contorted into a grimace of pain.

Kevin glanced quickly at his mother, then dropped to the floor to help Marguerite. "What happened?" he asked.

Marguerite looked at him ruefully. "She said I didn't get her dinner up quickly enough, and it was cold."

Kevin's jaw dropped as he stared at the plate of untouched food on his mother's tray. "But—for Christ's sake! You brought it up an hour ago, before we even started. Didn't she eat it?"

Marguerite shook her head quickly, but said nothing. Kevin stood up, glaring at his mother and the heavy cane still clutched in her hand. Suddenly he understood. "So you hit her, Mother? You sat there while it got cold, then called Marguerite up here so you could hit her with your cane?"

Helena's eyes narrowed dangerously, and when she spoke, her voice was a malevolent hiss. "Watch what you say, Kevin. You don't know her as I do. You haven't been here! You went away and left us alone! Don't you start criticizing now, young—"

"Oh, for Heaven's sake, Mother," Kevin snapped. "Stop behaving like a child. Marguerite, come on. Ruby can reheat it, or I'll do it myself. But you come back down and finish your dinner."

Marguerite started to get up from the floor, but before she had regained her feet, Helena's voice lashed out like a whip.

"No! I want her to do it, Kevin! If she's going to spend her life acting like a servant, who are you to stop her?"

Stunned, Kevin looked down at his sister.

Though her eyes had filled with tears, Marguerite said nothing. Instead, she simply pulled herself unsteadily to her feet, and picked up her mother's tray.

*   *   *

It was long after midnight when Kevin slid out of bed, careful not to disturb Anne, whose breathing had slipped into the regular rhythms of sleep hours before. Kevin himself had lain awake, feeling the house around him, his nostrils filled with the familiar scents of his childhood, the summer night heavy with the shrill sounds of tropical insects. All of it seemed so far in the past and yet was still so familiar.

But the image that hung in his mind was that of Marguerite, crouched painfully on the floor, betraying nothing of her pain and humiliation, quietly suffering her mother's fury. How long had it been like this? he wondered. And why had Marguerite never called him, never told him what was happening and what her life had come to?

Or did she even realize that her existence didn't have to be tied to a bitter woman who was living in the past?

Knowing he wasn't going to drift into sleep, he put on a light robe and went out into the broad corridor, closing the door behind him. He needed no lights—every inch of the house seemed familiar to him, and as he moved along the hall toward the main staircase, he remembered each of the rooms as he passed them.

Even when he was a child, the many guest rooms of the mansion had already begun to deteriorate, for the wide circle of wealthy friends his grandparents had once entertained had long since disappeared, along with the large staff of servants necessary to keep up the house in the manner for which it was designed. Though he hadn't yet looked at them, he was certain they were just as he remembered them, although no doubt more faded—the Blue Room, the Emerald Room, the Rose Room—all of them with their damask wallpaper, their matching carpets, their marble fireplaces.

He moved down the stairs, through the small reception room and into the main salon, instinctively sidestepping the bench of the grand piano. He switched on the crystal lamp on the table behind the Louis XVI sofa, and the room was suffused with a soft glow that couldn't quite wash the shadows away from the far corners. He crossed toward the double doors that led through a small solarium to the dining room, pausing for a moment to gaze up at the portrait of his mother above the fireplace.

Done in France by a society painter who had been the rage among touring Americans, his mother was posed in the formal costume of a danseuse of her day, her hair drawn back from her face, her high cheekbones needing no makeup to accentuate them. One hand was lifted gracefully, and her left leg was oddly bent, as if she were about to loft herself to her toes. Kevin stared at the picture for several minutes, trying to see in that youthful face any faint hints of the haggard and bitter harridan the portrait's subject had become.

There were none.

He moved on, then, pausing in the solarium, but passing quickly through the dining room and the butler's pantry to the enormous old-fashioned kitchen. Little here had changed since he was a boy. The ancient range still stood against the far wall, opposite the immense built-in iceboxes that had been electrified long before he was born. An array of enormous pots and pans, their copper still kept immaculate by Ruby, hung on the rack above the long counter, but he was certain they weren't used anymore, for next to the sink, stacked neatly in a draining rack, was the cookware Ruby had used for that evening's dinner—small pans, of a size to serve six instead of sixteen or twenty-six.

At last he opened the refrigerator, pulled out the remains of the roast, found some bread, and made himself a sandwich. He sat down at the table next to the window and listened for a while to the sounds of the house.

A light breeze had come up, and limbs brushed against the house's siding. Everywhere there were faint creaks as the old wood adjusted to the slightly cooler temperature of the night.

And then, slowly, he began to feel a creeping sensation on the back of his neck. The hairs stood on end and a faint chill passed over him.

A plank of the floor creaked loudly, and he started, turning quickly, not certain what to expect.

Ruby stood at the door to her room, her old eyes fixed on him, her expression strangely blank. She smiled faintly and moved toward him.

"Can't sleep, can you, Mr. Kevin," she said softly. "Just like when you were a boy. Well, I reckon you're gonna have to get used to more nights like that, now that you've come home."

Kevin frowned and shook his head. "Not many, Ruby," he replied. "And I haven't come home. My home is in Connecticut. I'm just here for a couple of weeks' vacation."

Ruby settled her weight into the chair opposite him, grunting slightly with the effort. "Not a couple of weeks," she said. "You're back, and you'll stay back. No Devereaux has ever left Sea Oaks yet."

Kevin cocked his head, his brows rising. "I did. I've been gone a long time, Ruby. I'm not coming back."

"That's not what Miz Helena says," Ruby countered. "She says you done come back and you going to stay. And you ask me, if that's what she says, that's what she mean. You'll stay."

Kevin's voice hardened slightly. "I didn't ask you, Ruby," he said. "But since you've taken it upon yourself to tell me, let me answer you. I don't give a damn what my mother wants, and haven't since I was eight years old. No more than she's given a damn what I want. So why would I stay? I love my family, and I love my life, and I have no intention of changing it. Certainly," he added, glancing meaningfully around the ancient kitchen, "not to live in this relic and try to pretend there's anything left in Devereaux for any of us. The town's dead, Ruby, and so is the house. When Mother's gone—if Mother's gone—I'll be gone too. But even if she lives awhile longer, I won't be staying."

Ruby said nothing, only watching him with her nearly black eyes. At last she heaved herself slowly to her feet and started back toward her room. She had nearly reached the door when she stopped and turned back.

"I understand what you're saying, Mr. Kevin," she said. "But I know what Miz Helena means. You *are* a Devereaux, Mr. Kevin, and you *will* stay at Sea Oaks. That's just the way things are. Don't try to fight it, Mr. Kevin. It won't do you no good at all. None." Before he could reply, she disappeared into her own room and silently closed the door behind her.

Kevin sat alone for a long time after Ruby left, then finally bit into his sandwich. It tasted dry, and the bread seemed to stick in his throat. Throwing the rest of it into the trash basket beneath the sink, he switched off the lights and went back upstairs.

But even after he was back in bed and had heard the clock in the hall softly strike the hour of two A.M., he was still awake.

Ruby's words had driven the last possibility of sleep from him, and now the tiredness in his body was accentuated by something else.

A cold knot of fear had begun forming deep inside him as he wondered if perhaps Ruby wasn't right.

Perhaps, indeed, his mother had determined that he should not be allowed to escape from Sea Oaks again.

Perhaps she intended to imprison him, just as she had imprisoned Marguerite.

Perhaps she intended to imprison them all.

CHAPTER 4

By Thursday morning Anne was beginning to grow used to the strange daily rhythm of Devereaux Island. Breakfast, she had learned, was served at exactly seven in the morning, and, like all meals, was constantly interrupted by the harsh buzzing that signaled Helena Devereaux's insistent demands for her daughter's attentions. After breakfast Ruby would go about her cleaning, moving heavily about the house. Anne was certain that each year fewer of the rooms were used. Most of them, indeed, were closed off, their furnishings draped with muslin dust covers, their heavy draperies drawn against the brilliant burning of the sun. Ruby would go slowly through the rooms still in use, dust cloth in her hand, but her ministrations had little effect—the house, though occupied by seven people now, was still imbued with the stultifying atmosphere of a museum. Even Julie and Jeff found themselves unconsciously lowering their voices when they were inside.

After breakfast Marguerite disappeared into her mother's room, where she would sit in a chair whose upholstery had grown shiny from constant use, reading quietly to Helena, who lay in her bed, snoring softly.

Unless Marguerite stopped reading.

Then the querulous tones of the old woman's voice would sound through the house as she berated her daughter. "I don't ask much," were the words she repeated most often. "I've taken care of you all your life—the least you can do is read to me a little now and then!" Once, Anne listened outside Helena's door, but all she heard after the old woman's furious outburst was the calm melody of Marguerite's sweetly modulated voice.

Before lunch Marguerite would change clothes, always appearing on the veranda as if she were prepared to greet twenty guests, though there was never anyone but the family in attendance. Somehow, even when Anne herself felt her clothes clinging damply to her skin, Marguerite always managed to look cool and fresh, her dark hair coiled up in a French twist held in place by a large tortoise-shell comb. On anyone else the ornament might have looked ridiculous, but the comb only accentuated Marguerite's graceful figure, and if she felt self-conscious about her pronounced limp, she never showed it. Yet, even on the veranda, there was no escape from the buzzer's demands. Indeed, Anne had quickly realized that the buzzer was only silent during the long hot afternoons when an even deeper somnolence fell over the house. Then Helena would drift into a fitful nap while Marguerite disappeared into the sewing room, where she would spend an hour or two at the ancient Singer.

Already, she had produced a sea-green shift for Julie, its waist loosely belted in white, which not only fit Julie perfectly, but set off her skin in a manner that lent her the same exotic beauty as her aunt's.

Each of the evenings was a repeat of the first one they had spent at Sea Oaks—a simple meal, ruined by Helena's continued demands for attention.

For Anne, unused to the southern heat, the days were turning into endless damp hells of boredom, which she spent searching for shelter from the oppressive heat. Once, on the third day of their visit, she'd driven across the causeway into the village, but quickly returned. The stark poverty of its dusty streets and failing businesses had only depressed her more, and by the time she returned to Sea Oaks she understood well why Marguerite seldom left the island and sent Ruby to do what little shopping was necessary. And so, on Thursday morning, she wasn't surprised when Julie, her expression almost guilty, asked her how much longer they would be staying.

Anne smiled sympathetically at her teenage daughter, knowing full well how she herself would have reacted to being stuck in such a place when she was fifteen. "It seems like weeks already, doesn't it?'' she asked. When Julie nodded, but said nothing, Anne sighed. ''I don't know what to tell you, darling. Your father keeps saying it'll just be another day or two, but knowing how your grandmother is . . .'' Her voice trailed off, and she could read the disappointment in Julie's eyes.

''It's just that there's nothing to do,'' Julie said softly. ''Dad keeps finding things around here to fix—''

''Which could certainly take a year or so,'' Anne observed archly, but Julie didn't seem to notice her mother's attempt at a joke.

''—and Jeff has Toby to play with, but I haven't met anybody yet.''

Her aunt's voice interrupted her. ''I intend to fix that this very morning,'' Marguerite said, stepping out onto the veranda. Julie flushed in embarrassment, but Marguerite tossed her niece's discomfort away with an airy gesture. ''My girls are coming this morning, and I thought you might like to join the class.''

Julie looked at her aunt uncertainly. ''I—I don't know. I've been taking ballet for three years, but—''

Understanding immediately, Marguerite squeezed Julie's hand. ''If you're worried that you might not be good enough, you can stop,'' she said. ''Every now and then I get a really good student, but most of them are . . .'' She hesitated, searching for just the right words. ''Well, let's just say they aren't all quite as motivated as they might be, shall we?'' She turned to Anne, winking. ''Still, whatever I can teach them, I'm happy to do. And even if you don't want to join the class,'' she finished, turning back to Julie, ''at least you can meet the girls.''

''I'd love it,'' Julie replied. ''And I'm sorry about what I said before. I didn't really mean for you to hear it. It isn't that I don't like it here—''

''Enough!'' Marguerite commanded, holding up her hand to stem Julie's words. ''You're not the only one who doesn't have anything to do around here, you know. That's one of the reasons I keep teaching—it gives all the girls something to do. Besides—'' But once again her words were interrupted by the sharp sound of Helena's buzzer, and almost automatically she turned and disappeared back into the stifling darkness of the house.

"I feel so sorry for her," Julie said, her eyes filling with tears. "Aunt Marguerite's so nice, and Grandmother's so mean to her. Why doesn't she just—" And then, before she spoke the word, Julie bit it back.

"Why doesn't she just die?" Anne finished quietly, and Julie turned to face her mother, nodding unhappily.

"I wish I didn't think that, but—"

"But you do," Anne finished for her. "And so do I, if it's any help. Of course, it would be nice if your grandmother was a sweet old lady we could all love, but the fact of the matter is that she's not. So you mustn't worry about what you might think of her."

"I don't even see why we came," Julie said, releasing the anger that had slowly built inside her over the last few days. "Grandmother won't talk to Jeff or me, and she hardly speaks to you. I don't even think she cares that Dad's here!"

"I know," Anne sighed. "But we're not just here for her. We have to think of your father too. If this visit will make him feel better about staying away so long, then it will be worth it. All right?"

Julie nodded, and Anne gave her a reassuring hug. "Now let's go up and find you something to wear to Marguerite's class. I think I have a running suit that'll fit you, if you don't mind dying of heat."

"Shoes!" Julie exclaimed. "I didn't bring any toe shoes!"

Anne smiled triumphantly. "Which is exactly what mothers are for. At the last minute I stuck in a pair. I couldn't believe you wouldn't be dancing at all." Together, they went into the house and started up the stairs, just missing being bowled over by Jeff, who was pounding down from the second floor, two steps at a time.

"Hey!" Anne cried out, swinging him off his feet. "Where are you going in such a hurry? Didn't I tell you not to run in the house?"

"But it's Toby," Jeff protested, squirming in his mother's grasp. "He's coming across the causeway, and he's got a fishing pole!"

"A fishing pole!" Anne repeated. "Well, I guess we can't get in the way of fishing!" She set Jeff back on his feet, then she and Julie went on upstairs.

As they passed the closed door to Helena's room, they could hear the old woman's voice, railing once more at Marguerite.

Self-consciously they quickened their steps, neither of them wishing to witness Marguerite's humiliation.

When Marguerite came up, Ruby had been waiting at the top of the stairs, her eyes stormy and her jaw set stubbornly. "She's refusing to eat her breakfast again, Miz Marguerite. I swear, I don't know what to do with her anymore. It's like she wants to starve herself to death or somethin'."

"It's all right, Ruby," Marguerite had told her. "Go on back to whatever you were doing, and I'll talk to her."

Ruby regarded Marguerite doubtfully. "Seems like every time you talk to her lately, she just starts callin' you names and treatin' you like dirt!"

Marguerite sighed tiredly. "I'm all right. And it can't go on forever, can it?" She opened the door and stepped into her mother's room.

"Where have you been?" Helena demanded instantly. "When I call you, I expect you to come, not dawdle around like a useless child!"

"I'm sorry, Mother," Marguerite said evenly. "I had to speak to Ruby for a moment—"

"Ruby!" Helena spat the word distastefully. "I don't see why we keep her around here! She's as useless as you are!"

Marguerite's eyes shifted away from her mother to the untouched breakfast that still sat on the tray bridging Helena's thin legs. "Was there something wrong with your breakfast?"

Helena's eyes raked Marguerite scornfully. "Was there something wrong with your breakfast?" she mimicked acidly. "How am I supposed to eat, with the house filled with strangers? That miserable little boy runs up and down the stairs as if this were a reform school—which is exactly where he belongs—and that wife of Kevin's keeps prowling around as if she owns the house! I won't have it! Do you hear me?''

"I'm sure everyone in the house heard you." Though she had intended only to think the words, Marguerite was shocked to hear them tumble from her lips.

Helena fairly quivered with rage. "How dare you speak to me like that?'' she demanded. "I've taken care of you your entire life! And what do I get in return? Ingratitude and impertinence! You apologize to me, Marguerite! This instant!''

Marguerite choked back the sob that rose in her throat, and stared miserably at the floor. "I'm sorry, Mother," she said softly. "I meant no disrespect!''

"Didn't you," Helena sneered. "You chatter those words like a parrot, child. Do you think I believe them? I'm not a fool, you know, even though you've always thought I was!''

"I told you I'm sorry, Mother," Marguerite whispered miserably. "I don't know what else I can do. But they're Kevin's family, and I'm sure they don't mean to disturb you—''

"They're not Kevin's family," Helena hissed. "*You* are Kevin's family. You and I! I don't know why he brought them here! And I won't have that woman poking around my house!''

"I'm sure Anne wasn't—''

But the old woman cut her off once more. "You don't know! I want you to go and make sure the nursery is locked. She was trying to get in there this morning. I heard her!''

Marguerite hesitated a second too long.

"Do it!'' Helena demanded.

Swallowing hard, her heart pounding with frustration and barely contained anger, Marguerite hurried out of the bedroom and down the hall to a door near her own. She was just trying the handle when the door to the room Kevin and Anne shared opened and Anne looked out.

"That room's locked," Anne said, and was surprised to see Marguerite's back stiffen and her hand drop away from the doorknob as if it had burned her. Frowning, she stepped into the hallway itself. "What is it, Marguerite? Is something wrong?''

Marguerite, her back still toward Anne, shook her head, then finally turned around. Her face was pale and her hands were trembling. "Marguerite, what is it?" Anne asked. "Something *is* wrong."

"H-How did you know this room was locked?" Marguerite asked.

Anne stepped back in surprise. "I—why, I tried the door earlier. That room is right next to Julie's, and I thought Jeff might like to be in it. He's so far down the hall, all by himself—I just thought he might like to be closer to the rest of the family, that's all." Her puzzled frown deepened. "Why? What's in that room?"

Marguerite's eyes suddenly took on a haunted look. "It—It's nothing, really. It's just that mother has some things in here she likes to keep locked up. She just wanted me to check it, that's all."

Anne's lips tightened. "Well, you can tell her that neither I nor my children have any intention of stealing anything," she said, then, seeing the hurt in Marguerite's eyes, wished she could take the words back. She crossed the hall and put her arms around her sister-in-law. "I'm sorry," she said quietly. "That was unkind of me, and unfair. It's just—well, maybe it's just the heat."

But Marguerite shook her head. "No, it's not, Anne. Let's not try to pretend we don't both know what Mother's like. And, of course, that's exactly what she was thinking, and she made me come down here to check the door." She forced a small smile. "Well, at least I can tell her it's still locked, can't I?" Giving Anne a quick embrace, she stepped away, then brushed a strand of hair away from her forehead.

Anne stayed where she was for a moment, watching Marguerite walk heavily back to her mother's room, her limp more pronounced than Anne had yet seen it. Then she turned back to stare speculatively at the locked door.

There was something else behind the door; she was sure of it. It wasn't just a collection of valuable furniture.

No, there was more to it than that. But what?

*　　*　　*

Julie stepped shyly through the enormous double doors that opened from the third-floor landing into the ballroom. It was the first time she'd been up here, and her eyes widened in awe.

Forty feet by sixty, the room covered most of the third floor. The ceiling rose fourteen feet above the floor, its plaster heavily molded into a series of garlands and rosettes. A massive chandelier hung from the center of each rosette, but the brass was heavily tarnished, and the crystals—many of them chipped, others missing entirely—were covered with a thick layer of grease and dust. Opposite the main doors from the landing a long wall was broken by four sets of French doors opening onto a balcony above the veranda at the front of the house, and heavy draperies hung limply at the sides of the doors. At either end of the room large windows provided panoramic views of the island and the sea.

The floor was smoothly fitted parquet in a pattern of rhombuses so intricate it made Julie dizzy, but the finish on the floor had long ago worn away, and no trace of its former polish remained. A thick carpet was rolled up against one wall, and Julie was certain that it hadn't been moved from its position in years.

In the far corner there was a grand piano, next to which stood an old phonograph console, the wood over its single speaker carved in the form of a treble clef. A short barre had been bolted to the wall between the windows at that end of the room, backed by a mirror whose silvering had flaked away in places, leaving a web of dark veins, and large, smudgy expanses in which a reflection was barely visible. A dozen chairs, their gilt frames badly marred and their red velvet seats all but worn through, were scattered near the piano.

Marguerite sat on the piano bench, softly playing a passage from Stravinsky's *Firebird*, and on the floor five girls moved haltingly through the difficult choreography their teacher had devised. When she glanced up and saw Julie, Marguerite abruptly stopped playing, stood up, and came across the room to draw Julie inside. Her hand still holding Julie's, she turned to face her students.

"Girls, this is my niece, Julie."

Quickly, she introduced Julie to each of the girls, but by the time she was done, Julie realized she only remembered the names of two of them.

Jennifer Mayhew, whose smile had been particularly friendly, and Mary-Beth Fletcher, who hadn't smiled at all.

"Why don't we finish what we were doing while Julie warms up, then we can all go to the barre and run through a few of the basics," Marguerite suggested.

"I warmed up downstairs, Aunt Marguerite," Julie replied. "I didn't want to take up any extra time."

Marguerite nodded appreciatively. "Then why don't you take the position nearest the piano, where I can see you clearly."

The five other girls glanced uncertainly at each other, but started toward the barre, Jenny Mayhew falling in next to Julie and leaning over to whisper in her ear. "She wants to see what you can do, but doesn't want to make you do it by yourself."

"And if there's any more whispering," Marguerite observed from her place at the piano, winking at Jenny, "the whisperer can do a solo for all of us."

Jenny giggled, and winked back at Marguerite, then took her place next to Julie.

"First position, girls," Marguerite directed, striking a chord, then beginning to play a simple tempo. "Second position . . . third . . . and turn!"

Julie began going through the movements, passing from one position to the next effortlessly, her arms moving gracefully as her feet fell naturally into the poses her aunt directed. The music seemed, as always, to flow directly from the piano into her fingertips, and then through her body until she felt it absorbed within her and her movements seemed to come directly out of the notes themselves. She closed her eyes and let her mind drift, enjoying the feel of the dance, the stretching of her muscles, even the pain in her feet as she rose up onto her toes.

And then, abruptly, the music stopped, and she opened her

eyes to see all the other girls staring at her. Her aunt was on her feet.

"Did—Did I do something wrong?" she asked, her voice anxious.

"Wrong?" Marguerite asked. "Hardly. You did everything nearly perfectly!" She turned to the other girls. "Why don't all of you sit down for a few minutes? I think we'd all enjoy watching Julie, and certainly we can all learn something from her." Her attention went back to Julie. "You've only been studying for three years?"

Julie flushed in embarrassment. "I've only been studying seriously for three years," she admitted. "But I've been taking lessons since I was six."

Marguerite's brows rose appreciatively. "Nine years! Then you must have a solo, don't you?"

Julie shrugged dismissively. "Just some things I've done in recital."

"Would you do one for us?" Marguerite asked.

Julie's eyes immediately scanned the other girls.

Mary-Beth Fletcher's eyes had narrowed slightly, and Julie saw her glance at the girl next to her, then whisper quickly into her ear. But Jennifer Mayhew was smiling encouragingly, as was one other girl, whose name suddenly came back to Julie: Tammy-Jo Aaronson.

"I—I guess I could," she said finally. "I have something my teacher at home choreographed. Do you have the music from *West Side Story*?"

"I do, indeed," Marguerite replied. She put on a record, and a moment later the opening strains of 'The Dance at the Gym' filled the ballroom, the vibrant rhythms strangely out of place in the faded nineteenth century grandeur of the ballroom.

Then Julie was alone on the floor, once more lost in the music, dancing with her eyes closed, swaying fluidly to the rhythms, her body moving effortlessly. Marguerite watched her niece with undisguised pride, seeing in Julie's every movement the heritage that had come to Julie direct from her aunt and grandmother. And as she watched, her eyes drifted over the other girls in her class.

Jennifer Mayhew and Mary-Beth Fletcher were her most promising students, but compared to Julie, it was obvious even to Marguerite's biased eye that neither of them had any real future as professional dancers. As for the others, Tammy-Jo Aaronson, a slightly overweight girl who never seemed to worry about anything at all, was at least willing to try.

Allison Carter—blond, and thinly pretty—was really only in the class because of her mother's social hopes for her daughter. But Allison didn't really care, either about her mother's ambitions or Marguerite's lessons. The fifth girl, Charlene Phillips, was present, Marguerite knew, simply because she was Mary-Beth Fletcher's best friend and did whatever Mary-Beth did.

And after this class, there would be no more. Marguerite had decided years ago that this group of girls would be her last. She would enjoy them while she could, and hadn't thought too much about what she would do when they grew up.

But it didn't matter, really, for she had them now, and she loved each of them for what she was. And now, for a while at least, there was Julie. In Julie she could see all the dreams of her youth, still vibrant and alive.

The music built to a crescendo, and Julie spun across the floor, her legs moving instinctively, her arms a graceful counterpoint. Then it was over, and after a moment she heard Jennifer and Tammy-Jo begin clapping. A moment later the other girls joined in.

Only Mary-Beth Fletcher sat still, her hands folded in her lap.

Marguerite rose from her chair and hurried across the floor to hug Julie.

"It was beautiful," she whispered. "I couldn't have done it better myself when I was your age." Then she turned back to the girls once more, and gestured Julie to take a bow. Julie performed a deep curtsey, then deliberately let herself collapse to the floor in a perfect parody of having lost her footing.

Mary-Beth Fletcher again refrained from joining in the response as the girls laughed. Instead she leaned over to whisper to her friend, who immediately cut short her own laughter.

Julie scrambled to her feet and grinned happily at her aunt. "Was I really all right?"

"Of course you were," Marguerite replied. "You were more than all right—everything about what you just did shows your talent. Except your eyes. Never close your eyes when you dance, Julie. Remember, you aren't doing it for yourself. You're doing it for an audience, and they want to see your eyes."

"But I always dance with my eyes closed," Julie protested. "At least, if it's a solo. I can feel the music so much better—"

"But you mustn't!" Marguerite proclaimed. "You must always be aware of the audience. Always!"

Slowly, the class resumed, but as Julie danced with the others, she felt her aunt's eyes on her; indeed, she could even feel the pride her aunt was taking in her, and when the hour was over, she wished she could go on for another hour. Even the heat in the ballroom didn't seem to affect her anymore.

But at last Marguerite ended the lesson and the girls began drifting downstairs. As she had earlier, Jennifer Mayhew fell in beside Julie.

"You're really good," she said, her voice frankly admiring.

"You're not exactly bad yourself," Julie replied.

Jenny shrugged. "I try, but when I watch you, I feel like I might as well forget it. Trying just isn't enough—you have to have talent too. And I guess we all know where you got yours."

Julie nodded. "I wish I could have seen Aunt Marguerite dance. Dad says she was really good."

Jenny nodded. "She still is. There's a lot she can't do, I guess, but she never stops trying to show us how."

Julie cocked her head, looking at Jenny carefully. "You really like my aunt, don't you?"

"Are you kidding?" Jenny asked. "Everybody likes Miss Marguerite. She always has time for us, and she's never mad at us, and she always seems to know just how we feel." Her voice dropped lower. "That's why most of us come—we all know we aren't ever going to be dancers, but it gives us an excuse to be with Miss Marguerite, and she always makes it fun.''

Suddenly Mary-Beth Fletcher, who was a few steps ahead, turned around and fixed her eyes on Julie.

"And she's never had favorites either," she said. "At least she hasn't until now!''

Before Julie could say anything, Mary-Beth turned away and hurried down the stairs. When she was gone, Julie looked at Jenny, the pain of Mary-Beth's words burning her eyes.

"Don't worry about it," Jenny told her. "Until you came along, Mary-Beth always thought I was Marguerite's favorite. And if it wasn't me, it would have been somebody else. Besides," she added, her grin suddenly flashing, "why shouldn't you be her favorite? You're her niece, and you're the best dancer." Then, without missing a beat, she changed the subject completely. "Hey, you want to go to the beach this afternoon? I'll introduce you to the rest of the kids."

Julie hesitated only a split-second, then nodded eagerly. "I'd love it. You don't know how bored I've been."

"I do too," Jennifer shot back. "Don't forget, I've lived here all my life. And it can get boooooor*ing*!"

By the time Jennifer left a few minutes later, Julie was feeling much better about Devereaux. Perhaps, after all, the trip wasn't going to be a total waste of time.

CHAPTER 5

"Kevin, what on earth are you doing?" Anne demanded. After searching the house, she'd finally found him behind the west wing, his shirt stripped off and his chest gleaming with sweat. A mound of tangled vines surrounded him, and when she spoke to him, he turned to face her with a triumphant grin spread over his dirt-streaked face.

"I can't believe it," he replied, dropping the big pair of hedge shears to the ground and planting his hands on his hips. "You know, when they built this place, they knew what they were doing."

Anne's brows arched skeptically. "If they knew what they were doing," she countered, "why is it falling apart?"

"That's just it," Kevin told her, his grin widening. "It isn't falling apart. Underneath the siding, the brick is as solid as ever, and even most of the siding just needs repainting and new nails. I thought this wall would come down when I went after the vines, but look!" He gestured toward the expanse of wall he'd stripped naked of twenty-five years of growth, and Anne's eyes reluctantly followed his gesture.

"I see buckled siding with no paint on it at all, two shutters that are about to fall on your head, and a rain gutter that's missing a whole section," she said. "And that drain pipe's coming down, those windows on the second floor are cracked, and if that's not dry rot down there by the foundation, then I've gone blind."

Kevin chuckled ruefully. "All right, so it's not pretty," he agreed. "But that isn't dry rot—I checked the basement, and the timbers are fine. Besides, the whole foundation's concrete, and it doesn't get dry rot."

Anne made a sour face. "Right. All it does is decompose," she pointed out.

"Except that it hasn't. And all the rest of what you see is just cosmetic. Every time I do something around here, I'm amazed. It's as though the house has been taking care of itself all these years, just waiting for someone to come along and give it a new coat of paint."

At his words a faint alarm sounded in Anne's head, and her eyes darkened as she looked at her husband. "Is that what you're thinking of doing next?" she asked. "Painting it?"

Kevin's grin faded slightly. "What if I am? It needs it, and—"

"And you only have another ten days of vacation," Anne reminded him. "It's one thing for you to fix a few things, but I hope you're not planning to spend the whole time working on this place."

"I wasn't, really, but why shouldn't I?" Kevin asked, his manner suddenly defensive. "My mother and sister live here, Anne. What am I supposed to do, just let everything go?"

Anne struggled with her conflicting emotions. In a way, of course, he was right—there was a lot that needed to be done to the house, and most of it was work Marguerite certainly couldn't do. And, obviously, there wasn't any money to hire people. But what about herself and the children? Weren't they entitled to have some fun with Kevin sometime during these two weeks? "It just seems a little strange to me that someone who didn't want to come down here at all is starting to act like he doesn't ever plan to leave," she said finally, then her heart skipped a beat as she saw a veil drop behind Kevin's eyes.

"You know that's not true," he said, but his voice seemed to Anne to lack conviction, and she suddenly had a feeling she didn't want to pursue the subject any further.

"Well, I didn't come out here to give you grief, anyway," she told him. "But something's bothering me, and I wanted to talk to you about it."

Kevin looked at her quizzically. "And you wanted to talk to me alone," he said, reading her mind.

Anne nodded briefly, then told him what had happened in

the upstairs hall that morning. "Do you know what's in that room?" she asked when she was finished. "There was something about the way Marguerite was acting that gave me the strangest feeling. Like there was something she didn't want me to see."

Kevin's grin returned, and his eyes glinted with humor. "So you think you've detected a mystery in the mansion?" he teased. "Well, I hate to burst your bubble, but if it's the room I'm thinking of, it was the nursery."

"The nursery?" Anne repeated. "*Your* nursery?"

"First Marguerite's, then mine," Kevin agreed. "And there's no mystery about it. If you want to see it, ask Ruby to unlock it for you."

But Ruby, who was slicing okra when Anne came into the kitchen a few minutes later, refused. "There's some things best left alone," she said, her eyes avoiding Anne's.

For a moment Anne considered demanding the keys, but then changed her mind. It was not, after all, her house, nor was Ruby her own employee. But for the rest of the day she found herself pausing repeatedly in front of the locked door, staring speculatively at it. And once, late in the afternoon, she felt eyes watching her as she stood in the hallway. But when she turned, the long corridor was empty.

Helena Devereaux's eyes blinked open in the darkness and she twisted her head automatically to look at the fluorescent hands of the clock by her bedside.

A little after midnight.

Usually she didn't waken until two-thirty in the morning, and then her wakefulness only lasted a few minutes. But tonight, as the sound of insects droned in the darkness outside her open window, she was certain that something was wrong.

The creatures of the night suddenly fell silent.

A floorboard creaked softly somewhere beyond the closed door to her room.

She listened intently for several seconds that seemed to stretch out forever, each of them marked by the abnormally loud ticking of the clock on the nightstand.

The creak came again.

For an instant she thought it must be Marguerite, but then knew it was not. Whoever was in the hall had stopped when the first floorboard creaked, and Marguerite would not have done that. So it was someone else.

Helena's eyes narrowed in the darkness as she remembered Anne standing in the corridor that afternoon, gazing at the door to the nursery. Her heart began to flutter as she understood what was happening. That woman was going to go into the nursery.

Her first instinct was to reach for the button by her bed and summon Marguerite, but even as she stretched, she changed her mind.

She would deal with this herself.

She swung her legs off the bed and reached for the limp silk wrapper that Ruby had dropped on the chair on the other side of the night table. Why couldn't the stupid woman leave it on the bed, where she could reach it?

Helena struggled to her feet, supporting herself against the bed table as she reached for the wrapper, then sat down on the edge of the bed while she put the garment on.

Finally, tying the belt around her waist and taking a single key from the drawer of her nightstand, she began making her way toward the door, edging along the wall to steady herself, her breathing growing harsher with every step.

But the rasping in her lungs didn't matter.

What mattered was keeping that woman out of the nursery!

She leaned against the wall for a moment while she caught her breath, then pulled the door open. The soft glow of a nightlight cast long shadows down the corridor, but there was no sign of Anne.

And then, from downstairs, Helena heard another floorboard creak, and instantly understood what Anne was doing. Slowly she started down the hall, her knees wobbling beneath her and her heart throbbing in her chest. When she finally came to the head of the stairs, she had to brace herself against the banister to keep from falling.

For a moment Anne was forgotten as Helena's eyes fell on the hated chair lift that had been her only means of getting from one floor to another for the last decade. She'd never intended it for her own use at all—indeed, she should have had it torn out after she'd finally forbidden Marguerite to keep using it so many years ago. But tearing it out hadn't been necessary, for once she'd told Marguerite that the chair was nothing but a crutch, her daughter had never tried to use it again.

So she hadn't torn it out, and when her own body began to fail her, she'd found she needed the lift herself. But not tonight. Tonight she only had to get to the nursery.

Get there before Anne did.

She started once more down the long hall, ignoring the sudden sharp flashes of pain shooting through her left arm.

Anne groped through the darkness of the first floor, still feeling guilty about what she was doing. But she hadn't been able to fall asleep that night, and long after Kevin had begun to snore softly beside her, she'd lain awake, the image of the locked door across the hall still hanging in front of her eyes.

"There's some things best left alone."

What could Ruby have meant?

What could there be in a nursery that required being locked up?

At last she'd left her bed, slipped out into the dimness of the hall and started toward the stairs. But each time a floorboard had creaked, she stopped short, afraid of being caught. But it was ridiculous! Caught doing what? She wasn't doing anything wrong!

And yet even when she had reached the bottom of the stairs, she hadn't turned on any lights, and now she found herself hesitating outside the kitchen door, listening for any signs that Ruby might still be awake.

At last satisfied, she pushed the door open and reached for the ring of keys that hung from a hook just inside the door.

The soft clink as it came free from the hook seemed to echo loudly through the kitchen, and she quickly silenced the sound with her hand, then hurried back toward the stairs.

She could sense something different as soon as she reached the second-floor landing. She paused once more, listening, but the house was quiet, and the insects outside had begun softly chirping once again. And yet, as she started along the corridor toward the nursery door, a sense of unease—stronger than the vague guilt she had felt earlier—pervaded her mind.

Perhaps she should give it up, and simply put the nursery out of her mind. But she knew she couldn't.

Steeling herself for whatever she might find, she walked quickly to the locked door and began trying the keys.

The eighth one fit.

She twisted it in the lock, then turned the knob and pushed the door open a crack.

Inside, the room was pitch black, and Anne felt along the wall for a light switch. A moment later the room filled with a brilliant white light, and Anne pushed the door wide.

And screamed.

A shattered crib stood brokenly propped against one wall, the remains of what had apparently once been a bassinet standing next to it. In one corner was a tiny rocking chair, with a full-sized duplicate of it only a few feet away.

Both chairs had had their upholstery slashed, and wads of cotton batting bulged from the rents in the fabric.

The remains of a heavy braided rug covered the floor, and a few pictures—hanging crookedly in broken frames behind shattered glass—decorated the walls.

And in the middle of the room Helena Devereaux stood, her eyes blazing, her body quivering with rage.

As quickly as it had come, the scream died on Anne's lips. Her eyes darted around the chaos of the all but destroyed room for a moment, then came to rest on the old woman. "I—I don't understand," she whispered, half to herself.

"Nobody *asked* you to understand," Helena's voice hissed. She took a step toward Anne, her hands, almost like claws, reaching out toward the younger woman. "Nobody asked you to come here and start poking around my house! You have no business in here, woman! Don't you think this room is kept locked for a reason? Or don't you care?"

"But what is it, Mrs. Devereaux?" Anne asked. "What happened to it? Why is it kept locked?"

"To keep people like you out!" Helena shrieked. She lurched toward Anne once again, tottering forward on her shaking legs, her finger pointing accusingly at Anne. "How dare you come in here? How dare you poke your nose into our affairs!"

Suddenly her eyes widened and she stepped back as if she had been stricken by a blow. Her face, already red, turned a deep scarlet, and then her hands clamped against her chest. She gasped—a horrible, rattling sound that seemed to jerk her whole body—then her legs crumbled beneath her and she dropped to the floor.

Her own eyes widening with shock, Anne stared mutely at the fallen woman for a moment, then dropped to her knees next to her mother-in-law and took her hand. Helena, her eyes glowering malevolently despite the pain that wracked her body, snatched her hand away.

"Don't touch me!" she rasped.

Panic rising out of the depths of her belly, Anne rose to her feet and turned toward the door, only to find Kevin, his eyes still clouded with sleep, staring at her uncertainly.

"Kevin!" Anne cried. "It's your mother! Something's happened to her! Hurry!"

"Her medicine," Kevin said, brushing past Anne and dropping to the floor beside Helena. "It's on the table by her bed. Get it!"

Her own heart pounding now, Anne rushed from the room and ran down the hall to Helena's suite, pushing open the door so hard it slammed noisily against the wall. She rummaged in the clutter on the night table for a moment, then found the small bottle of pills. She was just about to start back to the nursery when Marguerite, a robe wrapped tightly around her, appeared in the doorway.

"What is it?" Marguerite asked. "What's—" Then, for the first time, she saw the empty bed. "Anne? Where's Mother? What's happening?"

"The nursery," Anne said quickly. "I think—I don't know—it looks like a heart attack." She pushed past Marguerite, the bottle clutched in her hand. "Call an ambulance, Marguerite. Quick!" She raced back to the nursery, fumbling with the cap of the bottle as she ran.

"Water!" Kevin demanded.

Anne froze for a moment, staring down at Helena's face. Her complexion had gone dead white now and the fingers of one of her hands were twitching spasmodically, as if trying to grasp at some unseen object. Then, seizing control of herself once more, Anne hurried into her bathroom and returned with a glass of water just as Kevin was shaking three of the pills out of the small vial. He cradled his mother's head in his lap and tried to put the pills into her mouth, but Helena shoved his hand roughly away.

"No—" she gasped, her words barely audible through the labored raling of her strangled breath. "It's too late." Then her eyes opened wide and she stared up into her son's face. "Kevin . . ." she began, and her voice trailed away.

"I'm here, Mother," Kevin said. "Don't worry—you're going to be all right."

Helena's eyes fixed on his. "Promise me—" she whispered. "Promise me—" Then her body jerked reflexively as another spasm struck her heart.

"What, Mother?" Kevin asked. "What is it?"

Suddenly there was a small shriek from the doorway, and Anne looked up to see Marguerite, her face ashen, her knuckles white as she clutched at the door. "Is she—"

Anne shook her head. "Where's the doctor?"

"C-Coming," Marguerite stammered. She lurched into the room, her lame leg threatening to give way beneath her, and Anne hurried to her side, supporting her as she moved toward her stricken mother.

"No!" Helena gasped, her eyes lighting venomously on Marguerite. "Not her! Get her out! Out!"

Her eyes widening with shock, Marguerite stepped back, covering her mouth with her hand. "Mama," she cried. "Don't die, Mama. You can't . . ."

Once more Helena seemed to rally. "I *am* dying," she gasped. "Don't you want to watch me, Marguerite? Isn't that what you've been waiting for all these years?" Then her body contracted once more and her hands flew again to her breast. Writhing in pain now, she clutched at Kevin, her breathing reduced to short rasping gasps. "Promise me . . ." she managed once again.

Kevin drew a sharp breath as he heard his mother's words, but as her hands closed like twin vises on his, he could do nothing but nod.

"Marguerite," the old woman gasped. "Watch out for Marguerite. . . ."

Her eyes met his, and for the last time in his life Kevin felt the strange power of his mother's will reach out to close around him.

Even as she lay dying, he wanted to pull away from her, wanted to escape from her influence. But he couldn't. He couldn't escape her as a child, and he couldn't escape her now.

The last mighty stroke of the seizure took Helena then, and she screamed out loud as a searing pain exploded from her chest into every extremity of her body. A vein exploded in her forehead and an angry purplish stain spread beneath the skin. And then, as the scream died on her lips, her grasp on Kevin's hands relaxed, her hands fell away, her mouth dropped open, and her head lolled back on Kevin's lap. The anger drained from her eyes, and she stared sightlessly upward until her son gently closed their lids.

Marguerite, whimpering softly against the wall by the door, seemed to sense the change.

"M-Mama?" she asked, her voice uncertain now, and almost childlike. "Mama?"

Kevin looked helplessly up at his older sister. "She's gone, Marguerite."

"Noooo . . ."

The word was wrenched from Marguerite's lips in an anguished wail, and she pulled herself away from Anne's supporting grip to lurch across the room. Her lame leg twisted oddly sideways, she dropped to the floor and gathered her mother into her arms. "No, Mama," she whispered. "You can't leave me. You can't— You can never leave me, Mama. I won't let you! I won't let you!" Sobbing brokenly, she buried her face in Helena's still chest, then hugged her body tighter, as if trying to lend her own warmth to Helena's corpse.

Kevin started to reach out to her, but suddenly Ruby appeared at the door. She stepped forward quickly, her hand stopping his own. Their eyes met, and Kevin found his gaze held by the deep dark eyes of the old servant. "Leave her be, Mr. Kevin," Ruby said quietly. "She's got to deal with this in her own way. And she will, Mr. Kevin. She will."

Kevin tried to protest, but Ruby shook her head. "I know her, Mr. Kevin. I know her a lot better than you do. I been here all her life and know how she is. We got to leave her be."

Sighing heavily, she shifted to look down at the still, frail body that was all that was left of her mistress. "It'll be all right," she said almost to herself. "I'll make sure it is, Miz Helena. I'll make sure." Then, taking Kevin by the hand, she led him out of the ruined nursery.

Anne, who had stood stunned near the door through it all, stared numbly at Marguerite and Helena for a moment, then turned to go. But before she was quite out of the room, Marguerite spoke, her voice bleak and empty.

"She's left me, Anne," she said quietly.

Anne turned back then, and found Marguerite looking at her, her eyes unblinking and filled with a pain Anne had never seen before.

"How could she do that?" Marguerite asked then. "How could she leave me? I needed her, Anne. I *needed* her."

CHAPTER 6

Anne had watched in amazement as the cars streamed across the causeway on the afternoon of Helena Devereaux's funeral, but upon reflection, decided she really shouldn't have been surprised at the turnout. After all, even in the face of the obvious depression of the area, the Devereauxes had still been the first family of the county for nearly two centuries, and certainly the death of the matriarch would be considered an event of some note. And, she also realized, most of the people who came over to the island for the service hadn't actually seen Helena in better than a decade, and in all likelihood had no idea of what an evil-tempered harridan she had become. Certainly Marguerite would never have complained, and unless Anne had thoroughly misjudged Ruby, the old servant would have been just as discreet as Marguerite herself.

Now, standing in the suffocating heat of the July afternoon, Anne let her attention wander as the local parish priest droned on in what she considered to be an entirely fictional eulogizing of Helena's soul. Certainly the Helena Devereaux the priest was talking about bore no resemblance to the woman Anne had known during the last week. Finally, she tuned the priest out altogether, letting her eyes wander over the faces of the people whose own fortunes had been tied to those of the Devereauxes over so many generations. The group gathered in the small family graveyard a hundred yards below the house was nearly evenly divided between whites and blacks, and there were many faces that showed features of both the races. Nor, so far as Anne could see, were there any strains between them as white and black stood side by side at the grave.

To Anne's further surprise, the villagers didn't look nearly as poor as she had expected. Though a few of the men's faces reflected the deep lines of worry endemic to the very poor, for whom old age begins to show early in life, most of them seemed to be middle-class people who had fallen on hard times but expected their condition to be temporary. They were dressed in their best suits, and though the clothing was not expensive nor quite up to the latest styles, neither was it ragged or shining with age. Most of the village men wore dark suits similar to the one Kevin himself was wearing.

The women, for the most part, were reflections of their husbands. Their faces, too, had the weathered look of those for whom life had not been particularly easy, but she saw none of the hopeless bitterness created by the stark poverty of the hill country of West Virginia, through which she and Kevin had driven on their way to New Orleans ten years before. Indeed, as Anne felt the sun beating down, it occurred to her that in this part of the country anyone who spent much time outdoors was going to take on a weathered look.

There was also, she noticed, an odd similarity among the faces she was looking at. That, too, was understandable, for over the years these families must have intermarried to the point where most of the people at the funeral were cousins of one degree or another. She suppressed a small smile as she silently speculated on how many of them actually had Devereaux blood running somewhere in their veins, and suspected it was a far higher percentage than anyone in town ever admitted.

The priest fell silent, and Anne refocused her attention on the ornate coffin that rested on a small catafalque before the open door in the large marble crypt holding the remains of four generations of Devereauxes. Anne had studied the crypt earlier, reading the names of Devereauxes long gone. The earliest of them all had French names, but over the years some Scottish and Irish names had begun to creep in. Anne had been unable to read some of the inscriptions, for the marble mausoleum was deeply pitted by its exposure to the elements. But Helena's name was crisply clear, chiseled only the day before by a monument carver who had driven up from Charleston specifically to match Helena's epitaph to that of her husband Rafe, already entombed in the crypt.

The crowd murmured in whispered prayer as the pallbearers lifted the coffin from the catafalque and slid it into the dark recess of marble. Then Marguerite stepped forward, her slim figure swathed in a cascade of black chiffon, and placed a single rose on her mother's coffin. She stood still a moment, then reached out, touched the coffin with the tips of her fingers, and stepped back.

Kevin repeated the ritual, then; one by one, the mourners filed past the open crypt, speaking a soft word of encouragement to Marguerite, then moving on, drifting out of the cemetery and up the low rise to the mansion itself, where a cold buffet was already spread on the veranda. Anne, with Julie and Jeff flanking her, hung back until the last of the villagers had paid their respects, then stepped forward. First she, then each of the children, placed a flower on the coffin inside the crypt, amidst the other flowers. When they were done, Marguerite reached out to the crypt's heavy door, then hesitated. Her eyes damp, she turned to Kevin. "I can't," she said quietly. "I just can't do it, Kevin."

Understanding, Kevin moved to his sister's side, swung the door closed, and locked it with a silver key. Putting his arm around Marguerite, he led her toward the house.

"Is it all over?" Jeff asked in a loud whisper as Anne and the children, too, left the cemetery.

"It's all over," Anne assured her son, who somehow had managed to stand relatively still through the half hour of the service. "And I'll bet if you can find Toby, the two of you can get at that food before it's all gone." His face lighting up, Jeff raced ahead and disappeared into the crowd, then reappeared a second later with Toby Martin in tow. The two of them flew up the steps to the veranda and began piling food onto their plates. Anne grinned ruefully at Julie. "I have a feeling we might have trouble convincing Jeff to go home," she remarked. "Did you ever see anyone make such a close friend so fast?"

"Toby's nice," Julie replied. "In fact, most of the kids here are nice. They're not like the people we know in Connecticut."

Anne gazed at her daughter with mild surprise. "I thought you liked your friends."

"I do," Julie said quickly, flushing. "But everyone's different down here. They don't worry about who has the nicest house, or the most money, or any of that stuff."

"It's hard to worry about money if you don't have any," Anne pointedly observed.

"They're not that poor," Julie said. "Jennifer's father works in Charleston, and most of her friends' fathers do too."

Anne's expression turned uncertain. "But if they're all working, why don't they do something about their homes? The whole town looks like it's falling apart." When Julie's eyes clouded and she looked away from her mother, Anne's uncertainty deepened. "Julie? What is it? Is something wrong?"

Julie shrugged elaborately, then saw Jenny Mayhew, who was standing with another girl and three boys. "There's Jenny," she said, waving. "I'd better go say hello to her." She started away, but Anne stopped her.

"Julie, what's wrong? What is it?"

Julie hesitated once more, then her eyes, darkened by anger, met her mother's. "Maybe you'd better ask Daddy," she said. "Ask him why the town looks the way it does!" Before Anne could reply, Julie hurried up the slope and was swallowed up by the group of teenagers.

Anne stayed where she was for a moment, wondering what Julie could have been talking about. Still pondering the question, she, too, started walking up the gentle hill. But that afternoon she was not to find out what Julie's strange words had meant, for as she moved among the crowd of mourners clustering in the shade of the trees on the front lawn, she increasingly felt like an outsider. And, of course, she was.

All the people here—even her husband—shared a common heritage of which she knew nothing. And as she spoke to them, or tried to speak to them, she felt the chasm between herself and the people of Devereaux widening.

Not that anyone was rude to her. Indeed, she felt that most of them were going out of their way to be kind to her. But it was the kindness a native shows to an alien, not the kindness one friend shows to another.

Within thirty minutes Anne was certain that no matter how long a time she spent in Devereaux—even if it was the rest of her life—she would never fit in.

Long before the first of the mourners had gone home, she had slipped away to the shelter of the room she shared with Kevin.

And that, she decided as she stretched out on the bed, was the crux of the matter. This wasn't her room, and never would be. It was only the room she shared with Kevin, who, unlike herself, was a real Devereaux.

That was the way it was, and always would be.

But it doesn't matter, she told herself, closing her eyes against the afternoon sun. It doesn't matter, because in a few more days we'll be going home. . . .

"Did you ever see a dead person before?" Toby asked, staring mournfully at the plate of potato salad for which he suddenly had no appetite.

Jeff shook his head silently.

"It kind of made me feel funny," Toby admitted.

"Me too," Jeff agreed. But it had done more to him than just make him feel funny. He'd stood as quietly as he could all through the service, wondering what would happen when it was all over. He'd been glad they hadn't opened the coffin again before they put it into the crypt—it had been bad enough having it sitting in the library for three days, while everyone in town came by to peer down at the strange white mask that didn't quite look like his grandmother. He'd looked at the body a lot—whenever nobody came along to chase him out of the library—trying to figure out why his grandmother looked so much different now that she was dead. But even now that they'd buried her—if that was what you called it when you put the body in a stone box above the ground—he

still wasn't quite sure. But he knew that looking at the body
had been scary.

Even scarier was the way his Aunt Marguerite had looked
at him when she'd found him in the library yesterday. Her
face had been white and her hair messed up, and for just a
second she had looked to Jeff exactly like his grandmother.

But it was when she looked right at him that he felt
goosebumps all over his body. It was just the way his grandmother had looked at him when she was coming down the
stairs in the chair the first day he had been at Sea Oaks.

Like she wasn't sure who he was, and didn't care.

And she didn't care, Jeff had known instantly, because for
some reason—even though she didn't even know him—his
grandmother hated him.

And yesterday, for just a split second, that was how his
Aunt Marguerite had looked at him.

Just like she hated him.

He felt a chill run down his back, and quickly looked
around, as if his aunt had been able to read his mind just
now. But she was nowhere to be seen, so he nudged Toby
with his elbow. "Come on," he said. "Let's go down to the
beach." With Toby right behind him, he began threading his
way through the crowd once more, relieved that he didn't run
into his aunt.

Marguerite stood under the largest of the oak trees, the
faces of the people she had known all her life melding
together until she found herself uncertain of exactly whom
she was talking to. And then a tall figure emerged from the
throng, and suddenly Will Hempstead stood before her. Looming nearly a foot taller than Marguerite, he smiled gently
down at her, his eyes filled with concern. "Is there anything I
can do?" he asked, his voice dropping so that no one but
Marguerite could hear him. "If there's anything, Marguerite,
anything at all, you just tell me."

Marguerite smiled wanly and shook her head. "But it's
sweet of you to offer, Will. After all these years, and after

what happened, well . . .'' Her voice trailed up in embarrassment.

"It's all right," Will assured her. "I'm a lot older now, and so are you, but nothing's changed, Marguerite. I hope you know that."

Marguerite tipped her head up and met Will's eyes. "But it *has* changed, Will. Everything's changed, and nothing can ever be the way it was again." She could see that Will was about to say something else—something she wasn't sure she wanted to hear—and then she saw her brother a few yards away. "Kevin?" she called. "Kevin, come and say hello to Will Hempstead. You remember Will, don't you?"

Kevin excused himself from the group he was chatting with and strode over, his hand extended. "More likely that Will doesn't remember me. I don't think I've seen you since I was eight or ten years old." He grasped Will's hand firmly in his own. "What're you up to these days?"

"Law," Will announced. "As in capturing, not prosecuting."

"Will's the police chief," Marguerite explained, and Kevin thought her voice was suddenly a little too bright. "Everybody says he's got the right personality for the job, but I think they appointed him because he's so big nobody would dare to fight him."

"And I think you tease just as much as you did when you were a girl," Will Hempstead replied, but beamed at her words nonetheless. Then he turned his attention to Kevin. "Heard you were here. Lots of people are glad you're back."

Kevin shrugged. "Well, it's nice to feel welcome, but I'm afraid I won't be staying long. In fact, I think about three more days and we have to head back north."

Hempstead looked surprised. "Not staying?" he asked. "Well, now, that's not the way I heard it. Folks are saying you're bringing the wife and kids and moving down here to stay. And if you're not," he added, "I've got to say I'm sorry." He gave Kevin a broad wink. "I've seen that daughter of yours—prettiest girl we've had around here since Marguerite grew up. 'Course, she looks just like Marguerite, so I suppose you might say I'm a bit prejudiced.''

"Will!" Marguerite exclaimed.

"Well, it's true, isn't it?" Will demanded.

"Even if it is, this isn't the time or the place to be saying such things," Marguerite protested. Leaving Kevin and Hempstead alone together, she made her way across the lawn, her right hand pressed against her hip, her limp more pronounced than usual. Will Hempstead watched her go, his eyes taking on a faraway look.

"Still carrying a torch for her?" Kevin finally asked, and the police chief flushed deeply, but nodded.

"Guess I always will," he said. "And now that Miss Helena's gone—" He cut off his words abruptly, clearly embarrassed.

"Now that Mother's dead, you can come around again?" Kevin finished. Before Will could say anything, Kevin went on. "I wonder what she'll do now? Living with mother all these years—I have a feeling things might be rough for her for a while."

Hempstead shook his head. "She'll be all right. There isn't a soul in town who isn't crazy about Marguerite, even in spite of the old lady. All she has to do is ask, and folks'll flock around." Then his eyes pointedly met Kevin's. " 'Course it would help if her brother flocked around a bit, too, if you know what I mean. You're all the family she's got left, and she's going to need you. In fact," he added, "the whole town's going to need you. Or at least know what your intentions are."

Kevin shifted uncomfortably. "I know what you're saying, Will. And I intend to get Mother's affairs straightened out. But that shouldn't take too long, and once it's done, I'll be gone."

A third man joined the group. It was Sam Waterman, a white-haired lawyer who had looked after Helena Devereaux's affairs for nearly half a century. Kevin was not surprised to see that even today, despite the occasion, Waterman was dressed in his habitual white suit. "Did I hear you say you're leaving?" he asked Kevin, his voice sharp.

Kevin repeated what he'd told Will Hempstead, and the old lawyer listened in silence. But when Kevin was done, he shook his head.

"I wouldn't count on that," he said softly.

Kevin frowned. What could the lawyer be talking about? "I beg your pardon?" he asked.

"I wouldn't count on leaving," the lawyer repeated. "In fact, I wouldn't even think about it until tomorrow, when I'll be bringing the will out. And after that, you might just be changing your mind." Then, smiling genially, he turned and stepped into another conversation a few yards away.

Kevin stared after him for a moment, wondering what on earth the lawyer could have been talking about. Unbidden, the words Ruby had spoken the first night he was back at Sea Oaks came back to his mind.

"You *are* a Devereaux, Mr. Kevin, and you *will* stay at Sea Oaks."

Despite the shimmering heat of the afternoon, a chill passed through him.

Kevin was unable to sleep that night. Not only had Sam Waterman's words stayed in his mind, but after dinner Anne had told him of her cryptic conversation with Julie after the funeral. When she was done, he'd nodded. "It's the leases," he'd said, helping himself to a bourbon and water from the bar in the small library in the east wing. "No one in Devereaux owns the land his house or business is on."

Anne had blinked. "I beg your pardon?"

"Leases," Kevin had explained. "My family have always been fanatics about land. So when things got real bad at the end of the last century, they didn't sell land, they leased it—ninety-nine-year leases, which start running out in the next few years. Which means, legally, that every building in Devereaux, along with the land, reverts to us. That's why," he'd added, as shock began to register on Anne's face, "the town looks the way it does. Who's going to waste money fixing up a bunch of buildings that don't belong to them?

Nobody in town's broke, Anne. They just don't know what's going to happen next.''

Anne's eyes had narrowed. ''So that's what they all meant when they wanted to know what you were going to do?''

Kevin had nodded tiredly. ''Will Hempstead as much as asked me today, but I put him off.''

''And what are you going to do?'' Anne had asked.

Kevin shook his head. ''Sleep on it, I suppose. And see what Sam Waterman has to say. Then you and I and Marguerite can decide what's the right thing to do.''

Anne had held up her hands in protest. ''Not me,'' she'd said. ''It's all up to you and Marguerite. I've never been here before, I don't know any of the people involved, and, to be frank, I'm not too crazy about the place.'' When Kevin had given her a quizzical look, she'd added only half apologetically, ''What can I say? I watched the way everyone treated you and Marguerite this afternoon, and I felt the way they treated me. To them, you're part of Devereaux, and it doesn't matter that you don't live here anymore. You're part of *them*. But I'm not.'' When Kevin had tried to argue with her, she'd cut him off. ''Oh, they were polite enough. It's not that—it's just a feeling. I got the idea that deep down they feel that I'm an outsider, and they're right. So you and Marguerite decide what has to be done, and don't worry about me. I'm not a part of Sea Oaks, or Devereaux, and I never will be.''

They'd left it at that, and now Anne was sleeping peacefully beside him. But Kevin was still awake, his mind churning. Finally, knowing sleep was hours away, he got up and left the room. At the other end of the hall a streak of light glowed beneath Marguerite's door, and Kevin walked down and tapped softly. A moment later his sister told him to come in.

Marguerite was sitting up in bed, a pair of reading glasses perched on her nose. She took them off as he came in, then patted the bed for him to sit next to her.

''How are you holding up?'' Kevin asked.

''All right, I guess,'' Marguerite replied. ''Still numb, I suppose. But that will pass, and I'll get through it.''

"You always do," he said softly. "Sometimes you amaze me. How did you tolerate her all those years?"

Marguerite's eyes clouded slightly. "I loved her, Kevin," she said. Then, as he started to speak, she put her fingers to his lips. "I know how you felt, but I didn't. She took care of me, too, Kevin. After the—" She hesitated a second, then forced herself to go on. "After my accident she took care of me, you know."

"How could I forget?" Kevin asked, his bitterness suddenly clear in his voice. "She sent me off to military school so she could spend all her time with you."

Marguerite's eyes filled with tears. "Is that what you think?"

"Why shouldn't I? It's true, isn't it?"

Marguerite was silent for a long time, but at last, tiredly, she nodded. "I suppose it is," she agreed. "And I suppose it wasn't fair. But it was a bad time for me, too, Kevin. And in the end you got away from here. I never did."

Kevin reached out and took her hand. "Well, it's not too late. I suspect you can now do pretty much anything you want. If we sell Sea Oaks—"

Marguerite snatched her hand away. "Sell Sea Oaks?" she echoed. "Kevin, you're not thinking of doing that, are you? Where would I live? What would I do?"

Instantly, Kevin regretted his words. "I just said 'if,' " he assured her. "We certainly won't do anything you don't want to do."

"Well, I know I don't want to leave here," Marguerite told him. "I've lived here all my life. I won't say it's always been perfect, but it's my home, and I don't know if I could live anywhere else." Her voice took on a frightened edge. "I don't need much money—"

"Hey!" Kevin protested. "Take it easy. If it's what you want, and we can find a way, of course you'll stay here. And we shouldn't even be talking about it now. Let's wait until tomorrow and see what Sam's got to say. Okay?"

Marguerite looked at him for a moment, then smiled. "Okay." Then she glanced at the clock. "And I think you should be in bed. You're still my baby brother, and I can send you to bed if I want to, right?''

"Right," Kevin agreed, getting to his feet and leaning over to kiss his sister's cheek. "And keep the faith, sis, okay?"

"Don't I always?" Marguerite replied.

As Kevin left the room, she put her glasses back on and tried to concentrate on the book she'd been attempting to read. But it did no good. Without her mother, something was missing in the house.

Finally she reached over and switched off the light, then lay flat on the bed. In her right hip—the hip that had been so badly broken so many years ago—a burning pain began to radiate.

She tried to ignore the pain, tried to tell herself it didn't exist.

But, of course, it did exist. It was always there, lurking just beneath her consciousness, and on days like today, when something was upsetting her, the pain broke through, overtaking her entire body.

It had been going on like this for three days now, ever since her mother had died.

Every day the pain was becoming worse. . . .

It was the dream that woke Jeff up. He'd seen his grandmother, her cold eyes glaring at him, her bony finger pointing accusingly at him. But he didn't know why she was angry at him.

All he knew was that she wanted to hurt him.

Wanted to kill him.

Just as she reached out for him, her fingers circling his throat, he woke up.

He lay still in the bed for a few minutes, his heart pounding, and listened to the sounds of the house.

One by one he identified each of them.

The strange scratching sound—the one that sounded like

someone was trying to get in at the window—was just a branch brushing up against the screen.

The hollow thunking—the sound that on the first night had seemed ominous, like a ghost knocking at the door—was a loose shutter on the third floor, right above his room.

The creakings and groanings were just the house shifting, and he'd never been afraid of sounds like that—the house in Connecticut had them too.

But something had wakened him, and after he'd finally identified all the night noises, he crept out of his bed and went to the door. He pressed his ear up against the wood and listened carefully.

Nothing.

He went to the window and peered anxiously out into the darkness. There was a half-moon shimmering above the sea, and he watched the silvery streak that spread over the rippling waters, and the surf shining brightly in the moonlight.

Then he saw the movement.

He wasn't sure it was there for a second, because when he shifted his eyes to the place where he thought he'd seen it, it disappeared.

He shifted his gaze slightly, and he saw it again.

He closed his eyes for a moment, waiting for them to get used to the darkness, then opened them again.

And gasped, and his heart began to pound.

A hundred yards behind the house, in the cemetery, a pale white form seemed to be moving amid the tombstones.

A ghost.

His grandmother's ghost.

But that was dumb, he told himself. There were no such things as ghosts, except in movies.

Except that it was there, as clearly visible as his grandmother had been in his dream. He couldn't see it perfectly, for the branches of the oak tree kept swaying in the breeze, but every few seconds he could catch a glimpse of it, moving through the graveyard, circling slowly around the crypt.

His heart beat even faster, and he felt the cold knot of fear left over from the dream begin to harden in his belly.

What should he do?

Should he crawl back in bed and pull the covers up over his head? But what if the ghost had seen him, and came for him?

Julie.

Julie would know what to do.

His legs trembling, he went to the door and listened again. What if it were out there now, waiting for him?

He listened as hard as he could, but heard nothing. Carefully, doing his best to make no noise, he twisted the doorknob and pulled the door open a crack.

The hall was pitch dark, and his grandmother seemed to reach out of the blackness, trying to wrap her icy fingers around his throat.

He shrank back, panic closing in on him.

But he couldn't stay where he was. Not anymore.

Then he knew what to do.

If he turned on all the lights in his room and opened his door wide, he'd be able to see what was in the hall.

He turned the switch on the wall, and the chandelier over the center of the room came on. He opened the door again. Though the crack was only an inch wide, it was already better. Slowly, carefully, he widened the crack, and the shaft of light widened.

He looked both ways, peering into the dark shadows beyond the light. Then, taking a deep breath, he sprinted down the hall and burst through the door to Julie's room, hurling himself into her bed and pulling the covers up tight. Instantly, Julie sat up.

"Jeff?" she asked. Pulling the covers away from him, she glared down at him. "Jeff! What are you doing?"

Jeff swallowed the lump in his throat, and tried not to let his voice quaver. "Gh-Ghost," he managed. "There's a ghost in the graveyard, Julie!"

Julie stared at him. "What are you talking about?"

"I *saw* it," Jeff insisted. "I woke up, and I knew something was wrong, and when I looked out the window, I saw it!"

"*What* did you see?" Julie demanded.

"A *ghost*! It was all white, and it was just sort of floating around!"

Julie rolled her eyes. "That's dumb. There's no such thing as ghosts, and you know it."

"I saw it!" Jeff insisted. "If you don't believe me, just look!"

Suddenly Julie thought she understood. "You think you can make me get out of bed and go look out the window just so you can laugh at me? Well, you can't, so just go back to your bed, or I'm going to call Mom and Dad."

Jeff stayed where he was, his face set stubbornly. "I don't care," he said. "I know what I saw."

Julie hesitated. Always before, the threat to call their parents had put an end to Jeff's games. But this time he really looked scared. At last, sighing heavily but still curious, she got out of bed and went to the window.

The cemetery lay serenely in the moonlight, empty of anything but the crypt and a few headstones.

"There's nothing there," Julie said.

"There is too," Jeff said, staying where he was.

"There *isn't*," Julie insisted. "If you don't believe me, come look!"

There was a long silence, and finally Jeff left the bed and approached the window cautiously. Before he looked out, he slipped his hand into his older sister's. Then, at last, he screwed up his courage and looked once more into the moonlit stillness of the night.

The graveyard was empty.

He caught his breath, his eyes flooding with tears. "But it was there," he said. "I saw it. I know I did."

Finally, convinced that whatever he'd seen had truly frightened him, Julie led her brother back to bed. "Well, whatever it was, it's gone now. But if you want to, you can sleep with me tonight, all right?"

Jeff nodded solemnly, and let Julie tuck him in. A minute later she got into the other side of the bed and switched off the light.

For several minutes the room was silent. Then the hair on

the back of Jeff's neck stood on end and he felt a shiver run down his spine.

"Boo!" Julie cried, grabbing him from behind.

Jeff shrieked, then, despite himself, began to giggle. But long after his giggling had subsided and Julie had fallen asleep, the image of what he'd seen in the graveyard stayed in his mind.

It *had* been a ghost, and it *had* been real.

And if he'd stayed in his room, it would have come for him.

CHAPTER 7

"I did too see something!" Jeff flared. His jaw set stubbornly and his eyes narrowed to angry slits as he glared at his sister across the kitchen table.

But Julie only shrugged, and poured some molasses onto the stack of pancakes Ruby had just set in front of her.

"I didn't *say* you didn't see something," she replied, deliberately using the exaggeratedly patient tone she knew would make Jeff even madder. "All I said was that you didn't see a ghost. There's no such thing as ghosts."

"How do you know?" Jeff demanded. "Just because you say so doesn't make it so!"

"And just because you say so, doesn't either."

Ruby came over with an enormous plate of food and sat down to join the children. "What you two arguin' about so early in the morning?" she asked.

Before Jeff could say a word, Julie cut him off. "Jeff thought he saw a ghost last night. Did you ever hear anything so dumb?" But instead of nodding, as Julie had expected, Ruby turned to look at Jeff, her eyes glistening brightly.

"Down in the graveyard?" she asked. "By the crypt?"

Jeff's eyes widened with surprise, and he nodded. "It was all white," he breathed. "Almost like it was floating, or something."

Once again Ruby nodded. "That would have been Miz Helena," she said quietly. "I thought she'd turn up."

"Grandmother?" Jeff asked.

But before Ruby could reply, Julie broke out in laughter. "Oh, come on, Ruby, you've got to be kidding!"

Ruby swung around, and when her eyes fixed on Julie,

there was a darkness in them that made the laughter die on the girl's lips. " 'Round here, we don't kid 'bout things like that."

"B-But there's no such things as ghosts," Julie repeated, but her voice had lost most of its conviction.

"Aren't there?" the old woman asked. "Well, maybe where you come from there aren't. But things ain't the same down here. And if Jeff says he saw a ghost last night, I'd be inclined to believe him if I was you."

Jeff, emboldened, gazed up at Ruby with awe. "Did you ever see a ghost?"

Ruby's lips pursed for a moment, then, once more, she nodded. "I reckon I have," she said. "Fact is, I don't think there's many people on this island who haven't. Not if they've been here after someone dies, leastways. Happens every time. Happened when your grandfather died—I saw the specter myself."

Julie, her breakfast forgotten, looked out the window. Though the morning sky was bright and the heat was already beginning to make the air shimmer, she realized that she was shivering as she looked down the slope toward the family graveyard. For just a moment she almost imagined she could see—

No! She shook the strange sensation off and turned back to Ruby. "I still say there isn't any such thing as ghosts," she insisted, but suddenly wondered whom she was trying to convince—Ruby or herself.

Ruby peered at her through placid eyes. "You can believe what you want," she said. "It don't make no difference. I know what I've seen. And if Miz Helena came back last night, it wouldn't surprise me at all. There's people around here say all the Devereauxes come back. Some folks say they never leave this island at all, and that some nights—when the moon's just right—you can see all of 'em, wandering around the island."

Jeff's eyes were as large as saucers now. "But what do they want? What are they doing?"

Ruby shrugged elaborately. "Who knows? Maybe they just lookin' around, seein' to it that everything's all right." Her eyes narrowed then, taking on a faraway look, and the pitch of her voice dropped. "Or maybe they want something," she went on. "With the dead, you never know. But I know they're here, and I know when a Devereaux dies, he always come back, at least once."

"Wow," Jeff breathed. "Wait'll I tell Toby about this!"

"Tell him about what?" Kevin asked, coming in from the dining room and taking the last chair at the table.

"The ghost!" Jeff exclaimed. He was already on his feet, picking up the plate in front of him and carrying it over to the sink. "I saw Grandmother last night! Isn't that neat?" Then, before his father could say anything, Jeff was gone, banging out the back door and skipping down the steps two at a time.

Kevin watched him go, then turned to Ruby. "Mind telling me what that was all about?"

"You heard him," Ruby replied, pushing herself up from her chair and setting about fixing a stack of pancakes for Kevin. "Miz Helena. She come back last night, and Jeff saw her."

Kevin's expression tightened angrily. "For Christ's sake, Ruby! You aren't still scaring kids with those old stories, are you?"

Julie looked sharply at her father. "You mean you've heard it before?"

Kevin's head bobbed a single time. "Not since I was Jeff's age. She scared me half to death after my father died, telling me he'd come back and if I wasn't good, he'd punish me." His eyes shifted back to Ruby, and he noted her spine stiffen as she expertly flipped the pancakes. "And I won't have you scaring Jeff like that, Ruby."

Ruby spoke without turning around. "Didn't look to me like he was what you could call petrified," she muttered.

"He probably wasn't, now," Kevin replied. "But what about tonight? Or tomorrow night? I lost a lot of sleep over those stories when I was his age, and I'd just as soon he didn't have to."

"All's I did was tell him what I know," Ruby said stiffly as she set the plate in front of Kevin. "I don't see as how the truth can hurt anyone."

"But it's not the truth," Kevin shot back. "It's nothing but an old wives' tale."

Ruby turned to stare at Kevin, her eyes boring into his. "For someone who ain't been around here for an awful long time, you sure seem to think you know what's goin' on," she said. "But let me tell you somethin', young man," she added in a tone Kevin hadn't heard since he was a boy. "You don't know nothin'! You hear me? You don't know nothin'!" And then, back erect and head held high, she disappeared through the swinging door to the butler's pantry. A moment later Julie and Kevin could hear her angrily banging drawers closed.

Julie giggled softly and glanced at her father out of the corner of her eye. "For a second I thought she was going to spank you."

"For a second I did too," Kevin agreed. Then his grin faded and his expression grew more serious. "Did Jeff really believe her?"

Julie shrugged. "Who knows? He probably did—she almost had me convinced until you came in."

"Well, if she tells you any more stories, don't believe her," Kevin replied. "Ruby's a wonderful woman, but she's as full of superstition as everyone else around here."

Julie started to nod, then her eyes clouded. "But what if it's true?" she asked. "I mean, if everybody believes the same thing, there has to be a reason, doesn't there?"

But before Kevin could answer, Anne came into the kitchen. "There's a phone call for you," she said. "A boy. Someone named Kerry Sanders?"

Julie flushed red, then nodded eagerly. "I met him yesterday," she said, her voice tinged with excitement. "He said he was going to call this morning. He wanted to know if I could go to the beach with him and some other kids. Can I?"

Anne shrugged. "Why not?" When Julie was gone, she turned to Kevin. "So. Anything been going on this morning?"

Kevin shook his head. "Nothing worth talking about," he told her. "Just the staff, telling local ghost stories to the kids."

*   *   *

Sam Waterman prided himself on his ability to read the outcome of any meeting before he went into it. A lot of it, he knew, came simply from age—the older you got, the more you knew, and he was nearly eighty now. But there was more to it than that: he'd always had a knack for reading character, and that had always given him a little extra edge—if you knew whom you were dealing with, you knew how to approach him.

Today, however, he had no idea what he might be in for, and as he steered his car out onto the causeway to Devereaux Island, he shoved a Tums into his mouth to try to quench the ember of worry that had been burning in his belly all morning. The trouble was, he didn't know Anne Devereaux at all, and even Kevin, whom Sam had known since the day he was born, had become an enigma.

Part of it was the way Kevin talked now, in the harsh tones of a Yankee. Not a trace of the gentle drawl of South Carolina was left in his voice, and even his manner had changed. There was something that Sam could only call "clipped" about Kevin's manner. But, of course, the years in the North, where things moved so much more rapidly than they did in Devereaux, would have caused that. Sam chuckled softly to himself as he pulled onto the island. Hell, in Devereaux, things hardly moved at all! But still, he was about to toss something into Kevin's and Anne's laps without a clue as to how they might react to it, and Sam didn't like that at all.

Without thinking about it, he slowed the car, as if the few extra moments of delay might help the situation, but he still arrived at the mansion before he was quite ready. Still, there was nothing to be done except get on with it. If truth be known—and Sam was well aware that the truth was seldom, if ever, known—he should have come out here right after breakfast and gotten it over with. Nothing was going to change, and it might have saved a couple of cents on the Tums bill. Sighing heavily, he reached for the accordion file on the passenger seat, then got out of the car and made his way up the steps. As he was crossing the veranda, the front door swung wide and Marguerite came out. As always, she looked cool and fresh in the summer heat, but today Sam thought her eyes looked a bit clouded and her smile of welcome seemed just a little uncertain.

Maybe she knows, he thought, but then dismissed the idea from his mind. Helena Devereaux had never told anyone but him what she planned to do with her estate, and had sworn him to secrecy too. "It's not just a whim," she'd snapped when he suggested she discuss her plans with her only daughter. "Marguerite can't deal with things—never has been able to."

"Afternoon, Marguerite," Sam said now, noticing that whatever Helena had thought of her daughter, Marguerite certainly seemed to be dealing with things in a manner to be proud of. Even at the funeral she'd conducted herself with a remarkable calm. No, there wouldn't be any hysterics here. "Everybody ready for the reading?"

Marguerite stepped back to let the old lawyer precede her out of the sweltering heat and into the relative coolness of the house. "The children are out with their friends, and Kevin and Anne are waiting in the study."

Sam nodded briefly, and turned left into the west wing. At the end of the corridor was a large room with windows on all three sides, where the heads of the Devereaux family had always carried on the vast preponderance of their work. Sam, though he'd never asked Rafe Devereaux, had always wondered if the placement of the study was symbolic, since it was one of only two rooms in the house that offered a full view of all the Devereaux holdings.

The other room was the master suite, directly above the study.

Anne and Kevin stood up as Sam entered the room, and after greeting them, he immediately went around the desk and seated himself in the worn leather chair that had been there for the better part of two centuries. But the chair was as well made as the house, and didn't so much as creak as it accepted his weight. Sam carefully fit his wire-rimmed glasses over his nose, then slid a thin sheaf of papers out of the accordion folder. "Shall we begin?" he asked, peering at the three Devereauxes over the tops of his glasses. When no one objected, he began reading.

Ten minutes later it was over, and, as Sam had expected, a numbed silence hung over the room. Sam occupied himself during the silence by speculating on which of them would speak first. He had finally settled on Kevin when Anne's voice, tight with outrage, exploded shrilly through the tense silence.

"That's absolutely outrageous! She can't have left it all to Kevin! She *can't* have!"

"She not only can," Waterman observed mildly, "she has."

"But it's not fair," Anne protested. "What about Marguerite? She took care of Helena all her life! And now she gets nothing? Nothing at all?" Her eyes were flashing with indignation, and she reached out to grasp Marguerite's hand. "How could she do that?"

To everyone's surprise, it was Marguerite who answered her. "It's the way we've always done things, Anne," she said. Though her eyes were glistening damply, her voice held steady. "Our land has always passed to the oldest son. It was always the only way we could keep the land together. Daddy always said if you divide the land, you lose it. So, of course, it goes to Kevin now. I suppose I should have known, shouldn't I?"

"Does it really matter?" Kevin asked archly, speaking for the first time since Waterman had finished reading the will. "Apart from the island, and the town itself, is there anything left?"

"A couple of hundred acres," Waterman replied. "But it's not good for much—mostly swampland that no one wants."

"But we can sell the holdings in town, can't we?" Anne asked. "And split the money with Marguerite?"

"Possibly," Waterman agreed. "But it won't be simple—the leases don't run out for several more years, and there's a codicil."

"A codicil?" Kevin echoed. "You mean there's more?"

Waterman nodded, licking his lips nervously. "It's part of the will. I tried to talk Helena out of it but I couldn't. In fact, since she knew I was opposed to it, she had another lawyer draw it up." He faced Kevin squarely now. "I assume you're

aware of how much your mother wanted you to come back
here?''

Kevin nodded, but frowned in puzzlement. What was the
lawyer getting at?

''Well, I'm afraid she's found a way. Although she's left
everything to you, she's also stipulated that you must live
here at Sea Oaks and manage the estate, and I quote, 'to the
best advantage of the Devereaux family and the citizens of
Devereaux, South Carolina.' End of quote.''

Kevin's frown dissolved, to be replaced by a relaxed smile.
''Then we don't have a problem. All I have to do is take
Anne and the kids home, and Marguerite gets everything,
right?''

''Wrong,'' Waterman replied. ''Give your mother a little
more credit than that. She may not have been kind, but she
wasn't stupid either. If you refuse to live here and manage the
estate, then everything goes to the Fortress. Everything—the
land, the house, the bank accounts, the stocks—the whole
lot. If you won't live here, then Marguerite can't, either.''

A second shocked silence fell over the room. Marguerite's
fingers tightened on the arms of her chair, but she said
nothing. Anne looked dazed, as if she couldn't quite compre-
hend what had transpired. But Kevin's face was ashen, and
his jaw was clenched with fury. It took nearly a full minute
before he was finally able to speak. ''I gather you've already
found there's no way to break that codicil?''

Waterman spread his hands helplessly. ''It's very long, it's
very complicated, and it's very complete. She's covered every eventuality either she or the Charleston attorney could
think of, and as far as I know, it will hold up. I even thought
of burning it,'' he added. ''But it wouldn't have done any
good. The original isn't even in my hands.''

Anne blinked as if coming out of a deep sleep. ''But it's
obscene,'' she breathed. ''After everything Marguerite's done
for her, she leaves her nothing, and now she wants to force
Kevin to change his whole life too!''

Waterman sighed heavily. ''I agree with you,'' he said. ''I
did my best to talk her out of it, but she wouldn't budge.
And,'' he added, ''it's not forever.'' His lips stretched into a

thin, humorless smile. "Actually, it would have been better if she'd made it forever. That, a court would have ruled was unreasonable. But she got around that. You have to stay ten years. You have full control of the land, but if you sell any of it, the sales can't become final until the ten years are up. After that, you can do what you want."

"Generous of her," Anne remarked, making no attempt to conceal her bitter sarcasm.

"Not generous," Waterman contradicted quietly. "It was as far as she could go and make it stick. And she told me that she thought ten years was enough anyway. She said if she could get you back for that long, you'd stay on of your own accord."

Marguerite rose unsteadily to her feet and limped heavily across to Kevin. She put her hands on his shoulders and bent down to kiss his cheek. "I'm sorry," she whispered. "I'm so sorry. I didn't know anything about this. Nothing at all."

Kevin covered his sister's hand with his own. "It's all right," he told her. "I'm not sure what we can do about all this, but there has to be a way to sort it out. And we'll find it."

Marguerite managed a smile and bobbed her head. "I'm sure we will," she agreed, her voice quavering. "But right now I'm a little tired. If you'll all excuse me?" She glanced at Sam, almost as if asking permission to leave. When he said nothing, she turned and moved haltingly out of the study, pulling the door closed behind her.

"How could Helena have been this cruel?" Anne asked when Marguerite was gone.

Waterman shook his head and began packing the papers back into the accordion file. "I don't know," he said, though he wasn't sure Anne's question had required a response. "It just comes down to a question of control, I suppose. She never liked being out of control. She hated being sick the last years, and she hated having to be taken care of. Maybe she focused it all on Marguerite in the end."

"But what are we supposed to do?" Anne asked, her voice taking on a plaintive note. "Surely Kevin isn't really expected to stay here."

Once again Waterman's lips curled into a thin smile. "What the two of you do, of course, is entirely your own decision. But while you think about it, don't forget Marguerite." His eyes met hers. "And the rest of us," he added. "Don't forget the rest of us either. Whatever you decide, everyone in Devereaux is going to have to live with."

Five minutes later the attorney left, his car kicking up a thin cloud of dust as he drove away from Devereaux Island. Kevin and Anne watched until he was gone, his car disappearing across the causeway. Then, together, they turned and went back into the shadowy darkness of the mansion.

But it's not a mansion, Anne silently reflected as she closed the front door. *It's not a mansion at all. It's a prison.*

Marguerite paused at the top of the stairs to catch her breath and wait for the white-hot pain in her hip to ease a little. The pain had begun as she'd listened to Sam Waterman read the will, but she'd done her best not to show it. Instead, she'd simply gripped the arms of the chair harder and harder, until the ache in her hands and fingers took her mind off the pain in her hip.

She'd never thought about the possibility of having to leave Sea Oaks before. Always, since the days after the accident—when she knew she would never be able to dance again—she had assumed she'd live out her life quietly here, with her mother, in the familiar surroundings that had been the only home she'd ever known. Now, as the reality of her mother's will began to sink in, she realized that it wasn't just Sea Oaks she'd taken for granted; it was her mother too. And until just now, listening to Sam's voice as he read, she hadn't truly realized that her mother was gone, that she would never again hear the angry rasping of the buzzer, never again face her mother's angry countenance as she made the newest of her ever-increasing demands on Marguerite.

But Marguerite had accepted the demands willingly, accepted the constant interruptions in her day almost eagerly. Taking care of her mother, as her mother had taken care of her, had been the center of her life for more years than she cared to remember. And they hadn't been bad years for her, despite what everyone else thought.

And, of course, Marguerite knew what they thought, had long ago learned to read the thoughts behind the words when people spoke to her.

"How *is* your mother," said in the most solicitous tones and with the most sympathetic of expressions, meant, quite simply, "When is the old hag going to die?"

"How are you?" meant "How can you stand to put up with that nasty old woman?"

Marguerite had always appeared to accept the words at face value, never betrayed her resentment at other people's assumption that she must have hated her mother. For she did not hate her mother; indeed, she loved her mother, explaining the older woman's ever-growing bad temper as nothing more than a result of advancing age and retreating good health. Who, confined to a bed, wouldn't become irritable after a while?

And besides, Marguerite owed Helena far more than she had ever paid. Hadn't she disappointed her mother so many years ago, when she'd been clumsy enough to fall down the stairs and end the dream Helena had nourished for her since the day she'd been born?

Hadn't she turned, in that single moment, from the object of her mother's hopes into a burden her mother had been forced to bear?

And now her mother was gone, and even though Kevin and his family were there, the house would, for Marguerite, be forever empty.

Except, of course, for her girls.

She still had them. Would always have them, or others like them.

And Julie.

She mustn't forget Julie. There was so much of herself in Julie.

She started toward her room, a small smile playing around her lips as she remembered watching Julie dance. It was almost like watching herself again. . . .

A sudden movement at the end of the corridor caught her eye. Then she realized that someone was in her mother's room.

Frowning, Marguerite started along the hall, her lame leg dragging slightly, her step uneven, one hand brushing lightly against the wall to hold her balance. The door to the master suite was open, and Marguerite stepped through, then stopped.

The door to the immense walk-in closet where her mother's clothes hung neatly on padded hangers was thrown wide open, and Ruby was taking the garments off the hangers one by one, folding them, and packing them away into large cardboard cartons. Marguerite's eyes widened as she realized what Ruby was doing, and she gasped. Ruby turned to look at her, then went back to her work.

"I guess we can send these to the thrift shop," she said, surveying the long row of gowns. "I'm not sure who'd buy them, but I 'spose there's always someone—"

Her words were cut off as Marguerite snatched the dress she was holding out of her hands.

"How dare you?" Marguerite demanded, her eyes flashing with anger. "How dare you touch my mother's things?"

Ruby, startled, stepped back, nearly stumbling over one of the boxes. "Miss Marguerite, you can see plain as day what I'm doing. I'm packing up Miss Helena's things, just like I packed up Mr. Rafe's after he died." She reached out to take the dress from Marguerite, but Marguerite jerked it away.

"No!" she exclaimed, clutching the dress close to her breast. "I won't let you! Not yet!"

Ruby started to protest, but changed her mind when she saw the angry glow in Marguerite's eyes. She backed slowly away. "I'm sorry, Miss Marguerite," she said. "Maybe I should've waited til tomorrow."

As quickly as it had come, the anger seemed to drain out of Marguerite, and she relaxed slightly. But she did not give up the dress. "Yes," she said at last. "Tomorrow. Maybe you can begin the packing tomorrow. Or the day after. But not today." Her eyes took on a pleading look. "Please, Ruby?" she asked.

Ruby's tongue flicked over her lips for a second and her

eyes hooded. But at last she nodded. "All right," she said. "I'll wait a day or two. These dresses ain't going any further out of fashion than they already are." She turned then and started out of the room, but at the door she looked back.

Marguerite was in the dressing room now, standing in front of a mirror. Her mother's dress held up against her body, she stared at her image in the glass for a moment. Then, a mysterious smile spreading across her face, she bowed deeply in the style of a prima ballerina.

But the lameness in her leg made the bow clumsy, and pitifully grotesque.

Ruby hurried out of the room.

CHAPTER 8

Julie lay on her back, her right arm shielding her eyes from the sun. She could feel a slow trickle of sweat running down her side, and knew that soon she would have to go into the water, if only to cool off a little. The problem, though, was that she wasn't sure she had quite enough strength to make the few yards from her towel to the water's edge. The heat had closed around her like a blanket, wrapping her so tightly she could barely breathe. But around her the rest of the kids—the kids who had grown up here—didn't seem to be affected by it at all.

There were ten of them altogether, and Julie had decided early in the afternoon that she liked all of them except Mary-Beth Fletcher. And she'd tried to like Mary-Beth, too, even after the way Mary-Beth had acted at the dance class a week ago. But it hadn't been easy, because each time she'd started to approach Mary-Beth, the other girl had suddenly gotten involved with someone else and acted as if Julie weren't even there.

And then, an hour ago, she'd been sitting with Kerry, exploring the contents of the picnic basket that Ruby had packed for her, when Mary-Beth had dropped down onto the edge of Kerry's towel. Julie had offered her a sandwich, but Mary-Beth had shaken her head.

"We don't eat like northerners down here," she said, stretching out each vowel in an exaggerated drawl. "You go on and make a pig of yourself if you want to though. I'm sure it's just fine by me!"

Julie had felt herself redden with embarrassment, but had

said nothing, and a few minutes later, her flirting with Kerry getting her nowhere, Mary-Beth had wandered away.

Now Julie could hear Mary-Beth's voice again, this time talking to a couple of her friends. For a moment Julie was certain that Mary-Beth thought she couldn't hear her, but then she realized that exactly the opposite was true: Mary-Beth had raised her voice to make certain that Julie heard every word.

"I think maybe I'll quit dance class," Mary-Beth was saying.

"Quit?" Julie heard Jennifer Mayhew ask, her voice clearly reflecting her dismay. "Why?"

"I don't know," Mary-Beth replied in calculatedly offhand tones. Though Julie's eyes were closed, she could feel Mary-Beth staring at her as she continued. "Up till last week Miss Marguerite never had any favorites or anything like that, and it was fun. Now it looks like all we're going to do is sit around and watch that Yankee trash jump around while Marguerite drools like an idiot and tells us all how wonderful her niece is. Who needs it?"

Jenny Mayhew gasped indignantly. "Mary-Beth, that's not true, and you know it! Miss Marguerite isn't like that at all, and it's not Julie's fault if she's better than the rest of us. I should think you'd want to learn from her."

Julie could almost see Mary-Beth's simpering smile. "Well, aren't you the goody-goody all of a sudden!"

Then Julie heard another voice. "Jenny's not a goody-goody, and none of the rest of us are either. If you want to quit because you know you aren't any good, why don't you just say so? You don't have to blame Julie, or claim Miss Marguerite's different."

Mary-Beth's voice turned defensive. "I didn't say I was going to quit," she protested. "I just said I *might*. I'm just thinking about it is all. How come you're all jumping on me? And if you're all so crazy about Julie, why don't you go talk to her?"

Suddenly Julie could stand it no more. She sat up, blinking in the brightness of the sun, and turned to Kerry, who was sitting up on his towel next to hers, his strong jaw set in anger, his clear blue eyes flashing dangerously.

"Come on," she said. "Let's go in the water. If I stay here another five minutes, I think I'm going to pass out." She tried to stand up, but fell back onto the blanket, her legs weak with the heat. But as she heard Mary-Beth start giggling, Kerry reached down and took her hand, the strength of his powerfully built body easily pulling her upright.

"Just start moving," he said softly enough so no one else could hear him. He grinned encouragingly, brushing a lock of his curly blond hair off his forehead. "It's only a few yards, and as soon as you get in the water, you'll be fine."

A wave of dizziness swept over Julie. For a moment she thought she was going to faint, but Kerry's hand tightened on hers, and she let him lead her quickly down the beach. Feeling the coolness of the water close over her feet, she let go of Kerry's hand and plunged into a large wave that was rushing toward shore.

Instantly her head cleared and she felt the sticky layer of perspiration wash away. She swam underwater for a few strokes, then broke the surface, rolled over on her back, and looked around for Kerry. He surfaced only a few feet away and grinned at her. "Feel better?"

Julie nodded. "I thought I was going to pass out. How does everybody stand it?"

"The heat, or Mary-Beth?" Kerry teased.

"The heat," Julie replied. "Who cares what Mary-Beth says?"

Suddenly Kerry yelled at her, and Julie turned around just in time to see a breaker building up right behind her. Taking a deep breath, she grabbed her nose and ducked down just as the wave broke over her, and a moment later felt the water rush past her.

"You get used to the heat," Kerry told her after they'd both come to the surface again. "Another couple of weeks and you won't even notice it anymore." He grinned mischievously. "Same with Mary-Beth—another couple of weeks and you won't notice her anymore either. Besides, she's just messed up 'cause I invited you today."

Now Julie thought she understood. "Was she your girl-friend?"

Kerry shook his head. "No way."

"But she wishes she were?" Julie asked, and Kerry's face reddened with embarrassment.

"You want to talk all afternoon, or swim?" he demanded, splashing water in her face.

Julie splashed him back, and then all the rest of the kids except Mary-Beth Fletcher plunged into the water to join in the melee. Before long the group divided itself into two sides, but the sides kept changing as alliances were abandoned the moment an opportunity for a good dunk came up. And then, out of the laughter, Julie heard Kerry's voice shouting to her. "Julie! Look out!"

She whirled, but it was already too late. From out of nowhere an enormous wave had built up, and before she could dive into it or duck beneath the surface, the undertow had her in its grip and she felt her legs slide out from under her. She gasped for breath just as the wave hit her, knocking her flat then tumbling her along the bottom like a piece of waterlogged wood.

She struggled against it, fighting to regain her footing, but then she felt her feet tangling in seaweed, and the first twinges of panic closed around her heart.

It's all right, she told herself. I can swim, and it's only a wave, and the water isn't even over my head. All I have to do is let myself go, then stand up!

But how long could she go? Her lungs were bursting now, and she knew she couldn't hold her breath more than a few more seconds.

And the wave seemed determined to keep her at the bottom.

She lunged hard then, and her breath gave out. The spent air poured out of her lungs, but it was going to be all right! She felt her head break the surface and her feet connect with the bottom. She opened her mouth wide, taking in great gasps of air.

And water.

Another wave had already built behind the first, smashing

into her face, flooding her mouth, choking her throat with brine. She was coughing as she went under for the second time, and this time she knew she had no reserves of air to sustain her.

She was going to drown!

Panic overwhelmed her, and she began thrashing against the churning water, fighting against the current, searching for a foothold on the bottom.

Against her will, her lungs began to take in water.

And then, as she felt herself begin to black out, strong arms snaked around her body and lifted her out of the water. She struggled for a moment, then heard Kerry's voice.

"It's okay! You're okay, Julie, I've got you!"

Still coughing and choking, she threw her arms around him and clung to him as he waded through the surf, and up the beach. Finally he laid her on her towel, then dropped down next to her, rolling her over onto her stomach and pressing down hard on her back.

Saltwater spewed out of her lungs and disappeared into the sand.

A moment later it was over and Julie lay still, her chest heaving as she took in breath after breath of pure fresh air. It felt like hours before she finally trusted herself to roll over and look up at the circle of faces above her.

"Wh—What happened?" she asked.

Kerry gazed back at her, his blue eyes filled with worry. "It was my fault," he said. "I should have warned you. It was a rogue wave. They come in like that every now and then. Everything's real calm, and then all of a sudden a big one comes, and if you're not ready, it just knocks you out. Are you all right?"

Julie hesitated, then nodded. "I—I think so." She managed a weak grin. "But I sure thought it was all over for a second. If you hadn't gotten hold of me . . ." She fell silent, shuddering even at the thought, then realized she was shivering with cold despite the heat of the afternoon. "I—maybe you'd better take me home. . . ."

With the rest of the kids crowding around, Kerry picked

her up and carried her to his car, a battered and rusty Chevy convertible whose top was little more than a series of shreds held together by a mass of silvery duct tape.

"Maybe we'd better get someone else's car," he suggested, his voice anxious, but Julie shook her head.

"It's all right," she said. "I like your car."

"Then you're nuts," Kerry replied, but still grinned at her. "But that's okay—I like nutty girls." Slamming the door after making sure she was safely inside, he ran around and clambered into the driver's seat.

Neither of them heard Mary-Beth Fletcher's parting shot: "Why don't you just drive her right on back up North, where she belongs? And if you like her so much, go with her!"

Toby Martin stared suspiciously at Jeff. "What if we get caught?" he demanded.

They were inside the fort they'd finished building that afternoon—a shaky lean-to next to the garage, constructed out of rotting lumber scavenged from the collapsing slave quarters—and hammered together with a cache of rusty nails they'd found in the barn. There was a small door just big enough for them to crawl through, and it hadn't occurred to either of them that a window might have relieved the stuffy heat inside. But if they even felt the heat, neither was about to admit it. Since they'd finished the fort an hour ago, they'd been inside, securely hidden away from the world outside, talking about what Jeff had seen in the cemetery the night before.

"We won't get caught," Jeff insisted. "I'll sneak out after everyone else has gone to sleep, and we'll meet here. Then we'll watch the graveyard all night."

Suddenly, from outside, they heard a noise, as if something had moved in the underbrush. "What was that?" Jeff whispered. "Is there someone out there?"

Toby shrugged his shoulders. "I don't know. What'll we do?"

"Let's go look," Jeff decided. He dropped to his hands and knees and wriggled through the tiny hole in the wall. A moment later Toby followed him.

"What was it?" Toby asked. "Did you see anything?"

Jeff shook his head, his eyes searching the brush for any sign of movement. A few feet away he spotted a rabbit low to the ground, holding absolutely still. "Look!" he whispered, nudging Toby's ribs. "Over there! I'm gonna see if I can catch him."

Toby's eyes followed Jeff's, but it took a moment before he, too, spotted the rabbit.

And another moment before he realized why the rabbit wasn't moving. "Wait!" He yelled, but it was too late.

The ominous buzz of a rattlesnake hummed in the air, and Jeff froze, only his eyes moving as he searched for the source of the warning rasp.

It was only three feet away, a large, pink timber rattler, its thick coils wrapped tightly, its head bobbing dangerously as the rattle on its tail quivered with menace.

"Don't move!" Toby warned. "That's why the rabbit was holding still. If you don't move, it can't see you!"

"But . . . what are we going to do?" Jeff whimpered. His knees felt weak and he was sure he was going to collapse any second.

"I'll get someone," Toby said. "But if you move, he'll kill you for sure!" Leaving Jeff alone with the writhing creature, he turned and dashed up the driveway toward the house, screaming for help. The back door slammed open just as Toby got to the steps, and Kevin emerged.

"A snake," Toby screamed. "A big rattler's got Jeff down by the garage. Quick, Mr. Devereaux. Quick!"

Racing past the terrified boy, Kevin hurtled down the driveway to the garage, pausing only to snatch up a rusty shovel that leaned against the wall just inside its open door. A second later he found his son, still rooted to the spot, his face pale, his whole body trembling with fright.

"It's okay," Kevin said. "I'm here now, and it's going to be okay. Just stay still, Jeff. Can you do that?"

Jeff, too terrified even to speak, said nothing.

Kevin circled slowly around until he was behind the snake, then began approaching it, moving slowly and carefully, trying to make no sound that would alert the serpent to the danger from the rear. Step by step he drew closer, his eyes locked on the weaving head of the snake, which still stared at Jeff, its tongue flicking in and out as it tried to locate its prey.

Kevin raised the shovel, poising it to strike the moment he was close enough.

His foot came down on a twig, which snapped loudly. The rattler twisted and struck instantly, and Kevin leaped aside, bringing the shovel down with all the force he could muster. The blade of the shovel sank into the earth just as the snake's head struck it, and Kevin could feel the vibration of the blow as it came up the handle. Only slightly stunned from the impact, the snake recoiled, preparing to strike again. But this time Kevin was faster.

The blade of the tool sliced through the snake's body just behind its head, and the creature collapsed in mid-strike, its coils thrashing on the ground for a moment before it died.

Jeff, screaming, threw himself into his father's arms.

"It's all right," Kevin told him. "You're okay, and the snake's dead. It's all over."

"It was going to kill me, Daddy," Jeff sobbed. "I didn't even see it. It was just there!"

"I know," Kevin told him. "That's the way they are. You have to keep your eyes open all the time and make sure you look before you take a step. But you're okay."

Anne appeared around the corner of the garage, stopping short when she saw the still twitching remains of the rattler. "My God," she breathed, her eyes wide with horror. "What happened?"

"Nothing," Kevin assured her. "Jeff just ran into a snake, but he did exactly the right thing. In fact," he added, "I probably didn't even need to kill it. In another few seconds it would have lost interest and gone away. It was probably more frightened than Jeff."

Anne stared at Kevin indignantly. "How can you say that? It could have killed him!" She gathered her son into her arms and held him close. "Honey, are you all right?"

Jeff nodded, and wriggled out of his mother's arms. Now that it was over and the danger had passed, he was fascinated with the snake's body. "Can I keep it, Dad?" he asked, poking at the six feet of rattler with a stick.

Kevin chuckled, and used the spade once more to cut off the rattles. "Take those—when I was your age, I must have had a couple dozen of 'em."

"Awesome," Jeff said. He squatted down, gingerly picked up the rattle, then shook it.

There was a slight buzzing sound, and Jeff dropped the rattle as if it were red-hot, then self-consciously picked it up again. "You got one of these?" he asked Toby, who was standing a few yards away.

Toby nodded. "I have five. And one of 'em's even bigger than that."

"Really?" Jeff asked, his voice filled with awe. "Can I see?"

"Sure," Toby replied.

"When? Now?"

But before Toby could reply, Anne intervened. "Not now," she said. "Right now, I think you'd better both go in the house."

"Aw, Mom," Jeff began, but Anne shook her head.

"Maybe you're all over this, but I'm not. And until I am, I want you where I can see you, all right?"

Knowing better than to argue with her, Jeff started toward the house, Toby trailing along behind. Anne, though, stayed where she was, staring at the snake with revulsion. Finally, she met Kevin's eyes.

"How did you stand it?" she asked. "How can anyone stand it? The heat, the alligators, the mosquitoes, and now this!"

Kevin only shrugged. "Except for the alligators, what's so different than home? We get some pretty awful heat, and in case you didn't know it, we have rattlers too."

Anne's mouth fell open. "Oh, come on, Kevin—"

"But it's true," Kevin insisted. "There are timber rattlers all over the east. The only reason we don't see so many of them is because of all the development. And it wouldn't take much to clean them out of here."

Anne's eyes narrowed and a frown creased her forehead. "Clean them out? What are you talking about?"

Before Kevin could say anything, there was a loud honking, and they turned to see Kerry Sanders's car roaring down the dirt road from the causeway, a plume of dust spewing up behind him. It was when he slammed the brakes on as he reached the front of the house that they realized something was wrong.

Hurrying up the drive, they reached Kerry's car just as he was helping Julie out of the passenger seat.

Her face was pale, and her hair, a stringy mass of tangled locks, hung limply over her shoulders.

Anne stared at her daughter in shock. "Julie? Are you all right?"

Julie nodded, but wrapped a towel around herself. "I'm all right. I just got knocked over by a wave and started choking."

"Knocked over?" Anne repeated, her voice rising, "Honey, you look like you almost drowned."

"It's not that bad—" Julie started to object, but Kerry cut her off.

"It was pretty bad. She got hit by two waves, but I got to her in time. She's okay, but she says she's cold—"

"Shock," Kevin said. "Come on, honey, let's get you into bed and warmed up."

Anne stared at her husband. How could he take it so lightly? First a rattler threatened Jeff, and now Julie was brought home half drowned! And he was acting as if nothing had happened! What would it take for him to see that the best thing they could do was simply pack up their clothes and go back where they belonged? She opened her mouth, about to speak her mind, then suddenly thought better of it. Later, when they were alone and Julie was over the worst of her fright, she would talk to Kevin about it. And he would understand.

But a niggling doubt kept picking at her. What if he didn't understand? What if he was actually thinking of staying here? What would she do?

She didn't know.

Picking Julie up, Kevin strode up the front steps, Anne running ahead of him to open the door. But just as he got to the threshold, the door opened and Marguerite appeared. She stepped back to let Kevin and Anne pass, but blocked Kerry's way as he tried to follow. He stopped in confusion.

"C-Can I come in?" he finally asked.

Marguerite ignored his question. "What's happened?" she demanded. "What has happened to my niece?"

As clearly as he could, Kerry explained. "It was an accident," he finished. "I tried to warn her, but it was too late. I—"

But Marguerite didn't let him finish. "How dare you?" she asked, her eyes glittering with anger. "What do you mean, an accident? There are no such things as accidents, young man. We entrusted Julie to you, and what happened? You bring her home half drowned!"

Kerry's face reddened, and he took a step backward. "I—I'm sorry, Miss Devereaux," he began, but once again Marguerite cut him off.

"Sorry? You're *sorry*? My niece is a very special person, Kerry. She's a dancer who has a brilliant career ahead of her. Today all that could have been taken away from her because of you, and all you can say is that you're sorry?"

Kerry felt his temper rising. "Well, what do you want me to say?" he demanded. "It wasn't my fault, and I tried to warn her, and I got her out of the water and brought her home! What else was I supposed to do?"

"You should never have let it happen in the first place," Marguerite declared. "You're just like all the rest of the boys—no sense of responsibility at all! And how dare you speak to me the way you just did?"

The rest of Kerry's control snapped. "Me speak to you?"

he shouted. "What about the way you were talking to me? Now I see why Mary-Beth wants to quit your stupid classes. If you talk to the girls the way you talk to me, I'll bet they all quit!"

Marguerite lurched backward in the face of Kerry's anger and had to grasp the doorjamb to keep from stumbling. "Quit?" she gasped. "I don't understand—what are you talking about?"

"I'm talking about Mary-Beth Fletcher," Kerry said, his voice still quivering with anger. "She was talking about quitting your classes today, and everyone else was trying to talk her out of it. But now I see why she wants out." Turning, he stormed off the veranda, slammed back into his car, started it, and gunned the engine. Then he popped the clutch. The wheels spun in the grass for a moment before they caught, then left deep ruts as the car skidded across the lawn, slewed onto the road, and disappeared in a cloud of dust.

Marguerite, stunned, stood on the veranda until long after Kerry's car had disappeared from view.

What had he been talking about? Mary-Beth was going to quit her lessons? But it wasn't possible. She couldn't leave Marguerite. She couldn't!

Then, as the thoughts tumbled through her mind, Marguerite felt a touch on her arm.

She spun around, half expecting to see her mother standing there.

But, of course, it wasn't her mother—her mother was dead. She had to remember that and stop thinking that Helena was going to come back.

"R-Ruby?" she asked, her eyes blinking as they flooded with hot tears. "Oh, Ruby, what am I going to do? If Mary-Beth leaves me—"

"Now, now," Ruby soothed. "Don't you even think about that. We don't have to worry about Mary-Beth Fletcher. I always said she'd come to a bad end, and if she quits your lessons, I say we're well rid of her."

But Marguerite shook her head. "No," she breathed. "You

don't understand, Ruby. She can't leave me. I love her, Ruby. I love her, and she can't leave me. . . .'' Her voice trailed off and she took an unsteady step, leaning heavily on Ruby to hold her balance. "She can't . . ." she said once more.

"Then she won't," Ruby said firmly, leading Marguerite back into the house and closing the door behind her. "We'll fix it, Miss Marguerite. There's always ways of fixin' things."

Marguerite let herself be led into the small parlor, and settled into a chair, where she sat in silence for several minutes. "Yes," she said at last, coming out of her reverie. "We'll fix it, won't we? There are ways of fixing everything."

CHAPTER 9

Kevin waited until dinner was over and Ruby had begun clearing off the large dining room table before he brought up the idea that had been growing in his mind ever since Sam Waterman had left a few hours earlier. His whole family had known something was up, and all through the meal they wanted to know what he was smiling about. He hadn't told them, waiting until just the right moment. But finally, with a soft breeze wafting gently through the open French doors and the scent of wisteria perfuming the air, he decided the time was right. He turned to Julie, who was sitting at his right scraping up the last crumbs of Ruby's rhubarb pie. "What would you think," he asked, drawing each word out for the maximum effect, "of living here? I mean on a permanent basis?"

Julie stared at her father in shocked surprise, and her brow furrowed slightly. "You mean not go back home at all? Just stay here?"

"Well, of course we'd go home," he told her. He glanced toward Anne, and the first pang of doubt suddenly came over him, for instead of smiling encouragingly at him, she seemed to be stiffening in her chair at the opposite end of the table. He turned his attention quickly back to Julie. "We'd have to pack up, sell the house, and take care of a lot of details. But what I want to know is how you feel about living here."

Now Julie looked dazed. "I—I don't know," she stammered. "I mean—well, I just haven't thought about it, that's all."

"I think it would be neat!" Jeff declared, his eyes sparkling with excitement.

"And I," Anne said from the end of the table, her cool voice washing the glitter from Jeff's eyes, "would like to know what on earth you're talking about."

Kevin shifted his eyes to his wife and silently took a deep breath before he spoke. "I've just been thinking about our problem," he said. "And it occurs to me that even though Mother was trying to control me with her will, she might have done us all the biggest favor of our lives."

Anne's eyes flashed briefly toward Marguerite, who was sitting quietly, her own eyes fastened on her brother. "All of us?" she asked, her skepticism clear in her voice. "I'm not sure I'm following you."

"An inn," Kevin said, deciding it was time to lay his cards on the table. "We all know I've always wanted to run my own place, and it seems to me that Sea Oaks is perfect. It's way too big for a family, but we've got nine bedrooms—every one of them with its own bath—and plenty of space down here for public rooms. Not to mention the rest of the island. There's more than enough land for a golf course, condominiums, swimming pools, and tennis courts—the whole works!"

Anne stared at him as if he'd lost his mind. "Kevin, what are you talking about? It sounds like you're thinking of turning this place into another Hilton Head!"

"Exactly!" Kevin exclaimed, the enthusiasm for the project that had been building in him all afternoon spilling out. "Why not? I'm not saying it wouldn't take a lot of work and a lot of money, but everything we need to start is right here. We've got one of the best beaches on the whole coast, a house that's perfect for a small hotel—at least to start with—and all the land we need! And we already own it. And think of the benefits to the town—my God, if it's any kind of a success at all, land values would skyrocket, there'd be more jobs than we have people to fill them—"

But Anne didn't let him finish. She stood up abruptly, her face expressionless. "I think you and I had better talk about this later, when we're by ourselves," she said. "If you'll excuse me . . ." As her family sat in silence, she left the dining room, and a moment later her footsteps on the stairs echoed through the house. It was Julie who finally spoke.

"You goofed, Dad," she said. "How come you didn't at least talk to her about it first?"

Kevin knew his daughter was right, but the whole idea of the inn had seemed so perfect to him that he'd allowed himself to hope that Anne would see it too. But he also knew Anne hated surprises, and, even worse, hated the idea of having decisions made for her. And the way he'd been talking . . . He dropped his napkin onto the table and stood up. "I'd better go talk to her."

"Well, I still think it would be neat," Jeff said after his father was gone.

Julie hardly even heard her brother. Instead, she was looking at her aunt, who was sitting perfectly still in her chair, her eyes almost blank. "Aunt Marguerite?" Julie finally asked. "Do you know what this is all about? Why is Dad talking about turning your house into a hotel?"

Marguerite shook her head as if trying to clear something out of her mind, then managed to smile at her niece. "It's . . . well, it's not really my house anymore, darling," she said. "It's your father's now. And, well, there are some problems." As simply as she could, Marguerite explained the terms of her mother's will to the children. When she had finished, Julie was filled with indignation.

"But it's not fair!" she declared. "How could she do that?"

Marguerite shrugged. "I know it doesn't seem fair, darling, but life never is, really, is it? And what your father is doing is trying to find a way for us all to deal with Mother's will." Her eyes drifted around the room, lighting for a moment on each piece of furniture, then moving on. Finally she sighed quietly. "But a hotel," she mused. "I don't know—to fill the house with strangers—well, it just seems such a peculiar idea."

Now Julie cocked her head thoughtfully. "But it isn't, really, Aunt Marguerite. Daddy's right—this house would make a wonderful inn. And places like this are what everybody wants to find now. Daddy says everyone's tired of new hotels. They want to stay in places that have history, and are really old-fashioned, and—'' She fell silent with sudden embarrassment at her thoughtless remark, but her aunt only smiled at her.

''Yes, the house *is* old-fashioned,'' she said. Then she brightened a little. ''And certainly the kitchen is big enough to feed an army. Way back in my grandmother's day it wasn't at all unusual for there to be twenty or twenty-five people here for meals.'' Marguerite's face began to light up as she remembered the past. ''Even when I was a girl, we still had balls here. Everyone would come from miles around, and we'd hire extra staff, and the house would be all decorated like something out of a fairy tale. We'd have a little orchestra in the ballroom, and we'd dance all night.'' Her eyes, sparkling now, came to rest on Julie. ''Wouldn't it be wonderful if it could be like that again?'' she asked. ''Why, it would be just like it used to be, before—'' Abruptly she stopped talking and the light faded from her eyes.

''Before what?'' Julie asked.

But Marguerite only shook her head. ''Nothing,'' she said. ''It's just, well, sometimes I let my mind drift, that's all. And I mustn't do that.''

''Why not?'' Jeff asked. ''I do it all the time. I like to lie on my back sometimes, and look up at the sky, and pretend I'm a bird, or a cloud, or something. What's wrong with that?''

''Nothing, I suppose,'' Marguerite said, but her voice was vague, as if she were thinking about something else. ''But you can't let yourself do it too much. If you do, you can forget what's real and what's not. And then . . .'' Her voice trailed off, and once more her features took on the faraway look they'd had before. Jeff, who'd been watching her as she spoke, looked nervously toward his sister. But when he started to say something, Julie shook her head.

''Come on,'' she said. ''We better go help Ruby do the dishes.''

A few minutes later, when they were in the kitchen, Jeff looked up at Julie, his eyes serious. ''What's wrong with

Aunt Marguerite?'' he asked. ''How come she was talking so weird? And what's wrong with pretending?''

But before Julie could answer, Ruby spoke. ''Nothing's wrong with pretending. But your aunt wasn't pretending. She was remembering. And whenever she remembers all the good times she had, she remembers the bad ones too.''

Jeff glanced at his sister then back to Ruby. ''Bad times?'' he asked. ''What do you mean?''

Ruby seemed about to speak, then appeared to change her mind. ''Nothing,'' she said. ''I guess I was just talking.''

''How am I *supposed* to feel?'' Anne demanded. ''This afternoon I had to deal with your mother's insane will, my daughter nearly drowning, and my son being attacked by a rattlesnake. And what happens at dinner? You act as if the most wonderful opportunity in the world has just dropped into your lap!'' Her anger growing, she stood in the center of the bedroom, her eyes flashing. ''And you didn't even talk to me about it! That's the worst of it—you just made up your mind what you wanted to do, and now you expect me to go along with it! Well, I won't, Kevin. I simply won't do it.''

Kevin moved toward her, but Anne stepped back, effectively ducking away from his touch. ''I'm sorry,'' he said. ''Honey, I know I should have talked to you about it, but the whole idea just seemed so perfect that I couldn't imagine you wouldn't see it too.''

But Anne wasn't mollified. ''Perfect? For Heaven's sake, Kevin, do you have any idea what it would cost? Where are we supposed to get the money for this crazy idea?''

''We have the house—'' Kevin began, but Anne cut him off.

''Which is mortgaged to the hilt. We'll be lucky to break even on it, and you know that as well as I do!''

''This house,'' Kevin said hastily. ''I think I can mortgage it, but even if I can't, I think I've found a way around the will.''

Anne shook her head. ''You heard Mr. Waterman. There

isn't any way around ⌐he will. If there were, he'd have found it."

"But that's just it. It's not quite going around it. I think I can sell options to buy when the leases run out. I can sell them to the tenants—as many of them as want to buy their land—and I'll bet I can sell the rest to outside developers. Same thing with the land on the island . . ."

Anne stared at him as if he'd gone crazy. "But you can't do any of that," she objected. "You can't sell anything for ten years, and you can't even do that unless you stay here. And if you think I'm willing to do that—"

"Wait," Kevin pleaded, holding up his hand. "Will you please just wait and think about it? I know I was wrong not to talk to you about it right away, and I didn't really mean to present it the way I did. But I still think it's a way we can turn Mother's will to our own advantage. All I'm asking you to do is think about it. Can't you at least do that?"

Anne opened her mouth to voice still another objection, then changed her mind. What was she doing? Making her own mind up as unalterably as she thought Kevin had made his? She took a deep breath, then forced a small smile. "All right," she agreed. "I'll think about it. But I want to think about it myself, without you trying to talk me into anything."

"Just let me tell you how I think I can work it," Kevin began, but Anne shook her head.

"We'll talk about that tomorrow. Right now, I have to think about whether or not I can even live here. And there are the kids to think about too. What about school? I don't know much about South Carolina, but I know they don't spend a lot on education down here."

"I went to school here," Kevin pointed out.

"You went to the Fortress, and you know perfectly well you hated every minute of it." Suddenly she grinned, almost in spite of herself. "Pretty clever of your mother to threaten to leave everything to the Fortress, wasn't it? She must have known you'd do almost anything to keep that outfit from getting their hands on this place."

The corners of Kevin's mouth twitched slightly. "Nobody

can say Mother wasn't smart," he agreed. "But I hadn't really thought much about that aspect of it."

"Well, you'd better," Anne sighed, "because I have to tell you I think there's a pretty good chance they're going to get it." The grin faded from her face, and she met her husband's eyes. "I love you very much, Kevin," she said. "But I don't know if I can live here. I promised to think about it, and I will. But what if I decide I can't? What then?"

Kevin's stomach felt hollow. What, indeed, if she said she couldn't live here? What would he do? It came as a jolt when he realized he didn't know. He didn't know what meant more to him—his wife, his family, and the life he'd lived for twenty years—or this ancient mansion—the symbol of the unhappy years of his childhood, and now the possibility of a future he'd never been able to do anything but dream about. His mind raced, but before the right words came, it was already too late.

"Well," Anne said quietly, her voice trembling, "I guess I have my answer, don't I?"

It was past midnight, but the temperature had dropped only slightly and the light breeze that had stirred the air earlier had died completely. A heaviness lay over the house, and as Anne sat in the dimly lit living room, she felt the atmosphere closing around her, suffocating her. Outside, the night buzzed with the whirrings of insects, and she could hear them batting at the window, trying to get to the beckoning light of the table lamp.

She'd been sitting alone for hours now. Until ten-thirty, when the children had finally gone to bed, she'd felt their eyes on her, watching her warily. They'd already made up their minds, she knew. They wanted to stay.

And why shouldn't they? For Jeff the island was paradise on earth, acres and acres of wilderness to be explored, his own private beach, a house that was more like a castle to an eight-year-old. In his mind, everything about Devereaux and Sea Oaks was a fantasy come true.

For Julie it was much the same. She'd already made friends, friends she seemed to like better than the kids she'd known all her life. And, of course, there was Kerry Sanders—tall, blond, and blue-eyed, and he had already saved Julie's life. Even alone in the semidarkness Anne had to smile at the knowledge of how Julie must feel right now. Kerry, obviously, was destined to be the first big love of Julie's life, and Anne could well imagine the heartbreak Julie would go through if she were forced away from him. But it was a heartbreak she would get over, no matter what she thought right now.

Anne had felt Marguerite's eyes on her, too, though Marguerite had done her best to appear totally neutral. But what would Marguerite do if Anne convinced Kevin not to stay here? How could she live without the house and the income from the land and whatever holdings Helena might have managed to cling to over the years? She'd probably have to live with them in Connecticut.

Marguerite would hate it.

All of them, eventually, would hate it.

But what about me? Anne thought. She'd spent an hour wandering through the enormous house, trying to imagine herself living in the huge expanse of rooms. She'd run her hands over the furniture—furniture that had been in the Devereaux family for generations—and tried to imagine it all as hers.

She couldn't.

She wasn't a Devereaux—at least not a Devereaux of Sea Oaks—and never would be. You had to be born into the ability to be comfortable in surroundings such as these, and she wasn't. She had grown up in a small town in upstate New York, in a tiny five-room house her parents had barely been able to afford. From there it had been an apartment in New York shared with three other girls, and then she had married Kevin, never once understanding the kind of background he had come from. He'd talked of his family so little, and when he'd talked of them at all, it was with a bitterness that made Anne's heart ache. She'd known he'd grown up in military school—and hated every minute of it—and moved north at his first opportunity. And never, not once, had he intimated he might be willing to move back to South Carolina under any circumstances at all.

Yet here the circumstances were.

Of course, they wouldn't be living in the mansion, she reminded herself. At least not all of it. And it wouldn't be a mansion anymore. It would be a business, and Kevin, she knew, was perfectly capable of running it.

But they'd still have to live here, and Kevin would have to work twenty-four hours a day, at least for the first few years, and the children would have to go to school here, which, as far as Anne was concerned, was almost as bad as not going to school at all.

And in the end there was a good likelihood they would wind up broke, despite all of Kevin's expertise. In the hotel business it happened all the time.

And on top of all that there was the heat, the humidity, the unending insects, snakes, alligators—

No!

She almost screamed the word out loud. It was impossible, all of it. But how was she going to tell Kevin? And how was he going to react?

She closed her eyes for a few minutes, letting her mind drift, unwilling to deal right now with the possibility that her marriage could be dealt a fatal blow.

And all because of a vicious old woman's spiteful will. This was Helena's fault—all of it.

The clock ticked loudly, then struck the half hour, and Anne knew she should go to bed. Her mind was beginning to get fuzzy, and her emotions were taking over.

She didn't know at first why she was certain she was no longer alone in the room. It was just a feeling she had. She kept her eyes closed, listening.

Something creaked softly, something more than the constant shifting of the old house.

Whoever was in the room had come closer. But why didn't he speak? Anne's heart beat a little faster. She should open her eyes and look around.

She couldn't.

She had to.

The floorboards creaked again.

Steeling herself, Anne opened her eyes.

A few feet away, a figure stood, clad in white, staring at her.

Helena!

Anne gasped, sitting bolt upright, her heart pounding. But then the figure moved and she heard a voice.

"Anne? It's me. Marguerite. I—I thought you were asleep, and I didn't want to wake you."

Anne laughed weakly as her heart settled back into its normal rhythms. "Marguerite! I'm sorry. You frightened me half to death. I guess I *was* asleep, but all of a sudden I had this creepy feeling, and when I saw you, I thought you were Helena's ghost." She paused, giggling self-consciously. "Come back to haunt me, I suppose." She swung her legs off the couch and reached over to turn up the lamp. "What are you doing down here? I thought you'd gone to sleep hours ago."

"I couldn't sleep," Marguerite admitted, stepping out of the shadows and settling into the chair opposite Anne. "I was lying up there, thinking about Mother's will, and I kept getting more and more frightened." She gazed at Anne, her eyes wide. "I can't talk to Kevin about it—he already has so much to think about. But I'm scared, Anne. I don't know what to do."

"Scared?" Anne repeated. "Scared of what?"

Marguerite bit her lip and looked away for a moment, but then her eyes came back to Anne. "I'm afraid he's going to go away again," she said, her voice barely more than a whisper. "And if he does, I don't know what I'll do. I won't have anyplace to live, and no money. I—I just don't know what to do. And I know it isn't your worry—I know it *shouldn't* be your worry. But—But—"

"But of course it is my worry," Anne said immediately, her heart going out to her sister-in-law. "Whatever happens, it concerns all of us, and we all have to know how you feel too."

Marguerite blinked in the lamp light. "But that's just it, don't you see? I don't know how I feel. I can't imagine living anywhere but here, but I don't want you to do something you don't truly want to do. Oh, Anne! Kevin is all I have left. He and the children, and you. And I know how unhappy he used to be here. But if he goes now, and I lose the house—'' Her voice broke and she buried her face in her hands. Anne moved to her side and put her arms around the distraught woman. When Marguerite looked up again, her face was streaked with tears. "I can't lose it, Anne," she said, her voice choked. "I just can't. Please—you have to stay. You all have to. I—I need you!"

Anne tried to swallow the lump growing in her throat, and when she was finally able to speak, her voice was shaking. "We'll work it out, Marguerite," she promised. "One way or another, we'll work it out. But you won't be alone. All right?"

Marguerite hesitated, then nodded and dabbed at her eyes with a handkerchief. Finally she got to her feet and moved unsteadily toward the entry hall and the stairs. "I'm sorry," she apologized. "I feel like a perfect fool, really. But I couldn't help myself. I just had to come down and talk to you. I—I hope you don't mind too much."

"Of course not," Anne assured her. "Just go back to bed and try to get some sleep, and I'm sure that by tomorrow we'll all know what we have to do. I'll think about all of it, I promise."

Marguerite smiled. "That's good," she said. "I used to do that myself sometimes." She glanced around the large entry hall and shuddered. "Of course, sometimes I couldn't even think straight, not with all the memories here. So sometimes I'd take the car and go away for a while. Just get off the island for a little while, do you know what I mean?"

Anne nodded, then waited while Marguerite slowly climbed the stairs, finally going back into the living room to turn off the lamp. But to her surprise, Ruby was standing in the dining room door, her fingers clutching at a robe she had put over her shoulders. The old servant stared at her for a long moment, then shook her head.

"She got you," she said softly. "She got the whole lot of you, and she'll never let you go."

Instantly, Anne was certain she understood. "She's dead,

Ruby,'' she replied. "She's dead and buried, and there's nothing she can do to any of us. Whatever we do, it will be because we want to, not because of Miss Helena, or her will.''

But once again Ruby shook her head. "You'll stay. You'll all stay. That's the way she wants it, and she'll find a way to get what she wants.'' Then, leaving Anne standing alone in the living room which was still dominated by the portrait of Helena Devereaux, Ruby turned and plodded heavily back through the dining room toward her own small room behind the kitchen.

CHAPTER 10

The morning sky was slate gray, with thick clouds swirling up out of the southeast. Ruby, standing at the kitchen counter putting the finishing touches on a breakfast tray for Marguerite, glanced out the window and shook her head dolefully. "Seems like they might have warned us about this one," she grumbled. "Looks like its gonna be bad today. Don't expect Miss Marguerite will be down at all."

Julie looked up from the magazine she was leafing through while she ate her breakfast. "But what about class?" she asked. "And she was up earlier, wasn't she?"

Ruby shrugged dismissively. "Alls I know is that when it gets like this, her leg gets real bad. And if her leg gets bad, I don't know how she can teach her class. Besides," she added, nodding pointedly toward the storm brewing outside, "if this keeps up, nobody's gonna get across the causeway anyhow." She picked up the tray and started toward the kitchen door, but Julie promptly rose to her feet.

"I can take it up," she said.

Ruby hesitated a split second, the wrinkles in her brow deepening slightly, then smiled and handed the tray to Julie. "Well, I 'spose she might just like that."

Balancing the tray carefully, Julie backed through the swinging door to the butler's pantry, then went through the dining room and living room toward the main staircase. As she started up, she heard her mother's voice from the library in the far wing.

"Kevin, you can't expect me to make up my mind about something this important overnight! My God, first you spring this idea on me out of the blue, then you expect me to know how I feel about it the next day. It's just not fair."

123

"Honey, I'm not asking you to decide right now. I'm just asking you to let me explain it to you—"

"No!" Anne exploded. "You don't have to explain it—I'm perfectly sure that whatever plan you've come up with is perfectly reasonable. What I'm not at all sure of is whether I can live here. And I'm almost positive it would be wrong for the kids."

"But they *want* to stay—" Kevin began, but Anne cut him off.

"And Jeff would like it to be Christmas every day too! For God's sake, Kevin—they're *children*! You can't expect them to know what's right for them!"

Before her father could say anything else, Julie hurried up the stairs, unwilling to hear more. By the time she'd gotten to the top of the stairs and started down the hall toward Marguerite's room, the orange juice had slopped over the top of the glass, splashing onto the pile of toast next to the two fried eggs Ruby had put on Marguerite's plate. Her eyes stinging as she tried to control her emotions, Julie pushed the door to her aunt's room open, and slipped inside. Marguerite, dressed in a red satin robe, was sitting in a chair near her bed, her lame leg propped up on an ottoman. She smiled at her niece as Julie came into the room, but when she saw the glistening in Julie's eyes, her smile faded away. "Julie, what is it? What's wrong?"

Julie sniffled as she set the tray on the table next to her aunt. "Nothing, really, I guess. I just heard Mom and Dad, that's all. They're fighting about whether or not we can stay here."

Marguerite's eyes closed for a second and her head swung sadly back and forth. "I knew it," she said softly. "I knew there'd be trouble. I thought—well, never mind what I thought." Then she smiled again. "Aren't you nice to bring up my breakfast. But you didn't need to do it—Ruby could have brought it."

"I wanted to," Julie protested. "I—I'm sorry your leg hurts this morning. Ruby told me it always gets worse when there's a storm."

Marguerite managed a resigned smile. "There's nothing to

be done about it. But if I take it easy for an hour or so, I should be fine by the time my girls get here.''

Julie glanced nervously out the window. The wind seemed to have picked up, and the pines were starting to whistle, a low, keening sound that made Julie shiver. ''Will they really come today? Ruby says—''

Marguerite brushed her words aside with an airy gesture. ''Ruby's a terrible worrywart who's always sure the end of the world's just around the corner. And this is just a little squall. You watch—by ten o'clock every one of the girls will be here. And my leg will be fine.''

Julie frowned uncertainly. ''Maybe I should call Jenny and tell her not to come. She could call everyone else and—''

But Marguerite shook her head. ''That's absolutely ridiculous. If I didn't think I could handle it, I'd tell you so. And I certainly wouldn't want any of the girls to come out here if it were dangerous. But I'll be fine, and the storm will pass through. You should get downstairs and finish your breakfast. You can't dance right after you've eaten, you know. You'll wind up with a cramp.'' Julie started out of the room, but Marguerite stopped her. ''And Julie? Don't worry about your mother. I'm sure in the end she'll do what's right. We just have to let her work things out for herself. All right?''

Julie nodded uncertainly and left the room. As she started down the stairs, she braced herself for the angry sound of her parents' voices, but all she heard from the library was silence. When she got to the kitchen, though, she found her parents on either side of the breakfast table, their faces stony.

Neither of them spoke to her when she came in, and when she looked at Ruby, the old woman shook her head warningly. Quickly Julie backed out of the kitchen and started retracing her steps. But as she got to the stairs, Jeff came hurtling down. Julie grabbed him as he started to dart past, swinging him around to face her. ''If you're going to the kitchen,'' she said, ''you better not. Mom and Dad are in there, and they're having a fight. Right now they aren't even speaking to each other.''

Jeff's eyes widened in surprise. ''Mom and Dad never fight!'' he declared.

"Well, they're fighting now," Julie insisted. "And we better stay out of it. Okay?"

"But I'm hungry," Jeff complained, jerking his arm free from his sister's grip. "What am I supposed to do, starve to death?"

Julie rolled her eyes. "Do what you want. But if Mom and Dad start yelling at you, don't come running to me."

Jeff glared scornfully at Julie. "I won't!"

But five minutes later he crept into Julie's room, his face pale. "They're yelling at each other," he said, his voice quivering. "Mom says she won't ever live here, and Dad says we have to. What are we going to do?"

Julie shook her head. "I don't know," she said. "I guess there isn't anything we *can* do, except wait and see what happens."

"Well, it's not fair," Jeff replied. "All of us want to stay here except Mom. What's wrong with her?"

All Julie could do was shake her head and shrug.

At ten o'clock, just as it began to rain, Alicia Mayhew pulled her station wagon up in front of Sea Oaks and four girls poured out of it, hurrying up the steps to the wide veranda that fronted the old mansion. Jenny was about to make her own dash for the front porch when her mother glanced apprehensively at the lowering sky. "Maybe I ought to wait," she fretted. "It's looking pretty bad."

"What good will it do to wait?" Jenny asked. "If it gets much worse, you'd just have to stay here with the rest of us. And if it doesn't get any worse, you can come and pick us up."

Alicia reached over and squeezed her daughter's hand affectionately. "I just want to be sure you don't try to walk home in this. Or any of the other girls, either. Promise?"

"I promise," Jenny groaned. "Now will you stop worrying and go home? Everything's going to be fine." She jumped out of the car, slammed the door, then ran up the steps to the cluster of girls who were waiting for her. She waved once to her mother, then pressed the bell, certain that her mother wouldn't drive away until she and the other girls were inside the house. Sometimes, she reflected as she waited for Ruby to open the door, her mother acted as if she were still five years old. A moment later the door opened, and Jenny turned to wave once more. As she'd expected, the station wagon was just beginning to move down the driveway. Then, as a sheet of lightning flashed across the sky, instantly followed by a clap of thunder, she ducked into the house, closing the door behind her. The other girls were already starting up the stairs toward the third floor. "Where's Julie?" Jenny asked, and Ruby jerked her thumb toward the ceiling.

"In her room, I guess. And I'm not sure but what you girls wasted your time this morning. Miss Marguerite's not feeling so good today."

Jenny grinned mischievously. "She'd have to be dead before she'd miss a class." At that moment, as if to prove the truth of Jenny's words, Marguerite appeared at the top of the stairs, her back erect as always, her hair pinned up into a sleek chignon, a loose smock covering her leotard.

"And if you don't get up here and start warming up," she said, her eyes darkening as she regarded Jenny, "you'll be dead before the lesson is over."

As Jenny hurried up the stairs, Marguerite moved easily along the second-floor landing, her limp barely discernible. Ruby watched until Marguerite had disappeared from view, then started back toward the kitchen. But it was strange, she thought. For the last twenty years Marguerite's limp had gotten much worse when the weather turned bad. And this morning, when she'd found Marguerite already in the kitchen even before she herself was dressed, she'd been able to read the pain in Marguerite's face, and her leg had been so stiff she'd hardly been able to climb the stairs. Yet now Marguerite seemed to be perfectly fine.

A strange day, she decided as she pushed through the kitchen door. A very strange day.

*   *   *

The house seemed to be closing in on Anne. All morning, from the moment she'd awakened from a restless sleep, she'd felt the pressure all around her. It wasn't just Kevin, pressing her to make up her mind before she'd truly had a chance to think things through. It was the children too. She'd seen Julie's face during that quick moment when she had appeared in the kitchen, then backed away. Julie's eyes had rested on her for a moment, and Anne had been able to read the message all too clearly. "Why are you fighting with Dad?" Julie's eyes had said. "Why can't you do what the rest of us want to do?"

Then Jeff had come in, his face anxious, his eyes beseeching her. Just in time for him to hear her sounding like some kind of a shrew.

She'd almost given in then, almost agreed to Kevin's plan, despite her grave misgivings. And she had agreed to let him take her through the house, listening carefully to his plans for converting the mansion into a small hotel.

But all she had seen in room after room was an unending amount of work that needed to be done, and an equally unending stream of bills that would have to be paid. And in the end where would they be? Trapped on a tiny island.

That's when it had all closed in on her, and the huge rooms had become tiny, pressing in on her until she wanted to scream.

They were back in the library now, and Kevin was going over lists of figures he'd drawn up, estimating the cost of everything and trying to show her how it could all be paid for. But she couldn't hear him anymore, and not because of the storm howling outside, the wind whipping through the pines and magnolias, threatening to rip them up by the roots and fling them across the lawn and into the sea beyond. Even the house was shaking every now and then as the gusts battered against it. But it wasn't the storm that had made her deaf.

It was the house—closing in—and her own mind, screaming at her to get away, to think about it all somewhere else, someplace where she would be alone, where she couldn't see and feel everyone's eyes watching her, waiting for her to make up her mind. Then she remembered Marguerite's words from last night: ". . . sometimes I'd take the car and go away for awhile. Just get off the island for a little while . . ."

"I'm leaving," she said suddenly.

Kevin looked up at her, startled. "Leaving?" he echoed, his voice hollow. "But I thought—"

Anne shook her head. "Not permanently. But I have to get out of here. I have to get out of this house and off this island, and be by myself for a while." Her eyes flooded with tears. "I don't even feel like I can think anymore. I know what you want, and I know what the kids want, and Marguerite too! But I don't know what *I* want, Kevin! And it seems like every minute that goes by, I hate it here even more. And I don't even know why I hate it!" Her voice had taken on an hysterical edge, the words tumbling unbidden from her mouth. "I know it's a wonderful house, and I know it could be made into a beautiful inn! And I know you could do it! But I feel like I'm completely out of control. It's like your mother's got you, even though she's dead. She's got you, and the kids, and Marguerite, and now she wants me too! I know it sounds insane, but that's the way I feel! I feel like I'm going crazy, Kevin. I just have to get away. Now!"

Kevin reached out to take her by the arm, but she twisted away from him. "No!" she screamed. "Don't try to stop me! Don't even speak to me! Just let me go!"

Kevin stared at his wife. Her face was pale, her hands were trembling, and there was a wildness in her eyes he'd never seen before. He reached out to her again, but again she avoided his touch.

"Please," she said, her voice dropping to a whisper. "Just let me go. Just let me get out of here for a few hours." She turned away from him, hurrying out of the library. When he caught up with her, she was already in the foyer, struggling into a raincoat, searching in her purse for her car keys. She had the door halfway open when he reached out and pushed it closed.

"Not now," he said. "Honey, you have to wait—the storm's too bad. You won't even be able to get across the causeway—"

Anne shook her head. "I have to," she said. "I have to get out of here, and I have to get out now. If I can't get off this island, I'm going to go nuts." Her eyes locked on his. "I have to do this, Kevin. I'll be back in a few hours, or I'll call you. But I have to go now." Pulling the door open, she clutched the raincoat around her and stepped out onto the veranda. The rain, driven by the screaming wind, lashed at her, but she ignored it, leaning into the storm and stumbling down the steps. A moment later she disappeared around the corner of the house, and a minute after that Kevin saw their station wagon, with Anne at the wheel, move quickly down the driveway toward the road. Helplessly he watched her go until the storm had swallowed up the car.

He was just closing the front door when the sky seemed to explode with lightning, instantly followed by a clap of thunder so loud it made the windows rattle. And as the thunder faded away, the lights suddenly went out, plunging the house into a darkness almost as deep as night.

Damn, Kevin cursed softly to himself. Pushing the door closed against the force of the storm, he started toward the stairs to the basement. Perhaps it wasn't the electricity that was gone at all—perhaps it was only the main fuse to the house, overloaded by the bolt of lightning.

In the ballroom the music from the phonograph suddenly stopped. The bright lights of the chandeliers flickered once, then went out. The full fury of the storm was lashing at the house now, and one of the girls shrieked as the electricity gave out.

"It's all right," Marguerite said, her voice calm. "It's just a storm, and we've all gotten through them before. I'm sure the lights will be on in a minute and we can go on with our class."

"Why don't we just quit now?" Mary-Beth Fletcher asked, her voice taking on a belligerent tone. "All we've done anyway is sit here and watch Julie dance. I don't even know why we came today."

The rest of the girls fell silent, all of them watching Marguerite, but after only a second's hesitation she smiled at Mary-Beth. "I think maybe you're right. Maybe we ought to quit for the day and go downstairs and see if Ruby has anything to eat. How does that sound?"

The tension caused by Mary-Beth's words broke, and the girls began unlacing their toe shoes and drifting toward the door, groping their way through the darkness, toward the stairs. But when they finally got to the first floor and the rest of the girls started toward the kitchen, Mary-Beth stopped. "I'm going home," she announced. "I'm not hungry, and I'm sick of watching Marguerite gush over Julie, and I'm sick of these stupid dance classes."

Jennifer Mayhew glared at Mary-Beth. "Will you be quiet? Do you want Miss Marguerite to hear you?"

"Who cares?" Mary-Beth shot back. "She doesn't care about us anymore. All she cares about is her Yankee-trash niece, and I'm so sick of *her* I could throw up! So I'm going home."

"But you can't," Jenny protested. "You won't be able to get across the causeway."

"Well, I'd rather get washed off the causeway than stay here," Mary-Beth replied. She began pulling on her raincoat as Marguerite started making her slow way down the stairs from the second-floor landing. By the time she got to the entry hall, Mary-Beth was ready to go.

Marguerite stared at her in surprise. "Mary-Beth? Where are you going?"

"Home," Mary-Beth said, her eyes fixed on the floor. "I decided I'm going to quit dance class and I don't want to stay here any longer. So I'm going home."

Marguerite's face clouded. "But—But I don't understand. I thought you liked dancing—"

"Maybe I did," Mary-Beth replied, her voice sullen now. "But I don't anymore. And I don't like Julie, either. So I better go." She turned toward the door, but Marguerite stopped her.

"Mary-Beth, you can't leave now. Not in this storm, and not like this." Her voice took on a pleading note. "Please.

Stay at least until the storm passes. And let's try to talk about this. You can't leave this way. You just can't.''

But Mary-Beth shook her head. ''I'm not afraid of the storm, and I'm not going to change my mind,'' she said, her voice rising in anger. ''Why can't you just let me go?'' She turned, pulled open the front door, and strode out into the storm. Marguerite, stunned, watched her go, then, her hand unconsciously going to her right hip, which was suddenly burning with pain, went to the closet and pulled a mackintosh off one of the hooks.

Julie, who was still standing in the foyer, stared at her aunt. ''Aunt Marguerite, what are you doing? You can't go out there. Let me do it. Jenny and I can go after her.''

Marguerite shook her head. ''I have to do it,'' she said calmly. ''I have to do what's right.'' She smiled at Julie, her hand already on the door, and at Jenny, who had just come in to the entry hall. ''I won't be more than a few minutes,'' she promised. ''I'll just find her and bring her back.'' A moment later Marguerite, too, disappeared into the storm.

Anne braked to a stop at the end of the causeway, peering intently through the windshield. She could see practically nothing, for even with the wipers on high, the rain was far too heavy for them to be effective. Finally she rolled down the window and leaned out, gazing ahead toward the narrow strip of roadway that led to the mainland.

The wind was shrieking up the coast from the south now, and a constant spray of saltwater, driven off the heaving sea, stung Anne's face and clouded her vision. But the causeway still looked passable, though even as she watched a wave crested then splashed across the road. She closed the window and put the car in gear, then pressed on the accelerator, nosing the car out onto the narrow span.

She was a quarter of the way across when the engine started to cough. Quickly, she pressed the gas pedal to the floor. The car shook for a second, then the engine caught, hurtling the car forward into the cloud of spray.

And then, when she was halfway across, the engine coughed again, sputtered, and died. Anne slammed on the brakes, but their power had gone when the engine had stopped, and it took all her strength to bring the station wagon to a stop. Slamming the gear shift lever into park, she twisted the key, but nothing happened. Then she remembered, and quickly turned the key back then forward again.

The starter ground, but the engine refused to catch. She waited a moment, then tried again.

Still nothing.

The wind suddenly increased, and Anne felt the car sway slightly, and move an inch or two. A wave—larger than the rest—rose up from the south and smashed into the causeway, briefly flooding the road before washing on over to the north.

Anne twisted the key again. Once more the starter ground fruitlessly.

Without realizing quite what she was doing, Anne shoved the door open and made her way around to the front of the car, clinging to whatever handholds she could find. Fumbling, she reached for the catch that would release the hood. A moment later she was staring stupidly at the tangle of wires and hoses that ran around the engine like a maze.

None it it, she realized, meant anything to her. She had only a vague idea of how a car worked, much less of where to begin looking for the problem.

And then, as she stared blankly at the engine, another wave broke over the causeway, its force nearly knocking her from her feet. Gasping at the shock of it, Anne slammed the hood shut and made her way back to the driver's door.

A third wave struck her as she reached the door, and both she and the interior of the car were soaking wet by the time she got in and managed to pull the door closed.

She sat for a moment, staring out through the windshield.

The storm was building fast now, and the waves were washing over the road one after the other, keeping it constantly flooded.

The car had to start—it had to! There was no way she could walk through the storm. If the wind didn't blow her off the road, the waves would overwhelm her.

Panic starting to grow within her, she twisted the key once more.

The starter ground, but more weakly this time, and she realized the battery was wearing down. But the engine didn't catch.

Frantically her eyes searched the dashboard, looking for some clue as to what was wrong. Then she saw it.

The gas gauge seemed to pop out at her, far larger than it really was, as if she were viewing it through a telescope.

Empty.

The needle, which should have been on the full mark, was resting all the way over on the opposite end.

But it was impossible. The car had been full only two days ago. She'd filled it herself, and it had hardly been driven since.

And then, slowly, the truth began to dawn on her.

Someone had drained the tank.

Drained it!

But it was impossible. It made no sense! Why?

The panic that had been growing inside her burst loose now, and she leaned on the horn, silently screaming for someone to hear it, for someone to come to her rescue. But she knew it was impossible. Even she could barely hear the faint sound of the horn above the screaming roar of the storm, and the rain and spray were so heavy now that she could see neither end of the causeway.

She tried to regain control of herself, tried to force herself to be calm.

It would pass. It was only a summer squall, though it seemed to carry the force of a hurricane with it. And when it passed, she would simply get out of the car and walk the rest of the way to the village.

But the storm wasn't passing.

Instead its force continued to build. When she looked out to the south, the waves seemed mountainous.

And then, like a supernatural force, an enormous wave bore down on her, its swell rising ever higher until it crested, looming over the causeway for what seemed to be an eternity, then, finally, breaking.

It hit the car broadside, with the force of an oncoming locomotive.

The car shuddered, and Anne felt it slip sideways. For just an instant she thought it was going to hold, for there was the slightest hesitation before the inertia of the car finally gave way to the power of the wave.

And then, as if it had been seized by a huge hand, the car was picked up by the water and rolled.

A second wave, on the heels of the first, finished the job, rolling the car once more until it toppled over the edge and slid down the embankment.

Anne screamed as the car hit the water, and braced herself against the shock. Then the water closed over the automobile as it continued to roll, seized by the current and the storm-driven waves.

She had to get out, had to escape from the car before it filled with water.

She tried to shove the door open, but it was held tight by the weight of the water outside. She thought furiously now, and then knew what she had to do. Against every instinct in her mind and body, she had to roll the window down and let the water pour in until the pressure was equal. Only then would she be able to escape, either by forcing the door open or forcing herself through the open window.

Taking a deep breath, she began to crank the window.

Water gushed into the car, sluicing over her with what felt like the power of a firehose. She turned away from it, her breath coming in gasps now as she felt the water rising around her. The car seemed to be flooding much too quickly, far faster, indeed, than she'd thought possible.

Suddenly the car stopped rolling, and Anne realized it was lying on its side, the open window up. She still had a chance! And then, in front of her, the windshield shattered, caving in with a sudden rush as the sea began its final invasion of the automobile. Anne screamed once more, then gasped for a final breath before the last of the air was forced out of the car.

Now!

She had to get out now or it would be too late. She shoved at the door, and it moved slightly, then stuck.

The window!

She clawed at the open window, then shoved with her feet braced against the passenger door.

Up! She had to push straight up!

Her arms and head passed through the window, then her body. She twisted, trying to pull her legs after her.

She was going to make it. Only another second and she would be free.

And then she felt it happen: something wrapped itself around her ankle and jerked tight.

She knew what it was, knew instinctively, without even thinking about it.

The seat belt.

The wide strip of webbing that was meant to save her life. But it had turned on her now, twisting around her ankle, entangling her, holding her under the water's surface.

Her breath was burning in her lungs, but she reached down, fumbling with the thick strap, trying to find enough slack to free her snared leg.

The pressure kept building in her lungs, and the current of the heaving sea battered at her, pulling her fingers—fingers that felt clumsy and useless—away from the stiff material. At last her body revolted and her lungs spewed out her breath, then drew in the first agonizing draft of saltwater.

She'd lost.

At the very last moment she'd lost, and now she was going to die.

Water filled her lungs, and her body quickly leeched the last of the oxygen out of her blood.

A strange euphoria began to come over her, and suddenly she began to think of the sea as a friend.

A gentle friend, in whose softly swaying arms she was going to be borne away.

Her panic drained away then and she let herself relax, giving herself up to her new, and final, friend.

CHAPTER 11

The pain was burning furiously in Marguerite's hip now, but she did her best to ignore it, leaning into the wind, shielding her eyes from the lashing rain as best she could. She was on the road, slogging through the mud that sucked at her feet and threatened to bog her down entirely, but she had to go on. And then, barely visible through the torrent, she could just make out another figure.

"Mary-Beth!" she shouted, her words instantly lost in the howling wind. "Mary-Beth, wait! Please wait!" Whimpering against the pain in her hip and the almost complete numbness in her lame leg, she redoubled her efforts, breaking into an awkward run as she tried to catch up to Mary-Beth Fletcher. When she was still ten yards away, she called out again. "Mary-Beth! Wait!"

Mary-Beth hesitated, then turned around, and a moment later Marguerite caught up with her. Gasping for breath, Marguerite put out a hand to steady herself, but Mary-Beth backed away, and Marguerite almost lost her balance. "Mary-Beth, please," Marguerite gasped. "You can't go home now—it's too dangerous. Come back to the house."

Mary-Beth hesitated. She knew she'd made a mistake almost as soon as she left the mansion, and the wind had nearly knocked her down. But she'd made up her mind and wasn't going to change it. She just couldn't bear to go back to the house now and see the other girls looking at her, teasing her about losing her nerve.

Especially Julie. Julie, who'd come out of nowhere and instantly made friends with all of Mary-Beth's friends, danced better than Mary-Beth would ever be able to, and then taken

Kerry Sanders away from her too. No, she wasn't about to go back to Sea Oaks now. Not ever. She glared at Marguerite, her eyes flashing with anger. "I'm not going back," she shouted, her voice rising to carry above the storm. "Never! I hate you, and I hate Julie, and I'm leaving. And no one can stop me!" Once again Marguerite reached out to her, but Mary-Beth twisted away, clutching at the coat flapping around her legs. "I hate you," Mary-Beth lashed out once more. "I hate all of you, and I never want to see any of you again!" Then she was gone, the storm closing around her.

Marguerite stood in the middle of the muddy road, stunned by the girl's angry words, fiery pain throbbing in her hip, her heart pounding. Mary-Beth was leaving.

Leaving, and never coming back.

But she couldn't—she couldn't do that. She couldn't just turn away from Marguerite. It wasn't possible. There had to be a way to bring her back—there had to!

Once more she leaned into the storm, staggering against the wind now, pushing herself on. She had to get to Mary-Beth before she reached the causeway. If she didn't—

She put the thought out of her mind, unable to accept the idea that one of her girls might, indeed, leave her forever.

Mary-Beth stared at the heaving sea. The waves were huge, surging over the causeway with a raw, terrifying power that made her cringe. She couldn't possibly make it across. And the wind seemed to have risen even higher, threatening to lift her off her feet and hurl her into the churning sea.

A bolt of lightning flashed across the sky, and Mary-Beth screamed out loud as the crash of thunder rolled over her. She could feel its power against her chest, and clamped her hands over her ears until it had passed on, rumbling away, the sound lost in the screaming wind. She was crying now, wishing she'd never left the mansion, wishing she'd gone back with Marguerite when she had the chance. But it was too late now. She'd never be able to make it back to Sea Oaks—she was too tired from fighting the storm. She had to find shelter, find someplace to wait until the storm eased up.

There was a stand of pines fifty yards away, bending in the wind, a high-pitched keening springing from the trees, storm-lashed needles. If she could just get there, get to one of the trees, get a little protection from the storm. Holding her arms up to deflect the rain, she lurched toward the trees one step at a time.

Then she was there, huddling against one of the tree trunks; even the slight protection it offered a welcome haven from the maelstrom. She leaned against the tree, exhausted, her breath coming in short gasps, her heart still pounding.

Sea spray was mixed with the rain here, and she could taste the sharp tang of salt on her tongue. But at least she was safe.

Another bolt of lightning rent the sky, and a sharp crack—louder than a rifle shot—sounded above her. The tree she was leaning against split along its full length, knocking Mary-Beth to the ground. Almost instantly mud oozed through her coat and clothes, and she felt its cold sliminess against her skin.

She was sobbing now, crying brokenly as she wriggled away from the split tree, then pulling herself up to lean against the trunk of another. It wasn't just the storm that threatened her now. It was the woods too.

Around her she could hear branches breaking loose in the wind, crashing to the ground.

If one of them hit her—

She pulled herself to her feet. She had to get away, find someplace safe. Or someone—

Tripping, stumbling, she made her shambling way out of the stand of pines. Shreds of moss, ripped loose from the trees and driven by the storm, lashed her face, and once more she held her hands up in a futile effort to protect herself.

And then, with the instincts of a trapped animal, she sensed a presence nearby.

She stopped, listening carefully, but could hear nothing but the storm.

"H-Help!" she called out, her words sounding puny against

the raging of the wind and crashing of the surf. "Please—
someone help me! Please!"

And then, emerging from the storm, she saw a figure
approaching her. It was only a faint outline at first, but she
began calling out once more. The figure seemed to hesitate a
moment, then started once more toward her.

Mary-Beth fell to her knees, exhausted not only by her
battle against the storm, but her fear, as well. But in a minute
it would be over. Whoever was out there—whoever had come
to rescue her—would be with her in a few more seconds, and
she would be safe.

She gasped once more, struggling to control herself, to put
down the last of the panic that had engulfed her only seconds
ago. And then, finally, she looked up.

Looked up, ready to see a familiar face smiling down at
her, ready to have the last of the terror fall away.

Looked up to see an enormous rock, held high by two
trembling hands, descend down upon her, crashing into her
face.

She never knew whether the last sound she heard was the
sharp crack of a branch breaking above her head or the
equally sharp crack of her own skull, splitting and caving in
under the force of the stone as it smashed down upon her.

Julie flinched as yet another bolt of lightning slashed across
the sky and the house trembled under the force of the thunder
that followed immediately after. She tried not to show her
fear as she gazed at Jennifer Mayhew, who seemed completely unworried by the fury of the storm. "Where are
they?" she asked. "Shouldn't they have been back by now?"
Though it seemed to Julie as if an eternity had passed since
her aunt, followed a few minutes later by her father, had gone
out into the storm to search for Mary-Beth Fletcher, it had
actually been no more than thirty minutes.

But Jennifer didn't seem concerned. "They're fine," she
said. "We get lots worse storms than this. Wait till later on,
when the hurricanes come. That's when it really gets scary."

Tammy-Jo Aaronson rolled her eyes. "If it gets any worse than this, we're going to blow right into the ocean," she said. Nervously, she glanced into the shadowy corners of the dim living room. "I wish the lights would come back on. I hate it when this happens."

The other two girls in the room snickered softly. "Afraid Miss Helena's going to get you?" Allison Carter asked, her voice mocking. Instantly, Julie's eyes shifted to Allison.

"Why did you say that?" she asked, her voice quavering as she remembered the tale Ruby had told on the morning after her grandmother's funeral.

Allison grinned wickedly. "Everyone knows about the Devereaux ghosts," she said. "They always come back, and I heard that they're worst of all during storms. And when it gets real bad, they come up out of the cemetery and creep around in the house."

Jeff, who had been sitting quietly on the end of a sofa, stared at Allison, his eyes wide. "Wh-What do they want?" he breathed.

Allison turned to Jeff, and her voice dropped to a hoarse whisper. "Little boys," she said. "Little boys like you. And you'll never know when they're going to come. In fact," she added, letting her eyes dart toward the corners of the room, "they could be here right now, just waiting for you to wander away by yourself."

"Stop it!" Tammy-Jo Aaronson demanded. Then, as her friends all began giggling at the fear apparent in her voice, she tried to put on a brave face and managed to force a laugh. "That is so stupid—" she began, but then fell silent, her face draining of color as the French doors rattled loudly.

"Wh-What's that?" Jeff stammered, sliding off the sofa and edging closer to Julie.

Another bolt of lightning flashed. Outside the French doors, silhouetted against the thin curtains stretched over the glass, they could see a figure working at the handle.

One of the girls uttered a strangled whimper, and Jeff pressed up against his sister, his arms sliding around her waist. Then, as the thunder faded away, they heard a voice call out.

"Julie? Darling, unlock the door. I'm going to drown!"

The tension in the room broke instantly as they recognized Marguerite's voice. Julie ran to the door, twisting at the lock, then holding the door against the wind as her aunt slipped inside, her mackintosh dripping wet.

"The front door was locked, and I forgot my key. Didn't you hear me ringing the bell?"

Julie stared at her aunt for a second, then began to giggle. "How could we hear it?" she asked. "The electricity's out, remember? There isn't any bell. But where are Dad and Mary-Beth?"

"I couldn't make Mary-Beth come back," Marguerite said. "I tried to talk to her, but she wouldn't listen. She—" She cut her own words off and stared at Julie. "Your father?" she asked. "Why would I have seen him? Isn't he here?"

Julie shook her head. "He went after you," she explained. "He was worried about you being out in the storm and—"

Before she could finish, the front door opened, then slammed shut again, and Kevin, his clothes soaked and smeared with mud, appeared in the wide double doors between the foyer and the living room. He stared at Marguerite, his chest heaving as if he'd been running. "You're here," he finally managed, his voice gasping. "My God, I feel like I've been all over this island. Where were you?"

Marguerite frowned. "On the road, of course. But Mary-Beth wouldn't come back. She said she wanted to go home."

"In this?" Kevin asked, gesturing toward the storm outside. "My God, nobody could get across the causeway right now. It's completely flooded."

The girls exchanged nervous glances. "But then where is she?" Allison finally asked. "If she's not on the island, and she couldn't get off . . ." Her voice trailed off as she slowly realized the implication of her words.

"Now, let's not get ourselves worked up," Marguerite said quickly as she saw the girls' fear increase. "Kevin couldn't have searched the whole island—he hasn't had time. And she might have been able to get across. We—well, we'll just have to wait here, won't we? We'll wait here, and the storm will pass, and then we'll find out what's happened."

"I bet I know what happened," Jeff said, his eyes staring up at his father. "I bet the ghosts got her. I bet the ghosts came and found her and took her away."

Kevin stared quizzically at his son. "Whatever made you think of that?" he asked.

Jeff turned to stare at Allison Carter. "She told us," he said. "She said all the Devereaux ghosts come when there's storms."

Allison laughed out loud. "But I was only kidding," she told Jeff, and turned to Kevin. "Really, Mr. Devereaux, it was just a joke."

"But what if it wasn't?" Jeff asked. "What if it's true? What if Grandmother came back and took Mary-Beth? What if she killed her?"

A shocked silence fell over the room. "That's a terrible thing to say, Jeff," Marguerite said, her voice taking on a hard edge that made Jeff shrink back. "You should be ashamed of yourself, even thinking such a thing!"

Jeff stared at his aunt for a moment, blinking, then burst into tears and fled up the stairs.

CHAPTER 12

The storm was over, and a strange calm had settled over Devereaux Island. Everywhere, the land was littered with fallen branches and wind-scattered debris. The sea, still heaving in the aftermath of the storm, was covered with white-caps, and a heavy surf pounded steadily at the wide expanse of the beach. But the sky was clear, a deep blue tinged gray only to the north, where the storm was receding over the horizon. The wind had dropped to a stiff breeze, but even that was waning, and already the familiar heat was beginning to build. Steam rose from the land in a misty fog as the rainfall evaporated beneath the power of the sun.

Alicia Mayhew had come and gone, and the mansion was empty now of the girls who had waited out the storm for four long hours. Thirty minutes earlier, just as Alicia had arrived, the electricity had come back on and the phone began to work again.

Kevin had stopped Alicia on the veranda, just as she was ready to leave, and asked her if she'd seen Anne anywhere in the village, or perhaps their car.

Alicia had shaken her head. "But if I'd been her," she told Kevin, "I'd have headed inland." She shook her head in wonder as she remembered the power of the storm that had kept everyone in Devereaux shut up in their homes for most of the day. "I've seen squalls before, but that one was something else." Her eyes took on a look of worry. "I hope Mary-Beth is all right."

Kevin managed a grin. "From what Marguerite said, she must have been okay. She was mad about something, and she wasn't about to come back here."

Alicia's brows arched knowingly. "That girl's always mad about something. This time I suspect it had to do with your daughter. Mary-Beth's had a crush on Kerry Sanders for months now, but since he met Julie, he hasn't had eyes for anyone else. Well," she finished, glancing at her carful of teenage girls, "I'd better get home. Let me know when you hear from Anne, will you?" she added as she started down the steps. "I'd love to hear what she thinks of our little squalls."

Kevin shrugged ruefully. "I'm afraid it'll just add fuel to her fire. She's determined not to stay down here, and after this, I can't say I can blame her too much."

Alicia Mayhew turned back, surprised. "Stay here? You mean you're thinking of moving back?"

Kevin nodded. "It's all up in the air right now, but there seem to be a lot of good reasons to stay. It all depends on Anne. . . ." His voice trailed off, but Alicia nodded with instant understanding.

"She thinks we're living in the back woods, and that we're culturally deprived, right?"

Kevin reddened slightly, but nodded.

"Well, I can't blame her," Alicia sighed. "I guess we were, for a hundred years there. But things have changed." She smiled encouragingly. "Why don't I talk to her?" she suggested. "Maybe I can convince her at least to give us a try."

"I'd appreciate that," Kevin replied, as the phone in the entry hall rang shrilly. "I'd better get that. It might be Anne now." He waved to Alicia, and as she hurried down the steps, he went into the house and picked up the phone. "Hello?"

"Kevin? It's Muriel Fletcher. Is Mary-Beth still there?"

Kevin felt a tightening in his stomach. Mary-Beth should have been home hours ago. Then, speaking from one of the extensions upstairs, he heard Marguerite's voice.

"Muriel? You mean Mary-Beth isn't home yet?"

"No. She's there, isn't she?"

"N-No," Marguerite replied, and Kevin could hear the sudden worry in her voice. "She—well, I'm afraid she refused to stay. She was upset about something, and decided to walk home.''

"Walk?'' Muriel sounded shocked. "In that storm? My God, Marguerite, how could you have let her do something like that?''

Marguerite's voice was trembling. "I tried to stop her, but I couldn't, Muriel. She just put on her coat and walked out. I followed her and tried to talk her into coming back, but I couldn't. She—well, she ran away from me.''

"Oh, Lord,'' Muriel groaned. It wasn't surprising, really. Her daughter had always had a short temper, and even Muriel had had problems keeping her under control.

"I tried to find her again, but by the time I got to the causeway, she was gone,'' Marguerite went on. Then her voice took on a more hopeful note. "It didn't look too bad, really. The storm seemed to be letting up a little. But she must have gotten across. Otherwise, she would have come back to the house, wouldn't she?''

Muriel hesitated, trying to put herself into her daughter's mind. "No,'' she said at last. "She probably wouldn't. Not if she was angry. She'd have stayed outside by herself before she admitted she'd made a mistake.''

"Well, I'm sure she's all right,'' Marguerite insisted. "Perhaps she went to see one of her friends.''

There was another short hesitation, but when Muriel Fletcher spoke again, Kevin could hear her concern. "Maybe so,'' she said. "Anyway, I'll call around. And Kevin? Are you still there?''

"I'm here,'' Kevin replied.

"Would you mind taking a look around the island? I know it's a lot to ask, but—''

"Of course I will,'' Kevin replied. "I'll call you back in an hour or so.''

He hung up, and a moment later heard his sister's irregular step as she made her way down the second-floor hall to the head of the stairs. She looked down at him, her face a mask of worry. "I shouldn't have let her leave, Kevin,'' she said. "If something's happened to her, it will be my fault. I shouldn't have let her leave.''

"Hold on, Margie," Kevin replied, unconsciously using the nickname he'd called her when he was a child. "We don't know that anything's happened to her at all. I'll go out and have a look around—" But before he could finish, he heard a car door slam outside, and a moment later, the sound of heavy feet on the veranda. The bell rang just as he pulled the door open.

On the veranda, his expression somber and his eyes grave, stood Will Hempstead. Instantly Kevin knew something was drastically wrong, and he instinctively took a step backward.

"It's Anne, Kevin," the police chief said. "There isn't any easy way to tell you this. Her . . . well, her body just washed up on a shore little bit north of town. We don't . . . well, we don't exactly know what happened yet, but . . ."

Hempstead's voice droned on, but Kevin heard none of it. It wasn't possible. Anne couldn't be dead—she couldn't! She'd just gone for a ride, just wanted to be by herself. She was coming back. She was coming back any minute now, and she wouldn't be angry anymore. She'd be smiling at him, and telling him she'd finally thought it all through, and—

But she wasn't coming back. Something had happened, and she was never coming home to him, or to the children, again.

He dropped onto the wooden chair near the door and buried his face in his hands, his body wracked by the first sobs of his grief.

Even the creatures of the night seemed to have fallen silent.

The air was still, and the last of the storm-driven surf had long since died away. Only a gentle lapping sound drifted through the darkness, and Kevin, alone now in the room he had shared with Anne, sat by the window, staring out. His mind felt numb, unwilling to accept the truth of what had happened. He kept feeling a strange urge to talk to Anne, to call out to her as if she were in the bathroom, preparing herself for bed. Twice he'd heard a sound and looked up eagerly, ready for the door to open, for Anne to come into the room. But each time he'd caught himself.

It wasn't Anne.

It would never be Anne again.

They'd pieced together what must have happened. She hadn't even made it across the causeway. The wind and the sea had taken her, washing the car off the road, trapping her inside. But she'd gotten free, almost.

Will Hempstead's words still rang in his mind. "We found the car. She'd gotten out of it. Almost made it. But from the marks on her body it looks like the seat belt wrapped around her ankle and held her under. So stupid. So goddamned, fucking stupid!"

Kevin almost wished Will hadn't told him. In a way, it would have been easier if he could have believed she died instantly, knocked unconscious before she drowned. But to have been fighting to the very end, to be so close to surviving—

He shuddered, and tried to fight back the tears that overwhelmed him. Unable to stop himself, he gave in, sobbing silently for a few minutes until the wracking wave of grief ebbed once more. He opened the window, sucking the heavily perfumed air deep into his lungs.

It was the scent that did it, the strong odor that suddenly carried him back to his youth, the days before his father had died, when life had seemed wonderful to him. But then, when he was six, his father had fallen in the barn, broken his neck and died. After that everything changed.

His mother had suddenly turned all her attention to Marguerite. And Kevin couldn't blame her really, not now. Not from the perspective of his own maturity. After all, Marguerite had been so much like their mother. Her beauty, her grace, her talent . . .

Marguerite had suddenly filled his mother's life, and in her determination that her daughter should have the career she herself had missed, she had turned away from Kevin himself. Turned away from him, and finally sent him away to military school.

To the Fortress, where he had spent nine miserable months

each year, only to be sent away each summer to a camp in Maine.

Home—home at Sea Oaks—only for Christmas.

It shouldn't have been home anymore, not after all these years. And yet, as the gloriously sweet smells of the southern summer filled his lungs, he knew that it was home.

It was his mother he'd hated, not this place.

He wished Anne could have understood that, understood that the hatred for his home that he'd always expressed had never truly been directed toward the town, or the island, or the house.

Only toward his mother.

But his mother was dead now.

And so was Anne.

All he had left was Sea Oaks. Sea Oaks, and his dream. The dream he'd hoped Anne would share with him and help him make into reality.

Slowly, as he gazed out over the island and felt the house around him, he realized that his decision was finally made. For without Anne, there truly was no longer a choice. He was needed here, and his roots were here, and here, with his children and his sister, he would stay.

Stay, and survive.

But Anne, he knew, would never leave him. Nor, he realized, would the fact ever leave him that after twenty years of happiness, their last moments together had been moments of anger. Anger, and bitterness. That, he knew, was something he was going to have to live with the rest of his life.

"I'm sorry," he whispered into the night. "Oh, Anne, I'm so sorry. If only—"

But he didn't finish the sentence, for there were no "if onlys" left. All that was left was reality, and the strange emptiness within him.

Marguerite moved slowly down the hall, trying not to disturb the silence in the house. She paused outside Kevin's door for a moment, listening. There was silence, but as she was about to tap softly at the door, the stillness was broken by the strangled sound of an uncontrolled sob, and Marguerite hesitated.

What could she say to him? What could she say to relieve the pain he must be feeling?

Nothing.

Her hand, poised a few inches from the door, dropped to her side, and she moved on.

The pain in her hip had eased this afternoon, and her limp wasn't too bad. It was the passing of the storm, of course. Her limp was always better after the storms had passed.

She came to Jeff's door, listened again, then let herself inside without knocking. The boy lay in his bed, his eyes wide open, staring at the ceiling. She crossed to the bed and leaned down, gently stroking his cheek.

He turned his face away.

"I'm sorry, darling," Marguerite said, lowering herself gingerly to the edge of his bed. "I'm so sorry about what's happened."

Jeff looked at her with angry, tear-filled eyes. "It's not fair," he said, his voice quavering. "Why did Mommy have to die? It's just not fair!"

"I know," Marguerite crooned, reaching out to touch him again. "I know how you feel, and I want you to know—"

But once again Jeff turned away from her, pulling the covers over his head and curling himself into a tight ball. "Leave me alone!" he cried, his voice muffled by the blankets. "You're not my mother! Just leave me alone!"

Marguerite's hand jerked back as if she'd been stung. She sat still for a second, wondering what to do, then sighed heavily and got to her feet. She reached down to pat the boy once more, but he shook violently under the covers, wriggling away from her touch. A moment later, nodding vaguely to herself, Marguerite left the room, silently closing the door behind her.

She walked slowly along the corridor, coming at last to Julie's room. She paused a moment, listening again, then rapped softly at the door. There was a moment of silence, then she heard Julie's voice, clear, but strained: "C-Come in." Marguerite placed her hand on the knob, twisted it and pushed the door open. Julie, her eyes red with tears, sat on the bed, a pile of pillows supporting her slumped back. Marguerite stood still for a moment, her heart reaching out to the girl.

Like me, she thought. She looks so much like me when I was her age.

She took a step forward, then another, then was beside her niece. She felt Julie's arms slip around her neck, felt Julie's face press against her bosom.

"What am I going to do?" Julie sobbed, tears flooding down her face. "Oh, Aunt Marguerite, what's going to happen? I—I feel so sad and so—so alone. I can't stand it, Aunt Marguerite. I just can't stand it. . . ."

"Hush, darling," Marguerite whispered into Julie's ear. "It's going to be all right. I'm going to take care of you, my darling. I'm going to take perfect care of you, and you're never going to be alone again. Never, ever again."

Slowly, she felt Julie relax in her arms, and the girl's sobbing began to ease. Marguerite rocked her for a moment, very gently, and a small lullaby drifted from her lips.

She stayed there for hours, long after Julie had finally fallen asleep, watching her niece, reaching out now and then to stroke her cheek, to brush a strand of hair away from her brow.

It was going to be all right, Marguerite thought silently to herself as dawn finally began to break. She would take care of them all now; take care of Kevin and Jeff.

And Julie.

She would take care of Julie, just as Helena had taken care of her.

Yes, everything was going to be fine now. . . .

CHAPTER 13

For two weeks a strange sort of paralysis hung over Sea Oaks, as if Anne's death had drained the energy out of the mansion. A cold numbness had engulfed Kevin, and for the first few days after the funeral—a small funeral, since few of the people in Devereaux had come to know Anne in the short time she'd been there—he found himself doing nothing at odd times of the day. He would begin some small task, perhaps nothing more than clearing the overgrowth from a section of the garden, when he would suddenly become aware that time had passed—time he had spent in some private world, a world in which his wife still dwelt, still stood close to him, almost close enough to touch. But he couldn't touch her, not quite, for even in those times of silent, unmoving retreat, he could never quite reach her. They were painful times, for when they ended, Kevin would find that his memories had only left him more bereft, and as he continued whatever small chore he had assigned himself, he would be acutely aware of the emptiness within him. And yet, as the days went on, he knew he had to stop retreating, stop blaming himself for the argument that had hung unresolved between him and Anne when she died. He still had his children, and Marguerite, and Sea Oaks. Slowly, each day, he forced himself to do a little more, to turn more of what little energy he had toward the real world, and less toward the private world of his own grief.

Now, his own wounds slowly healing, he could also see the progress in the mansion. The grounds around the house, so long left unattended, had been cleaned out, and the gardens once more looked as if they had been planned and cared for. The peeling paint had been chipped away and carefully sanded, so that the house was ready for the painters who would begin working in another week or two. But what he really needed to do was begin working on the interior, something he had been almost unconsciously putting off. It wasn't that he didn't know exactly what he wanted to do, for he did. In his mind's eye he had already decided exactly how each of the rooms should look, and even the renovations of the third floor, where he, Marguerite, and the children would eventually be living, were laid out in perfect mental detail, ready to be committed to paper by the architect from Charleston he had commissioned only yesterday. And yet, despite his mental planning, he had still delayed the actual work inside the house, for each day, as he moved from room to room, he could almost hear his mother's voice, whispering to him:

"This is my house. You have no right to change it. It should stay just as it is, just as I left it."

The practicalities of the situation—the fact that Marguerite, he, Julie, and Jeff were each occupying rooms, and that Marguerite had begged him to put off doing anything to the nursery or their mother's suite—had been only an excuse. There were still three other rooms he could work on, rooms as badly in need of stripping and sanding as the outside of the house had been. Indeed, some days, after he'd finished work and spent a few minutes wandering through the mansion, he had wondered if it was truly possible for him to accomplish what he'd set out to do.

And yet, after long conversations with Sam Waterman, he knew that it was. Between them they'd come up with a scheme that would make all the financing he needed available to him, so long as he stayed at Sea Oaks. In the end they had had to take out a performance bond, guaranteeing his compliance with the residency clause of the will. Everything he owned beyond the estate now had a lien against it; every asset he had would be held in escrow for ten years. In return he was able to sell options on the land on the mainland, exercisable in ten years, which would raise more than enough cash for the renovations necessary to the mansion and enough capital to tide him over until the hotel began showing a profit.

And the profit, he was pleased to discover when he finished his financial projections, was going to be far beyond what he'd initially hoped for. Since he owned the island free and clear and would have no mortgage debt to service, even a forty percent occupancy of the nine bedrooms he would start with would put him at the break-even point. After that it was clear profit. And so in two weeks the crews would come in to begin the renovations to the interior.

This morning he had to talk to Marguerite about his plans. He could put it off no longer.

And he could put the children off no longer either. He knew he'd been neglecting them, forcing them to deal with the loss of their mother as best they could while he nursed his own wounds. It hadn't been fair, and yet, in the first days of wrenching grief, he'd been able to do nothing else. Still, he'd been aware of what was happening, of how each of them was dealing with the tragedy.

Julie, almost overnight, had seemed to grow up. Even on the morning of Anne's funeral there had been a maturity about her he'd never seen before. Without anyone asking her, she'd begun looking after her brother, making sure he took his bath each day, seeing to it that his room was reasonably clean and finishing the job herself, just as her mother had. At the funeral she'd stood next to Jeff, holding his hand, kneeling beside him to comfort him when his tears had finally gotten the best of him. And that night, when Kevin went upstairs, he'd found Julie coming out of Jeff's room. She'd just tucked him in, she'd told him, and read to him. Forcing a smile, she'd added self-consciously that she hadn't done it just for Jeff—it made her feel better too. And yet, sometimes when he watched Julie covertly as she sat quietly reading a book or watching television, he'd been able to see the hurt in her eyes, the grief she was trying so hard to control. Once, when they were alone together in the library, he'd tried to talk to her, but after only a few words she'd shaken her head.

"I don't want to talk about it," she'd said. "Not right now. Maybe in a few days. But right now, if I talk about Mom, I'll cry, and if I start crying, I won't be able to stop. And then Jeff will start crying, too, and I won't be able to take care of him." Her eyes had met his. "I have to take care of him, Dad. Mom would have wanted me to."

Now, as he started up the stairs in search of Marguerite, Kevin knew that Anne would have wanted him to take care of Jeff too. And in that he'd failed. But he didn't know what to say to Jeff. How could he explain to his son that he'd let the boy's mother go out into a storm that he knew was dangerous, that he, Kevin, had let her die? Jeff would hate him for that—almost as much as Kevin hated himself—and he couldn't bear the idea of that. And so he'd found himself almost avoiding his son, and watched the child retreat within himself. In the last few days, in fact, Jeff had said practically nothing to Kevin, only telling him where he was going when he left the house and what he was going to do. But it's going to change, Kevin told himself as he knocked on Marguerite's door. The real work on the house is going to start, and all of us are going to begin a new life. And it's going to work.

"Come in," Marguerite called softly, and Kevin pushed her door open to find his sister still in her dressing gown, sitting by the window with a book in her lap. She looked up and smiled at him apologetically.

"I know I should have been dressed hours ago," she said. "But it's so hot, and I don't really have anything to do that I can't put off for a day, and I just thought—"

"I'm afraid I have something that can't be put off," Kevin broke in, perching on the edge of Marguerite's bed. "It's the renovations. They have to begin in two weeks."

Marguerite gazed at him blankly. "Only two weeks? But I thought—well, I suppose I thought it would be months."

Kevin's shoulders moved in a helpless gesture. "I can't wait for months. But I have a problem." He explained his plans to her, leading her through the changes he envisioned for the first floor and the new construction on the third. "The problem is this floor," he finished. "I'm not asking you to give up this room—at least not yet—but I have to start doing something with the rest of it."

Marguerite blinked. "But there's the Rose Room, and the Green Room—"

"And the nursery and Mother's rooms," Kevin broke in,

deciding to confront the issue head on. Marguerite paled slightly, and Kevin could see her body tense. "I can't do it one room at a time. The expense would be astronomical. Which means that we're going to have to clean out Mother's things. As for the nursery . . ." he began, then deliberately let his voice trail off. Not once since their mother had died had Marguerite been willing to discuss the ruined nursery. But it could be put off no longer.

Marguerite was silent for a moment, then winced as a burst of pain shot from her hip down the length of her crippled leg. She did her best to ignore it, then finally came to a decision and stood up, her leg threatening to give way beneath her. "I know you've been wondering about the nursery," she said at last. She took a deep breath, and when she spoke, her eyes avoided her brother. "I did it. I . . . well, I suppose I always hoped that someday I might get married and have a baby, and . . . well, I guess that room was my way of keeping my hopes alive. I—I just started working on it one day. First I was just going to paint it, but then it just kept on going, and after a while I'd made curtains and furnished it and gotten it all ready." Her eyes suddenly came to rest on him, glistening. "And then Mother destroyed it. She said it was just a fantasy and I had to forget about it. So she ruined it one day." Her voice began to tremble. "She broke all the furniture and shredded the upholstery and smashed the pictures. And then she locked it up and forbade me ever to go into it again."

Kevin gazed unbelievingly at his sister. "And you didn't?" he asked, his voice betraying his incredulity.

But Marguerite only shook her head. "I—I couldn't," she admitted. "I suppose I thought that after mother died I might put it back together again." She fell silent for a moment, then went on. "But I'm almost fifty, aren't I? I'm not going to get married, and I'm not going to have a baby, and I'm not crazy. So take the nursery and do what you want with it. It's time I gave it up completely."

Kevin swallowed the lump that had risen in his throat. "I—I'm not sure what to say—" he began, but Marguerite held up her hand in protest.

"Don't say anything. I feel foolish enough as it is. Ruby and Mother understood, of course, and I hope you can too. But it's over now. I'm not going to get married, and everything is going to change, and I have to change too." Her eyes met his again, and Kevin thought he saw something strange in them for a moment. It was a quality of fear, or desperation, but almost as soon as it came into her eyes, it was gone.

"What about Mother's rooms?" he finally asked, his voice low.

Marguerite hesitated only a moment, then nodded. "I'll take care of it," she said. "I'll start this morning."

Kevin stayed a moment longer, thinking there was something he should say to his sister, some gesture he should make to let her know he understood how much she was giving up, but in the end he could find no words. Saying nothing, he kissed her, then left her alone.

When he was gone, Marguerite stood still for a moment, feeling his kiss on her cheek, then unconsciously brushed it away. Her hip throbbing now, she hobbled to the door and made her way down the hall to her mother's rooms. She went into the little parlor first, moving slowly through the room, her fingers brushing over the polished mahogany of the furniture, pausing for a moment at a large rosewood music box which she could still remember from her childhood. How she had loved to tip its lid open and watch the slowly turning metal disk as the soft melody resonated off the sounding board. She almost opened it now, but then turned quickly away, her eyes blurring with tears. She moved on, then, into the bedroom, automatically making minor adjustments to the clutter on the dresser top, putting things as her mother had liked them. At last she found herself in Helena's dressing room, standing in front of one of the large closets, her eyes wandering over the long row of dresses—long out of fashion— that her mother had always refused to dispose of.

Suddenly, not certain what she was doing or why, she reached out and took one of the dresses off the hanger.

She remembered the dress well. It had been one of her mother's favorites—a party dress, one her mother had worn when Marguerite was only a little girl. Made of silk, it was an emerald green and had been cut on the bias, so it had clung to Helena's body in voluptuous folds, falling almost to the floor.

Holding it to her body, Marguerite turned to face the mirror. The dress draped against her, she stared at her own image.

She could see the resemblance, even after nearly half a century. In the mirror was a woman who looked now very much as her mother had looked then.

Taking off her dressing gown, Marguerite slipped the dress over her head.

Jeff stood in the corridor, peering through the slightly open door to his grandmother's room in rapt fascination. He wasn't sure how long he'd been watching. In fact, he hadn't really started out to watch at all. He'd been headed downstairs, on his way to meet Toby Martin, when he noticed that the door to his grandmother's room was ajar and had come to see why.

And there was Aunt Marguerite, standing in front of the mirror, holding an old-fashioned dress up and staring at herself. Then, as he watched, she'd put it on, moving slowly as she stared into the mirror. Finally, unaware of him standing just outside the door, she went to his grandmother's dressing table and started combing her hair, piling it up on top of her head and shoving it full of large hairpins.

It made her look strange, and Jeff was beginning to feel he shouldn't be watching at all when he felt a hand on his shoulder.

He jumped violently, about to yelp in surprise, when Ruby's hand clamped over his mouth and she spun him around to face her.

"What are you doin' up here?" Ruby demanded, her voice low, but nonetheless clear.

"N-Nothing!" Jeff said as the old woman's hand fell away from his mouth. "I wasn't doing anything. I was just—"

"Just spying on your auntie," Ruby finished for him, her

voice a severe whisper. "Didn't your mommy ever teach you not to do things like that?"

Jeff tried to twist out of her grip. "I wasn't," he protested. "I just saw something in here and came to see what it was."

Ruby regarded the boy carefully for a moment, then released his shoulder from her grasp. "All right," she said. "But you run along downstairs and mind your own business."

A vast surge of relief flowed through Jeff as he realized he was going to face no punishment. He scurried along the hall, then disappeared down the stairs.

But Ruby remained where she was, her eyes glued to Marguerite as the other woman sat in front of the mirror, her hands flying as she arranged her hair in imitation of the style that had been Helena's favorite so many years ago.

Kevin pushed his chair back from the kitchen table, took his plate to the sink and scraped the remains into the strainer, then rinsed the plate before putting it into the big commercial dishwasher that had been installed the day before, and which Ruby had been complaining about ever since. "Don't see why we need it," she'd grumbled even as the plumber had been hooking it up. "Plenty of people around here wouldn't mind washing dishes, if they got paid for it." Now, as Kevin dropped his plate into the gleaming stainless steel machine, she pointedly looked the other way.

"I have to go into town to see Sam," Kevin spoke. "Anyone want a ride?"

Jeff shook his head. "Me and Toby are gonna work on the fort."

" 'Toby and I,' " Kevin corrected automatically. "Julie?"

"Some of the kids are coming out to the beach," she said. "Jenny, and Kerry, and I don't know who else."

"Our beach?" Marguerite asked, her brows arching. Julie, her own eyes suddenly worried, turned to her aunt.

"Isn't it all right?" she asked. "I mean, after Grandmother died you said—"

"Of course," Marguerite broke in. "I didn't mean it that

way. You know your friends are welcome. It's just that—''
She hesitated, her eyes going to Kevin as if for help, but
when he didn't seem to sense what she was getting at, she
turned back to Julie. "Well, I just wondered if you should be
seeing Kerry again, so soon after . . ." She couldn't quite
bring herself to finish her thought, and her voice trailed off,
but Kevin suddenly understood.

"I think it would be good for her," he decided. "We all
need to keep busy, and see people, and if Julie can have a
good time with her friends, she certainly ought to."

"But so soon . . ." Marguerite repeated, and now Julie
looked pleadingly to her father.

"It's not too soon," Kevin told his sister. "Things aren't
the way they used to be, and life goes on." He smiled
warmly at his daughter. "You have a good time," he told
her. "And if you want to ask Kerry to stay for dinner, do. It
would be good for all of us to have some company for a
change."

"Can I ask Toby?" Jeff asked, his voice eager, and Kevin
actually found himself laughing for the first time since Anne
had died.

"You bet," he replied. "Ask anyone you want." He
glanced at his watch then, and started toward the door. "If I
don't get out of here, I'm going to be late." But Marguerite
stopped him before he could leave.

"Kevin, I—well, I've been thinking. About Mother's rooms.
I know what I said this morning, but I've changed my
mind."

Kevin's eyes clouded. "Changed your mind? But I thought
we'd agreed. Marguerite, I need the rooms. I—''

"I know you need the rooms," Marguerite interrupted.
"But I can't let you have Mother's. Not yet. I . . . well, I just
can't." She hesitated briefly, then went on. "I've decided to
move into Mother's rooms myself, Kevin. You can have my
room, and the nursery. With the other rooms, that will make
five. Surely that's enough for now, isn't it?"

Kevin looked sharply at his sister. "You don't have to give
up your room. Not yet, anyway. I thought we'd decided—''

"But I want to give it up," Marguerite insisted. "I'll just

move into Mother's rooms for a while. It'll give me time to go through her things and decide what to do with them. Then, by the time the third floor's ready, I'll be ready too. It'll work out fine. Really it will!''

Kevin thought about it for a moment, then shrugged. "If it's really what you want," he agreed. Then something else occurred to him. "What about the chair lift?" he asked. "Is there any reason not to get rid of it? It's an eyesore, and that generator Mother had installed in the closet could go downstairs to run the furnace if the electricity goes out."

Marguerite hesitated a moment, then shrugged. "I—I guess it doesn't matter," she said at last. "Do whatever you want."

Then Kevin was gone, and a moment later Julie, too, left the kitchen, heading upstairs to get ready for her afternoon at the beach.

Jeff stuffed the last of his sandwich into his mouth, then slid off his chair and started toward the back door, but before he could even open it, Marguerite spoke.

"Where do you think you're going, young man?" she asked.

The cold sharpness in her voice made Jeff freeze in his tracks and slowly turn around. "Ou-Outside," he stammered. "Toby's meeting me at our fort."

"Is he?" Marguerite asked. "Well, I'm afraid he's going to have to wait. You have some work to do, don't you?"

Jeff stared blankly at his aunt. "What?" he asked.

"You can clear off this table, and help Ruby with the dishes."

Jeff blinked. What was she talking about? He never did the lunch dishes. He and Julie helped with the dinner dishes, but Ruby always did the lunch dishes herself.

"It's all right," he heard Ruby saying. "Let the boy go, Miss Marguerite. There's not much of a mess, and I can—"

"No!" Marguerite snapped, her eyes never leaving Jeff. "It's time he learned to do a few things around here. He's already spoiled, and I don't see—"

Jeff's temper suddenly snapped, and he glared angrily at his aunt. "I'm not spoiled!" he yelled. "And you're not my mother, and you can't tell me what to do!"

Marguerite rose to her feet, her own eyes flashing. "How dare you speak to me like that?" she demanded. "How dare you?" She took a step toward Jeff, but he backed away.

"Don't you come near me!" he yelled. "You're crazy! That's what you are. I saw you this morning, and you're crazy!" Then he pushed his way through the screen door and fled down the back-porch steps, running down the hill until he disappeared into the thick stand of moss-covered pines.

When he was gone, Marguerite stayed where she was for a moment, then turned and limped stiffly toward the butler's pantry and the rest of the house beyond.

Ruby, her eyes clouded with worry, watched her go, but said nothing.

Maybe I'm wrong, she told herself as she began clearing up the lunch dishes and loading them, without thinking, into the dishwasher. Maybe it's nothing at all. Maybe she's just on edge.

And yet, as she went about her chores, she knew she wasn't wrong, and that Marguerite wasn't simply on edge. No, it was more than that.

Perhaps a lot more.

Julie lay on the sand, Kerry sprawled out beside her. It was a quiet day, for all the kids gathered on the beach were friends of Mary-Beth Fletcher's, and as they had gathered on the island, each of them had wondered what might really have happened to her. But none of them had felt much like talking about it, and in the end they had decided not to talk about Mary-Beth and to try to have a good time.

The sun beat down on Julie, but instead of making her feel weak, it felt good against her skin. She could almost feel her tan deepening beneath the light coat of coconut oil she'd smeared on an hour ago. Around her she could hear quietly laughing voices, and a little earlier she had even caught herself laughing as Kerry plunged for a Frisbee somebody had thrown, missed, and dropped face first into the sand.

Aware of someone kneeling down next to her, she opened her eyes, squinting up at Jennifer Mayhew.

"I *love* this beach," Jenny shouted happily. "It's clean, and it's wide, and there's nobody here!"

Julie giggled. "Well, we better enjoy it while we can, 'cause I heard Dad talking to Mr. Waterman the other day. They were talking about a golf course and condominiums and all kinds of things."

Kerry sat up, his brows furrowing thoughtfully. "Does your dad really think it'll work?" he asked, with concern. "My dad says he can't imagine why anybody would want to come out here. I mean, all it is is a bunch of flats."

Julie shrugged. "What's Hilton Head like? It was the same thing. And if Dad says it's going to work, then it's going to work." She grinned at Kerry. "Besides, you grew up here—everybody hates where they grew up. Or at least they do if they've got any imagination. But look at this beach. Jenny's right—it's great! And when we get done with the house, it's going to look just like it used to, only better." She giggled. "Maybe we could even restore the old slave quarters and turn them into rooms."

Kerry looked shocked for a second, then realized she was only kidding. "Well, I hope it works," he said. "And so does everybody else," he added, scrambling to his feet and brushing the sand off his chest and legs. "At least your dad's trying to do something with this place. Everybody thought your grandmother just didn't care."

Julie's smile faded away. "I don't think she did," she said. "I think she wanted everything to stay the way it was, and never realized that everything had changed anyway. She even treated Ruby like she was still a slave," she added, her eyes rolling scornfully. "I don't even see why Ruby stayed around."

Kerry grinned mischievously. "Same reason," he teased. "She just doesn't know she's *not* still a slave."

"That's terrible," Julie shouted, slinging a handful of sand at Kerry, then jumping up to chase him down the beach. "If I thought you meant it, I'd never speak to you again."

"And if I had meant it, you shouldn't ever speak to me

again," Kerry replied, letting Julie catch up with him. "Come on. Let's take a swim. And this time, watch out for the waves. I don't want to have your aunt mad at me again."

They splashed through the water, diving into the gentle breakers that were washing up onto the beach, then began swimming out past the surf line. Soon they were in gently swelling water, and if Julie put her feet down, she could just touch the bottom, feeling the now-familiar grass brushing against her legs. She floated on her back for a while, closing her eyes against the sun, then shrieked as Kerry sneaked up on her, ducking her beneath the surface. She came up spluttering, and spotted him swimming away from her. Kicking hard, she chased after him and had almost caught up with him when she felt something bump against her leg.

She let out a shout, more from surprise than anything else, and Kerry instantly stopped swimming and turned back.

"What is it?" he called.

"I don't know!" Julie shouted back. "Something just bumped into me. Like a fish or something!"

"I bet it was a turtle," Kerry told her. "They come in to feed on the grass, and they lay their eggs on the beach. If it bumps into you again, try to grab it."

"Grab it?" Julie exclaimed. "Are you nuts? What if it bit me?"

Now Kerry was laughing. "They don't bite. They just try to swim away, and if you lift them out of the water, they keep on flapping their legs. They're funny!"

Julie's eyes narrowed suspiciously. "If you're lying to me—" she began, but before she could finish, she felt the light bump again. Without thinking it through, she reached down into the water and felt for whatever had hit her.

Her hands closed on an object, firm, but not quite hard. She frowned while trying to bring it to the surface, but for a moment it stuck. Then it gave way and came up, breaking the surface.

It was not a sea turtle, but Julie knew immediately what it was.

It was Mary-Beth Fletcher.

Her face was bloated, and much of the flesh had long since been torn away by feeding sea creatures.

What was left of her hair was a tangled mass which seemed to wrap itself around Julie's hands, as if seeking to grasp onto her.

Both her eyes were gone, and the empty sockets stared vacantly at Julie. Even as she watched, a worm wriggled out of the depths of Mary-Beth's skull, then fell into the water.

Screaming, Julie tried to hurl the corpse away, but the hair was twisted around her fingers and she couldn't shake her hands loose. Then, as her stomach began to churn and her screams grew into an hysterical wailing, Kerry was beside her, tearing at the tangled hair that trapped her hands, pushing wildly—almost futilely—at Mary-Beth's hideous remains as they bobbed grotesquely in the calmness of the summer sea.

Julie never knew exactly how she got to shore.

CHAPTER 14

The small sitting room adjoining Helena's bedroom gleamed softly in the diffused light that poured through the sheers over the windows, and Marguerite smiled softly as she surveyed her work. Every piece of furniture had been polished to perfection, the last of the accumulation of dust wiped away. She'd done her best to cover the most worn areas of the Victorian sofa with an assortment of the shawls her mother had loved so much, but had been unable to do anything about the peeling wallpaper. Perhaps, if she looked hard enough, she could find the same pattern somewhere in one of the decorating shops in Charleston. But still, for the first time in years the room looked exactly as she remembered it from the days of her childhood.

It had always been her mother's favorite room in the house, and now that it had been cleaned and polished, Marguerite could understand why. Part of it was the light. The room faced away from the afternoon sun, and the indirect light seemed to make the rosewood and mahogany of the furniture glow as if lit from within. Nor was this room ever as hot in the afternoon as the rest of the house. But it went beyond the light and the temperature—there was an old-fashioned atmosphere, as if somehow the passing years had been shut out. In this room—like her mother before her—Marguerite could almost imagine that nothing had changed at Sea Oaks, that outside the cotton fields were in full bloom, covering the island in white, and that the fields went on, sweeping across the mainland as far as the eye could see. She could almost feel the house around her humming with life as servants went about their business, preparing for a ball.

Perhaps there would be music tonight.

She pictured the ballroom, its chandeliers sparkling brilliantly as all the friends of the Devereauxes danced the long summer night away. And then, at dawn, a breakfast would be laid out, the dining room table laden with omelets, melons, and great bowls of strawberries.

She could almost hear the music now, the thin strains of soaring violins—

Marguerite was suddenly jerked out of her reverie. It wasn't music, it was something else. She listened sharply and heard it again. The same sound.

It wasn't violins.

It was a siren—a siren coming closer. She went to the window, pulled the curtain aside and leaned out. Far in the distance, just leaving the village, she could see an ambulance, closely followed by the black and white shape of the town's only patrol car. As she watched and listened, the ambulance turned onto the causeway and the sirens grew louder.

Marguerite's heart skipped a beat as she thought of Julie, who was spending the afternoon on the beach with her friends.

Her friends, and that boy—

She remembered what happened the last time Julie had gone to the beach with Kerry Sanders.

Her heart pounding now, she hurried out into the corridor and began a painful progress toward the stairs. "Kevin!" she called. "Kevin, where are you? Something's happened!"

By the time she reached the top of the stairs, Kevin was looking anxiously up at her from the entry hall. Next to him was Joe Briggs, the contractor he'd hired to carry out the renovations. Ignoring Joe, Marguerite's eyes fixed on her brother. "There's an ambulance coming," she cried, her voice shaking. "Something's happened to Julie! I know it!"

She started down the stairs, clinging to the rail to keep her balance, but by the time she got to the bottom, Kevin was already gone, dashing outside through the French doors in the dining room, Joe Briggs right behind him. As Marguerite came into the dining room herself, Ruby emerged from the kitchen.

"What's going on?" Ruby demanded. "Where are they going?"

"The beach," Marguerite gasped. "Help me, Ruby. Something's happened at the beach. There's an ambulance coming, and Will's car, and—" She broke off, reaching out to Ruby. "It's Julie! I just know it's Julie. Help me, Ruby. I have to get down there."

Immediately Ruby was at her side, taking her arm to steady her. "Now just calm down, Miss Marguerite," Ruby admonished her as they left the house and started making their way down the rise toward the stand of pines. "Nothin's happened to Julie. If anything had happened to her, Kerry Sanders would have been here first thing!"

But Marguerite barely heard Ruby's words. The sound of the wailing siren filled the air now, and she could see the ambulance and police car bumping across the ground on one of the overgrown roads that had served the island years ago, when the fields were under cultivation.

Her hip was throbbing with pain, but in her hysteria she ignored it, half leaning on Ruby and half pulling her as she hurried toward the beach. Abruptly the siren was cut off. Marguerite felt a cold knot of fear tighten in her belly.

It's too late. It's too late, and Julie's already dead.

"Hurry!" she yelled, breaking into an ungainly run, her right leg held stiff against the pain that threatened to topple her at every step.

Muttering to herself, Ruby did her best to keep up with her frantic employer.

They broke through the pines and were on the beach, Marguerite's eyes searching the knot of teenagers who crowded around Will Hempstead. Then she saw Julie, crumpled on the sand, Kevin beside her, holding her. On her other side was Kerry Sanders, crouched on the sand, watching helplessly as Julie sobbed into a towel that covered her face. But where were the men from the ambulance?

Frantically Marguerite searched for them, then found them. They were not with Julie.

They were a few yards farther down the beach, pulling something out of the surf.

Then, it wasn't Julie.

Marguerite took a deep breath, released it, then let the tension flow out of her body along with the expelled air before moving again.

A minute later she dropped to the sand, pulling Julie into her arms, cradling the sobbing girl's head against her breast. "My darling," she breathed. "My poor darling. What is it? Tell me what's happened?"

Julie said nothing, only shaking her head as her sobs built, and pulling her legs up against her chest. Her whole body quivered as if she'd been seized by a chill, and her arms wrapped around Marguerite, clinging to her with a passion that grew out of terror.

"It's Mary-Beth Fletcher," Kevin told her, his voice tight, eyes slightly glazed. "They found her. She was in the water, and she bumped up against Julie. Julie—she—" His voice broke and he shook his head.

"Julie pulled her out, Miss Marguerite," Kerry Sanders finished, his eyes avoiding hers. "I thought it might be a turtle, and she was trying to catch it."

Marguerite's eyes widened in horror. "Dear God," she breathed, and her arms tightened protectively around her niece. "It's all right," she whispered into Julie's ear. "It's going to be all right, my darling. I'm here, and I won't let anything hurt you. Nothing at all . . ." Still rocking Julie gently, she fixed her eyes darkly on Kerry Sanders. "Go home," she said, her voice taking on a harsh edge. "Just go home, and leave us alone."

The words struck Kerry almost like a physical blow. He stayed where he was for a moment, then got to his feet and started walking uncertainly away. Then Kevin was beside him, laying an arm across his shoulders. "It's all right, Kerry," he said, leading the boy a few yards down the beach. "She's just upset, and worried about Julie."

Kerry looked at Kevin and shook his head. "It's not that. She did the same thing when I brought Julie home the day the wave hit her. She acted like it was my fault. And maybe she was right that day. Maybe I should have been watching more carefully. But—" His voice broke, and he struggled to control the tightness in his throat. "But what was I supposed to do today? I didn't know Mary-Beth was—" He fell silent, unable to finish the sentence.

"Of course you didn't," Kevin assured him. "And when she thinks about it, Marguerite will understand it wasn't your fault."

But Kerry shook his head. "No, she won't," he said, his voice carrying a bitterness beyond his years. "She always liked me, before Julie came. But now everything's different— now she acts like she hates me. But I didn't do anything, Mr. Devereaux."

"No one says you did," Kevin told him. "You might as well go home now, and come out tomorrow, or the next day. Everything will be fine—you'll see."

But Kerry didn't go home. Instead, he moved farther down the beach to join his friends as they watched the medics wrap Mary-Beth Fletcher's corpse in a sheet of plastic, then load it into the ambulance. Only when they were done with Mary-Beth did they finally turn their attention to Julie, giving her a shot to counteract the effects of her shock, then loading her onto a stretcher to carry her home. Finally, as the medics left the beach, with Marguerite following closely behind, Kerry found himself standing next to Jennifer Mayhew. "What happened to Mary-Beth?" he asked. "Does anybody know?"

Jennifer shook her head. "I heard Will Hempstead talking to the driver. He said he doesn't think they're going to be able to find out. He says . . ." Jennifer paused a moment, and when she spoke again, her voice was steady, though her face was still pale. "He says she was in the water too long and there's—there's not enough left of her to tell what happened."

"Shit," Kerry said softly and shook his head. "Come on. We might as well get out of here." But as he and Jennifer were walking toward his car, the sheriff stopped him.

"Kerry?" he said. "How come Bobby Hastings came all the way into town to call me? How come he didn't just go up to the mansion?"

Kerry just stared at Hempstead. It was Jennifer Mayhew who finally answered his question. "He was scared," she said, her voice almost shy. "We were all scared, and Julie was crying, and Bobby didn't know what to do."

"And I was afraid of Miss Marguerite," Kerry blurted, his eyes on the ground. "I was afraid she'd be mad at me and think it was all my fault. And I was right. Anyway, I told Bobby to go get you."

Hempstead's eyes narrowed. "You were afraid of Marguerite?" he echoed. "But that's crazy. She likes all the kids. She always has."

Now Kerry faced him. "The girls," he said. "She likes the girls, Mr. Hempstead. But she doesn't like me."

He turned away and started once more toward his car. A moment later Jenny Mayhew followed him.

"I bet Aunt Marguerite killed her," Jeff said. He and Toby Martin were back at their fort, guiltily consuming the warm Cokes and stale cookies that Jeff had swiped from the kitchen that morning. They'd heard the sirens and run down to the beach to see what was happening, then watched in fascination as the men from the ambulance pulled the body out of the waves. They'd tried to sneak up close to get a good look, but one of the ambulance men had shooed them away, and after that they'd just hung around, careful to stay out of the way but trying not to miss anything that had happened. Once, Jeff had tried to talk to his father, but his father, too, had brushed him off, saying he was busy and would talk to him later. And all Julie's friends had simply ignored him, acting like he and Toby weren't there at all. So after they'd taken Julie up to the mansion, and the ambulance had left, they'd come back to the fort behind the garage to try to figure out what had happened to Mary-Beth Fletcher.

Now Toby stared at Jeff, his eyes wide. "Miss Marguerite wouldn't hurt anybody," he said. "Why would she want to kill Mary-Beth?"

"Because she's crazy," Jeff replied, reaching into the brown paper bag to fish out another cookie. "I saw her this morning, and she was acting real weird. She was putting on my grandmother's clothes and combing her hair funny and everything.''

Toby frowned thoughtfully. ''Maybe she was playing dress-up,'' he said. ''My sister does that all the time.''

Jeff made a scornful face. ''Your sister's only five. Aunt Marguerite's a grown-up. Grown-ups don't play dress-up. Unless they're crazy. And did you see how she was acting with Julie?''

Toby's frown deepened. ''She was just trying to take care of her. Julie was crying, wasn't she?''

Jeff's eyes rolled as if Toby were some kind of an idiot. ''She was acting just like she was our mother,'' he said. ''And she was doing that to me today too. She was trying to tell me what to do and everything!''

''So what did you do?'' Toby asked.

Jeff shrugged as if what had happened with his aunt after lunch were nothing. ''I told her she wasn't my mother and that she couldn't tell me what to do.''

''Wow,'' Toby breathed, his eyes wide at his friend's nerve. ''What did she do?''

''Nothing,'' Jeff announced, though he didn't add that he hadn't stayed around to find out, but had instead fled from the kitchen before either his aunt or Ruby could catch him. ''Anyway, I think she's crazy, and I bet she killed Mary-Beth Fletcher.''

Toby looked at Jeff uncertainly. He liked Jeff a lot—in fact, ever since Jeff had come to Devereaux, they'd been best friends. But he'd known Miss Marguerite as long as he could remember, and she'd never seemed crazy to him. Whenever he or any of the other kids ran into her in the village, she always bought them a Coke or some candy or something, and then sat and talked to them just like they were grown-ups. His mom always said Miss Marguerite must be lonely out there in that big old house, and Toby always felt sorry for her. ''How come she'd want to kill Mary-Beth?'' he asked at last.

''How should I know?'' Jeff replied, exasperated. ''Nobody knows why crazy people do things. That's why they're crazy.''

''Then I guess you two are about as crazy as anybody I

know," Ruby said from outside the fort, and the two boys froze, their faces taking on guilty looks as their eyes searched for a place to hide the stolen cookies and Cokes. "Anybody who'd sit in there in heat like this got to have a few screws loose." Her face appeared in the tiny crawl hole, regarding them suspiciously. "So that's where my cookies and Cokes went," she said. "I got cold ones in the kitchen, and if the two of you can sit still for half an hour, I just might make some fresh cookies. Those should've been fed to the birds two days ago. Now come on out of there, both of you."

She withdrew her head from the crawl hole, and Jeff and Toby crept out, still not sure whether Jeff's thievery was going to be punished or not. But Ruby only took each of them by a hand and began walking them up the hill toward the back door.

Fifteen minutes later, as Ruby slid the first sheet of chocolate chip cookies into the oven, the door to the dining room opened and Marguerite stepped into the kitchen.

"I thought I asked you to make some iced tea for—" she began, but stopped short when she saw what Ruby was doing. "Cookies?" she asked, her voice taking on a querulous edge. "For Heaven's sake, Ruby, Julie can't have cookies! She needs something cold! I asked you to make iced tea for her!"

"It's in the fridge," Ruby said placidly, nodding toward the huge refrigerator. "Seems to me she won't want it till she wakes up anyway, and I got a couple hungry boys here that don't look sleepy at all."

For the first time Marguerite noticed Jeff and Toby sitting at the kitchen table, and as she looked at them, Jeff was certain he saw a flash of anger in her eyes. But then her expression cleared and she smiled at them. "Well, we certainly don't want them starving right here in our kitchen, do we?" she said. She leaned down to kiss Jeff on the cheek, but he shrank away. "Are you still mad at me?" she asked.

"N-No," Jeff stammered, embarrassed in front of his friend, and trying not to let his sudden fear show in his voice but failing.

"Well, I wish you wouldn't be," Marguerite said, reaching out to stroke Jeff's hair. "I know I shouldn't have talked to you the way I did earlier, but I guess I just wasn't feeling quite myself."

Jeff shifted uneasily in his chair and tried to duck his head away from his aunt's touch. "It's okay," he mumbled. Then: "Is Julie still crying?"

Marguerite shook her head. "She's asleep now, and you and Toby must be very quiet. You don't want to wake her up, do you?"

Jeff glanced toward Toby. "We're not making any noise. And anyway, when Julie's asleep, nobody can wake her up. It's like she was dead or something."

Marguerite's face paled and the muscles around her mouth tightened. "What a terrible thing to say! You mustn't even think such a thing. And after what's happened—"

"Oh, now, he didn't mean anything by it," Ruby interrupted, her voice smooth. She gently slipped between Marguerite and Jeff to place the bowl with the remains of the cookie batter in front of the two boys. "Now, you go on back upstairs, and soon as Julie wakes up, you just push the buzzer and I'll bring up some iced tea and maybe a cookie or two."

For a moment Marguerite looked as if she was about to object, but then seemed to change her mind. Then she was gone, leaving the boys alone with Ruby once more. Silently Ruby went back to her work, but Jeff looked at Toby with knowing eyes.

"See?" he whispered. "First she acts all sweet, then she's mad. She's nuts!"

Ruby turned to face Jeff, her eyes smoldering. "I didn't say nothin' before 'cause I don't believe in listening in on other folks's private conversations. But don't you start calling Miss Marguerite crazy, you hear me? I just don't want to hear that!"

Jeff, his eyes round, blushed a deep red, then quickly bobbed his head. A moment later Ruby went back to her work as if nothing had happened.

* * *

Jeff hadn't been able to sleep at all. It seemed that ever since he'd gone to bed, the house had been filled with strange sounds, sounds he hadn't heard before. There was a slight wind blowing, and he tried to convince himself that what he was hearing wasn't anything more than the trees brushing against the house, but he knew he didn't believe it, because all the sounds hadn't come from outside.

Some of them had come from inside the house itself, and he was certain he knew what they were.

It was his aunt, moving around the house, stopping outside his door to listen, then moving on.

He'd been sure of it, listening to the strange, uneven footsteps that had been indistinct at first, then clearer. He could picture her, moving along the hall, leaning against one of the walls, stopping in front of each door, listening.

What did she want?

Once, when he heard her stop outside his room for what seemed like an eternity, he pulled the sheet up over his head, afraid that she was going to come inside. But then, finally, she'd gone away again, and after a while he'd tried once more to go to sleep. But he could still hear her, moving up and down the hall, and every now and then he was sure he could hear doors opening and closing.

Now the night seemed to be filled with sounds, and he could no longer distinguish one from another. But all of them seemed impossibly loud, and finally he put his hands over his ears, trying to shut them out.

They were still there.

No, they weren't there at all. He was only imagining them, like the time he woke up from a nightmare but the dream seemed like it was still there, and all the monsters that had surrounded him while he slept were still coming at him, reaching out for him, even though he was awake.

Now he could even hear his own heart pounding, but that seemed to drown out the rest of the noises, and he began to be afraid that if he couldn't hear them, whatever was making the noises might be able to sneak up on him.

The door.

Had he locked the door?

He crept out of bed and moved silently across the floor, then turned the key in the lock. He froze as the bolt slid home, but suddenly the sounds seemed to have stopped. Beyond his door the house was quiet now.

He started back toward his bed, but then a flicker of movement caught his eye.

He knew what it was even before he went to the window to peer out into the darkness of the night.

His grandmother's ghost, come back once more.

Unconsciously holding his breath, he crept close to the window.

There was only a faint glimmer of moonlight, but even in the near total·darkness he could see the shimmering white figure in the cemetery.

What should he do?

And then he knew.

Ruby.

If he could get downstairs, get to Ruby, she would know what to do. Last time she had believed him when he'd told her what he saw, and tonight she would believe him too.

His sister wouldn't, and his father wouldn't.

Only Ruby.

He went back to the door and listened carefully. From the hall outside there was only silence. His fingers trembling, he twisted the key in the lock, then listened again.

More silence.

He pulled the key out of the lock, then bent over and pressed his eye against the tiny hole.

A faint glow showed, and he knew that a nightlight had been left on, so at least he wouldn't have to make his way through the darkness.

Taking a deep breath, he opened the door, slipped out of his room, looked both ways, then ran for the staircase. Before he even had time to think about what he was doing, he was downstairs, through the living room and dining room, pushing his way into the kitchen and Ruby's room beyond.

He tapped softly at her door, and a few seconds later, tapped louder. At last he heard her voice. "Who's out there? What's wrong?"

"It's me," he whispered. "Jeff. Can I come in?"

He could hear the rustling of a sheet inside, then shuffling steps before the door finally opened and Ruby peered out at him, her eyes sleepy. "What's wrong, honey?" she asked. "What are you doing down here?"

"It—It's Grandmother," Jeff whispered, his eyes wide and his voice quavering. "She's in the graveyard again."

Ruby blinked, then nodded and came out of her bedroom, closing the door behind her. "Well, let's you and me have a look," she said, and took Jeff by the hand. She led him back through the kitchen, and when they were in the dining room, went to the French doors and pulled one of the curtains aside. Together they looked out into the darkness.

The strange white figure was still there, moving slowly toward the crypt, its arms outstretched.

"Wh-What's she want?" Jeff asked, his voice barely audible.

"The child," Ruby replied, letting the curtain fall back in place. "They found Mary-Beth Fletcher today, and she's come for her soul." She pulled Jeff away from the window and started back toward the stairs. "Now let's get you back in bed where you belong. She won't hurt you—it's not you she's after. So we'll just get you back in bed, and don't you pay her any mind at all. All right?"

"But—But what if she comes in the house?" Jeff asked plaintively as Ruby led him up the stairs. "Why can't I sleep with you tonight?"

"She won't come in the house," Ruby assured him. "And you don't need to sleep with me, do you? Aren't you a big boy?"

Jeff bit his lip and let Ruby tuck him into his bed. "C-Can I leave a light on?" he begged. "Please?"

Ruby hesitated, then nodded. "Don't see any harm in that." She went to the closet, opened the door, and pulled the chain that hung from the bare bulb on the ceiling. Then she closed the door until only an inch of light spilled out of the closet to spread reassuringly across the floor. "How's that?" she asked.

"O-Okay," Jeff stammered.

Ruby moved back toward the bed and lowered herself into

the chair next to the bed table. "Maybe I'll just sit here a minute," she said. "No point hurrying back to bed, now I'm wide awake."

Jeff, relieved at not being left alone but not quite willing to admit it, said nothing, and a moment later Ruby began to hum a soft lullaby. After a few minutes Jeff closed his eyes and let the quiet song soothe him.

Ten minutes later, when Jeff's deep and steady breathing told her he was asleep, Ruby quietly turned off the light in the closet and left the room, closing the door silently behind her.

She paused in the wide corridor for a moment, then moved down to Marguerite's door, where again she paused, this time to listen.

Silence.

Finally she went back downstairs, feeling the familiarity of the house around her. She moved quickly now, needing no light to guide her, knowing every inch of the house perfectly. But in the dining room she paused once more to look out the French doors toward the graveyard.

The ghostly figure was still there, moving strangely in the faint light of the moon, moving with a strange rhythm, almost as if it were dancing.

Ruby finally returned to her bed, but that night sleep did not come easily back to her. She kept wakening from strange dreams, dreams out of the past—the past she had hoped was long forgotten.

CHAPTER 15

Julie lay in her bed the next morning, only a sheet covering her. She wasn't certain what was causing the strange fogginess in her mind—the suffocating heat, or the pills the doctor had given her the day before and insisted she keep taking through today. She had awakened twice during the night, each time with the hideous specter of Mary-Beth hanging in the darkness, empty eye sockets staring accusingly at her. It had taken all of Julie's willpower to keep from screaming out loud, and the second time it happened, just before dawn, she wanted to go down the hall to her aunt's room. But she had decided it was a childish urge, and forced herself to stay where she was, finally falling asleep again only when the gray light of the rising sun washed the last remnants of the vision of Mary-Beth from the dark screen of the night.

Now she lay in the damp heat of the morning, a sticky film of perspiration covering her body. Outside she could hear a mockingbird singing, and every now and then there were footsteps in the hall. Her father had come in earlier, and her aunt, but neither of them had stayed more than a couple of minutes, telling her she should go back to sleep. But it was too hot to sleep, and besides, there was the dream of Mary-Beth. The memory still sent chills through her body, despite the enervating heat.

When she heard a car pull up the driveway, she automatically glanced at the clock.

Five minutes before ten.

Of course. There was to be a dance class today, and the girls were arriving.

She pushed the sheet away and sat up, swinging around to

place her feet on the floor. But even before she tried to stand, a wave of dizziness overcame her and she had to lie back down. She was just sitting up again when there was a soft tap at the door and she heard Jennifer Mayhew's voice calling softly through the thick wood.

"Julie? Are you awake?"

"Come in," Julie called back, surprised at the weakness of her own voice.

The door opened and Jenny, dressed for dance class, peered inside. Her eyes widened as she stared at Julie. "You look just awful," she breathed, then flushed with embarrassment.

But Julie only smiled, though the smile felt as weak as her legs. "I don't feel real good either," she admitted. "When I heard you guys coming up the driveway, I thought I'd get dressed, but I can hardly even stand up."

Jennifer came into the room and closed the door behind her. "Are you sick?"

"I think it's the pills Dr. Adams gave me. They make me all woozy and put me to sleep, but every time I fall asleep, I dream about Mary-Beth. And it's so hot." She glanced at Jenny out of the corner of her eye. "Did . . . did everybody come?"

"Three of us did," her friend replied, instantly understanding what Julie was really asking. "Me, Allison Carter, and Tammy-Jo." She made a sour face. "Charlene said she couldn't ever come to the island again. She came over to my house last night and carried on like it was the end of the world."

"She was Mary-Beth's best friend," Julie pointed out.

"But she didn't even *see* Mary-Beth," Jenny retorted. "As soon as you started screaming, she went all to pieces, and she wouldn't go anywhere near Mary-Beth when they pulled her out of the water. But the way she's been carrying on, you'd think it was her that found Mary-Beth, not you!"

Julie shuddered as the memory suddenly came flooding back to her, and Jenny flushed again and wished she could take back her words. But before she could say anything else, the door opened and Marguerite appeared.

"Ten o'clock," she announced to Jenny. "Time for you to

be getting upstairs.'' Then she smiled affectionately at Julie. "And you should be asleep.''

"It's too hot,'' Julie replied. "Can't I come upstairs and at least watch?''

Marguerite shook her head. "Dr. Adams wants you in bed all day today. But if you're better tomorrow—''

"I'm not sick,'' Julie reminded her aunt. "It just scared me, that's all. And the pills make me feel strange—''

"If Dr. Adams wants you to have them, then I'm sure there's a reason,'' Marguerite interrupted with a sudden severity that Julie had never heard before. But before she could protest any further, Marguerite had left her room, beckoning Jenny to follow her.

"I'll come back after class,'' Jenny promised.

Then Julie was alone again.

A few minutes later she heard the faint sounds of the piano upstairs as Marguerite began to play.

The heat in the ballroom was nearly suffocating, though the French doors to the balcony stood wide open. Not a breath of air was moving, and the faded draperies hung limp, their thick, velvet folds only adding to the heavy closeness inside the large room. The three girls at the barre did their best to keep up the pace of their warm-up exercises, but Jenny Mayhew was beginning to think she might faint. And besides the penetrating heat of the morning, the class seemed wrong today.

It wasn't simply that Julie wasn't there. More than that, the girls were feeling Mary-Beth Fletcher's absence. Mary-Beth had been absent from the class last week, too, but then there had been at least the possibility that Mary-Beth was still alive, even though no one really thought so. After yesterday even that possibility was gone.

Nor had Marguerite even mentioned Mary-Beth Fletcher. She had simply led Jenny up the stairs to the ballroom, where the other two girls were waiting, seated herself at the piano and had begun playing the music that always accompanied the warm-ups. But as she played, Jenny was certain that the beat was faster than usual, and she was finding it difficult to keep up as she moved skillfully through the five positions.

"Right arm a little lower, Jennifer!" she heard Marguerite call as she turned into fourth position and felt the familiar ache in her legs as she moved her right foot forward exactly twelve inches, placing it precisely in line with her left, heel to toe. "That's right. Fifth position!" Automatically Jennifer's right foot moved back to touch her left, and her right arm swept upward so her fingers almost met above her head. "Straight!" she heard Marguerite call. "Keep your legs straight!"

"But it's too hot," Allison Carter complained, her arms dropping to her sides and her legs relaxing into a more normal position.

"It's hot under the lights of the stage," Marguerite replied, never skipping a beat. "Half of the dance is simple endurance, and if you can't develop that endurance, you'll never be a dancer."

Now Tammy-Jo Aaronson let her arms drop, too, then collapsed into a chair, wiping her face with a towel. "But I don't want to be a dancer," she complained. "All I ever wanted to do was learn a little bit about it and have fun. But it's not fun anymore!"

Marguerite stopped playing and slammed the lid of the piano shut. The loud report of the heavy piece of wood startled Jenny Mayhew, and she felt a sharp twinge in her Achilles tendon as her left leg jerked reflexively. She dropped to the floor and immediately began massaging her ankle.

"Fun?" Marguerite demanded, her voice growing strident. She rose from the piano bench and limped toward the three girls, who were now exchanging worried glances. "Who ever told you dancing was fun? Ballroom dancing is fun, and I suppose for some people dancing to rock music is even fun. But the ballet is not fun! It is an art, and it takes years of discipline to perfect. Years! Do you think I enjoyed it when I was your age?" She paused for a split second, her eyes flashing. "Of course not," she went on. "But I knew why I was going through it. I knew why my legs hurt and my feet were sore and my ankles swollen. But I never complained. Never!"

Jenny Mayhew, her ankle forgotten in the face of Marguerite's sudden wrath, scrambled to her feet and instinctively moved closer to Allison and Tammy-Jo, who were watching the teacher with frightened eyes. But Marguerite seemed not to notice.

"I worked when I was your age," Marguerite went on, her voice echoing shrilly in the expanse of the ballroom. "It didn't matter how hot it was, or how tired I was, or how much my legs hurt. I kept dancing, because I had to! I had to!"

"Well, I *don't* have to!" Tammy-Jo said, her voice breaking as her eyes filled with tears. "I don't want to be a dancer, and I never did. I only came because of my friends. And look what happened. Mary-Beth's dead, and Charlene won't come anymore, and I don't blame her! It isn't any fun anymore, and I'm going home."

Marguerite froze, her face pale as she stared at the girls. "But you can't—" she began, her voice dropping to a whisper. Before she could finish, Allison Carter was on her feet too.

"She can too," she said. "And so can I." Her face stormy, she turned to Jenny. "I'm going with Tammy-Jo," she said. "It's too hot, and I'm tired, and I don't want to stay." She untied the ribbons of her dancing shoes, pulled them off, and shoved them into her tote bag. A minute later she was lacing up her sneakers and shrugging into the T-shirt she'd worn over her leotard that morning. By the time she was done, Tammy-Jo Aaronson, too, was ready. "Are you coming?" Allison asked Jenny as she and Tammy-Jo started toward the door.

"I—I don't know. . . ." Jenny stammered, her eyes shifting unhappily between her friends and Marguerite.

Marguerite, her face ashen now, her whole body trembling, reached out toward Jenny, as if trying to touch her. But there was something in her eyes—a strange burning light—that made Jenny shrink away. "I—I'm sorry," she whispered. "I have to go with them.'' Her voice took on a pleading note, as if she were begging Marguerite to understand. ''They're my friends,'' she finished, her own voice trembling now. ''I have to go—'' Her voice broke, and she felt the hot sting of tears in her eyes as she pulled her dancing shoes off and shoved her feet into a worn pair of loafers. Then, feeling ashamed of what she was doing, she hurried out of the ballroom, catching up with Allison and Tammy-Jo when they were halfway down the stairs. When they came to the second-floor landing, she looked uncertainly at the closed door to Julie's room. ''Shouldn't we say good-bye to Julie?'' she asked, but Tammy-Jo shook her head.

''I just want to get out of here. I knew Charlene was right—we shouldn't have come at all today.''

Turning away from Julie's room, the three girls hurried down the last flight of stairs and out the front door.

In the ballroom Marguerite stood perfectly still, staring at the empty chairs where only a few moments ago her students had been sitting. ''You can't,'' she breathed, her voice barely audible. ''You can't leave me . . . you can't.''

She blinked, and felt a wetness that made the room blur around her, so that she was forced to shut her eyes tightly against the tears. When she opened them a moment later, her vision had cleared.

Everything had changed.

A cool breeze floated in from the open windows, and the sheer curtains, snowy white and freshly pressed, billowed gently. The room sparkled with light, and around her people were dancing. But there was no music.

Drifting as if in a trance, she moved over to the old phonograph and took a record from the top of the stack next to it. A moment later, as the needle began scratching its way through the worn recording, Marguerite heard the room fill with the clear strains of an orchestra.

Slowly, alone in what appeared to her to be a crowded room, she began to dance. . . .

*   *   *

Jeff looked sullenly around the dimly lit basement of the mansion. It seemed like he'd been down here forever, helping his father go through all the junk that appeared to fill every corner. The heat outside had penetrated even the cellar, and dust hung in the air, choking Jeff's lungs. "Why do we have to stay here?" he asked, looking up at his father. "I hate it!"

"I thought you liked it," Kevin replied. "When we first talked about staying here, you wanted to."

"That was before," Jeff said. "When Mom was here, it was fun. But it isn't any fun anymore." His voice began to crack, and he rubbed his fists in his eyes. "It's too hot, and Mom's dead, and I hate it here. I want to go home!"

Kevin set down the large box of cast-off clothes he had just picked up to carry upstairs, and knelt down so his eyes were level with his son's. "Hey, champ," he said, his voice gentle, "I know it's tough. I miss your mom, too, you know. We all do. But there isn't anything we can do about that. Even if we went back up North, that wouldn't bring her back."

Jeff sniffled, then wiped his nose with his sleeve. "I know," he mumbled. "But I still hate it here." He was about to say something else, when the door at the top of the stairs opened and Ruby called down.

"Will Hempstead's here," she said. "Wants to talk to you."

Kevin glanced up with a flash of irritation and almost told Ruby to tell the police chief to come back later. Then he thought better of it and stood up, giving Jeff's head a quick rub. "How about that?" he asked, forcing a light tone into his voice. "Just as we're getting sick of being stuck down here, Mr. Hempstead comes along. Come on, let's go see what he wants." He started up the stairs, and Jeff, only somewhat mollified by escaping the hot confines of the basement, trailed along.

They found Hempstead in the library. When he turned to face Kevin and Jeff as they came in, his eyes were grave.

"Will," Kevin greeted him, extending his hand and trying

not to show the sudden twinge of anxiety he felt at the expression on the police chief's face. "Good to see you."

The police chief shook Kevin's hand perfunctorily, then dropped it. "Thought I'd come out and tell you the autopsy on Mary-Beth Fletcher's done." He paused then, nodding toward Jeff, and didn't go on until Kevin had sent the boy out of the room. But neither of the two men noticed Jeff leave the door to the library ajar. "Couldn't tell much, really," he said when they were alone. "She'd been in the water too long and—well, you saw her. Anyway, the final report's going to show that it was an accident. If the storm was strong enough to take a car off the causeway, Mary-Beth wouldn't have had much of a chance at all."

"Then it's over," Kevin replied, relaxing.

Hempstead shook his head. "I wish it were. But with this kind of thing—well, I'm afraid there's some talk going around."

"Talk?" Kevin echoed. "What kind of talk?"

Hempstead shifted his weight uneasily from one foot to the other. "Well, I'm afraid it's about Marguerite. There're some people saying that since Marguerite was the last person to see Mary-Beth, and since they'd had some kind of fight—"

"It was hardly a fight," Kevin interjected. "All Marguerite was doing was trying to talk Mary-Beth into waiting out the storm. Surely people aren't saying—"

Hempstead cut him off with a gesture. "In towns like this there's no telling what people'll say. That's why I wanted to come out and talk to you about it. You might hear some gossip, and I just wanted you to know that that's all it is. There isn't any evidence that anyone did anything to Mary-Beth, and I certainly don't even intend to talk to Marguerite about it. I've known her too long, and I know she'd never do anything to any of the kids. The whole idea's just plain ridiculous. But there's always a few gossips, and they always have to find something to talk about."

Kevin nodded. "You're sure you don't want to talk to Marguerite?" he asked. "She's upstairs."

Hempstead shook his head. "No use upsetting her," he said.

The two men left the library, and Kevin frowned as he saw Jeff scuttle out of sight. But he said nothing, instead walking the police chief out to his car. They chatted briefly, then Kevin stepped back as the black and white car pulled down the driveway and onto the road to the causeway. As he started back into the house, Jeff came out to the veranda.

"Can't we go to the beach, Dad? How come we have to work all the time?"

Kevin cocked his head and winked at his son. "Because if we don't we'll all starve to death. Now, come on. We're almost finished down there, and once we've got all the junk cleaned out, we'll knock off. Okay?"

Jeff silently followed his father back to the basement, but as Kevin once more began hauling crumbling cardboard boxes toward the foot of the stairs, he said, "I bet everybody's right. I bet Aunt Marguerite *did* kill Mary Beth Fletcher." He clapped his hands over his mouth as he realized he'd just admitted his eavesdropping.

Kevin turned to stare at his son. "Aside from the fact that you shouldn't have been listening to a private talk, what on earth would make you say something like that?"

Jeff glared up at his father, his eyes stormy. "Because she's crazy," he said. "She's crazy, and I bet she killed Mary-Beth, and killed Mommy too!"

"Jeff!"

But Jeff wouldn't be stopped. "Well, it's true!" he yelled. "I saw Aunt Marguerite in Grandmother's room, and she was acting real crazy. And when you're around, she always acts like she likes me, but she doesn't. When you and Julie aren't around, she yells at me and tries to boss me around, and tries to act like she's my mom! But she's not. She's a crazy person, and I bet she killed Mom and Mary-Beth. And I bet she wants to kill me too!"

Before he even thought about what he was doing, Kevin's hand lashed out and struck Jeff across the face. "Don't you ever talk that way again," he said. "Aunt Marguerite loves you very much, and she'd never want to hurt you!"

"It's not true!" Jeff shouted, tears streaming from his eyes, his hand pressed to his stinging cheek. "She hates me, and she's going to kill me!'' As Kevin raised his hand once more, Jeff shrank away, taking a step backward. Losing his balance, he fell over, screaming in pain as his head struck one of the posts that supported the floor above.

His anger draining away as suddenly as it had come over him, Kevin stared helplessly at his son for a second, then reached down and picked him up. Jeff was screaming now and blood was streaming from a cut on the back of his head. Kevin charged up the stairs, Jeff clasped to his chest, calling out for Ruby. By the time he got to the top of the stairs, Ruby was there, waiting for him. Her eyes took in the situation at once.

"Take him to Dr. Adams," she said. "Go on, take him now. I'll call ahead and tell him you're coming."

"He—He fell," Kevin stammered, his face pale as he still held his son. "I was yelling at him, Ruby. I—I even hit him, and he fell down and hit his head."

Ruby brushed his words aside. "Don't tell me. Just get him on into town and get that head sewn up. And don't worry—cuts on the head bleed like crazy, but there ain't nothin' to them. Now, get along with you." She hustled Kevin out the door, then hurried to the phone as Kevin loaded Jeff into Marguerite's Chevy and started toward the village.

Julie woke up from a restless sleep and heard the car pulling away from the house. For a moment she thought it must be Mrs. Mayhew taking the girls home, but when she got out of bed and moved shakily to the window, she saw her aunt's car with her father at the wheel, moving toward the causeway. And then, as the sound of its engine died away, she heard the faint notes of scratchy music drifting down from the ballroom above.

Her friends must still be in the house, and the lesson was running overtime.

She put on her bathrobe and went to the door. Her legs felt stronger now, but her mind was still fogged from the pills. Outside her room she leaned against the wall for a moment, waiting for a slight dizziness to pass. Then she started along the hall, toward the stairs to the third floor.

She climbed the stairs slowly, pausing several times to catch her breath, but at last she reached the top and the small foyer that led through double doors to the ballroom.

Both the doors were closed, but she could hear the music clearly now.

Putting her hand on one of the doors, she pushed it open and stepped inside, expecting to see Jennifer, Allison, and Tammy-Jo on the floor, while Marguerite stood near the barre, watching them carefully, offering small corrections and words of encouragement.

Instead she saw that the room was empty save for Marguerite herself, who was in the middle of the floor, her eyes closed, her arms held aloft as she moved her body through a series of halting dips and turns.

Her right leg, made stiff by the long-ago accident, jutted out from her hip at an unnatural angle, and as she moved, her whole body jerked grotesquely as the lame leg refused to do her bidding.

Julie gasped, and her hand flew to her mouth as she watched the strange parody of a dance. But then, as she was about to slip away, Marguerite's eyes suddenly opened.

"Come," Marguerite said, her voice echoing in the empty room. "Come and dance with me."

She moved toward Julie, her arm extended, and clasped Julie's hand in her own, drawing her out onto the floor.

"Position one," Marguerite commanded.

Automatically Julie's feet turned outward, heels together, and her arms fell gracefully to her sides, her elbows bent so that her curving fingers nearly met.

Marguerite, her stiff leg resisting her mind's commands, tried to force herself into the position, but her body twisted around on her left leg and she staggered before Julie caught her arm.

"You can't, Aunt Marguerite—" she began, but her aunt ignored her.

"I must," she breathed. "I must dance. It's all I have . . . all I ever wanted." Once again she tried to force herself into the graceful pose, and a searing pain shot out from her hip as her body protested. Her eyes welled with tears.

"Don't, Aunt Marguerite," Julie protested. "You'll hurt yourself. Wh-Where are the girls? Jennifer promised—"

"They'll be back," Marguerite said. She took a step forward, then turned, her left knee bending as she dropped into a stiff curtsey, while her crippled right leg, twisted at an odd angle, stretched out behind her. "I know they'll come back. They won't leave me. I know they won't."

Julie's mind struggled in the fog of the sedative. Come back? But where had they gone? What was wrong? What had happened?

She was still trying to make sense of the strange scene in the ballroom when she felt a hand on her arm. She turned to see Ruby looking at her, her eyes filled with worry.

"You shouldn't be up here," the old housekeeper said. "You should be in your room, honey. You should be resting."

Julie shook her head as if trying to clear it of the strange fog. "But what's wrong?" she asked. "Where are my friends?"

Ruby gently eased Julie toward the door. "They're gone, child. The class is over for today, and they've gone home."

"But—But Aunt Marguerite . . ." Julie's eyes searched Ruby's face, imploring her. "Ruby, what's wrong with her? She's acting so strange. She's—"

"Shh," Ruby said, holding a finger to her lips. They were in the foyer now, and Ruby pulled the door closed behind them, then led Julie to the stairs. "She'll be all right," she said, though her voice was trembling. "We just have to leave her be, that's all."

"But what's wrong with her?" Julie insisted. "Why is she acting like that?"

Ruby sighed, then shook her head. "Things have been hard for her," she said at last. "She's like you, honey. She's just lost her mother. And there's Mary-Beth too. Miss Marguerite sets a lot of store by her girls, you know. And to lose one like that . . ." Her voice trailed off as they came to Julie's room. Ruby guided her back to her bed, tucking the sheet around her once more, then patted her hand reassuringly. "Now, don't you worry about her. She'll be all right, and so will you. You just go to sleep, and when you wake up, you'll have forgotten all about it.''

She waited a few minutes, and then, once more, the sedative overcame Julie, and her eyes closed. Only when she was certain that the girl was asleep did Ruby leave the room. But instead of going back downstairs to her work, she climbed back to the third floor and opened the door to the ballroom just wide enough to peer through.

Marguerite, her eyes closed, was still hobbling around the dance floor, her arms held high as if she were embracing an invisible partner.

The sense of unease she'd tried to conceal from Julie flooded back to Ruby. As she started back down the stairs, she tried not to think of what she knew she must do.

But perhaps this time it wouldn't be so bad.

Perhaps this time Marguerite wouldn't need to be locked up

CHAPTER 16

Julie woke up late in the afternoon, her body sticky with sweat and her mind vaguely disoriented. At last she rolled over to look at the clock on her bedside table, and was shocked to see that it was nearly six. It seemed only a few minutes ago that she'd fallen asleep—could it really have been seven hours? But it must have been—the strange fogginess she had felt this morning was gone, so the pills must have finally worn off. She lay in bed for a few minutes, waiting for the last vestiges of sleep to clear out of her mind, then got up and went to the window. Her father was down by the barn, his shirt off and his skin glistening as he wielded a rusty scythe against the overgrown weeds that choked the small paddock beside the barn. Julie called out to him, and he looked up and waved.

"How you feeling?" he shouted, his words drifting up on a gentle breeze coming in from the sea.

"I'm fine!" Julie called back. "I'm going to take a shower and then I'll be down." Before her father could protest, she turned away from the window and went to the bathroom. She stripped off her limp nightgown, turned on the cold water, took a deep breath and stepped into the cool spray. The shock instantly cleared her mind of the last traces of sleepiness, and as she felt the clean water wash the perspiration from her skin, her memories of the morning came back to her.

Jenny Mayhew had been there, and some of the other girls, but she couldn't quite remember what she and Jenny had talked about. And then, a little later, she'd gone up to the third floor.

But it had been strange.

Her friends were gone, and Marguerite had been dancing by herself. But there had been something strange about her aunt, almost as if Marguerite hadn't known quite who she was.

She frowned, lathering herself with soap, and tried to remember more. But there didn't seem to be any more. Just a sort of half memory, like a dream.

Her frown cleared and she grinned to herself. That was it—it had been a dream. Aunt Marguerite couldn't dance, and surely if she'd really gone up there, Marguerite would have known who she was. It must have been the pills, and the music.

She stepped out of the shower and toweled herself dry, then went back to her bedroom and found a clean pair of jeans and one of her father's old shirts. Dressed she went downstairs to the kitchen, where Ruby was fixing supper. The aroma of Cajun food filled the room, and Julie lifted the lid off a pot on the stove to peer at the gumbo bubbling inside. Ruby glared at her disapprovingly.

"What are you doing up? You're supposed to be in bed."

Julie shook her head. "I'm not sick. I feel fine, and I'm not taking anymore of Dr. Adams's pills. All they do is make me woozy and give me nightmares." She pulled open one of the drawers near the door to the butler's pantry. "Is it time to start setting the table?"

Ruby shrugged. "It isn't gonna set itself. But only do it for three. Your aunt won't be down for supper."

Julie's brows knit into a frown. "Is something wrong?"

"Seems like not much is right today." Ruby's eyes rolled heavenward. "You in bed after yesterday, then your brother bumpin' his head, and now Miss Marguerite, gone to bed with her hip."

Julie's frown deepened. "Wh-What happened?" she said, the dream she'd had that morning suddenly coming back to her.

Ruby shook her head dolefully and began peeling radishes into the sink as she spoke. "Seems to me you ought to know—you were there. Fool woman was tryin' to dance. She knows she can't do that kind of thing no more. But some time there's just no talking to her. Just like her mother, sometimes.''

A chill went through Julie. Then it hadn't been a dream. But why hadn't her aunt recognized her? ''Ruby? Is . . . well, is there something wrong with Aunt Marguerite? I mean, besides her hip?''

Finally Ruby turned to face Julie, but her eyes were opaque. ''Now what makes you ask a question like that?''

''It's just—'' Julie began, then fell silent, uncertain how to explain what had happened. ''It's just that this morning, when I went upstairs, it seemed like something was wrong. Aunt Marguerite looked sort of well, sort of strange, I guess. She was talking to me, but it seemed like she didn't quite know who I was. You know, like I was someone else or something.''

Ruby said nothing for a moment, then turned back to the sink. ''I guess maybe sometimes the pain gets to be too much for her,'' she replied at last. ''But if I were you, I wouldn't worry too much about it. She'll be all right.''

''Maybe I should go up and see her.''

Ruby shook her head again. ''Just let her be. When her leg starts hurtin' her, all she wants is to be left alone. I'll take a tray up to her after a while, and by morning everything will be fine again.''

The back door opened then, and Kevin, mopping the sweat off his torso with a T-shirt, stepped into the kitchen. He stopped short when he saw Julie, then cocked his head and looked at her critically. Finally he grinned. ''Well, at least you're back in the land of the living. Have you seen your brother yet?''

Julie shook her head. ''Ruby says he bumped his head.''

'' 'Bumped' hardly describes it,'' Kevin replied ruefully. ''He fell in the basement and cut himself. There was blood all over the place. Didn't you hear him screaming?''

Julie shook her head.

''Well, you were the only one in the county who didn't, then. Anyway, he's fine now.'' He winked. ''Of course, I had to bribe him with a movie tonight.''

Julie brightened. ''Can I go too?''

"Are you sure you feel up to it?" Kevin asked, his eyes narrowing. "Dr. Adams said you should take it easy."

Julie rolled her eyes in exasperation. "I'm all right," she insisted. "It's not like I'm sick. And I hate those pills." She turned on her most appealing smile, and knew immediately the argument was over. "Please?"

Kevin shrugged. "Fine with me. It's time the three of us did something together." He started out of the room, then turned back, his grin in place again. "And when Jeff comes down, be sure to fuss over the size of his bandage. But don't believe him when he tells you I was beating up on him."

"Beating up on him?" Julie repeated. "Why would he say that? You never beat up on us."

"Well, I'm afraid I did give him a whack," Kevin said, his voice more serious. "Not much of one, but it startled him and he tripped. But to hear him tell it, we're talking major child abuse."

Julie giggled. "I'll tell him about the time you spanked me with the ruler after I broke your new fishing rod. He'll think one whack is nothing."

"Thanks, I guess," Kevin said darkly, then disappeared through the door.

Two hours later, with Jeff wearing a new baseball cap to cover up the large plaster bandage over the stitches on the back of his head, the three of them set out for the movies.

"You're sure it's all right?" Kevin asked Ruby as they were heading out the back door. "If Marguerite's not feeling well—"

"She'll be fine," Ruby assured them. "I've been taking care of her since she was a baby, and I don't figure I can't take care of her now. You all get along and have a good time." She waited by the back door until they were gone, then went to the counter and began preparing a tray for Marguerite. At last, uncertain about what she would find upstairs, she picked up the tray and pushed her way out of the kitchen.

*   *   *

Marguerite sat stiffly on the bench in front of the vanity table, examining her image carefully in the mirror. Her hair, swept up in back, was arranged on top of her head in a clean, spiraling twist, held in place by a large, ornately carved tortoiseshell comb. Her eyes were heavily shadowed, the lids edged in black, the lashes themselves coated with a thick layer of mascara. Her lips were crimson, the brilliant red made even brighter by the pale powder with which she had coated her face. Just below the right corner of her mouth she had placed a single dark spot.

Now, satisfied at last with her face, she reached for her mother's jewelry box and began to go through the pieces one by one. She remembered them all, remembered them from her childhood, when she had stood silently by the door to this room, watching Helena get ready for one of her parties.

Sometimes, if she'd been very, very good, her mother would let her try on some of the jewelry. Marguerite could still remember the string of jet she had loved so much, winding it three times around her neck, then staring in rapture at the glistening black beads, which seemed to catch the light and throw it back in her eyes, almost making her blink with their brilliance.

But her mother had always made her take off the necklace.

Now there was no one who could make her take it off.

She found it at the bottom of the box and gently separated it from the other pieces in which it had become entangled, then held it to her throat. Finally, her fingers trembling, she wrapped it around her neck, fastening the clasp with the ease of habit, even though it had been more than forty years since the necklace had last been against her skin.

Suddenly the door opened, and she felt a flash of anger. She glanced up in the mirror and saw Ruby standing at the door, her eyes wide as she stared back at Marguerite.

"What are you doing here?" Marguerite demanded without turning around.

Ruby flinched, but then stepped forward. "I brought you a tray of supper, Miss Marguerite," she said. "I thought you might be hungry."

Marguerite was silent for a moment, her eyes still fixed on

Ruby's reflection. When at last she spoke, her voice held an edge of petulance that sent a chill through the old housekeeper. "Where is Julie? Why didn't Julie bring my tray?"

Now it was Ruby who was silent. She set the tray down on the table by the window, then turned to look at Marguerite once more. "Julie's gone to the movies," she said, keeping her voice level. "She went with her father and her brother."

Marguerite's jaw tightened and her eyes narrowed. "She didn't ask me if she could go—" she began, but Ruby cut her off.

"She's not your daughter," she said, her voice low but firm. She took a step forward. "And what do you think you're doing? Why are you wearing all that makeup? You tryin' to make yourself look like your mother?"

Marguerite said nothing, but her face grew even tighter.

"You don't want to do that," Ruby went on, her voice taking on a soft, soothing tone. "You want to be yourself, Miss Marguerite. You want to be the nice woman you are. You don't want to be Miss Helena, do you?" She was behind Marguerite now, her hands on Marguerite's shoulders, rubbing gently. "Why don't you just come over and sit by the window for a while and have a little supper. I made gumbo for you. You know how much you love gumbo. Just come on over and have a little somethin' to eat, and you'll be fine. Just fine . . ."

For a second Ruby thought she felt Marguerite relax beneath her touch, but then Marguerite whirled on the stool, knocking Ruby's hands away. Then her own hand snaked up, slapping Ruby hard across the face.

"How dare you talk to me like that?" she hissed, her voice taking on all the venom her mother's had once been able to command. "You mind your manners, Ruby!"

Ruby gasped and stepped back, her right hand going to her cheek, rubbing at the stinging bruise she felt already beginning to swell. "Don't you hit me," she said, her voice dropping. "I've taken care of you for a long time, and I'm gonna go on taking care of you. But I ain't gonna let you hit me, and I ain't gonna let you talk to me that way. You're not your mother, and don't you forget it. And don't you start thinking Julie's your daughter either. You think I'm going to let you start in with her the way your mother started in with you? 'Cause if that's what you think, you better think again!''

Marguerite was on her feet now, her eyes blazing, her hip throbbing madly. But she ignored the pain as her hand closed on a heavy perfume bottle. In a single, quick motion, she lifted it off the table, hurling it at Ruby.

Ruby dodged the bottle, and heard it crash against the wall. She stepped forward now, her own hand coming up to strike Marguerite across the face. "I told you not to do that," she said, her voice dangerous. "What you want? You want to be locked up again? Is that what you want? Because I'll do it."

"Stop it," Marguerite hissed. "Just stop it, and leave me alone. I'm fine. I'm just fine!"

"Fine?" Ruby echoed. "Is that why you moved in here to Miss Helena's room? 'Cause you're fine? That's why you got all that makeup all over your face, just like Miss Helena used to wear when you were a little girl? And look at your hair! Just like hers! You ain't fine, Miss Marguerite!"

"Don't talk that way," Marguerite cried, her hands covering her face. "Mama loved me. Just get out of this room and leave me alone!"

Ruby shook her head. "I can't do that, Miss Marguerite. I can't never do that. Who's going to look after you? You're going into one of your bad times, Miss Marguerite."

"I'm not," Marguerite wailed, her words choking in her throat. Sobbing, she lurched across the room and fell onto the bed, burying her face in the pillows. Ruby was suddenly beside her, her hands gently stroking Marguerite.

"That's right," she said. "You let it out. You know you can't keep everything bottled up—you know what happens to you."

Marguerite rolled over, away from Ruby's touch, then glared furiously at the old woman. "There's nothing wrong with me," she spat. "Nothing wrong with me except you. Staring at me all the time, looking at me like you think I'm crazy! But I'm not!"

"Now you calm down," Ruby replied. "You just get hold of yourself before I have to tell your brother what's happening to you. He don't know nothing about your bad times. But you think he'll stay here with those kids if I tell him about you?''

Marguerite cowered on the bed. ''He—He won't believe you—'' she began, but Ruby shook her head.

''He'll believe me,'' she said, her voice like ice. ''Maybe nobody would have believed me twenty years ago, but times have changed, Miss Marguerite. I couldn't stop your mother from doin' what she did, but I can stop you from bein' just like her. And I'll tell Mr. Kevin if things get bad with you. I'll tell him, and he'll believe me if I show him the room downstairs where Miss Helena locked you up. You see if he doesn't believe me! You see how long he stays here!''

''No,'' Marguerite sobbed, her voice breaking now. ''I'll be good, Ruby, I promise. Don't tell him—please don't. I—I couldn't stand it if you told him and he went away.'' Her eyes suddenly darted around the room, as if she were searching for something. ''Why do they always go away?'' she sobbed. ''Mother went away, and Mary-Beth. Even Anne wanted to go away.'' She fell back against the pillows, her body heaving.

Suddenly, with numbing clarity, Ruby understood. ''You killed them, didn't you?'' she breathed. ''You killed Anne, and you killed Mary-Beth Fletcher too.''

''They were going to leave me,'' Marguerite sobbed. ''They were going to leave me. I couldn't let them, Ruby. Don't you understand? I just couldn't let them leave. . . .''

Ruby backed away from the bed, stunned. So it was true. She'd thought of it before—just a fleeting thought that she'd instantly rejected, unwilling to face the possibility that Marguerite could have done such a thing. But she'd known.

She'd known, and had done nothing.

But now she had to do something. She had to get help, get help for Marguerite, and for herself. If she didn't—

''I'll call Dr. Adams,'' she said softly. ''I'll just call the doctor, and he'll come out. He'll take care of you.''

She turned away and started for the door, then heard Marguerite moving. She turned then, but it was already too late. Her eyes burning madly, Marguerite was upon her, hurtling herself toward Ruby, her hands outstretched, her fingers curled into angry claws. Ruby gasped and tried to duck aside, but Marguerite lurched into her, knocking her off balance. She stumbled and fell to the floor, feeling a sharp pain in her ankle.

Then Marguerite was upon her, scratching at Ruby's face, pummeling her fists against the housekeeper's head.

Ruby tried to defend herself, tried to use her arms to protect herself from Marguerite's fury, but it was impossible.

Marguerite stared unseeingly down at Ruby's face. She had to stop her, stop her before she told Kevin, and Kevin took Julie away from her. And he would too.

He'd take Julie away from her, just like her mother took her baby away from her, and took her dancing away from her—took everything away from her, until there was nothing left of herself except a shell.

An empty shell.

All those years of feeling dead inside.

All those years of having nothing.

Nothing except a few hours each week with her girls, who came to her for dancing lessons.

But they left too. They grew up, and went on with their lives, and left her alone with her mother.

And even her mother had left her.

Taken everything she had, then left her.

But no one else would ever leave her again. Not Ruby, or Kevin, or Julie.

Certainly not Julie.

Whatever happened, she'd keep Julie.

Just as her mother had kept her.

Except that Ruby wanted to ruin it all. But it wouldn't happen. She wouldn't let it happen. Her fingers sank deep into Ruby's hair, and closed into fists.

Her arms stiff, she began rocking back and forth, smashing Ruby's head against the floor over and over again.

Dimly, as if from a great distance, she could hear Ruby's screams, but she ignored them and kept rocking.

It was like riding a rocking horse.

She could remember it from when she was a tiny little girl.

You had to sit straight and hold the reins just right. And then you started rocking, and the horse's head would go up and down, up and down.

Up and down.

There was a strange, compelling rhythm to it, almost like swaying to a melody—punctuated by the hollow thump of Ruby's head striking the hardwood of the floor.

Ruby was silent now, and her arms had dropped away from their futile struggle against Marguerite. Then, slowly, her energy beginning to drain away, Marguerite stopped rocking and let go of Ruby's hair. She looked down once more.

Ruby's eyes were closed, and for a moment Marguerite was certain she was dead. But then she felt Ruby's chest heave slightly under her weight.

She had to do something.

If Kevin came home and found Ruby—

Downstairs.

She had to get Ruby downstairs, where Kevin wouldn't find her.

She got up, heaving herself off Ruby's inert body. Her hip felt almost numb now, as if the pain had finally burned itself out, and she dragged herself to the chair where one of her mother's dressing gowns lay. She slipped into the robe, then used the belt to tie Ruby's hands together.

Grasping the belt with both her own hands, she hauled Ruby to the door of her room and out into the corridor. She paused for a moment, trying to catch her breath, then started slowly toward the head of the stairs, moving Ruby a few feet at a time. Once, she thought she heard Ruby moan, but decided it must have been something else, for as she stared down into the unconscious face, she saw no sign of movement. Indeed, she thought Ruby looked almost peaceful. . . .

She came to the head of the stairs and worked Ruby around so that she was sitting up, her back resting against the wall next to the chair lift that hadn't been used since her mother had died. She bent over then, slipping her hands under Ruby's armpits. Taking a deep breath, she heaved upward and to the right, and then Ruby's bulk shifted onto the chair.

Using the free end of the belt, she tied Ruby to the chair,

then turned the power switch on. Below her, in the closet, she could hear the faint hum of the lift's machinery. She pressed the button, and a metallic clanking sound echoed in the entry hall. There was a rattle, and the chair slowly began to descend the wide staircase.

Marguerite moved stiffly beside it until it came to the bottom, automatically shifted itself into neutral, and fell silent. Untying the belt from the chair, she let Ruby slip back to the floor, her eyes still closed.

She grasped the belt around Ruby's wrists once more and dragged her toward the stairs to the basement. It was easier now, for the floor of the entry hall was polished hardwood and there was less resistance than there had been on the carpeting upstairs. She came to the narrow door to the basement, opened it, poised Ruby at the top of the stairs, then pushed.

Ruby rolled down, her body tumbling grotesquely, then sprawling out on its back at the bottom.

Her breath coming in gasps now, Marguerite made her way to the foot of the basement stairs, stepped over Ruby, and pulled the string on the overhead light fixture.

A harsh white light from an unshaded bulb filled the basement, momentarily blinding Marguerite. But then her eyes adjusted to the light and she gazed around until she saw what she was looking for.

A small door, almost invisible, in the far corner of the basement.

Dragging Ruby behind her, she started toward the door. When she was in front of it, she stopped.

It had been years since she had been down here.

Years since the weeks—or had it been months?—after the accident, when her mother had kept her locked up down here, locked up in the dark, locked up until she understood that she had been sick and that without her mother she would never have gotten well at all.

She could still hear her mother's voice coming through the door, hanging in the darkness.

"I could have sent you away. I could have sent you away

forever. But I didn't. I love you. I love you, and I kept you at home, where you belong.''

Where you belong . . . where you belong . . .

The words still echoed, and as she reached for the door-knob, her fingers trembled.

At her feet, Ruby moaned softly.

Marguerite twisted the knob, but the door wouldn't open.

Then she saw the heavy padlock, hanging from its hasp.

Her right leg half dragging now, she made her way up to the kitchen and found Ruby's key ring hanging on the hook just inside the kitchen door. Snatching it off the hook, she hobbled back to the basement. She began fumbling with the keys, searching for the right one. And then, after what seemed an eternity, one of the keys slipped into the lock and it fell open in her hands.

She opened the door.

The room inside was tiny.

A wooden bed with a thin cotton pad was against one wall, a wide shelf opposite it—the shelf where, while she'd been sick, she'd eaten the meals that Ruby brought to her twice a day.

All she could remember of the room was the feel of that hard bed where she'd lain, hour after hour, week after week, waiting to get well, waiting for the pain to stop.

And finally the worst of the pain *had* stopped, and she'd come out of the room in the basement and never gone back to it.

But it had always been there, waiting for her. . . .

Ruby moaned again, and then her eyes flicked open for a moment. ''No,'' she mumbled. ''Oh, no, please . . .''

Marguerite stared down at her, then leaned over and grasped the housekeeper's hands once again. Pulling hard, she hauled Ruby over the threshold and, ignoring the pain in her leg, lowered herself to the floor.

She wrapped the free end of the soft satin belt around Ruby's neck and began to pull it tight.

Tight, and then tighter . . .

Ruby's eyes popped open and began to swell out of their sockets. One of her hands came up, groped toward Marguerite, then fell away. Her fingers twitched for a second, then were still.

"It's going to be all right now," Marguerite whispered softly as she put the lock back on its hasp and snapped it closed. "Everything's going to be all right. I'll have my home, and I'll have my little girl to take care of me, and nobody will ever leave me again. Never, ever again . . ."

An hour later Marguerite, dressed in one of her mother's favorite gowns, the string of jet beads around her neck, was back in the ballroom. Humming softly to herself, she raised her arms and bowed as gracefully as she could to the dancing partner only she could see.

"I dance well," she breathed as she let herself be taken into the invisible arms. "But not as well as my daughter. My daughter is going to be a star someday." She smiled gently, a faraway look in her eye. "I'm going to see to that. Yes, someday Marguerite is going to be a star. . . ."

CHAPTER 17

Kevin steered Marguerite's old Chevy off the causeway and turned left up the road toward the house. The car, coughing in protest as he pressed the accelerator, lurched forward, and Kevin shook his head dolefully. "We're going to have to get a new car," he said to no one in particular. "This one's about to fall apart."

"Can we get a convertible?" Jeff immediately asked from the backseat. "They're neat."

"I think another station wagon might be a little more practical," Kevin replied. Glancing ahead, he frowned. Silhouetted against the clear sky, Sea Oaks loomed like a dark and heavy mass, leavened only by a single light from the west end of the second story. "How come Ruby didn't leave the lights on for us?"

"Why would she?" Julie asked. "This is the first time we've gone out at night."

A couple of minutes later Kevin pulled the Chevy into the garage, switched off the wheezing motor, and swung the splintering door closed. Julie and Jeff were already in the kitchen when Kevin caught up with them, and Jeff was rummaging through the refrigerator, searching for something to eat.

"Not now," Kevin told him, pushing the refrigerator door closed. "It's past eleven, and you've already had a chocolate malt. Time for bed."

"Aw, Dad," Jeff moaned. "Ruby said she was going to make a pie tonight. Can't I have just one piece?"

Kevin glanced quickly around the kitchen, then glared at his son with mock severity. "If Ruby had wanted you to eat her pie, she would have left it out for you. Now, off with you!" He smacked Jeff's bottom gently, and the boy scooted out of the kitchen. When he was gone, Kevin smiled at Julie. "How about you? If I can find that pie, want to split a piece with me?"

Julie shook her head. "I shouldn't have had that sundae. I'll swell up like a balloon."

"Suit yourself," Kevin replied. He checked the back door to make certain it was locked. "If you're going up, make sure your brother brushed his teeth, will you?"

"Who has to make sure? He never brushes them unless I stand right there while he does it."

Kevin turned to look at Julie, his head cocked slightly, as if he was seeing her for the first time. "And you do that?" he asked, his voice choking with sudden emotion.

Julie shrugged, then nodded, blushing slightly with self-consciousness. "S-Someone has to do it," she said, her voice trembling.

Kevin bit his lip, then put his arms around his daughter, holding her close. "I know," he murmured. "But it should be me, not you. I guess I haven't been—"

Julie squeezed him hard, and spoke before he could finish. "I know how much you miss Mom," she said. "We all miss her. And I don't mind looking after Jeff. You have to look after all of us, and take care of this place and everything. What was I supposed to do?" she asked, looking up into her father's eyes. "Ask you if you wanted me to help with Jeff?"

"But you're only fifteen—"

"Almost sixteen," Julie reminded him. "And sometimes, since Mom died, I feel like I'm thirty. All of a sudden everything's different, and I can't act like a baby anymore. But Jeff's only eight. Someone has to look out for him."

Kevin's throat constricted, and for a moment he thought he was going to cry. "Thank you," he whispered, his voice hoarse. Together they moved out of the kitchen and through the house to the bottom of the stairs. "I'll check around down here, then come up," he said. He chuckled, but there was a hollowness to his laugh. "I was going to say I'd tuck you in, but I guess you don't need that anymore, do you?"

Now Julie truly did blush, though her father couldn't see it in the darkness of the house. "It's still kind of nice," she said, "every once in a while, anyway." Kissing her father on the cheek, she skipped up the stairs.

Kevin moved through the house slowly, checking the windows and doors. But as he went from room to room, he had a growing sense of unease, as if something in the house weren't quite right. When he came back to the kitchen for one last look, he knew something was amiss.

The dinner dishes, though neatly scraped stacked, and ready to be put into the dishwasher, were still on the counter next to the sink, and in the sink, soaking in cold, soapy water, were the pots and pans. Kevin stared at the mess for a moment, then crossed the kitchen and tapped softly at Ruby's door.

He waited a long moment, but there was no answer.

He tapped again, louder this time, but when there was still no answer, he twisted the knob and pushed the door open.

Ruby's bed, still made up, was empty.

Frowning, he closed her door, walked quickly through the house, mounted the stairs, and strode down the length of the hall to the closed door to what had been his mother's room. A light shone under the door, so he knew Marguerite was still awake.

He rapped sharply.

"Come in," he heard Marguerite call.

Opening the door, he stepped into the bedroom. Marguerite, lying in bed with only a sheet thrown over her nightgown clad body, smiled at him. Her eyes were twinkling, and her hair, cascading down over her shoulders to frame her face, made her look oddly young. "I heard the children come up," she said. "Did you have a good time?"

Kevin nodded. "Fine," he said. Then: "Are you feeling better? You look like you are."

Marguerite's smile broadened, and she stretched languorously in the bed. "I feel wonderful," she said. "The pain in my hip's almost not there tonight. I almost feel like I could dance again. I've just been lying here feeling good about everything. Didn't you ever feel that way?"

"But where's Ruby?" Kevin asked, ignoring his sister's questions. "The kitchen isn't cleaned up, and she's not in her room."

The smile faded from Marguerite's lips and her eyes darkened. "She's gone," she said, her voice taking on a slight edge. "She got a call just after you left. Some family problem, she said. Anyway, she brought me up my supper and then just took off!"

"Ruby?" Kevin said, his voice doubtful. "That doesn't sound like her. Even when I was little, she was always here—"

Marguerite cut him off with an impatient gesture. "Well, that was a lot of years ago, wasn't it? Back then you could count on people." She sighed heavily. "Sometimes I don't know what I'm going to do about her. It seems like she gets worse and worse. To take off tonight, when I wasn't feeling well—I swear, Kevin, sometimes I wonder if we shouldn't just fire her and try to find someone reliable. Mother always said—"

"Mother always said something bad about everyone," Kevin broke in. "And we certainly aren't going to fire Ruby."

Marguerite suddenly relaxed. "No, of course we aren't," she agreed, her voice gentle again. "And I suppose everyone has a right to have family problems now and then, don't they?" She reached out to Kevin, squeezing his hand gently. "And it's not as if I don't have anyone to take care of me, is it? There's you, and Julie . . ."

Kevin nodded. "And Jeff."

Marguerite laughed lightly, her voice tinkling like a tiny bell. "Of course," she added. "And Jeff. I mustn't forget him, must I?"

"As if he'd let you," Kevin replied. He bent down and brushed his sister's cheek with his lips. "Well, I'm glad you're feeling better, anyway. Have a good night's sleep, and I'll see you in the morning. But right now I'd better get downstairs and clean up the kitchen."

"You don't need to do that," Marguerite protested. "Julie can take care of it in the morn—"

But Kevin shook his head firmly. "I'll do it tonight. Julie's got enough to do, especially if Ruby's going to be gone for a while. See you tomorrow.''

Then he was gone, and Marguerite stretched luxuriantly once more.

She *did* feel good tonight, she decided. In fact, for the first time in years and years, she felt truly wonderful. . . .

Julie wasn't certain exactly what it was that had awakened her. Indeed, she wasn't quite sure she had been asleep at all. After she'd put Jeff to bed, she'd come to her room, put on her pajamas, then sprawled out on top of the covers to read for a while. Though she'd opened the window wide, the slight breeze there had been earlier had died away, and the humid air hung heavily around her, making it impossible to concentrate on her book. Finally she'd put it aside, lying on her back to stare at the ceiling as she let her mind drift. A little later her father had come in.

"Why didn't you tell me?" Julie complained when he'd told her of Ruby's absence. "I could have helped you with the dishes. All I've been doing is lying here pretending it's cool." She grinned at him. "But it doesn't work. The more I think about it, the stickier I get. Did Ruby leave any lemonade in the refrigerator?"

They'd gone downstairs together, then sat in the kitchen talking for a while, until Kevin finally found himself unable to stifle any more of his yawns. "Some of us didn't sleep all day," he'd remarked as he put the glasses in the dishwasher.

For the next hour or so Julie had lain once more on her bed, trying to drift into sleep but unable to.

The insect noises seemed to be amplified tonight, though the sea, nearly silent, was only a soft and distant lapping. Twice she heard an owl hooting softly in the darkness, and once, a little while ago, a sudden silence had fallen in the night, as if a dangerous presence had come near. But then, slowly, the crickets had once more begun their soft chirruping, and then the frogs had joined in the chorus, until once more the air vibrated with their sound.

Now, wide awake, Julie was almost certain she would get no sleep tonight.

She took a deep breath, rolled off the bed, and wandered over to the window. The moon was low, a brilliant silver orb hanging over the sea, its reflected light streaming across the surface of the water like a shimmering highway.

Far out, a boat crossed the path of the moon, and Julie watched it until it disappeared, swallowed up in the darkness of the horizon. Then, out of the corner of her eye, she saw a strange movement.

She frowned, shifting her gaze, but at first saw nothing. Then, slowly and indistinctly, she began to make out a form moving through the moss-hung trees near the cemetery.

It was nothing, she told herself, for when she looked directly at it, it disappeared entirely. It was only when she looked away that she could see it again, all but indistinguishable at the very edges of her vision. She turned away and forced herself to go back to her bed, but the memory of the strange vision stayed with her, and try as she might, she couldn't convince herself that it had been nothing.

Jeff's words came back to her, echoing in her mind. "I know I saw something, and I know it was a ghost!"

At last, almost in spite of herself, she got up again and went back to the window.

The figure was clear now, for it had emerged from the trees and moved into the graveyard.

The moon shone full on it, and it glimmered brightly as it dipped and turned among the graves, at last coming to rest beside the crypt, where it sank down, huddling against the ground.

Julie felt her heartbeat quicken, and suddenly the heat of the night seemed to drain away as a chill passed through her body. She watched, frozen, for a moment, then tore herself away from her window, hurried out of her room and down the hall to Jeff's room. Without knocking, she pushed the door open, went to her brother's bed and shook him.

"Jeff?" she whispered loudly. "Jeffy, are you awake?"

The little boy stirred, then opened his eyes and gazed

sleepily at the indistinct figure of his sister. "What's wrong?" he mumbled. "What do you want?"

"The ghost," Julie whispered, her voice trembling now. "I think it's out in the graveyard again."

Instantly Jeff came fully awake. He slid out of bed and darted to the window. He gazed out for a moment, then beckoned to Julie. "It's her," he whispered. "It's Grandmother."

Almost reluctantly, Julie joined her brother at the window and peered out into the night. The strange ghostly figure was still in the cemetery, moving slowly among the grave markers, almost as if searching for something.

"B-But it *can't* be a ghost," Julie whispered hoarsely. "There aren't any such things."

"Then what is it?" Jeff challenged. "I'm telling you, it's Grandmother's ghost, and Ruby says it's here because somebody died."

"No," Julie protested. Now that she wasn't alone, her fear seemed to abate. "I don't believe it. It's something else. It has to be—"

"It's not!" Jeff declared. Then he turned to stare at his sister, his eyes challenging. "If it's not a ghost, why don't you go down there and find out what it is?"

Julie swallowed, trying to clear the lump from her throat. "I—I don't want to," she said.

"You mean you're afraid to," Jeff crowed.

"Well, aren't you?" Julie demanded. "I don't see you running down there to find out what it is, either."

The two of them stared at each other for a moment, and finally Jeff looked away. "Wh-What are we going to do?" he asked, his voice drained of the bravado of a moment ago.

"We'll get Dad," Julie decided. "He'll know what it is."

Together they left Jeff's room and crept down the corridor to their father's room, letting themselves in without bothering to knock. A moment later Kevin switched on the bedside lamp and blinked at his children, who stood before him with pale faces and frightened eyes. Julie, who had seemed so mature only two hours earlier, now looked almost as young as Jeff.

"What is it?" Kevin asked. "What's wrong?"

"G-Grandmother," Jeff stammered. "She's in the grave-yard again."

Kevin frowned at his son. "Now come on," he said. "I thought we went all over that—"

"But it's true, Dad," Julie broke in. "I—I saw it too. I don't know what it is, but there's something in the graveyard, and—" She fell silent, suddenly feeling foolish. "Well, it looks like a ghost."

"Well, it isn't," Kevin sighed, swinging himself out of bed and jamming his arms through the sleeves of his robe. "It might be a deer, or someone trying to play a trick on you, but it isn't any ghost."

"Whatever it is, it's not a deer!" Jeff said. "Come on. You can see it from Julie's room."

His children behind him, Kevin crossed the hall to Julie's room, went to the window and peered out into the darkness.

The graveyard was empty.

He turned to the kids, his brows arched skeptically. "Well?" he said, tipping his head toward the window. "Take a look and please tell me what you see."

Reluctantly, Julie and Jeff approached the window and looked out. Moonlight still illuminated the island, and the gravestones stood out in stark relief. But except for the crypt and the surrounding headstones, the cemetery was empty.

Julie's eyes searched the pines where she had first seen the strange figure, but now there was nothing there except the hanging moss draping the limbs, and the deep shadows cast by the trees themselves. "B-But I *saw* something," she insisted, her voice trembling. "Dad, I know I did. We both saw something."

"You imagined you did," Kevin corrected her. "But what-ever happened, there certainly isn't anything out there now. So I want both of you back in bed. Okay?"

Julie, chagrined, nodded mutely and went back to her bed. But Jeff didn't move. Instead, he stared at his sister with pleading eyes.

"C-Can I sleep with you tonight?" he asked.

"Oh, for Heaven's sake," Kevin began, but Julie didn't let him finish.

"It's okay, Dad. Really. I don't mind if he sleeps with me."

Kevin started to object, then shrugged his shoulders. "Okay," he said. "Suit yourselves. But no more nonsense tonight about ghosts, all right? See you in the morning." Without waiting for either of his children to reply, he left Julie's room, closing the door behind him. Five minutes later he was once more sound asleep.

But in Julie's room both the children lay awake, listening to the sounds of the night, their nerves on edge.

"We saw it," Jeff finally said, his voice echoing oddly. "I know we saw it, and I know what it means. It means somebody's dead."

Julie said nothing, but for the first time, she didn't argue with her brother about what he'd seen, or what it might mean.

After all, tonight she'd seen it too.

Kevin and Julie were already in the kitchen when Jeff came downstairs the next morning. He slid onto his chair and stared with disgust at the bowl of cold cereal in front of him. "Where's Ruby?" he demanded. "How come we aren't having eggs and pancakes?"

Kevin, his mind already involved with the complexities of the estimates on the remodeling of five of the upstairs bedrooms, glanced at his son. "Ruby's not here," he explained. "Which is why we're all eating cold cereal without complaining."

Jeff made a face. "I hate this junk." He poked at the cereal with his spoon, then reached out and slid the sugar bowl across the table. Spoonful by spoonful he began emptying its contents onto his cereal, then added some milk. As he spooned the first scoop of the sticky mess into his mouth, he peered guiltily at his father out of the corner of his eye, but his father didn't appear to notice what he was doing. "I bet

Ruby's dead," he suddenly announced, and Kevin laid aside the estimate he was studying.

"I beg your pardon?" he asked.

Jeff stared solemnly at his father. "I bet Ruby's dead," he repeated. "I bet that's why Grandmother came back last night."

Kevin's eyes narrowed slightly. "I'm not following you."

Jeff's expression turned exasperated. "Ruby says the ghosts always come right after someone dies. So if Grandmother came back last night, and Ruby's not here, that means she's dead."

Kevin shook his head tiredly. "Well, if she's putting ideas like that into your head, maybe she'd better not come back at all," he observed wryly.

Jeff's exasperation deepened. "How can she come back when she's dead?" he demanded.

Kevin took a deep breath, got to his feet, and added his cereal bowl to the collection of dishes next to the sink. "Look," he said, his tone finally betraying annoyance. "I'm going to explain this to you one more time, and then I don't want to hear any more nonsense. Whatever you saw in the cemetery last night—or thought you saw—it wasn't a ghost. Not of your grandmother, or of anyone else." Jeff stared up at his father, his lips forming a tight line, but he said nothing. "There are no such things as ghosts. And as for Ruby, she had a problem with her family and had to go take care of it. I'm sure she'll be back today, or maybe tomorrow. But she's not dead. Clear?"

Jeff, knowing from his father's tone that he'd better not argue, nodded. "I guess," he agreed, sliding off his chair, but his voice carried no conviction.

Kevin, thankful for even that small a concession, gathered his papers together and started out of the kitchen. "I'll be in the library for a while," he told Julie. "If you need help with anything, just holler."

"We'll be okay," Julie replied. When her father was gone, she tossed Jeff the dishrag. "Wipe the table, okay?"

Jeff shrugged, but said nothing, and began carefully wiping off the scarred top of the kitchen table. Without looking up, he spoke again.

"Know what I bet?" he asked, his voice low, so his father wouldn't hear him.

"What?" Julie asked, knowing that no matter what she said, Jeff was going to tell her anyway.

"I bet Aunt Marguerite killed Ruby," Jeff went on. Now he looked up, his eyes wary as he glanced at the kitchen door. "I bet that after we went to the movie last night they had a big fight, and Aunt Marguerite killed Ruby and buried her out on the island somewhere."

"Jeff!" Julie exclaimed. But before she could say anything else, Marguerite spoke, her voice cold.

"That's a disgusting thing to say, Jeffrey."

Jeff whirled. To his horror, his aunt was standing just inside the kitchen door, staring down at him, her eyes blazing angrily. He gasped and took a step back.

"If I ever hear you say such a thing again, Jeffrey, I shall have no choice but to—"

But Jeff was already gone, slamming out the back door and streaking down the hill toward the grove of pines. Marguerite, her hand suddenly going to her hip, limped to the door. "Come back!" she shouted. "You come back here!"

"He didn't mean it, Aunt Marguerite," Julie pleaded. "Really he didn't. He's just a little boy, and he's always making up stories like that. But he didn't mean it."

Marguerite, her back stiff, said nothing for a moment, but then she turned and smiled at Julie. "Perhaps he didn't," she agreed. "But I'm afraid I've never quite understood small boys." She paused then, and when she spoke again, her voice had taken on a strangely distant tone. "Perhaps Mother was right," she said, her brows knitting thoughtfully. "She always said little boys were more trouble than they're worth. And I'm not sure she was wrong. No," she finished, "I'm not sure she was wrong at all."

CHAPTER 18

"Well, I know how we can find out," Toby Martin told Jeff. They were scuffing along the beach, and Jeff had just finished repeating to Toby what he'd already told his father and sister—that he didn't believe his aunt's story about where Ruby was. "Let's go see Emmaline. She'll know where Ruby is."

Jeff squinted in the bright sunlight. "Who's Emmaline?"

"Ruby's sister," Toby replied, his eyes rolling as if he couldn't imagine anyone in Devereaux not knowing Emmaline Carr's identity. "She lives out past Wither's Pond. Come on."

They left the beach and made their way through the maze of paths that led across the island, then came to the causeway. Jeff paused for a moment, frowning uncertainly. "Maybe I better tell my dad where I'm going."

Toby looked at him scornfully. "You're not going anywhere. Just into town. Who cares?"

Jeff considered it for a moment, then shrugged. They wouldn't be gone very long anyway.

At the mainland end of the causeway Toby turned left. They walked for a while along the main street of Devereaux, then Toby turned right on Atlanta Avenue and started inland. The village seemed to peter out after only a couple of blocks, giving way to an area of small farms, each of them no more than a few acres surrounding a sagging farmhouse, many of which looked abandoned. Finally Toby turned off the road entirely, following a footpath that led through a thicket of mossy pines, and past a stagnant pond covered with a thick layer of green slime. Jeff stared at it for a moment, but when a large snake suddenly dropped out of a tree to disappear below the water's surface, he ran to catch up with Toby. Then, in a small clearing carved out of the thicket, they came to a house.

Except as far as Jeff could see, it wasn't really a house at all. It was no more than a shack, really, built out of weathered boards, its floor supported a few feet above the ground by a crumbling foundation. It had a rusting tin roof, and there were torn screens over the glassless windows. The door stood open, but no light emerged from within.

Jeff stared at the sagging cabin in awe. "You mean someone really lives here?" he asked.

Toby shrugged. "Lots of people live in places like this." He took a step forward and shouted toward the cabin, "Emmaline? You home?"

There was a long silence, and Jeff glanced nervously around the little clearing. The image of the snake was still vivid in his mind, and he could almost feel one of the serpents slithering out of the trees, drawing closer to him. "M-Maybe we better go back," he whispered. "I don't like it here."

But Toby shook his head vehemently. "We came to talk to Emmaline, and we're gonna talk to her," he insisted, then his voice rose to a shout. "Hey, Emmaline! Come on out!"

There was another silence, then Jeff heard the sound of feet shuffling across the floor. A moment later a gnarled old woman dressed in a thin cotton dress that looked as if it might once have been blue, but was now washed and bleached to a grayish-white, appeared at the door. A tattered apron was tied around her waist, and a bandana around her hair. Her feet, bare of any socks or stockings, were shoved into a pair of frayed mules. Jeff couldn't tell exactly how old she might be, but her face was deeply lined, and when she peered out at him, her eyes narrowed to suspicious slits.

"Who's that?" she demanded, her voice rasping and rattling in her throat. "Who's yellin' at me?"

Even Toby drew back, but then he tried to make himself look braver than he felt. "It's me. Toby Martin."

The old woman's lips tightened and she raised her arm to shake a trembling finger at Toby. "Don't you get in no mischief out here," she warned. "I may be old, but I ain't dead yet!" Then her eyes shifted to Jeff. "Who be you? Don't believe I recognize you."

"J-Jeff," Jeff stammered. "Jeff Devereaux."

Emmaline's brows rose slightly. "Well, ain't that somethin'. A Devereaux comin' all the way out here just to visit old Emmaline." She fell silent for a moment, and when she spoke again, her voice sounded almost angry. "What you be wantin'?"

"W-We're looking for Ruby," Jeff quavered, fighting his urge to turn around and run away from the crumbling shanty and its strange occupant.

"How come you lookin' here? She don't live here."

Jeff felt a lump rise in his throat. "Aunt Marguerite said—" he began, but the old woman cut him off.

"Who cares what she says?" Emmaline demanded. "She's just plain crazy, and that's the truth, no matter what folks around here think!"

The two boys exchanged a nervous glance. "But she says Ruby went to see her family," Jeff finally managed to say.

Emmaline's black eyes glittered. "Ruby ain't got no family 'cept me, and she's not been here for months and months." She raised her hand again and beckoned the two boys forward. "You might as well come inside," she muttered. "If you ain't come to throw rocks, least I can do is give you some tea or somethin'."

"W-We better not," Toby breathed, the last of his air of nonchalance disappearing as he glanced nervously at the darkness within the little cabin.

"Scared?" Emmaline asked, her lips spreading into a twisted grimace of a smile which exposed dark gaps between the few teeth that still remained in her gums.

"N-No," Toby lied.

"Then come in," Emmaline demanded. "You want to know all about Miss Marguerite Devereaux, you got to come inside. I ain't standin' out here all day."

She turned away and disappeared back into the shack, leaving Toby and Jeff to stare uncertainly at each other.

"What should we do?" Jeff finally asked. "Will she hurt us?"

"I—I don't know," Toby replied. "Nobody hardly ever even talks to her anymore." A look of sudden determination came into his eyes. "If we run away now, we'll never find out where Ruby went," he decided. "Come on."

Almost against his will, Jeff let himself be led inside the cabin. There was an old easy chair—its upholstery torn and its stuffing bursting out—and a scarred wooden table with three chairs. But the cabin appeared to have been swept out that morning, and as Jeff gingerly perched himself on one of the chairs at the table, he could see a bed, neatly covered with a patchwork quilt, in the other room. "All's I got is some tea," Emmaline muttered, putting a steaming cup in front of Jeff and sitting down opposite him, her eyes squinting as she examined him in the shadowy light. "So you're Jeff," she said, easing herself into the chair opposite the boy. "Well, I guess Ruby wasn't too far wrong about you. Bright as a new penny, is what she said, and that's about what you look. 'Course, I don't rightly—"

"I thought you said you hadn't seen Ruby," Jeff asked.

"Didn't say that. All's I said was she warn't here. Ain't seen her for a couple of weeks now."

"Then where would she have gone?" Jeff piped.

Emmaline pursed her lips and her scowl deepened. "Well, now, I don't rightly know. Fact is, I ain't seen her at all for a week."

Jeff turned to Toby, his eyes shining triumphantly. "See? I told you Aunt Marguerite was lying! I bet she *did* kill Ruby!" Then he clapped his hands over his mouth and looked fearfully up at Emmaline. But to his surprise, Emmaline didn't look angry. Instead, she was nodding almost thoughtfully.

"I knew somethin' like this would happen," she said, half to herself. "I told her and told her to watch out for that sweet-actin' Miss Marguerite, but she wouldn't listen. Said Miss Marguerite was all better now and wouldn't hurt nobody!"

Jeff's eyes widened. "B-Better?" he asked. "What was wrong with her?"

Emmaline's lips narrowed into a thin, hard line. "Near's I can tell from what Ruby told me, your auntie was crazy as a bedbug, a long time ago. It was that accident that did it. If it was an accident.''

Now Toby, too, was listening in fascination to the old woman. ''You mean when she broke her hip?'' he asked.

''That warn't the half of it,'' Emmaline observed. ''Fact is, she was in a family way when she fell down them stairs, and she lost the baby. And that's what drove her crazy— t'warn't her hip at all!''

''C-Crazy?'' Jeff whispered, all of his own suspicions about his aunt suddenly congealing into a tight knot of fear. What if everything he'd said was actually true?

''Don't suppose nobody told you that,'' Emmaline continued darkly. ''Miss Helena sure never told anyone, and neither did Ruby, 'cept for me. Said no one else would believe her, and I 'spect she was right, the way things was back then. Anyway, Ruby told me a long time ago what happened. They kept your auntie locked up out there.''

''Aunt Marguerite?'' Jeff breathed. ''Wh-Where?''

''Down in the cellar. Miss Helena wouldn't even take her to the hospital after she fell down the stairs. Told Ruby she'd let Miss Marguerite die before she let anyone find out she was pregnant. So they just put her to bed, but then she lost the baby and just went crazy. That's when they locked her up down in the basement. There's a little tiny room down there— way at the back—that you can't hardly see. And that's where they kept her till she calmed down.'' Her voice took on a distant tone then, and her eyes clouded as if she were looking into the past. ''Miss Marguerite was a little spitfire before that,'' she said. ''Never knew a girl with so much spirit. Always in one kind of a scrape or another. But then afterwards—'' She fell silent, then poured herself another cup of strong tea from the dented pot at her elbow. ''Well, after that she just turned real sweet. Butter wouldn't melt in her mouth, and everybody started thinkin' she was some kind of saint.'' She shook her head, her eyes narrowing. ''But not me. I always told Ruby that people don't get over somethin' like what happened to her—it just festers inside 'em, and finally they come apart. And you mark my words,'' she finished, her eyes suddenly fixing on Jeff. ''Your auntie's gonna come apart some day, and if somethin' happened to Ruby, you can bet she done it."

Ten minutes later Jeff and Toby left Emmaline's tiny shack in the woods and started back toward the village. "Did you believe her?" Jeff asked when they were well away from the little clearing.

Toby shrugged. "I don't know. Lots of folks think she's kind of nuts. She sure looks like she is."

Jeff nodded, but his brows knit into a deep frown. "I still gotta tell my dad," he said as they came to the outskirts of Devereaux. "But I bet he won't believe me. Will you come with me?"

Toby shook his head. "Not me," he said. "I'm not ever goin' out there again."

Jeff gasped. "You think Emmaline's right, don't you?" he demanded. Toby said nothing, scuffing his feet unhappily in the dirt. "But what am I going to do?" Jeff wailed. "If you won't even come with me—" Abruptly he fell silent as he saw his aunt's battered Chevrolet parked in front of the general store. "I bet Dad's in there," he yelled, breaking into a run. "Come on! Let's find him."

But Kevin wasn't in the store. Instead they found out he'd gone upstairs to Sam Waterman's office. When they went up to the second floor, though, the lawyer's secretary wouldn't let them into her employer's office.

"Whatever you need to tell him can wait," she declared. "I'm sure it can't be a matter of life and death, now can it?"

Jeff tried to tell her that that was exactly what it was, but she only smiled tolerantly and pointed to a chair.

"If you want to wait, you can sit there," she said, turning back to her typewriter. "But I won't tolerate any fidgeting, or any noise."

The two boys settled down to wait, and the minutes dragged by, each of them longer than the one before.

Kerry Sanders pulled his car up in front of Sea Oaks and stared nervously at the old mansion. Maybe he should have called before he came out, but he was almost sure that if Marguerite Devereaux answered the phone, she wouldn't let him talk to Julie at all. So instead, he'd just gotten into his car and crossed the causeway, deciding that even if Marguerite wouldn't let him see Julie, at least he might be able to find out how she was. To his surprise, it was Julie herself who answered the door when he rang the bell a few seconds later.

"Hi," she said, her eyes sparkling happily as she recognized Kerry on the veranda.

"Hey, you okay?" Kerry asked, his voice reflecting his concern.

Julie nodded, and held the door wide. "I'm fine. Come on in." But as Kerry stepped into the entry hall, he saw Marguerite at the foot of the stairs, staring at him with cool disapproval.

"I—I thought maybe I could take you to the beach, or something," Kerry stammered, his eyes flicking past Julie toward her aunt.

"The beach . . ." Julie echoed, her eyes clouding.

"Not the one out here," Kerry said hastily. "The one on the channel. You've never been there, have you? There's hardly any surf at all, and the beach is kind of narrow, but—"

"I'd like that," Julie said, her expression clearing. "I'll go tell Aunt Marguerite—"

Just as she turned, Marguerite spoke, her voice carrying clearly from the foot of the stairs. "If you feel good enough to go to the beach, you should feel good enough to practice your dancing," she said coolly. "Surely you don't have time to waste with the likes of him." Her lips tight, she nodded toward Kerry, but pointedly avoided using his name. Kerry, his face flushing, said nothing.

Julie's smile faded. "But it's too hot to dance," she argued. "And didn't Dr. Adams say I should take it easy? I'm just going to lie on the beach for a while. I won't even go in swimming."

"I just don't think you ought to," Marguerite insisted. "After what happened day before yesterday—"

"But that's over," Julie replied. "And I didn't go anywhere yesterday, except to the movie with Daddy. Please? Just for a little while?"

Marguerite looked as though she were about to forbid her to go at all, but then seemed to think better of it. "Well, I don't suppose I can stop you," she sighed. "But promise me you won't go into the water. If anything were to happen to you, I don't know what I'd do." Her voice cracked. "I know it sounds silly, but just promise me. Please? I—I think of you just as if you were my own daughter, and I worry about you—"

"I promise," Julie said, snatching at the opportunity before her aunt had a chance to change her mind.

Kerry waited in his car while Julie ran upstairs to find a towel, but as he sat beneath the blazing sun, he could sense Marguerite's eyes still on him, almost feel the hostile vibrations emanating from her. At last Julie emerged from the house and jumped into the seat beside him. Kerry started the engine and drove quickly down the driveway to the road. When he spoke, his eyes stayed on the road, avoiding Julie. "Can I ask you something without you getting mad at me?"

Julie glanced over at him, her eyes puzzled. "Sure," she said. "Why should I get mad at you?"

"I don't know," Kerry admitted. "It's . . . well, it's about your aunt."

"Aunt Marguerite? What about her?"

"It's the way she's acting, I guess," Kerry said, his face reddening slightly. "I mean—well, she always used to like me, but ever since I've been hanging around with you, it seems like she hates me. But I haven't done anything." Finally he looked over at her. "It just seems like she's acting kind of weird, that's all."

Julie suddenly remembered the incident yesterday on the third floor—the one that at first she'd thought was a dream. "I—I don't know," she finally admitted. "Sometimes she seems kind of strange to me, too, but then she seems to be just like anyone else." Haltingly, she tried to tell Kerry what had happened the day before. "It was really weird," she finished. "But I was so fogged out from the pills, I'm not even sure what really happened."

"So what are you going to do?" Kerry asked, slowing the

car as they approached the causeway. "Did you talk to your dad about it?"

"It didn't seem like any big deal," Julie replied, shrugging. "But I keep thinking about it, and I keep thinking about the way Aunt Marguerite acts when I'm dancing. She seems to think I should be a big star or something, and I don't even want to be."

They saw a figure waving at them, and as Kerry brought the car to a halt, Jenny Mayhew ran up, panting. "I was just going out to your place," she said, grinning at Julie. "Are you okay?"

"I'm fine," Julie assured her. "But how come you didn't stop in to see me after class yesterday?"

Jenny's grin faded and she suddenly looked uncomfortable. "Didn't Marguerite tell you?" she asked.

"Tell me what?"

Jenny's eyes dropped. "We didn't stay for the whole class," she said. "It was real hot, and Miss Marguerite was making us work real hard, and—well, Tammy-Jo got kind of mad, and we all went home early." Her eyes met Julie's once more. "That's really why I was going out to your place," she added. "To apologize to Marguerite."

"Apologize to her?" Kerry asked. "Why? If it was too hot up there, she should have sent you all home anyway."

Jenny shook her head. "Maybe she should. But she said we shouldn't worry about the heat, and I guess she was right. If you want to dance, you can't say you're not going to do it just because it's too hot!"

Julie giggled. "But that's what I just did," she said. "She wanted me to practice my dancing, but I told her it was too hot and that I was supposed to take it easy." She glanced at Kerry, then giggled again. "No wonder she was mad at you. Everybody left yesterday, then today you came and took me away from her too."

"I didn't take you away from her," Kerry protested. "For Christ's sake, just because she's your aunt doesn't mean she owns you."

"Well, sometimes she acts like she owns me," Julie replied. "She acts like she has my whole life planned out for me—"

"Julie!" Jenny exclaimed. "That's not true. She's just proud of you 'cause you dance better than any of the rest of us."

"But I don't care," Julie said, her voice taking on a note of exasperation. "Dancing's fun, but it's not my whole life. Sometimes Aunt Marguerite acts like it should be. In fact, that's what Kerry and I were talking about just now."

Jenny frowned. "What are you talking about? You mean you're going to quit too?"

Julie realized she hadn't really been thinking about that at all, but now she shrugged nonchalantly. "I might," she said. "But so what if I do?"

"But she counts on you," Jenny told her. "She counts on all of us. I don't really care about dancing either, but I love Miss Marguerite, and just having all of us around makes her so happy."

"Except for yesterday," Julie reminded Jennifer. "It doesn't sound like anyone was having a very good time."

Jenny's eyes rolled scornfully. "Well, that was Tammy-Jo's fault, not Miss Marguerite's. For Heaven's sake, they'd just found Mary-Beth the day before. Nobody was feeling very good. Maybe we shouldn't have been having a lesson at all." She stepped back from the car, but her eyes remained fixed on Julie. "And if you decide to quit going to her classes, I think you're mean."

"I didn't say I'd decided," Julie protested. "I just said I was thinking about it, that's all."

"Well, let me know when you make up your mind," Jenny said, her eyes flashing angrily. "It's starting to look like I'm going to be the only one left, isn't it?"

Before Julie could say anything else, her friend was gone, walking quickly up the road toward Sea Oaks.

"Maybe we should go back," Julie fretted as Kerry put the car back in gear. "I don't want Jenny mad at me."

But Kerry shook his head. "She'll be all right. Marguerite's always been crazy about her." He let the clutch out and started across the causeway. A few minutes later they were lying side by side on the beach bordering the channel. "Now,

isn't this better than spending the afternoon up in the ballroom?'' Kerry asked.

''Mmm-hmm,'' Julie sighed. Then she sat up and stared out
at the sea, a shiver running through her as she remembered
what had happened two days ago. ''But I'm still not going in
the water. I don't know if I'll ever want to again.''

Marguerite was sitting on the veranda in front of Sea Oaks,
staring unseeingly out over the island. She shouldn't have let
Julie go off with Kerry Sanders like that, she thought. She
should have kept her home, the way her own mother had tried
to keep her home when she was Julie's age. But she'd been
like Julie, headstrong and willful, and look how she'd ended
up. Her mother had tried to stop her, tried to save her, but
she hadn't listened—

A figure was coming along the road from the causeway,
and Marguerite stood up, taking a step forward. Pain shot out
from her hip—the pain that had been throbbing for more than
an hour now, ever since Julie had left. But now Julie was
coming back.

And she was alone!

She moved across the veranda and down the steps to the
lawn as the figure drew nearer.

But it wasn't Julie. It was Jennifer Mayhew.

Marguerite's hip sent a sharp, jabbing needle shooting
down her right leg, and as she remembered what had happened in the ballroom yesterday, remembered the girls—*her*
girls—running away from her, the fingers of her right hand
began massaging her aching muscles.

She turned away, starting back up the steps to the veranda.

''Miss Marguerite?'' Jenny called. ''Miss Marguerite, wait!''

Marguerite stopped, but stood where she was, her back
still toward Jenny.

''I—I came to apologize,'' Jenny said, and the unhappi-
ness in her voice made Marguerite turn around to look at her.
Her eyes were glistening with tears. ''I—well, I wanted to tell

you I'm sorry I left with Tammy-Jo and Allison yesterday, and that even if Julie decides to quit, I won't.''

She ran forward and flung her arms around Marguerite. But Marguerite still didn't move. "Julie?" she breathed. "What are you talking about?"

Jenny tipped her face up. "I was just talking to her," she said. "She was on her way to the beach with Kerry Sanders, and she said she was thinking about quitting dancing."

Marguerite's eyes glazed over, but when she spoke, her voice was calm. "I'm sure you must be mistaken," she said. "Julie won't give up the dance. It means everything to her—everything."

"But she said—"

Marguerite placed a gentle hand over Jenny's mouth, cutting off her words. "I'll talk to her," she said. "When she comes home, I'll talk to her, and I'm sure we can straighten out whatever's wrong." Then she smiled at Jenny. "But since you're here, why don't we go up to the ballroom. I can give you a lesson, just the two of us, to make up for yesterday."

Jenny blinked in surprise. A lesson now? But she didn't have her leotard, or her shoes, or anything else she needed. "I—I don't know," she said. "I told Mom I'd be home—"

"But you must," Marguerite insisted. "You've come all this way, and I'm all alone. You mustn't go right now." Her voice took on a pleading note. "You mustn't."

Jenny hesitated, and for the first time noticed something odd in Marguerite's eyes. Though Marguerite was looking at her, Jenny had the strangest feeling that she wasn't really seeing her.

"Please," Marguerite said. "Just for a little while."

There was a tone of pathos in Marguerite's voice that twisted Jenny's heart, and she mutely nodded.

"Let me have your arm," Marguerite said as she led Jenny into the cavernous stillness of the great house. "I'm afraid my hip's a bit bad this morning. . . ."

Her voice trailed off, and her right hand clutched at Jenny's left arm, her fingers squeezing so hard Jenny winced in pain. They started up the stairs, moving slowly. At the second-floor landing Marguerite stopped to catch her breath.

"M-Maybe you should have used the chair lift," Jenny suggested, but Marguerite shook her head.

"I'm not dead yet," she said, her eyes taking on a look of almost grim determination. "And if I can't walk, then I can't even hope to dance, can I?" Renewing her grasp on Jenny Mayhew's arm, she mounted the stairs toward the third floor.

Ten minutes later Jenny knew she'd made a mistake. Ever since they'd come into the ballroom and Marguerite had put a scratchy record on the old phonograph, a growing sense of worry had begun to creep up on her.

Marguerite's eyes looked even stranger now, and instead of watching Jenny dance and gently correcting her when she made a mistake, Marguerite herself was dancing, moving stiffly around the room in a limping parody of a waltz, her arms held high, her head tipped back with her eyes closed, as if she were being held in the arms of an unseen partner.

Finally, her unease growing into the beginnings of fear, she edged toward the door. Instantly Marguerite stopped dancing, and her eyes, glowing with a strange light, fixed on Jenny. "Don't go," she said. "You can't go now."

Jenny's heart began to race and she felt dizzy. "I—I have to," she whispered. "I didn't really come for a lesson today. I don't have my shoes, or my leotard, or—"

"But it doesn't matter," Marguerite said. "All that matters is that you dance." She crossed the room, her right leg moving stiffly, her body twisting oddly with each step. "Dance with me," she commanded, her hand grasping Jenny's and pulling her out onto the floor. "Listen to the music, and dance. . . ."

Clutching Jenny's hand in her own, Marguerite forced herself into the first position of ballet, her unseen partner of a moment ago apparently forgotten now. "Position one!" she commanded, twisting her lame leg outward, the veins of her forehead standing out as she fought against the pain the movement caused in her malformed hip. "Turn your feet out, Marguerite! Out!"

Jenny stared at Marguerite, stunned. What was happening? Didn't Marguerite even know who she was?

"Position two!" Marguerite demanded. Her arms came up, but her right leg, throbbing with pain now, refused to move.

Jenny watched in horror as Marguerite battled against her own disfigured body. "Stop it," she cried, her voice breaking as a sob rose up in her throat. "Please stop it, Miss Marguerite. What are you trying to do?"

Marguerite's hand snaked up, slashing across Jenny's face. "Do not speak," she hissed. "When I am teaching you, you will not speak!"

Her voice had taken on a strangely familiar tone, but for a moment Jenny couldn't place it. And then she remembered.

How many times had she heard that voice echoing through this house, calling out, demanding, commanding? But it wasn't Marguerite's voice at all.

It was her mother's voice—Miss Helena's voice—calling out to Marguerite, demanding her presence, commanding her every action. But now Miss Helena's voice was coming out of Marguerite's own throat.

"No," Jenny whimpered. "Oh, no . . . ." She started toward the door. "I—I have to go," she whispered. "I'm sorry . . ."

"No!" Marguerite screamed. "You can't go. Not now! You can't leave me! I forbid it!"

Her tears flowing now, Jenny fled from the ballroom, lurching toward the head of the stairs. And then, just as she got there, she heard Helena Devereaux's voice once more, crackling out of Marguerite's throat. "You won't leave! I will not permit it!"

At the same instant that the words slashed at her ears, she felt two hands against her back and a great weight, pushing her forward.

She teetered for a moment, tried to grab for the banister, but missed.

Then she was tumbling, plunging head first down the steep staircase.

She hit the bottom, but the sound she heard—the last sound she would ever hear—was not that of her head striking the wooden floor of the landing.

Instead, it was the sharp crack of her own neck breaking.

CHAPTER 19

"But I'm tellin' you, Dad, that's what she said. Isn't it, Toby?" Jeff looked expectantly at his friend, as if Toby's corroboration would convince his father. The three of them were sitting in the back booth at the drugstore. An uneaten hamburger sat limply in front of Jeff. "How come you won't believe me?"

Kevin shook his head tiredly. He'd already explained to Jeff three times that Emmaline Carr's story was just too strange to be believed. Marguerite locked up in a hidden room in the basement? It was ludicrous! But what wasn't ludicrous was the fear in Jeff's eyes. "Look," he said at last. "How's this? We'll all go out to the house, and I'll ask your aunt about it."

Jeff's jaw set stubbornly. "Toby won't go out to our house anymore," he announced. "He's too scared of Aunt Marguerite. And I'm scared of her too."

"But that doesn't make any sense," Kevin insisted. "Your aunt loves you. She wouldn't hurt you for anything in the world."

"Yes, she would," Jeff argued, his eyes stormy. "She's only nice to me when you're around. If I'm all by myself with her, she acts like she hates me."

Kevin took a deep breath, knowing that once Jeff had made up his mind, he wasn't about to change it. "Okay," he sighed. "I'll tell you what—you go home with Toby for a while, and I'll go out to the island by myself. I'll have a talk with your aunt and see if I can find out where Ruby really is."

"Will you come and get me later on?" Jeff asked uncertainly.

Kevin shook his head. "You managed to walk all the way out to Emmaline's house. You can manage to walk back home." He slid out of the booth and dropped twenty dollars on the table. "You guys can pay the bill out of that, and there's enough left over for a movie. Okay?" The two boys, their eyes fastened on the ten dollar bill, bobbed their heads mutely. "And be home by supper time," Kevin admonished his son. "By then I'll have this all straightened out."

He strode out of the drugstore into the dusty heat of the afternoon. The clouds from the southeast were drifting over the village now, and the temperature seemed to have dropped a degree or two, but Kevin's shirt still clung damply to his body as he climbed into his sister's Chevy and started the engine.

It's the heat, he decided as he crossed the causeway toward the island. The heat gets to people after a while, and they start imagining things. But a story about Marguerite being locked up down in the basement of Sea Oaks? Alone in the car, he shook his head.

He found Marguerite sitting on the veranda, sipping a glass of lemonade. She smiled as he came up the steps, and when she rose to her feet, her limp was almost imperceptible.

"Still getting better?" Kevin asked, and Marguerite nodded, her smile broadening.

"I don't know what it is." She glanced up at the sky, then shrugged. "Usually it gets so much worse when a storm's coming. But today it seems just fine. I suppose I should count my blessings, shouldn't I?"

Kevin's brows arched. "I wish more people in this town would do that," he observed. "Instead of making up stories about other people."

Marguerite's smile faltered. "Making up stories? What sort of stories?"

Kevin hesitated, wondering how to begin. "Well, Emmaline Carr, for one. It seems Jeff and Toby went out to see her today."

"E-Emmaline?" Marguerite said, with the trace of a stammer. "Why would they want to go out and see Emmaline? Everyone knows she's strange in the head. Living in that shack, with no water or electricity . . ." Her voice trailed off and her head bobbed sympathetically. "Sometimes I feel so sorry for her," she went on. "Except for Ruby, she doesn't have anyone else in the world."

Kevin frowned. "But then Ruby doesn't have anyone but Emmaline, does she?" he asked.

Marguerite blinked. "I—why, I don't know. . . ." Then her voice took on a note of impatience. "Kevin, what are you trying to get at? Did Emmaline say something to Jeff?"

"I'm afraid she did," Kevin replied. Slowly he repeated the story Jeff had told him a few minutes ago. As he spoke, the last traces of Marguerite's smile disappeared and her eyes began to blaze with indignation.

"But that's terrible," she said when Kevin was finished. "How could Emmaline say such things about me? I've never done anything to hurt her—nothing at all. Why, she must have scared poor Jeff half to death."

"But where is Ruby?" Kevin finally asked. "If she didn't go to Emmaline's, where *did* she go?"

Marguerite's right hand fluttered at her bosom. "Well, I'm sure I don't know," she replied. "Perhaps she was lying to me. She's like that, you know. Mother always said you couldn't trust a word Ruby said. Not a word—" Abruptly she fell silent. As Kevin turned toward the front door, she asked, "Where are you going?"

Kevin turned to look at his sister, his eyes troubled. "Nowhere," he said. "I'm just going to have a look around the house, that's all."

He stepped into the gloom of the house, closing the door behind him. He paused for a moment, feeling the atmosphere. For a moment he noticed nothing different: the house seemed as it always had. But then, as he started through the living room toward the dining room and the kitchen beyond, he began to feel a strange sense of something being amiss.

Somehow, though he knew he was alone in the house, it did not feel empty. There was a sort of presence in the house, and as he crossed to the dining room, his neck began to tingle. He stopped walking, spinning around as if expecting to catch someone staring at him.

But the room was empty.

And then he knew what it was. The portrait of his mother still hung above the fireplace, and it was his mother's eyes he'd felt watching him, as if she were still alive and in the room. He paused for a moment, staring at the portrait.

It looked so much like Marguerite that a chill passed through him. His mother and his sister, he realized, could almost have been the same woman, they were so much alike.

Except that they weren't. His mother had been hard, cruel, and unloving. Even now he could remember the dream he'd had—the dream of being locked away in a tiny room, with his mother coming to kill him.

A tiny room.

That's what Jeff had said was in the basement—a tiny room, where Marguerite had been locked up.

He shook his head. It was crazy—it made no sense. He chuckled out loud, deciding the heat was now getting to him, too, but his small laugh echoed hollowly in the expanse of the room, mocking him.

Turning away from the portrait of his mother, he hurried on to the the kitchen.

Dirty dishes were piled in the sink, and the remains of Marguerite's solitary lunch still sat on the kitchen table, as if his sister expected Ruby to reappear at any moment to clean up the mess. Then Kevin's eyes fell on the door to Ruby's room.

Uncertain what to expect, he strode to it and opened the door.

It was exactly as it looked last night—the bed still neatly made up, Ruby's nightgown still hanging from a hook on the open closet door.

But then Kevin noticed some other things—things he hadn't noticed last night.

On the table in the corner behind the door, he saw a tray.

On the tray a supper was laid out—a plate of gumbo, cold and congealed, and a small salad, its lettuce limp and already beginning to shrivel.

A supper, as if Ruby had been about to eat alone in her room when—

When what?

Kevin rejected the thought flitting around the edges of his mind, and continued his inspection.

On the shelf high up in the closet, he found a suitcase, its top still thickly coated with dust.

No empty hangers hung on the clothes bar, nor did anything seem to be missing when Kevin inspected Ruby's drawers.

Suddenly the nightgown hanging from its hook stood out from the scene.

If Ruby had gone somewhere, wouldn't she have taken her nightgown with her? Wouldn't she have taken *something* with her?

And she certainly wouldn't have left a full meal, uneaten, sitting on a table in her room.

A knot of fear congealing in his belly, Kevin left her room and retraced his steps back through the dining room and living room.

His mother's eyes seemed to bore into him as he passed the portrait, and he quickened his step until he came into the entry hall. Marguerite was standing just inside the front door, and as Kevin started toward the door below the main stairs—the door that led to the basement—she spoke, her voice quavering.

"Wh-Where are you going?"

Kevin turned to face her, his eyes meeting hers. "Downstairs," he said.

"B-But you mustn't," Marguerite whispered. Once more her hand was fluttering at her bosom, but suddenly it dropped to her hip, and when she took a step forward, her limp was suddenly more pronounced. "Please, Kevin—don't go down there."

The knot of fear tightened its grip on Kevin, but he shook his head. "I have to," he said. Then he pulled the door open, tugged the string overhead, and started down to the cellar, the white light of the naked bulb overhead glaring coldly. He was already at the bottom of the stairs when he heard Marguerite's uneven footsteps as she slowly followed him.

*　　*　　*

He stared at the door numbly for a moment. It was still half hidden, almost lost in the shadows behind the furnace, and he understood now why he hadn't seen it before. Until a couple of days ago it must have been completely lost behind the mass of cardboard boxes that had been stacked there. He must have uncovered it himself just yesterday.

Indeed, if he hadn't let himself become so angry with Jeff, he surely would have seen it.

He could feel Marguerite now, just a few steps behind him, and hear her breathing coming in strange, half-strangled gasps. He turned to her, but her face was lost in shadow, the naked bulb above the stairs forming a brilliant halo behind her head.

"What's in there, Marguerite?" he asked, deliberately keeping his voice low. But still his words seemed to echo ominously, hanging heavily in the air.

"N-Nothing," Marguerite stammered. "There's nothing in there, Kevin. Really—"

"Then open it," Kevin said. "If there's nothing in there, then there's nothing to hide, is there?"

Marguerite seemed to shrink back. "No," she whispered, her voice taking on a childish whine. "I can't go in there. Please don't make me. Please?"

Kevin's heart began to race, and the cold knot of fear in his belly turned to ice. "Why?" he asked. "Marguerite, why can't you go in there?"

"I can't," Marguerite pleaded. "It's where Mama kept me. It's where she kept me during the bad times, when I was sick. Don't make me go in there, Kevin. Don't make me."

Taking a deep breath, Kevin stepped to the door and tried the lock. It held firm, hanging from its hasp and glittering dully in the light from the bare bulb.

"I need the key, Marguerite."

Marguerite bit her lip, and took an unsteady step backward, her hands clasped behind her back. "I—I don't have it," she whispered. "Ruby has all the keys. I wasn't ever allowed to have them. . . ."

Dear God, Kevin thought. What did Mother do to her? But he said nothing. Instead he stepped around Marguerite and hurried up the stairs.

In the kitchen he began rummaging through the drawers, searching for the ring of keys that Ruby always kept close at hand. And then he heard the door swing open and turned to see Marguerite, her eyes glistening strangely. Next to her, on a hook just behind the door, hung the ring of keys. He stepped forward and took it in his hand.

"No," Marguerite begged, the word strangling in her throat. "Don't go back down there, Kevin. Please don't."

Part of Kevin wanted to give in to his sister, to put the keys back on the hook and never go into the basement again. But he couldn't do that. Whatever was down there, he had to see it. He shook his head and stepped around Marguerite, starting back toward the stairs.

His back was already to her when she took the butcher knife out of one of the open drawers, concealing it in the folds of her skirt.

As she started once more after Kevin, the burning pain from her hip washed over her in throbbing waves, each one worse than the last. Descending the stairs, she had to clutch tightly to the railing, for her right leg, totally numbed by the pain now, was almost useless.

Kevin fumbled with the keys, trying one and then another. Most of them wouldn't go into the lock at all, and the ones that would, refused to twist as his fingers worked at them.

He was only vaguely aware of Marguerite now, only half sensing her presence as she stood behind him, her eyes, smoldering darkly, fastened on his fingers as he worked.

He tried the next to the last key, and suddenly the lock fell open in his hands.

He stared at it vacantly, a fragment of his mind wishing that none of the keys had fit.

Then, his hand trembling, he lifted the lock from its hasp and pushed the door open.

It swung slowly, creaking on its hinges, and from over his shoulder a shaft of light from the bare bulb above the stairs illuminated the tiny cell.

The first thing he saw was Ruby.

Propped up on the wooden cot, her eyes wide open and staring blankly at him, she still had the belt of Marguerite's robe knotted around her neck. One arm was outstretched, and her fingers seemed to be reaching out to him, pleading with him for help.

On the floor, her body twisted, lay Jennifer Mayhew. Her eyes, too, were open, staring sightlessly upward. Her head was wrenched back against one of her shoulders, and her arms sprawled lifelessly outward, the fingers of her left hand barely brushing against one of Ruby's legs.

"My God," Kevin groaned, involuntarily stepping back, then turning to face Marguerite. "What have you done?"

Marguerite stared at Kevin, her eyes wild. "Ruby was going to tell," she murmured. "She was going to tell on me, and make you go away. And Jenny was going to leave me. You understand, don't you, Kevin? I would have been all alone. . . ."

Kevin stared at her, shock numbing him. Then he stepped toward her.

"You're going to tell too," Marguerite suddenly cried. "You're going to tell, and take Julie away from me!" She raised her right arm, and the blade of the knife glittered evilly in the glare from the light. "I won't let you!" she screamed. "I won't let you take Julie. I won't!"

She hurtled herself forward, and Kevin, his body refusing to obey his mind, stared at her mutely, watched helplessly as the knife arced through the air.

The blade slashed into his chest, but for a moment he felt nothing at all. And then, as hot blood began gushing out of the wound, a strange heat seemed to emanate from the hardness of the blade in his body. His eyes widened and he began to sink to his knees, then felt himself twist around as Marguerite jerked the knife free.

Then he felt it again, a searing pain this time as the knife stabbed into his back. He tried to roll away, tried to call out his sister's name, but it did no good.

And then, as the knife slashed into him once again, he

remembered the dream—the dream he'd had when he was a boy, and then again only a few weeks ago.

The dream, in which his mother was going to kill him, and he'd tried to call out to his sister.

He looked up now, and saw his mother's face looming above him.

Except it wasn't his mother at all. It was Marguerite.

· And he was calling her name, but no sound came out. Only a hot, salty stream of blood boiled from his lips.

His lungs were filling with blood now, drowning him.

He was dying, and there was nothing he could do to save himself.

As his life ebbed away, he thought about the dream once more, the dream he had been certain held some deep meaning.

But the meaning hadn't been deep at all, for the dream had not even been a dream.

Instead, it had been a premonition, and now he was living it out.

It had been a premonition of his own death, down here in this dark and hidden room, and now it seemed as if he'd been waiting all his life for this moment when his mother would come to kill him.

Except it wasn't his mother at all.

It was his sister, who had somehow in her own madness become his mother.

Become his mother, and now become his children's mother too.

And as he died, he knew that she would kill them, just as she had killed him.

For him, the nightmare was over.

For his children, it had just begun.

CHAPTER 20

Alicia Mayhew glanced at the clock on the dashboard of her car, then up at the lowering sky. It was nearly three o'clock, and she'd distinctly told Jenny to be home no later than two. They were due at Alicia's brother's home in Charleston in thirty minutes, and even if she found Jenny within the next couple of minutes, they would still be late. And the storm wouldn't help, either. If Jenny got caught out in the rain—

She braked the car to a stop, for across the street Kerry Sanders and Julie Devereaux had gotten out of Kerry's worn convertible and were struggling to put the top up. "Julie?" Alicia called. "Julie!"

Julie looked up, then smiled and waved to Mrs. Mayhew. "Hi!" she called back.

"Have you seen Jenny?"

Julie shook her head. "Not since this morning. She was going out to see Aunt Marguerite."

Alicia frowned uncertainly. "But she said she was going out to see you—"

"We saw her on the road, right at the end of the causeway," Julie explained. "But it was mostly Aunt Marguerite she wanted to see. Isn't she home yet?"

Alicia's lips tightened and she shook her head impatiently. "I guess I'd better run out there," she sighed. She shifted into Drive, pressed the accelerator, and the car moved forward just as the first drops of rain began to fall. She waved to Julie and Kerry, but neither of them saw her as they struggled to get the torn top to Kerry's car up before the rain began in earnest.

Why, she wondered as she started out onto the causeway, couldn't kids ever learn to keep track of time?

*   *   *

It was going to be all right now, Marguerite Devereaux told herself as she gazed into the mirror of her mother's vanity. Everything was going to be fine. Kevin wasn't going to leave—not ever again—and she was safe. Sea Oaks was hers now. Sea Oaks, and Julie, and . . .

She paused.

And Jeff, she finished.

She mustn't forget Jeff. But he wasn't part of it—he didn't belong here, any more than Kevin had belonged here. It should be just her and Julie. Herself and Julie, just as it had been her mother and herself for so many years.

She would have to decide what to do about Jeff. Perhaps she should ask her mother.

She gazed into the mirror once more, examining her carefully applied makeup. It had taken her nearly an hour to get it exactly right, but her brows were finally tweezed to a thin line and darkened nearly black with one of her mother's eyebrow pencils. Her cheeks, heavily rouged, seemed to glow beneath a thick layer of almost white powder, and her lips were covered with a smear of bright red.

Carefully she wrapped one of her mother's old rats into her hair so that it formed a thick roll over her forehead. The rest of her hair, cascading in soft waves down to her shoulders, softened her face, framing it so that the rouge-enhanced planes of her cheekbones stood out dramatically. At last satisfied, she went to the closet and selected one of her mother's favorite dresses. Bright red, it had wide shoulder pads and a tapering bodice held snug by a wide, black patent-leather belt. As she slipped the dress carefully over her head, she remembered the last time her mother had worn it, more than forty years ago.

It had been a day much like today. A storm had been threatening, and her mother had been expecting guests for tea. Marguerite had hovered in a corner of the room, watching her mother dress, until Helena had finally noticed her and sent her upstairs to practice her dancing. "We have a recital tomorrow, and you want to be perfect, don't you?"

Just as Julie should have been practicing her dancing today, she reflected as she inspected herself in the full-length mirror on the closet door, instead of running off with that boy. She would have to do something about that—

The sound of the front door bell drifting up the stairs interrupted her reverie. Marguerite waited for a moment, certain that Ruby would answer it. But then, shaking her head slightly as she remembered that for now, at least, she would have to take care of such things herself, she checked her reflection in the mirror once more and hurried toward the top of the stairs. The pain in her hip had eased once again, diminishing to an annoying ache, and as she started down the stairs, her right hand rested only lightly on the banister. As the bell sounded for the second time, she drew the door open and gazed out at her unexpected visitor. "Alicia," she said, her lips widening into a smile of welcome. "Why, what a surprise. Won't you come in?"

Alicia Mayhew stared at Marguerite. What on earth had she done to herself? Her face was covered with a harsh mask of makeup, and that dress . . .

Alicia hadn't seen a dress like that since she was a little girl, when her mother and all her mother's friends had worn the same kind of clothes that Joan Crawford had worn in the movies. "I—I just came out to see if Jennifer was still here," Alicia stammered. Then, realizing she was staring at Marguerite, she self-consciously forced her eyes away, looking into the depths of the house. But Marguerite didn't seem to notice that she had been staring.

"Jennifer?" she asked, her voice taking on a note of concern. "Here?"

Alicia nodded. "I just saw Julie and Kerry, and they said Jenny was coming out to see you. She was supposed to be home an hour ago."

"Well, I don't know what to say," Marguerite replied, holding the door wider. "I've been here by myself all day, ever since Julie left." She smiled, the understanding expression of one worried mother to another. "I don't know what to do with her sometimes. There's so much she needs to do, but she just seems to want to run off with Kerry all the time."

Alicia shook her head distractedly, only half hearing what Marguerite was saying. "But Julie was so certain she was coming out here . . ."

"Well, I'm afraid she must have changed her mind," Marguerite said. "But I'm certain she'll be here tomorrow."

"T-Tomorrow?" Alicia echoed. "I-I'm afraid I don't understand."

"For the recital," Marguerite told her. "You mean Jennifer didn't tell you about it? But I've been planning it for weeks and weeks . . ."

Alicia cocked her head slightly. "I-I'm afraid Jennifer didn't say a word about it," she said. "And I don't see how she can be here, since we're supposed to be in Charleston tonight and tomorrow."

Marguerite's face crumpled in disappointment for a moment, but then her smile came back. "But I'm certain she'll be here," she said. "I know she was counting on seeing my little girl dance, and I can't imagine she'll miss it." She reached out and squeezed Alicia's hand reassuringly. "You come back tomorrow, and see if I'm not right."

"But I need to find her today—" Alicia began, but Marguerite shrugged helplessly.

"Perhaps she went to visit Allison or Tammy-Jo," she suggested. "You know how teenagers are—you never quite know what kind of trouble they're going to get into."

Alicia hesitated, and a small sigh escaped her lips. "I suppose you're right," she agreed. "Well, I'm sorry to have broken in on you like this—"

"But it's all right," Marguerite assured her. "You know I always love to have company." She held the door a little wider and glanced anxiously up at the sky and the slanting rain. "You're sure you won't come in? It looks like it's going to be pouring in a few more minutes."

Alicia shook her head. "I'd really better not. I've got to find Jenny and get down to Charleston." She hurried down the steps and across the driveway to her car, shielding herself from the rain as best she could. Slamming the door, she started the engine, turned on the wipers, and put the car in gear. But before she pulled away from Sea Oaks, she glanced up once more at Marguerite still standing at the door. What on earth had gotten into her, dressing herself that way? She looked so strange. . . .

But she didn't have time to worry about Marguerite Devereaux right now. Not until she found Jenny, anyway. And when she did find Jenny—

She glanced at her watch once more. It was nearly four now, and the storm seemed to be getting worse. If she didn't find Jenny soon, there would be no point in starting for Charleston at all. The storm would put an end to that. She pressed the accelerator hard, and the wheels of her car spun free on the slickness of the road, already turning to mud.

Marguerite watched Alicia go, then started back into the house. Suddenly she stopped, her eyes fastening on her car, which was standing next to the house, its windows wide open. Rain was beginning to blow into it, and soon it would be soaking wet. She hurried inside and reached for her keys, which should have been on the hook just inside the coat-closet door.

But they weren't there.

And then she remembered. She'd given them to Kevin that morning. But where was Kevin?

The basement. That's where he was, down in the basement with Ruby and Jennifer. . . .

She hurried downstairs and was back a few minutes later, the car keys clutched in her hand. Taking an umbrella against the rain, she hurried outside and backed the car into the garage, then swung the heavy wooden door shut. Just as she got back to the house, the first bolt of lightning flashed in the sky to the southeast, followed a few moments later by a low roll of thunder.

The wind began to pick up, and as Marguerite closed the front door, the moss-hung pines around the old house began to moan softly to each other.

Jeff pounded up the road from the causeway, his shirt pulled up over his head to protect him from the rain. It was coming down hard now, and the wind was starting to whip the wet cloth into his eyes, nearly blinding him. But he was almost home, and he could see the lights already on in the big house at the top of the rise. He ran even faster, then slipped as he turned the corner into the driveway, sprawling out into the sticky mud. Picking himself up, he tried to scrape the mud off his pants, then gave it up and started running again. A minute later he burst into the house, slamming the front door behind him.

"Dad?" he yelled. "Dad, I'm home!" He leaned against the wall, panting, then began pulling off his muddy shoes. But as he set them down next to the front door, he suddenly became aware of the silence in the house. He listened carefully, then again called out for his father.

There was no answer.

"Dad?" he said once more, his voice dropping as he felt the first stirrings of fear deep inside him. "Wh-Where are you?"

There was still no answer, and the silence in the house began to close in on him. He took a step toward the staircase, then froze as there was a sudden clanking sound, followed by the scrape of gears meshing. As he watched, the chair lift from the second floor began making its slow descent.

Jeff swallowed hard, but the lump in his throat only grew as he saw the lift come slowly down the stairs. Then it came around the curve, and he found himself staring up at his Aunt Marguerite.

Except it didn't look like his aunt.

The woman in the chair had her hair combed strangely, so that it looked old-fashioned, and her face was covered with makeup. He frowned then, and his heart began to race as he realized who his aunt looked like.

His grandmother.

She wasn't as old, and she wasn't as wrinkled, but the face was the same, and when she looked at him, it was like looking into his grandmother's eyes.

"Wh-Where's my dad?" he managed to whisper as the chair lift came to a halt and Marguerite rose to her feet and stepped off it.

"He's not here," Marguerite told him. "He had to go back to town for something." She took a step toward him, and Jeff shrank away from her.

"He didn't either," Jeff replied, his voice trembling now. "He was going to come back here and find out what you did to Ruby."

"Ruby?" Marguerite echoed, her voice sounding hollow in the large space of the entry hall. "Why, Jeff, darling, what are you talking about? I didn't do anything to Ruby."

"Y-Yes you did," Jeff quavered. "Emmaline told me, and I told my dad. I told him all about you."

Marguerite's eyes narrowed. "All about me?" she repeated. "But there's nothing to tell. And you shouldn't tell stories, Jeff. Don't you know what happens to small boys who tell stories about people?" She took a step toward him, and Jeff cowered back against the door.

"You leave me alone," he whimpered. "Just leave me alone!"

"Now, now," Marguerite said, her voice suddenly soothing. "Why would I want to hurt you? Aren't you my little boy now? Don't I love you? Why would I want to hurt you?"

She was close to Jeff and reaching out to him, and Jeff could feel his heart pounding.

"No!" he shouted. "Don't you touch me!"

His sudden yell startled Marguerite, and she stepped back. Instantly Jeff darted around her and raced toward the stairs, his feet drumming on the hardwood. Then he was on the stairs themselves, bounding up them two at a time, his heart thumping in his chest. He got to the second-floor landing, then raced down the hall to his room, slamming the door shut behind him and twisting the key in the lock. Only when he was certain the door wouldn't open did he run to his bed and throw himself on it, wrapping himself in the quilt folded at the foot of the bed. For a few minutes all he could hear was the racing of his own heart and the panting gasps of his own breath, but after a while his heartbeat slowed and his breathing returned to normal. He listened for a few minutes, certain that any second he would hear his aunt's strange, lopsided gait as she came after him.

But the seconds dragged on, turning into minutes, and Jeff heard nothing.

Once again the house seemed filled with a strange and ominous silence, broken only by the sound of the rain outside as it slashed against the windows.

Kerry Sanders pulled the old convertible to a stop in front of Sea Oaks. The rain was coming down in sheets now, and a steady stream of water was running through a tear in the canvas, draining onto the backseat. He glanced over his shoulder in disgust. "Guess nobody's gonna ride back there for a while." Then his gaze shifted to the house. "Want me to come in with you?"

Julie shook her head. "I don't think you better. You know how Aunt Marguerite feels."

"She's not gonna be mad at you, is she?" Kerry fretted. "I guess maybe I should have brought you back earlier—"

"It's all right," Julie insisted. "It isn't even five yet. It's not like we stayed out till midnight or something. And Daddy should be home, anyway, and he'll fix it with Aunt Marguerite." She put her hand on the door handle, but didn't open it. Instead she turned once more to Kerry. "Do you think Mrs. Mayhew found Jenny?"

Kerry shrugged. "I don't know. But it sure sounds like something weird is going on—I mean, when we saw Jen, she was coming out here."

"M-Maybe she changed her mind," Julie suggested. "Maybe after what I said about Aunt Marguerite . . ." Her voice trailed off, but her eyes, too, went to the house, where a single light glowed from the living room window. Other than that, the house seemed dark.

"You're sure you don't want me to come in?" Kerry said again. "I mean, if you're scared of your aunt—"

"No," Julie decided. "I'm not scared of her. She just wasn't feeling well yesterday, that's all." As if to emphasize her words, she opened the car door, but Kerry took her hand

and pulled her toward him. Before she knew what was happening, he was kissing her.

She stiffened, then felt a tremor run through her body as his lips caressed her face. He held her close for a moment, then suddenly released her, and when she looked at him, he was blushing with embarrassment.

"I—I don't know why I did that," he said, and Julie put a finger over his lips.

"It's all right. I'm glad you did." She smiled at him as she slid out of the car. "But let's hope Aunt Marguerite didn't see us," she added, giggling softly. "See you tomorrow!" She slammed the car door and ran to the house, ducking her head low against the rain.

Neither she nor Kerry saw Marguerite standing stiffly at one of the living room windows, her eyes smoldering darkly. By the time Julie was inside the house, Marguerite had moved back to the large wing-back chair near the fireplace, where she had been sitting when she heard Kerry's car grind up the drive.

Julie shoved the front door closed behind her and did her best to dry her hair with the beach towel. But as she threw her head back and ran her fingers through her damp hair, she paused, standing perfectly still.

Something in the house had changed.

It felt emptier than usual, as if something were missing.

It felt wrong.

Tentatively she took a step toward the double doors to the living room. Seeing Marguerite sitting on the chair by the fireplace, she let herself relax slightly.

"Aunt Marguerite?" she asked, unconsciously dropping her voice to little more than a whisper. "I'm home."

For a split second she didn't think her aunt had heard her, but then Marguerite stood up and turned to face Julie. "I know," she said. "I saw you just now."

Julie felt herself flush, and bit her lip. "Where's Dad?" she asked. "And Jeff?"

Marguerite hesitated. "Your father had to go back to town," she said. "And Jeff's upstairs, sulking." She stepped forward then, and for the first time the light from the lamp fell full on her face.

Julie gasped. "Aunt Marguerite," she breathed. "Wh-What's wrong? You look—" She had been about to say "terrible," but suddenly caught herself.

"Do you like it?" Marguerite asked, her right hand moving up to lightly brush against her own cheek. "I—well, I didn't have much to do today, and I thought I might just try something new."

"It—It's different," Julie managed. "I guess I just wasn't expecting it, that's all."

"And I think it suits me," Marguerite went on, almost as if she hadn't heard Julie. "It's the way Mother used to look, and she was so beautiful." Her voice took on a faraway tone. "So very beautiful. And I look so much like her." Her eyes, which had been flickering about the room, suddenly came to rest on Julie. "And so do you," she breathed, her voice barely audible now. "You're so much like Mother . . . and like me. . . ."

"I—I'd better go up and see Jeff," Julie stammered. "What happened? Why is he mad?"

Marguerite stiffened, then seemed to relax. "I'm not sure," she said at last. "I suppose I must have said something to him, though I can't imagine what. But he's a little boy, isn't he? And I've never understood little boys. I think when Kevin gets back, I shall have to talk to him about Jeff. I'll have to decide what to do with him. . . ."

Her last words were spoken to herself, for Julie was hurrying up the stairs to the second floor. A moment later she knocked softly on her brother's door.

"Jeff? It's me—Julie. Can I come in?"

There was a short silence, then she heard Jeff scuttling across the floor. There was a click as the key turned in the lock, then the door opened a crack and Jeff peered fearfully out at her. When he recognized his sister, he opened the door to let her in, then closed it again, relocking it.

"Jeff!" Julie exclaimed as he tried the door once more before turning to face her. "What's wrong? Aunt Marguerite says you're sulking. And how come you've got the door locked?''

"Because she's crazy!" Jeff said. "She killed Ruby, and she killed Daddy, and she wants to kill me too." He hurled himself into Julie's arms, clinging to her. "Didn't you see her?" he sobbed. "Didn't you see what she looks like?"

"Oh, good grief," Julie said, picking her brother up and carrying him to the bed, then plumping him down against the pillows. "Of course I saw her. And she does look a little strange, but that's just because she was experimenting with her hair and makeup."

"It's not!" Jeff insisted. "She looks just like Grandmother, and she came down in the chair lift and stared at me all funny. I'm scared of her!"

"Well, you don't have to be," Julie insisted with a lot more conviction than she felt. She remembered her shock when she'd first seen the lamp light strike her aunt's face. And Jeff was right—in a strange way, her aunt *did* look very much like their grandmother. "And what do you mean, she killed Daddy and Ruby? Ruby went to visit her family, and Dad's in town. She just told me so."

"That's what she told me too," Jeff wailed. "But it's not true. I saw Daddy in town and told him all about Aunt Marguerite, and he was coming out here to—"

He fell silent as there was a loud rapping on the door.

"Julie?" they heard Marguerite's voice calling from the other side of the door. "Are you in there?"

"Y-Yes, Aunt Marguerite," Julie called back.

"Well, I need you, dear. I'm trying to get supper ready and I need you to help me. And maybe Jeff could set the table. I'd like to have it all ready by the time your father gets back."

Julie looked at Jeff, who was still cringing against the pillow. Once again she remembered the strange feeling she'd had when she'd come into the house a few minutes ago.

And yet just now—when her aunt had spoken—there'd been nothing odd about what she'd said. How could Jeff even think she might have killed their father, or Ruby, or anyone

else? It just wasn't possible. She got off the bed, making up
her mind.

Going to the door, she twisted the key and pulled the door
open. Marguerite stood in the hall, looking worried.

"I don't know what we'll do if your father can't get
home," she fretted.

Julie frowned. "Not get home?" she asked. "Why wouldn't
he be able to?"

Marguerite was silent for a moment, then nodded toward
the window. "The storm, dear. If it gets much worse, there
won't be any way to get to the island at all. Then the three of
us will be all alone here."

As if to punctuate Marguerite's words, a bolt of lightning
flared in the sky outside and a sharp clap of thunder shook the
house.

And the wind began to howl.

CHAPTER 21

Alicia Mayhew flinched as a sheet of lightning crackled across the sky, immediately followed by a roar of thunder that made her car tremble. She leaned forward, straining to see through the rain that pounded the windshield, but it was useless. All she could see beyond the impotently flapping wipers was a deluge of water that was already beginning to flood the street. Then, barely visible to her right, she saw the indistinct shape of the tired wooden building that served as the Devereaux town hall. Sighing with relief, she angled her car into a parking space in front of the hall, then braced herself for the quick dash from the car to the building itself. Taking a deep breath, almost as if she were preparing to dive into a swimming pool, she opened the car door and jumped out, already dashing toward the town hall as she slammed the car door shut. "Damn," she swore to herself as her left foot slid out from under her on the slick sidewalk. A sharp pain shot up her leg, but she caught her balance, ignoring the pain until she was inside the building and the door was closed behind her, cutting off the noise of the raging storm.

Stopping to catch her breath, she massaged her sore ankle for a moment, then gingerly tested her weight on it. Nothing seemed to be broken, and the pain didn't increase as she tried to walk, so she hobbled awkwardly down the hall to the police department, which comprised only two rooms, neither of which included a jail. In the event anyone in Devereaux had to be incarcerated, Will Hempstead simply drove him down to the county seat at Beaufort. Alicia fleetingly wondered what on earth Hempstead would do in the event that someone needed to be locked up during a storm like this.

As if he'd read her mind, the police chief grinned up at Alicia from the chair upon which he was perched, tipped so far back the chair threatened to fall over, his feet propped comfortably on his desk. "Hope you don't want anyone busted today, Alicia. Even if I wanted to, I don't see how I could make it to Beaufort through this."

Alicia shook her head. "It's Jennifer," she said, glancing at Hempstead's deputy, Frank Weaver, who was sitting at an adjacent desk. She turned back to Hempstead, imploring now. "I can't find her, and I'm worried. I—well, I'm almost certain something's happened to her."

Hempstead's feet dropped to the floor and he brought his chair upright as he leaned forward, the twinkle in his eyes gone. "What do you mean, 'happened'?" he asked.

"I—I don't know," Alicia stammered. She perched nervously on the edge of the chair opposite Hempstead, then speaking slowly and choosing her words carefully, tried to explain exactly what had happened. Even as she told him, she realized that she sounded more like a dithering worrier than a legitimately concerned parent. Still, Hempstead listened patiently, and when Alicia was finished, he glanced at the clock. It was barely six P.M.

"So she was due home by two-thirty?"

Alicia nodded.

"And you went looking for her around three, is that right?"

Once again Alicia nodded.

"Been home since then?" Will Hempstead asked, his voice dry. "Or given a call?"

Alicia's eyes narrowed slightly. "Of course I have, Will. I'm not a fool, and you know it. I've called home from everywhere I've been, and Jennifer's not there."

Hempstead glanced out the window at the raging storm. "Well, if she got caught out in this, she could have holed up most anywhere—" he began, but Alicia shook her head.

"I don't believe that. She was already late before the storm even started. And that's not like Jennifer, Will. She's always on time, always exactly where she's supposed to be." Her voice had taken on a nervous shrillness, which she struggled to control. Finally she met Hempstead's eyes. "If you want to know the truth," she said, "I'm afraid something might have happened to her out at Sea Oaks."

"Sea Oaks?" Hempstead asked, and though he kept his voice neutral, Alicia could see a shadow come over his eyes. "I'm not sure I'm following you, Alicia."

Alicia ran her fingers impatiently through the wet strands of her graying hair, pushing a few wisps that had fallen over her forehead back into place. "I'm talking about Marguerite," she said, her eyes locking on Hempstead's once more. There wasn't anyone in town who didn't know Will Hempstead had once been in love with Marguerite Devereaux, and a lot of people still thought he carried a torch for her. "She—well, when I was talking to her, she looked very strange."

"Strange?" Hempstead asked, his voice suddenly cool. "Just what do you mean by 'strange'?"

"N-Not anything she said," Alicia replied. "At least I didn't think so—not at first. But she was wearing a dress that was so old it must have been her mother's." She tried to describe how Marguerite had looked, but finally shook her head. "I can't really tell you. She—well, she looked like she was dressed up for some kind of part."

"But what did she *say*?" Hempstead pressed.

Alicia bit her lip. "Not much, really. Just that Jennifer hadn't been there, but that she was supposed to be there tomorrow. She said she was having some kind of recital or something and—"

"And you thought that was strange?" Hempstead interrupted, his voice clearly reflecting his doubt. "For Christ's sake, Alicia, she's a dance teacher. She has recitals all the time. How many times have you been out there for them? Five? Ten? Dozens?"

Alicia sighed heavily. "I know all that, Will. But, well, this was different. For one thing, Jennifer never mentioned a recital to me, and she would have if there'd been one scheduled. She wouldn't have wanted to miss it, and she didn't say anything when I suggested we go up to Charleston to see my brother for a couple of days."

"And that's all?" Hempstead asked.

Alicia shifted uncomfortably. "And there's Muriel Fletcher," she breathed, this time unable to meet Hempstead's eyes when she spoke.

"Ah," Hempstead grunted. "I was wondering when you were going to come to that." He leaned forward now. "Look, Alicia, I know everything that Muriel's been saying about Mary-Beth, and I'm telling you, there's not a shred of evidence to back her up. If you want, you can look at the coroner's report yourself. All we can tell for certain is that she drowned, and that she banged her head on something. But it could have been anything, Alicia. Most likely she smashed her head on a rock when she got swept off the road. But—"

"But you're not going to do anything," Alicia finished for him. "That's what it boils down to, isn't it, Will?"

Hempstead shrugged helplessly. "What do you want me to do, Alicia? Jennifer's only been gone a few hours. Hell, she hasn't even missed dinner yet! Legally, I can't even take a missing-person report till day after tomorrow." He nodded toward the window. "And you don't really expect me to try to go out to Sea Oaks in that, do you?" The windows rattled as a gust of wind buffeted the building, and Hempstead turned back to face Alicia. "I'm sorry," he said. "The best thing you can do is go home and start calling everyone you know. The odds are Jennifer lost track of time, and when she realized she was late, she holed up somewhere. Hell, she's probably been trying to call you all afternoon."

Alicia took a deep breath, then stood up. "All right," she said, struggling against the anger rising within her. "I'll go home. But I know how you feel about Marguerite Devereaux, Will. Everybody in town does. And just because you're in love with her, it doesn't mean she couldn't have done something." Picking up her purse, she left the office. When she was gone, Hempstead turned to Frank Weaver.

"I don't know," Hempstead sighed. "What's the town coming to when people start thinkin' someone like Marguerite could hurt anybody?"

"So what are you going to do?" Weaver asked.

"Check around, I guess. Won't hurt to go talk to a few

people—see if I can figure out what happened to Jenny. But I'm sure not going to try to go out to the island in this mess. Even if I wanted to, I'm not sure I could make it.''

Then, shrugging into a bright yellow slicker, he followed Alicia Mayhew out into the storm.

"Isn't this nice?'' Marguerite asked as she settled herself into a chair at one end of the long dining room table. Julie and Jeff were seated on either side of her, the best silver and china in the house carefully arrayed at each place. The storm was howling outside, and the evening was almost as dark as night. But the chandelier above the dining room table glowed brightly, and the old Waterford crystal on the table seemed to come alive with refracted light.

"How come there's no place for Dad?'' Jeff demanded, but when he spoke, he kept his eyes on his sister.

"I already told you,'' Marguerite said, her voice taking on the trace of an edge. "Since he's not home now, I don't think we can count on him coming home. After all,'' she added, "we wouldn't want the same thing to happen to him that happened to your mother, would we?''

Jeff's eyes widened, and even Julie flinched. "But why hasn't he called?'' Julie asked. "If he couldn't get back, he'd call us, wouldn't he?''

"Perhaps the phones went out,'' Marguerite suggested. Instantly Jeff slid off his chair and ran through the living room to the foyer, where he picked up the phone.

"It works,'' Jeff called. "I'm gonna call the police.''

"The police!'' Marguerite exclaimed. "For Heaven's—'' But before she could finish her sentence, a bolt of lightning struck, instantly followed by a crash of thunder so loud it shook the house. Jeff dropped the phone and jumped back, and then, as the thunder faded away, the lights suddenly went out and the house was plunged into near blackness.

In the dining room Julie ran to a window and peered out. A moment later another bolt of lightning shot across the sky and she could see what had happened.

Halfway down the drive a tree, smoke still drifting from its top, had fallen across the power lines. "It's not going to come back on," she told her aunt. "The lines are down, and there's a tree lying across the driveway."

Marguerite took a deep breath. "Very well," she said. "It certainly isn't anything for us to get upset about. We have plenty of candles."

"The phone doesn't work now, either," Jeff said as he came back to the dining room. He looked at his sister with frightened eyes. "What are we going to do?"

"We're going to go on with our dinner," Marguerite stated. She found a box of matches on the sideboard and began lighting the candles in the twin candelabra on the table. A few seconds later the room was bright again, this time with the warm glimmer of the candles.

"I think this is rather nice," Marguerite said as she re-seated herself. "It reminds me of when I was a girl. I remember once when I was your age, Julie. We had a storm just like this one, and the lights went out that night too. Mother and I sat here all by ourselves, eating our supper."

Julie frowned uncertainly. "Where was Dad?" she asked. "Wasn't he here?"

Marguerite's eyes clouded, then she smiled thinly. "Oh, no," she said. "By then he was gone. It was just Mother and me, and after dinner we went up to the ballroom." She closed her eyes, and her voice took on a strange, lilting melody as she reminisced about the times so many years ago. "Mother was young then—younger than I am now. And she'd dance and dance, and I would watch. So beautiful—it was all so beautiful then, before . . ." Her voice trailed off. Jeff glanced uneasily at his sister.

"What's wrong with her?" he whispered. "How come her eyes are shut?"

Marguerite's eyes suddenly snapped open, and she turned to glare at Jeff. "What are you doing here?" she demanded, her voice rasping harshly. "Why aren't you at school?"

The color suddenly drained from Jeff's face and his eyes widened with fear.

"Th-There isn't any school, Aunt Marguerite," Julie said. "It's summer vacation, remember?"

Marguerite didn't seem to hear her. Instead, her eyes fixed balefully on Jeff. "I didn't tell you to come here," she hissed. "When I'm ready, I'll send for you."

Jeff slid off his chair, his whole body trembling with fright. Without saying a word, he fled from the room, charging up the stairs.

There was a long silence at the table, then Marguerite slowly turned, blinking, to look at Julie. "Where's Jeff?" she asked. "Isn't he going to finish his dinner?"

Julie stared at her aunt. "B-But you just told him you didn't want him here."

"Not want him?" Marguerite echoed. "But darling, of course I want him. He's my little boy, isn't he? Why wouldn't I want him?"

Julie felt her heart skip a beat, and her throat tightened. "But you said . . . you wanted to know why he wasn't in school."

Marguerite paused, and once more her eyes clouded. Then her expression cleared. "But, of course," she said. "He's almost nine, isn't he?"

Julie hesitated before nodding uncertainly. What was her aunt talking about?

"Then, of course, I'm right," Marguerite went on. "It's time for him to go, isn't it? I shall have to send him away, and then things will be the way they're supposed to be." She smiled then, her eyes fixing on Julie. "After Jeff is gone, it will be just you and me, won't it? Just the two of us, like it's supposed to be. . . ."

Still smiling, as if enjoying some secret only she held the key to, Marguerite went on eating her supper.

Alicia Mayhew paced nervously in the living room of her small house on Macon Street. It was eight o'clock now, and still there was no sign of Jennifer.

She'd long since run out of people to call; indeed, she felt as if she'd talked to everyone in town. And all of them had said the same thing.

First there had been Marian Phillips, Charlene's mother. "I don't know about the other girls," she'd said. "But after what happened out there the other day, Charlene says she'll never go back to the island again, and I don't really blame her."

Paula Aaronson had gone further. "Apparently there was some kind of a problem yesterday at their lesson. Tammy-Jo said Marguerite was acting very strange. The girls left early yesterday, you know."

"Left early?" Alicia had repeated. It was the first she'd heard of it. "But why?"

"I don't know, really. Tammy-Jo simply said that Marguerite was, well, 'weird' was the word she used. Of course, Marguerite's had a lot of shocks lately, and I suppose Tammy-Jo could have been exaggerating."

"But what about the recital tomorrow?" Alicia had asked.

"Recital? Why, I don't know. Just a moment." There had been a long silence, and then Paula had come back on the line. "Tammy-Jo doesn't know anything about a recital, and she says if there is one, she isn't going."

"I see," Alicia had breathed, then called up Diana Carter. But Allison's mother had not heard anything about a recital. Nor had she seen Jenny.

Now, with no one left on her list, she reluctantly dialed the Fletchers' number, and a moment later recognized Muriel Fletcher's voice, sounding strained, coming over the line.

"You already know what I think," Muriel told her, barely able to keep her voice under control. "And don't tell me what Will Hempstead thinks, because I already know. But he's in love with Marguerite, and always has been."

"I know," Alicia agreed. "But it just seems so unbelievable. To think that Marguerite might have—" She fell silent then, but Mrs. Fletcher finished her thought.

"That Marguerite might have killed her?" she asked, her voice trembling. "That's what I thought at first. But the more I think about it, the more I wonder. Mary-Beth was impetuous, but she wasn't stupid. If it hadn't been safe to cross the causeway, she wouldn't have tried. She'd have stayed on the island.''

"But why?" Alicia pressed. "Marguerite loved Mary-Beth. She loves all the girls—''

"Except that she's changed," Muriel said. "Will Hempstead won't believe me, but it's true. Mary-Beth was going to quit going to Marguerite's classes, you know. She didn't even wanted to go that day, but the rest of the girls talked her into it. And she and Marguerite had a fight, you know. She'd said she was quitting, and Marguerite tried to talk her out of it.''

Alicia felt a knot of fear forming in her stomach. Only that morning, before she'd left to go out to the island, Jennifer had talked about how the other girls were feeling.

"I don't think I'd go back either, except it would hurt Miss Marguerite so much," Alicia recalled her daughter saying. "But Tammy-Jo's right. It *isn't* as much fun as it used to be, and Miss Marguerite *is* more interested in Julie than she is in the rest of us.''

"Well, of course she is," Alicia had observed. "Julie's her niece, and she dances better than the rest of you.''

But now, remembering that conversation, an unbidden thought crept into the back of her mind.

What if Jennifer had changed her mind and told Marguerite she'd decided to quit the class?

No! She forced the thought away.

"If you ask me," she heard Muriel Fletcher saying, "there's been something strange about Marguerite ever since her mother died.''

"But she's dealt with it so well," Alicia replied.

"Which is exactly what I mean," Muriel went on. "For Heaven's sake, Alicia, Marguerite lived with that miserable woman her whole life, and for the last twenty years Helena treated Marguerite like dirt. You'd have thought she'd have been tickled pink when Helena died, even if she was her mother. But what did she do? First she acted as if nothing had happened at all, and then I heard she started talking about how much she missed Helena and what a wonderful mother she'd been!''

"But that's not so strange," Alicia pleaded, her voice taking on a desperate note. "Lots of people do that."

"Well, perhaps they do," Muriel said, her voice crisp. "But all I know is that the more I think about it, the more certain I am that there is something very, very wrong with Marguerite Devereaux. And in my heart I'm absolutely certain she's responsible for Mary-Beth's death."

Suddenly there was a flash of lightning and a crash of thunder, and then, as the lights in the house flickered, the phone went dead in Alicia Mayhew's hand.

"Damn!" she swore out loud. "Damn, damn, damn!"

She rattled the hook on the phone for a moment, but already knew from long experience that the phone would be dead for the rest of the night. Indeed, they'd be lucky if the lights didn't go out too. Finally, frustrated, she dropped the receiver back on the hook and went to the window to stare out into the raging storm.

The wind still seemed to be growing stronger, and the rain was coming down in torrents. If Jennifer was out there somewhere . . .

Then her eyes filled with tears as she realized that deep down inside, she didn't truly believe that Jennifer was anywhere out in the storm.

Deep in her soul she was certain that Jennifer had, indeed, gone to Sea Oaks that morning.

And for some reason Alicia could not yet understand, she'd never left.

Alicia numbly dropped onto the sofa in her tiny living room and prepared herself to wait for whatever news might eventually come. And yet, even as she began her vigil, she already knew how it was going to end.

She was going to be told that her daughter—her beloved Jennifer—was dead.

"Noooo!"

She screamed the word out loud, a wail of despairing anguish. But even had the storm not been raging outside, there would still have been no one to hear her, for since Jennifer's father had died ten years earlier, Jennifer had been all Alicia had in the world.

After tonight she would have nothing.

Unless . . .

Unless she was wrong.

She had to be wrong, she told herself. She had to hold onto hope, had to cling to whatever scrap of faith she could muster that Jennifer might still be alive.

She had to weather the storm.

CHAPTER 22

Jeff clutched the quilt around him, but even the warmth of its down filling couldn't abate the chill that had seized his body. He wasn't certain how long he'd been huddled on the bed, how long it had been since Julie had come in and tried to tell him he shouldn't worry, that everything was going to be all right. But it seemed like forever, and the candle flickering in its holder on his bed table had burned halfway down. When he'd first fled to his room from the dinner table, he'd been certain that his aunt would come for him right away. He'd cowered in his room, his ear pressed to the door, listening for her footsteps on the stairs. But after a while, when he'd heard nothing, he finally retreated to the bed, his entire body trembling with an icy fear.

She was going to kill him.

He was certain of it now. She didn't want him here, and she was going to send him away.

But why? He hadn't done anything. He hadn't done anything at all!

A bolt of lightning split the sky, and for a second the room was filled with brilliant white light. Then the clap of thunder crashed into the house as the light faded away, and Jeff whimpered softly, huddling deeper into the quilt. The rain, which had been beating steadily against the windows—driven almost horizontally by the wind—grew even heavier for a moment, then abruptly stopped. The silence left by its cessation had a strange hollowness to it, made all the more eerie by the wailing of the wind, crying through the trees like the lost souls of the damned.

And then, above the wind, Jeff finally heard the sound he'd been waiting for.

Uneven footsteps moving up the stairs.

Pulling the quilt tight around him, he slid off the bed, crept to the door, and pressed his ear against the wood.

He could hear it more clearly now, and as the ominous rhythm grew louder, he could picture his Aunt Marguerite, her right hand on her hip, her left grasping the banister, pulling herself step by step toward the second floor.

Then he heard her come to the landing, and there was a moment of silence even more terrifying than the soft thumping of her crippled leg. But the silence ended, and cold sweat broke out on Jeff's body as he heard the footsteps approach his door.

She was outside now, he was certain of it. And once more the heavy tread had stopped.

What was she doing?

He gasped—a choking whimper—as the doorknob turned only a few inches from his eyes. Shrinking back, he stared at the key in the lock.

Had he locked the door?

He searched his mind frantically, but couldn't remember. He'd turned the key too many times, each time trying the door, but then, a moment later, doubting his own memory and checking it again.

What if the last time he'd unlocked the door, and forgotten to check it?

The knob kept turning, and then he heard a soft click as the latch slid free of the strike plate.

The door moved a fraction of an inch, and Jeff pressed his hand to his mouth to keep from screaming out loud.

The door stopped moving, and there was a barely perceptible pause before unseen hands suddenly rattled the door, the sound resounding through the room with the intensity of drums.

"Why is this door locked?" he heard his aunt call, and there was something strange about her voice as it penetrated the thick oak of the door. "I've told you I won't have you locking this door, young man! Open it this instant!"

Jeff shrank back from the door once more, the quilt sliding off his shoulders and dropping to the floor. His eyes flooded with tears, and he backed away across the room.

"Do you hear me?" Marguerite's voice grated. "Open it!" Once more the door rattled loudly, and Jeff leaped toward the bed, seizing one of the pillows and pressing it against his chest.

The door rattled once more, then there was a moment of silence. Suddenly, miraculously, he heard footsteps again, getting softer as his aunt moved away from his door.

He rushed back to the door and once more pressed his ear to the wood. Where was she going?

The footsteps seemed to be receding down the hall. Was she going to her own room? He counted her steps, his heart racing.

Four

There was a pause, and he strained to hear the sound of a door. But a moment later the steps began again.

. . . seven . . .

Another pause, another silence.

. . . ten . . .

. . . fifteen steps.

A door opening and closing.

Thirty feet.

But that was just since he'd been counting. How many steps had she taken before?

But it didn't matter, for he knew where she'd gone.

She was in his grandmother's room. But what was she doing, and how long would she be in there? He stood frozen by the door, not knowing what to do.

Minutes ticked slowly by, and his heartbeat began to ease, but the same thought kept churning through his mind.

She was going to come back for him. He had to get out, had to hide. . . .

Julie—he had to get to Julie.

With trembling fingers he reached for the key, but just as he touched it, he heard a door far down the hall close with a soft but distinct thump.

And then, once more, the uneven footsteps as Marguerite made her way back down the corridor.

But this time she didn't pause at his door. Instead the footsteps began to fade away again, and finally he heard her on the stairs once more. And then he knew.

She was going back downstairs to get the keys.

He could see them in his mind's eye, hanging on the hook by the kitchen door.

One of them would fit this room.

His heart was pounding again, drowning out the sounds of the storm outside. He could no longer hear Marguerite's footsteps.

Now!

He wrestled with the key, and the bolt slid free. Jerking the door open, he suddenly stopped.

The corridor should have been completely dark. Instead it glowed softly with flickering candlelight.

That was what the pauses had meant. His aunt had stopped to light the candles that always stood on the small tables scattered along the length of the broad corridor.

The mere presence of the soft light eased his fear somewhat. He started toward Julie's room, then stopped as an idea came to him.

Conquering the last of the panic inside him, he took the key out of the lock, closed his door, then locked it from the outside. Slipping the key into his pocket, he raced down the corridor to Julie's room and tried her door.

To his relief, it was unlocked, and he pushed through it, then shut it quickly and twisted the key beneath the knob.

"Jeff?" he heard Julie ask. "What are you doing?"

He turned, his face pale. In the dim light of a small oil lamp, Julie was staring at him curiously.

"She—She went back downstairs," Jeff managed to say, his voice quavering. "She went down to get the keys, and then she's going to come back. She's going to come back and kill me!" Sobbing, he hurled himself into his sister's arms. "What are we going to do?"

"Shh," Julie soothed, stroking her brother's hair with gentle fingers. "She's not going to kill you—"

"She is!" Jeff insisted, his eyes imploring his sister. "She hates me, and she's going to kill me!"

Julie bit her lip. What could she say to the terrified boy? Even she had been frightened at the dinner table, when her aunt had started talking so strangely. But then Marguerite seemed to calm down, and she'd thought maybe—just maybe—everything was going to be all right after all. "She's not going to kill you," she insisted once more, struggling to keep her own voice even. "All we have to do is wait for Dad to come home, and everything will be all right. You'll see."

But Jeff shook his head. "He's not coming home," he sobbed. "He's not ever coming home, 'cause he's already dead. And she's going to kill us too!"

Harold Sanders frowned as the loud banging on the front door was repeated. Who the hell would be out in weather like this? Carrying his beer with him, he went to the door, opened it a crack—bracing it against the wind with one foot—and peered out. Standing on the front porch, water streaming off his yellow slicker, was Frank Weaver. Harold's frown deepened, and he pulled the door open far enough for the deputy to slip through.

"What the hell's goin' on, Frank? It's not fit for man nor beast out there tonight."

"Might have someone missing, Hal," Weaver replied. "Got a few questions I'd like to ask Kerry, if it's all right with you?"

"Kerry?" Hal Sanders repeated, taking on a guarded look. "You're not tryin' to say my boy's in trouble, are you? 'Cause if you are, you're gonna have me to deal with first!"

Edith Sanders, wiping her hands on her apron, came in from the kitchen just in time to hear the last thing her husband said. "Don't be silly, Hal," she told him. "Kerry's never been in trouble in his life, and you know it. I'm sure there's some mistake." She turned to Weaver, her eyes questioning.

"Now, take it easy, both of you," the deputy assured

them. "It's not Kerry we're worried about. But Jennifer Mayhew hasn't turned up at home, and near as I can tell, she ain't anywhere in town, either. But I hear Kerry talked to her this morning, and I just want to hear what he's got to say."

The elder Sanders's expression immediately cleared, and as Edith called upstairs to her son, Hal offered the deputy a beer. Weaver shrugged. "Don't mind if I do." He was just popping the tab of a Bud when Kerry Sanders appeared in the kitchen door.

"Mr. Weaver?" Kerry asked. "What's wrong? Has something happened to Jennifer?"

"Well, now, I don't rightly know," the deputy replied. "But I can tell you Alicia Mayhew's pretty het up. She says you talked to Jenny this morning."

Kerry nodded. "Julie and I both did. We were just coming across the causeway, and she was coming the other way. She was going to see Julie's aunt."

Weaver nodded. "Did she say why?"

Kerry nodded, then repeated the conversation he and Julie had had with Jennifer. When he was finished, the deputy looked troubled.

"And you're sure she actually went on up to the mansion?" he asked.

Kerry shrugged. "I guess so. She said she was, and she was walking that way when we left. And if she hadn't, she'd have found us at the beach, wouldn't she?"

"Who knows?" Weaver asked rhetorically. Then: "What about Marguerite Devereaux? Did you see her when you were out there?"

Kerry hesitated, then nodded, his face coloring. "I saw her," he said, his voice taking on a slight bitterness the deputy immediately seized upon.

"Something wrong between you and Marguerite?"

"I—I didn't think so," Kerry stammered. "At least, there wasn't until I started hanging around with Julie. Ever since then, it's like she hates me or something."

"So she *was* acting strange?" Weaver pressed.

Kerry swallowed nervously. "I—I'm not sure. She didn't want Julie to go to the beach with me. She kept talking about how Julie didn't have time to waste like that. She said Julie should be practicing her dancing."

"Hunh," the deputy grunted. "Well, I don't suppose we can hang her for that, can we?"

Kerry's brows furrowed. "What's going on?" he asked.

The deputy shrugged. "Don't know as anything is, really. But Alicia says Marguerite looked real strange when she was out there, and kept talking about a recital tomorrow. Said she was sure Jennifer would be there. But Alicia never heard about it before, and now she says the more she thinks about it, the more worried she gets."

"Does—Does she think Marguerite might have done something to Jenny?"

"Well, now, I guess she does," Weaver replied.

For the first time since Kerry had come into the kitchen, Hal Sanders spoke. "So what are you doin' here, Frank? How come you're not out on the island, having a look around?"

Weaver turned to stare at Hal. "You kidding?" he asked. "You seen what it's like outside? No way am I going to try to get out there tonight."

"But—But what about Julie?" Kerry asked.

"What about her?"

"If something's wrong with Marguerite—"

"If something's wrong with Marguerite, which isn't really likely, all things considerin', it'll keep till morning," Weaver said. "And Kevin's out there too. He can take care of things." He finished his beer, then crumpled the empty can with a quick squeeze of his right hand. "Well, I'd better be gettin' back to the office. Will's gonna want to know what I found out."

He shrugged back into his slicker, and a moment later was leaning his heavy frame into the storm as he hurried back to his car. Harold Sanders, who had walked to the front door with Weaver, waited until the police car was gone before he went back to the kitchen. But when he got there, he noticed that something was bothering Kerry.

"What is it?" he asked, laying a hand on his son's shoulder.

"I just don't like it," Kerry said. "I didn't like it when I dropped Julie off this afternoon, and I still don't. I keep having a feeling that Jenny's mother's right, and there's something going on out there.''

Hal gave Kerry's shoulder a squeeze, then slapped him gently on the back. "Well, whatever it is, it can wait till morning, as Frank said. And it's none of your business anyway," he added.

But Kerry shook his head. "I just wish someone would go out there and take a look around," he said.

"But you heard Frank," Hal replied. "You can't get out there."

Kerry nodded absently, and started back upstairs. But as he got to his room, he made up his mind.

Perhaps the cops wouldn't try to go out to the island tonight, but that didn't mean he couldn't.

Grabbing his keys from his dresser and pulling a slicker out of the closet, he headed back downstairs.

Marguerite, oblivious to the storm, opened the kitchen door and stepped out into the driving wind. It was completely dark now, and the rain had started again, lashing out of the sky, plastering her hair to her face, and washing her makeup away in smearing rivulets of color that looked almost like bloodstains against her pale skin. Her hip was burning with pain, and every step was a nightmare of searing needles being driven through her right leg. But she shut the pain out of her mind and groped her way down the steps. The path down the gentle slope was a sea of mud, and she could feel it squishing between her bare toes as she limped on. She'd taken off her mother's dress, replacing it with a long white robe that had also been her mother's. Its soft chenille clung damply to her body, and it felt heavy on her shoulders, but she plodded on, oblivious to it all, until she came to the gates of the small cemetery.

A bolt of lightning flashed down from above, and Marguerite flinched, then covered her ears against the crash of thunder that threatened to overwhelm her. But as the explo-

sion of sound died away to a boiling rumble, she lifted the
latch of the gate, opened it, and stepped through into the
graveyard itself. She moved forward numbly, her right leg
dragging through the mud now. With each step her legs
threatened to give out beneath her, and she had to steady
herself, reaching out to the weathered grave markers as she
staggered toward the crypt.

At last she was there.

Her fingers reached out, brushing against the cold marble,
and then, fumbling in the pocket of her robe, she brought out
a large key. She inserted it into the slot in the heavy door of
the crypt and turned it. A moment later the door swung
open.

"M-Mama?" Marguerite asked. Her voice was tiny, childlike, and as she reached for her mother's coffin, her fingers
trembled. "I-I'm sorry, Mama," she whimpered. "I didn't
mean to do it—I didn't mean to do any of it. But the bad
times came again, Mama. The bad times came, and you
weren't here to take care of me. And they were going to lock
me up, Mama. They were going to lock me up and leave me
alone, and I couldn't let them." Her eyes filled with tears,
but the rain washed them away as quickly as they came. "I
know I'm a bad girl, Mama. I know I'm the worst girl in the
whole world. But I didn't want to be, Mama. I didn't ever
want to be." She sniffled, and her hand moved slowly over
the coffin, caressing it. "All I wanted to do was dance,
Mama. I wanted to dance, and I wanted to please you, and I
never could. And so you left me. They were all going to
leave me, Mama. They were going to leave me and lock me
up, and I couldn't stand it. But I don't know what to do,
Mama. Tell me? Please, Mama . . . tell me what to do." Her
voice broke then, and she felt a strangling in her throat. "Tell
me, Mama. You're all I have. You're all I ever had. . . ."

She was silent then, and the storm whirled around her. But
she felt none of it, for deep within her own mind, all her
energies were concentrated on bringing her mother back to
life. And slowly, very slowly, Marguerite submerged her
own personality, and, out of the depths of her subconscious,
resurrected her mother's soul.

*   *   *

"Look!" Jeff cried out. He was at the window of Julie's room, his face pressed against the glass. Sheets of water poured down the windows, and for a moment all Julie could see were formless streaks. But then, as lightning glowed briefly in the distance, she saw the pale form in the cemetery, near the crypt. "She's back," Jeff whispered. "Grandmother's back. It—it means someone else is dead."

"No," Julie insisted, but as she peered frantically out into the storm, her heart began to race. And then, as both the children pressed against the glass, the whole universe seemed to light up with the power of a thousand searchlights. A sheet of brilliant light flashed across the night sky, the darkness washed away in a shadowless glare.

And in the graveyard the ghostly figure looked up.

Julie and Jeff gasped in shock as they recognized the visage of their aunt shining palely in the bright glare, her face framed by a sodden mass of hair, her right hand pressed against her hip while she leaned her weight against her mother's crypt.

And then the light was gone as a wave of thunder rolled across the sky, shaking the mansion to its foundations, making the windows rattle in their frames.

"It's her," Jeff whimpered. "It's not Grandmother at all. It's Aunt Marguerite."

"It's always been her," Julie breathed, her voice quavering in the pitch-black darkness that followed the lightning. "There isn't any ghost—"

"But she always comes after someone dies—" Jeff whispered, then fell into a shocked silence as he realized what he'd said. When he was finally able to speak again, his voice was barely audible. "She *did* kill them," he whispered. "That's why she's out there now. She killed Daddy."

"No," Julie wailed, her voice taking on a note of desperation. "We don't know that. Jeff, Daddy didn't even come home tonight—"

But her words died on her lips as another flash of lightning struck outside, lashing down from the sky to split open the roof of the garage. At the same moment a gust of wind screamed through the pines, and suddenly the wooden doors of the garage flew open, jerked off their hinges and were sent tumbling across the driveway, smashing against the house itself.

And inside the garage, briefly illuminated by flickers of lightning, Jeff and Julie saw their aunt's battered Chevrolet. Mutely, they stared at each other, both of them instantly knowing what it meant.

Their father had, after all, come home that day.

Come home, and never left again.

Marguerite stood in the rain, feeling the cool water washing over her face. It felt good. Felt so good to be alive again, and whole. And there was so much to do. . . .

A flash of lightning blazed across the sky, and she peered up to the second floor of the house.

A face was pressed against one of the windows—the face of a little boy.

But that wasn't right.

There shouldn't be a little boy in the house.

Only herself. Herself and her daughter. And Marguerite was safely locked up in the little room of the basement, where she would stay until she was willing to listen to reason. Imagine, blaming her mother for what had happened to her—

But what was Kevin doing up there? She'd sent him away—sent him away months ago, when she'd decided what had to be done about Marguerite. But now he was back, and if he found his sister—

She began stumbling toward the house, the mud dragging at her right leg, threatening to throw her off balance. And her hip hurt. But why should it hurt? There was nothing wrong with her—had never been anything wrong with her!

She concentrated on the face in the window, though the lightning had long since faded and even the thunder was no more than a distant drumroll. But she could see it still.

Kevin's eyes, staring at her, accusing her.

But not for long. He should have stayed away, stayed in school, where she sent him. He wasn't supposed to come back yet—wasn't supposed to come back for a long, long time, when everything that had happened would be long forgotten.

But if he found his sister—found her locked up down in the cellar—

No! He wouldn't find her—she wouldn't *let* him find her! She'd stop him—stop him any way she could.

All her mother's hatred burning brightly inside her, Marguerite struggled on toward the house, and when she finally reached the kitchen and leaned against the door she'd closed behind her, it was more than the storm that she shut out.

Along with the wind and thunder and lightning, she closed the last vestiges of her own personality out as well.

Though it was Marguerite's body that began making its way toward the stairs in the entry hall, it was Helena Devereaux's spirit that pressed her onward.

CHAPTER 23

There was a sudden lull in the storm outside. The wind dropped off, and the rain slackened to a soft drizzle. And then, out of the strange silence that fell over the house, the ominous sound of Marguerite's uneven gait resounded hollowly as she began to climb the stairs.

Jeff—cowering back against the window, his eyes round and terrified—gazed up at his sister. "What are we going to do?" he whispered. "She's coming!"

"Maybe she's not," Julie whispered back, but her voice held no conviction, for she was now as frightened as Jeff.

They heard Marguerite reach the top of the stairs, then pause. A moment later the footsteps began again. Holding their breaths, Julie and Jeff listened.

And the footsteps grew quieter; Marguerite was going the other way. Finally, after what seemed an eternity, they heard the door at the far end of the hall open and close, and they knew that their aunt had gone back to her mother's room.

"What should we do?" Jeff pleaded.

Julie's mind churned. Outside, the wind was coming up again, and once more the rain pounded on the windows. A bolt of lightning rent the night, followed by a sharp clap of thunder. She looked fearfully toward the window, not certain what was more frightening—the idea of staying in the house with her aunt, or going outside to face the wrath of the storm. "I don't know," Julie said at last. "M-Maybe she's forgotten about us. Maybe she went to bed."

Jeff pressed his ear against the door, listening, but could hear nothing above the renewed fury of the storm. And then there was a sharp knock on the door and Jeff leaped back, his face turning ashen.

"Open this door!" Marguerite commanded, and both children knew at once that something in their aunt's voice had changed. It had risen sharply from its usual tone, and taken on a rasping harshness. "How dare you try to lock me out! How dare you!"

The children watched as the knob turned back and forth and the door rattled in its frame as Marguerite shook it. Then the rattling suddenly stopped and there was a moment of silence.

"W-What's she doing?" Julie stammered.

Then a faint tinkling sound drifted through the door, and they both knew.

"It's the keys," Jeff wailed, and as if to confirm his words, they heard a metallic scraping and saw the key to Julie's door drop to the floor as another key slid into the slot from the other side. Jeff held his breath once again as Marguerite tried to open the lock.

The key didn't fit, and a second later they heard it being withdrawn, only to be replaced by another.

"We have to *do* something," Jeff wailed. He was sobbing with terror now, his eyes darting back and forth between his sister and the lock that was the only thing between him and his aunt.

Once again Julie wracked her brains, and then knew what she had to do. Her legs trembling, she crossed the room and picked up the key that lay on the floor. A moment later, as Marguerite withdrew the third key from the lock, Julie quickly inserted her own and twisted it a quarter of a turn.

"What are you doing?" Jeff demanded, his voice strangling on the panic that threatened to overwhelm him. "Don't unlock it!"

"I'm not," Julie whispered back. "I just turned the key a little bit so it won't fall out. But now she can't get one in from the other side! We're safe!"

As if to prove her words, there was a scraping sound from the other side of the door, and the key that now protruded from the lock beneath the doorknob wiggled but didn't drop out.

A moment after that Marguerite began pounding on the door, shouting her demands that the door be opened at once.

Her eyes wide with terror, Julie grasped her brother's hand in her own and backed away from the door.

The pounding went on, and Marguerite's furious voice continued to rave, but her words were indistinct now, lost in the raging fury of the storm.

"We're safe," Julie whispered. "It worked—she can't get in!"

They sat on the edge of Julie's bed, huddled together, trying to shut out the manic pounding at the door. And then, as suddenly as it had begun, the pounding stopped. Julie tensed, waiting for it to begin again, but the seconds ticked by and all they heard was the raging of the storm.

"Wh-What's she doing?"

"I don't know," Julie whispered, her mind racing. Then, in a flash, she knew.

Her little bathroom that connected to the room next door! Was the other door locked? She didn't know!

Yelping as she realized that her aunt must have remembered the connecting bath, too, she let go of Jeff and raced to the bathroom door. She twisted the knob and pushed, but the door stuck for a moment. She hurled her weight against it then, and it flew open.

Ten feet away, at the other end of the small bathroom, was the other door. There was no key in this lock, only a small knob that threw a bolt. If she could just get to it in time—

She threw herself toward the door, her fingers reaching for the knob.

Too late.

Just as she reached it, the door opened.

Marguerite, her face lit eerily by the small hurricane lamp in her hand, stood staring at Julie, her eyes smoldering with madness.

* * *

Kerry heard the murmur of his parents' voices in the parlor as he slipped through the kitchen, then pushed the back door open to duck out into the rain. The wind, coming straight out of the east now, drove a stinging lash of rain into his face, and he tucked his head low as he ran the few steps to his car and jumped into the driver's seat. He slammed the door shut and twisted the key in the ignition.

The motor ground for a few seconds, coughed, then caught, and he pumped the accelerator a few times, then put the car in gear. Backing down the driveway, he slewed the car into a sharp turn, slamming the transmission into low gear, then letting the clutch pop. The rear tires, already nearly bald, lost their grip on the wet pavement, and the car skidded wildly for a moment before Kerry regained control of himself and eased up on the gas pedal. The engine slowed, and a moment later he felt the tires catch. The car surged down the street.

He was on the main highway, approaching the intersection with the causeway road, when a gust of wind suddenly clawed at the torn canvas top of the car. There was a loud tearing sound, and suddenly the top was gone, nothing left of it but tatters of canvas lashing wildly in the wind. The rain poured down on Kerry now, but he ignored it, squinting his eyes against both the dark and the rain as he struggled to see ahead.

The intersection loomed up, and he pulled the car into a shuddering right turn. Once again the tires threatened to lose their grip on the pavement, but Kerry eased up on the gas, and the wheels held steady. And then the causeway was ahead of him, all but lost in a wind-whipped lather of rain and foam.

He slowed the car, leaning forward to peer through the windshield, but could see nothing. Finally he brought the car to a halt, then stood up, thrusting his head and shoulders through the scraps of canvas that still clung to the metal skeleton of the convertible top.

A bolt of lightning flashed, and for a split second Kerry could see the causeway clearly. It was awash with water, but he was almost certain he could see the pavement all the way across to the island. He dropped back into the driver's seat, then hesitated as he remembered what had happened to Anne Devereaux only a few weeks ago. But this storm was different, he realized.

The storm that had claimed Anne, and Mary-Beth Fletcher, too, had boiled up from the south, the winds running parallel to the coast, pushing water ahead of them. Those surges had built up the waves that broke over the roadway, sweeping Anne's car with them.

But tonight the wind was shifting wildly, right now it was coming out of the east, so that it was the island itself the pounding waves were battering. Here, in the temporary shelter of the mass of Devereaux Island, there was a momentary respite from the most dangerous waves.

Making up his mind, Kerry put the car in low gear and eased the clutch out. The battered convertible trembled as a gust of wind hit it, then began moving slowly out onto the causeway.

Julie stared at her aunt, her heart beating wildly. Marguerite seemed to have aged in the hour since Julie had last seen her, and there was a haggardness about her face that even the thick layers of fresh makeup didn't cover.

Her eyes, heavily circled with dark shadow, burned brightly, and her whole face seemed to glow in the candlelight like some strange Halloween mask that was lit from within.

She wore one of her mother's dresses, with a red skirt that flowed nearly to the floor, and a black lace bodice, buttoned to the neck, with long sleeves that ended in festoons of more lace around her wrists. The string of jet beads hung around her neck, their facets glinting brightly as they caught the light of the candle.

"How dare you?" Marguerite demanded, her eyes fixing furiously on Julie. "When I tell you to do something, I expect to be obeyed!"

Julie shrank back, but Marguerite's right hand snaked out and grasped her by the wrist. "I—I'm sorry, Aunt Marguerite," Julie whispered. "I—I couldn't hear you."

"Couldn't hear me?" Marguerite parroted, her voice taking on the mocking edge of sarcasm that had been one of her mother's most effective weapons. "If you couldn't hear me, it was because you weren't listening, wasn't it?" When Julie's response was not instantaneous, Marguerite's grip on her niece's wrist tightened. "Wasn't it?" she demanded once more.

"I—I guess so," Julie stammered. Her mind was reeling now, as panic welled up inside her. What could she do? Her eyes searched the tiny bathroom frantically, searching for something—anything—she could use as a weapon. But Marguerite jerked on her arm, whirling her around to push her out of the bathroom and into the bedroom, where Jeff, nearly paralyzed with fear, stood at the head of Julie's bed, his arms wrapped around the bedpost.

"You," Marguerite said, her voice dropping sharply, her eyes fixing accusingly on the terrified child. Jeff shrank back against the wall.

Dragging Julie with her, Marguerite crossed the room, her right leg moving stiffly, only barely supporting her weight. Setting the hurricane lamp on the bed table, she grasped Jeff's arm and started toward the door, "Open it!" she commanded, shoving Jeff forward. A small cry of pain escaping his lips, Jeff fumbled with the key, then managed to twist it in the lock and pull the bedroom door open. Pushing the children ahead of her, never releasing her grip on their arms, Marguerite herded them into the candlelit hallway. "What am I going to do with you?" Marguerite mumbled as she limped painfully down the long corridor.

"D-Don't hurt us, Aunt Marguerite," Julie managed to gasp, and slowly Marguerite's head swung around and her eyes fixed on Julie. Her lips twisted into a strange rictus of a smile.

"Hurt you?" she asked. "I won't hurt you, my darling. Why would I hurt my darling little girl? I love my little girl. My little girl is all I have and all I love—"

She stopped abruptly and her eyes clouded as she stared at the closed door to the nursery. Once again her hand tightened on Julie's wrist, her fingers, like claws, digging deeply into the flesh of Julie's arm. "Open the door," she whispered, her voice suddenly trembling as her breath began to come in panting gasps.

Silently Julie obeyed her aunt's instructions, removing the heavy ring of keys from the pocket of Marguerite's dress, then trying them one by one in the door until finally one of them fit and she felt the bolt of the lock click back. Her hand shaking, she turned the knob of the nursery door and pushed it open.

With sudden violence Marguerite hurled Jeff into the little room. Losing his balance, he sprawled on the floor and screamed with pain as he felt a sharp twist in his ankle. Ignoring his cries, Marguerite pulled the door shut, locked it, then dropped the keys back in her pocket.

"Wh-Why did you do that?" Julie quavered. "Why did you lock him in there?"

Marguerite gazed at Julie contemptuously. "What would you have me do with him?" she said. "He's just like all little boys. Always poking their noses in where they're not wanted, always in the way."

Then she was moving again, part of her weight leaning heavily on Julie, dragging her right leg forward until it was even with her left, then striding ahead on her left leg, only to drag the right one forward once more. When they came to the landing, she paused, drawing in deep gasps of air as she tried to catch her breath. "Upstairs," she said at last, and with renewed strength began climbing the flight of stairs that led to the ballroom.

Julie, her mind almost numb with fear now, let herself be guided up the stairs and into the ballroom itself. Marguerite reached into the pocket of her dress and brought forth a box of wooden matches. Striking one, she lit a stub of a candle that stood on top of the piano and turned to glare at Julie. "Are you ready?" she asked.

"R-Ready? For what, Aunt Marguerite? Wh-Why are we up here?"

"To dance!" Marguerite spat the words at Julie. "We have to rehearse, my darling. You don't want to look bad tomorrow, do you?"

Julie stared blankly at her aunt. What was she talking about? Tomorrow? There wasn't anything happening tomorrow, was there?

As if reading her thoughts, Marguerite's eyes narrowed. "Don't you remember? You have a recital tomorrow. All your friends will be here, and you are going to dance for them!"

She seated herself at the piano and opened the lid over the keyboard. For a moment Julie wanted to flee, wanted to run out of the ballroom, down the stairs and out of the house. She could hide in the storm, hide all night if she had to—

And then she remembered Jeff. If she left, what would her aunt do to her brother?

She couldn't leave, not as long as Jeff was locked in the nursery.

A moment later, as Marguerite struck the first chords on the out of tune piano, Julie forced her feet into the unnatural pose of the first position of classical ballet. . . .

Kerry was almost across the causeway when the wind suddenly shifted and the car shuddered as a mass of air struck it. Hands tightening on the wheel, he slowed the car to little more than a crawl. He was feeling his way along the narrow strip of pavement, the blacktop completely invisible beneath the torrents of rain and wind-whipped foam. The headlights glowed brightly, but the glare of the rain nearly blinded him, and the windshield wipers were useless. Just as he felt the tension inside him reach the breaking point, he felt a slight bump as he left the blacktop of the causeway and dropped onto the dirt road of the island. He pressed the accelerator then, and the car shot forward before skidding madly in the soft mud of the road.

He fought the car, spinning the wheels back and forth, and the tires found a grip on a patch of gravel. The car moved forward a few yards, but Kerry slammed on the brakes.

Just ahead of him a huge pine branch, its layer of moss stripped away, lay across the road, blocking his way. Cursing out loud, he set the brake and got out of the car, stumbling through the rain and mud. He glared angrily at the branch for a moment, kicking out at it with a shoe that was heavy with mud. Then, regaining control over himself, he bent down and grasped the branch with both hands. Straining, he tried to lift it free from the sucking mud, but it wouldn't budge. "Shit!" he exploded once again. Sighing heavily, he found the end of the branch where it had torn loose from the tree and began dragging it to the side of the road. For a moment he thought this, too, was going to be futile, but then the branch gave slightly, there was a strange sucking noise, and it pulled free. He dragged it off the road into the brush. His hands sticky with fresh sap now, and his clothes covered with mud, he returned to his car.

Slowly and carefully he began making his way along the road once again, the car slipping from side to side, threatening to lose the road entirely on every curve. At last he came to the driveway of Sea Oaks and started up the gentle rise toward the mansion itself.

He could see it now, looming against the sky. Here and there, glimmering through some of the windows, he thought he could make out the flickering light of candles.

Perhaps, after all, everything was going to be all right.

Fifty yards from the house he came to the tree that had fallen across the driveway. Abandoning the car, he began walking the last few yards.

Marguerite saw the bright flickering of lights playing across the ceiling of the ballroom and abruptly stopped playing. Julie, caught in midstep by the sudden silence, faltered, then caught herself just before she would have collapsed to the floor. She turned to look at Marguerite, and for the first time saw the glow of lights streaming up through the French doors that opened onto the balcony above the veranda. "Wh-What is it?" she asked. Her heart was pounding again, but this time with excitement.

Someone had come—someone had come to help her! She

ran to the window, pressing her face to the glass as she tried
to peer out into the storm.

The twin headlights nearly blinded her, but she didn't care.
Someone was here, and she was going to be all right!

She felt Marguerite's hand close on her shoulder, and a
split second later felt herself being spun around. There was a
sharp crack as Marguerite's right hand slashed across her
face, and Julie's eyes stung with sudden tears.

"How dare you?" Marguerite hissed. "How dare you
invite a beau out here at this hour? What will people say?"

Her fingers closing around Julie's arm, she started toward
the door, dragging Julie after her. Julie tried to struggle, but
Marguerite turned, her free hand slashing across Julie's other
cheek. "Did you think I wouldn't know?" Marguerite raged,
her voice shaking with fury. "Do you think I haven't always
known what you were doing with that boy? Filthy, that's
what you are. A filthy, degenerate slut! And after all I've
done for you!"

"No," Julie wailed. "I haven't done anything, Aunt
Marguerite."

"Liar!" Marguerite screeched, slapping Julie yet again.
"I'll teach you to lie to me!" Twisting Julie's arm up behind
her back, Marguerite pushed her toward the stairs, and Julie
had to grasp tightly to the banister to keep from falling as she
stumbled down to the second floor.

They came at last to the landing, and Marguerite pushed
her again, propelling her along the corridor until they were at
the nursery. Never releasing her grip on Julie, Marguerite
fumbled in her pocket for the key ring, then began trying the
keys in the nursery door. At last she found the right one.

Shoving Julie through the door, Marguerite pulled it closed
again and locked it once more.

Breathing heavily, but knowing what she must do, Marguerite slowly made her way toward the head of the main
staircase.

CHAPTER 24

As soon as he heard the lock click on the nursery door, Jeff ran to his sister, dropping down on the floor next to her. "What happened? What did she do to you?" he whimpered.

"She—She was making me dance," Julie told him. "She kept talking about a recital tomorrow." She sat up, rubbing gingerly at her left knee, the skin of which had scraped away when she hit the floor. She winced at the stinging in the raw flesh, then got to her feet and rushed to the window. "There's a car outside," she told Jeff. "Someone's come to help us!" She pressed her face to the glass, but the headlights were gone and the sky outside was once more pitch black. "Where is it?" she pleaded. "Didn't you see it, Jeff?"

Jeff shook his head. "I didn't see anything."

"But it was there!" Julie insisted. "It was coming up the hill, and you could see the headlights on the ceiling." A flash of lightning suddenly shot across the sky, and Julie saw what she was looking for. In the driveway, just beyond the fallen tree and only partly visible around the corner of the house, was a car.

Kerry Sanders's car.

She gasped, instinctively clutching Jeff's hand as thunder rolled over the house. "It's Kerry! He's here, Jeff. We're going to be all right!" As the thunder died away, there was another flash of lightning, and she could see Kerry himself. His shoulders were hunched against the storm, his head low as he fought his way uphill, his feet slipping on the slick drive, his clothes drenched and smeared with mud. A wave of relief flooded over Julie, replaced a split second later by renewed panic.

"We've got to warn him!" she cried. She began struggling with the window, trying to lift it.

"The lock!" Jeff screamed. "You have to open the lock!"

Julie stared dumbly at her brother, then understood what he was talking about. With fumbling fingers she groped at the latch between the two halves of the casement, whimpering with frustration when it refused to turn.

"The other way!" Jeff yelled. "You're turning it the wrong way!"

Shoving his sister aside, he reached up and hooked his thumb around the tab on the latch, then pulled to his right. Instantly the latch came free, and he tried to raise the window. "Help me!" he shouted when the wooden frame held fast. But even with Julie's help, it did no good. The wood of the window frame, soaked with rain, had swollen into a tight seal, jammed tight within its casement.

"What are we going to do?" Julie moaned. A sheet of lightning briefly illuminated the night, and she realized she had only a few seconds left. Kerry was almost to the corner of the house now, and in another moment would start toward the front door.

"Bust it!" Jeff exclaimed. He ran to the small rocking chair and began dragging it. "Help me!"

Julie stared dumbly at her brother for a moment, then understood. Grabbing the rocking chair, she pulled it next to the window, lifted it by the arms, took a deep breath, and smashed its runners into the casement. There was a crash as the old wood exploded outward and shards of glass dropped to the floor. A few long pieces, tapering to evil points, still remained, and Julie battered at them with the chair until they were gone. Then, ignoring the wind and rain lashing through the gaping hole where the window had been, she leaned out, raising her voice to scream into the wind.

"Kerry! Kerry, wait!"

But even as she shouted, she knew it was useless. Her words seemed to evaporate into the chaos of the storm, sounding muffled even to herself. And when the next flash of lightning came, and she could no longer see Kerry Sanders, she knew she had failed. Sobbing with fear and frustration, she turned away from the window. "What are we going to do?" she gasped, her voice choking. "She's crazy, Jeff. And she's going to kill Kerry! I know she is!"

Jeff, his eyes desolate, could only gaze mutely back at his sister.

Kerry darted up the steps, then paused on the veranda. Water poured off him, and he shivered as the wind whipped around him. Through the windows in the front of the house, he could see a few candles flickering brightly. And yet there was no other movement inside the house.

But they must have seen his headlights coming up the road. Why wasn't Julie already at the front door, waiting for him?

He'd been right—something *was* wrong.

He tried to swallow the fear rising like bile in the back of his throat. What should he do?

Part of him wanted to turn away, to go back to his car and start back to the mainland. But it was too late for that—the wind was coming steadily out of the south again, and waves, piled high by the force of the gale, would be breaking over the road, making it impassable.

Besides, even if he could get back to the mainland, by the time he found help and returned to the island, whatever was happening inside the house would already be over and done with. Screwing up his courage, he crossed the veranda and pounded on the front door.

Marguerite stood uncertainly at the foot of the stairs. The hollow pounding on the front door seemed to batter at her, and she whimpered softly to herself.

He shouldn't have come—he knew he was supposed to stay away. Hadn't she warned him what would happen if he kept coming out here, sniffing around her daughter like a rutting dog? And he was nobody—nothing but a sharecropper's son whose father had worked for her husband. How dare he think she would ever allow him to marry her daughter? As if she would ever allow Marguerite to marry anyone!

The pounding continued, and she could hear him shouting now, calling out, pleading to be let in.

Slowly a smile came to her lips.

She would let him in, all right. But it would be the last time.

Turning away from the stairs, she began hobbling slowly toward the kitchen.

Kerry's fists were beginning to hurt from pounding on the door. What was happening? Why wasn't someone answering? Couldn't they hear him? He shouted Julie's name, but the wind seized his words, scattering them into the trees. He moved down the veranda and peered in the living room windows.

The room, barely illuminated by five candles on the large coffee table in front of the fireplace, seemed empty. But just as he was about to turn away and go around to the back of the house, he saw movement in the dining room. A second later he recognized Marguerite's uneven gait as she stepped through the large double doors that separated the living room from the dining room. He rapped on the glass and shouted once more. He saw Marguerite pause and look uncertainly around. He rapped harder, and then, suddenly, she saw him. For a moment her expression froze, but then she nodded to him and a half smile curled around her lips.

She pointed to the front door.

The tension drained out of Kerry's body as he hurried back to the door. He'd been wrong! He'd been wrong about all of it. They were in the kitchen, that was all. And Julie was fine.

He waited impatiently, shivering in the wind, and at last heard the rattle of the lock as Marguerite opened it. Then the door itself opened and Marguerite stood framed by the oversize doorway, her face lost in the shadows.

"So you've come," Kerry heard her say.

"I was worried—" Kerry began, and abruptly fell silent.

There was something strange about Marguerite's voice. There was a hardness to it he'd never heard before. Indeed, she hadn't really sounded like Marguerite at all. For some reason it reminded him of old Helena Devereaux's harsh, demanding voice. "M-Miss Marguerite?" Kerry stammered uncertainly. "Are you all right?"

A bolt of lightning flashed across the sky then, and in the brilliant glare of its light, Kerry saw Marguerite's face clearly.

It was a grotesque mask of makeup, smeared and blotched, made even more hideous by the black lace of her bodice. In the white glare of the lightning she seemed a hideous creature out of a nightmare, and suddenly Kerry's fear flooded back in an icy chill.

She was staring at him now, her eyes glittering insanely. "Why wouldn't I be all right?" she demanded.

Kerry shrank back. Something *was* wrong—something was far more wrong than he had even imagined. This wasn't the Marguerite Devereaux he had known all his life, not even the Marguerite who had seemed to turn against him in the last two weeks. This was someone else, someone he didn't know at all.

"Scream," Jeff told his sister. "If you scream loud enough, he'll be able to hear you when she opens the door."

Julie stared numbly at her brother. If Kerry couldn't hear her from outside, through a broken window, how would he ever hear her through the thick door of the nursery, and all the way downstairs?

But she had to try—she had to do something. If she didn't—

A vision of her aunt's face flashed into her mind, the twisted mask of fury that had distorted Marguerite's features even beyond the strange makeup that had ruined her beauty.

Hurling herself toward the door, she began pounding on it, and both she and Jeff raised their voices to the loudest scream they could muster.

*   *   *

The roll of thunder following the bolt of lightning faded away, and Kerry was about to run from the veranda.

Then he heard the scream—muffled almost to the point of inaudibility—and took an instinctive step forward.

Instantly, the knife Marguerite held concealed in the folds of her skirt came up. Kerry recognized it too late.

He froze in mid-step, his eyes wide as he watched the knife arc down toward his chest. Each instant seemed to hang before him like an eternity, and his mind churned with confusion.

What was happening? Was she trying to kill him? But she couldn't be—she *wouldn't* be! Why? What had he done to her?

Even as the knife descended upon him, he realized the truth. It wasn't Marguerite at all who was killing him. It was someone else, someone she'd dredged up out of the depths of her mind, and it was that person who was killing him.

She was not Marguerite, and he was not Kerry. Instead he had got caught up in a mad fantasy, and none of it was real.

Except the knife.

The knife was real, and Kerry felt himself in suspended animation as it sank into his chest. He felt the cold metal slip between his ribs, felt his lungs tear as the blade ripped through them.

He felt the knife being torn out of him, and he staggered, his legs betraying him as shock began to move out from the wound, paralyzing his limbs, sapping the strength from his body.

Then the knife struck again, and this time he felt it enter his heart.

He pitched forward, his vision going black as he died. The last thing he saw was the scarlet gash of Marguerite's mouth, twisted into a vicious parody of a victorious smile.

Marguerite's heart pounded with wild elation as she watched the life drain out of the face in front of her. The eyes were opened wide, and she'd seen every one of the fleeting emotions that had passed through them. First the fear, the shock as he'd recognized who she really was. He'd almost gotten away from her then, almost turned to flee out into the night, where she knew she'd never be able to follow him—not with the strange burning in her hip that kept her from walking properly. But then she'd heard her daughter screaming from upstairs, and seen the boy turn back.

His eyes were puzzled then, as if he didn't know what he'd done, why she had to punish him—punish him and her daughter too. But then the puzzlement had vanished as she'd raised the knife, and he'd stared at it in fascination as she plunged it into his chest then jerked it out only to strike once more.

Then, finally, the light in his eyes had gone out, and she'd known he was dead, known it even before his body pitched forward and she stepped aside to let it fall to the floor at her feet.

She smiled once again as the force of his fall drove the knife even deeper and its point, covered with his blood, emerged out of his back.

Her fingers, twitching with pleasure, went to her bodice, and she felt the warm stickiness of his blood on the lace of her blouse. But that was all right. She could change her clothes if she wanted to—upstairs, hanging in her closets, were racks and racks of them. And it had been so long since she'd worn them, so many years since there had been a ball upstairs.

She stepped over the body at her feet and pushed the door closed against the storm. She could still hear her daughter screaming and pounding her fists against the door upstairs.

As well she might, considering what she'd done. She would have to be locked up again, just as she'd been locked up before, in the little room down in the cellar.

But there was so much to be done first. So very, very much . . .

Humming softly to herself, Marguerite bent down and grasped Kerry Sanders's arms, then began dragging him across the floor of the entry hall toward the bottom of the stairs.

Blood, still oozing slightly from his wounds, smeared across the floor, but Marguerite didn't notice it at all. Finally reaching the foot of the staircase, she paused for a moment to catch her breath. Then she threw the switch to activate the chair lift.

Nothing happened.

She frowned uncertainly, then remembered. Of course it didn't work—the electricity was off. She chuckled hollowly then, remembering that they'd thought of this years ago, her daughter and herself, when she'd been confined to the second floor. It was Marguerite who had come up with the idea.

"We'll put in a generator," she'd said. "Just a little one in the closet under the stairs. Just in case."

And tonight, finally, the case had come.

She picked up the hurricane lamp that stood on the newel post and went to the door beneath the stairs. Inside, tucked away in a corner, was the generator. She stared at it for a moment.

Would it even work? If it had been left to that worthless Ruby to look after, it probably wouldn't.

She studied the directions printed on the orange metal of the machine's gas tank, then fumbled for a moment as she searched for the choke. Finally, bracing herself uncomfortably, she pulled on the rope that emerged from the side.

On the third pull the little motor caught, coughed, then fell into an uneven idle that smoothed out when she adjusted the choke.

She turned one more switch and the machinery of the chair lift hummed into life.

She left the closet and returned to the foot of the stairs. She pressed the button, there was a familiar clanking sound, and the chair began descending toward her from its place at the second-floor landing.

Julie and Jeff, their throats sore and their voices hoarse, finally stopped screaming. The nursery was cold now, and the wind was whipping the curtains beside the broken window, but they were oblivious to it all, their ears pressed to the door as they strained to hear what was happening downstairs.

The wind slackened for a moment, and suddenly in the empty silence that replaced the howling of the storm, they heard the sound of machinery.

"Wh-What's she doing?" Jeff whispered, fearfully clutching Julie's hand.

"I don't know. It sounds like the chair lift. But it can't be—there isn't any electricity."

Then Jeff remembered the generator his father had shown him in the closet under the stairs.

"But why?" Julie asked after he had told her about it. "What does she need the lift for? She never uses it—she hates it."

"How should I know?" Jeff complained. "And where's Kerry?"

But Julie made no answer to Jeff's question, and he didn't ask it again, for both of them were already certain that Kerry was dead.

They didn't know how, and they didn't know why, but they were both absolutely positive that it had happened.

Their Aunt Marguerite had killed him.

The chair lift rattled to a stop at the bottom of the stairs, and Marguerite leaned down, sliding her hands under Kerry Sanders's arms. Her right leg sprawled awkwardly across the floor, she rested her weight on her left leg, crouching low to keep her balance. Finally, straining with the effort, she pushed herself upward, lifting Kerry's limp body into the chair. She held it in place for a moment, catching her breath, then let go.

The body swayed, nearly falling off the chair. She caught it at the last moment, then paused, uncertain what to do.

And then she knew.

Grasping the handle of the knife that still protruded from Kerry's chest, she pressed her weight against it, driving its sharp end into the banister at Kerry's back. Then, leaving the body pinned to the stair rail like an insect on a board, she gathered her skirts around her and hurried down the stairs to the cellar, carrying the hurricane lamp with her.

In a few moments she was back, a long length of clothesline clutched in her free hand. Setting the lamp back on the newel post, she began wrapping the rope around Kerry's body, tying it tightly against the back of the chair. When she was finally satisfied, she jerked the knife free of the banister and Kerry's body settled slightly, his shoulders drooping, his right arm falling from his lap so that his fingers almost brushed the bottom stair.

Once again Marguerite pressed the button, and the chair began moving slowly upward, its gears grinding loudly as it bore its grisly cargo aloft.

Marguerite, one hand clutching Kerry's shoulder for support, mounted the stairs next to the lift, keeping the sedate pace of the chair, oblivious to the small rivulet of crimson blood that ran down Kerry's arm and dribbled in large droplets onto the carpet that covered the stairs.

They came to the second-floor landing, but instead of stopping the chair there, Marguerite let it continue, jerking around the corner to the second flight, then grinding in protest as it hit the rust that had gathered on the upper set of rails during the years of disuse.

A high, keening wail accompanied the chair on its final ascent, and then it clanked loudly as it came to a stop once more.

Marguerite struggled with the rope, her fingers slipping off the blood-covered knots. But slowly she began working them loose, and at last the rope came free and Kerry's body tumbled to the floor. Grasping his hands in her own, she began dragging his corpse into the ballroom.

Julie and Jeff stared at each other in horror. They'd listened in silence as the chair lift had ground upward, then felt a moment of relief as it had clanged to a stop. But a few minutes later they'd heard a soft thump above them, as if something had fallen. Their eyes met, and though neither of them said a word, they both knew what had happened. It was Jeff who finally dared to speak, as the wind outside began to scream once more through the pines and a renewed torrent of rain battered at the house.

"She killed him," he whispered, his voice choking with terrified sobs. "She killed him, and she took him upstairs, and she's going to kill us too."

Julie was unable to make any reply at all, for she knew that what her brother had said was true.

And then, after what seemed like an eternity of silence from beyond the nursery door, the machinery suddenly came back to life and they heard the chair lift begin its slow descent once again.

CHAPTER 25

The storm seemed to find new strength, and once more the night was shattered by jagged daggers of lightning and the house shuddered under the force of the thunder that followed each flash. A tall pine only ten yards from the house shrieked in protest as a bolt of lightning struck its top, splitting its trunk to the root. Julie screamed out loud as the thunderclap crashed in her ears, then shrank back, clutching the small coverlet from the broken crib tight around her.

"We've got to get away from here!" Jeff shouted over the roar of the storm.

"How?" Julie sobbed. "There isn't any way out."

But Jeff was already at the smashed window, squinting into the darkness as he tried to find a means of escape. As another bolt of lightning slashed through the storm, he saw a way. Eight feet away, toward the corner of the house, a thick mass of wisteria climbed the wall. Here on the second floor there was a narrow ledge, no more than six inches wide, which ran the full length of the house. If he could get onto the ledge and cling to the house itself as he inched his way to the vines—

"I can do it!" he yelled. "I know I can!"

His shout of bravado roused Julie. Still clutching the quilt around her shoulders, she moved toward the window.

"Look!" Jeff whispered, his voice quivering with excitement now instead of fear. "There's some vines there. All I have to do is go along the ledge."

"But you can't," Julie protested. "There's nothing to hang onto."

"Yes, I can," Jeff insisted. "There's all kinds of cracks in

303

the siding. And if I can get out of the house, maybe I can get across the causeway too."

The memory of her mother flashed into Julie's head. "You can't get across. Not in this—"

"Kerry got across," Jeff replied, his jaw setting stubbornly. "If he could do it, so can I."

He climbed up onto the windowsill and swung his legs out, then rolled over so he was on his stomach, his head and shoulders still inside the nursery. He felt with his toes, then found the ledge. A moment later, his weight on the ledge but his balance maintained only by his hands clinging to the sill, he grinned at his sister. "See? It's easy."

"Don't!" Julie wailed. "You'll fall, Jeff."

"I won't either," Jeff told her. "And even if I do, I bet it won't hurt me. All it is is mud down there, and I've jumped off higher stuff than this."

He began edging his way toward the vines then, moving his feet slowly and carefully, testing the strength of the ledge with every step before trusting his weight to it. In a few seconds he was away from the window, only his right hand still clinging to its broken frame. He winced as he felt a fragment of glass slash his fingers, but let out no cry. Then, with his left hand, he began groping for a finger hold on the wall itself.

His heart sank for a moment as he felt nothing but the smooth surface of the siding, but then, barely within reach, he found a small crack. His fingertips dug in, and with the wind lashing at him, he took a deep breath, let go of the window frame, and began inching his way once more along the ledge.

He froze as the sky lit up around him, then pressed his body to the wall as a rumble of thunder made the house shake beneath his feet. As the thunder died away, he began creeping once more toward the vines.

He was three feet away when his left foot slipped and he felt himself lurch downward, the palms of his hands scraping across the wet siding. Just before his balance completely gave way, his fingers found a crack and he clutched wildly, his heart pounding, his breath frozen in his lungs. Trembling, he found his foothold once again, then moved quickly, scuttling like a crab to the relative safety of the vines.

His clothes were soaking wet, and he huddled in the vines for a moment, waiting for his heart to slow and his breathing to return to normal. At last he gripped the thick trunk of the ancient wisteria and abandoned the ledge.

Instantly he felt the vine tearing away from the wall, its tendrils loosing their grip on the old wood of the siding. Half climbing, half falling, he slithered to the ground. Just as his feet touched the wet earth, the mass of vines fell away from the house, collapsing in a tangled heap on top of him. He thrashed helplessly for a moment, but the vines seemed only to tighten around him, and he felt fingers of panic reaching out to him.

Marguerite emerged from the ballroom, humming softly to herself. She paused at the top of the stairs for a moment, her eyes darting around the small foyer outside the double doors as if she were searching for something that wasn't there. Then her tuneless melody suddenly stopped and she murmured out loud, her words instantly lost in the moaning of the wind outside.

"My guests—I must attend to my guests."

Seating herself on the chair lift, the bloodstained rope coiled neatly in her lap and the hurricane lamp held high, she pressed the button on the arm of the chair. The lift jerked once, then began its stately descent to the first floor.

When it came to a stop two minutes later, Marguerite stood up, staggering slightly as her lame hip protested, then caught her balance and went to the cellar door. Opening it, she held the lamp high as she started down the stairs, a soft glow of candlelight filling the dark reaches of the basement, casting eerie shadows on the walls and floor. Coming to the bottom of the stairs, Marguerite moved deliberately toward the small, nearly hidden chamber at the back, then reached into her pocket and fished out the key ring.

A moment later the lock snapped open and she pushed the door wide.

Holding the lamp high once more, she peered vacantly at the carnage within.

"It's time to go upstairs," she said softly, a smile playing at her lips. "In a little while the recital will begin."

She glanced around, and finally set the hurricane lamp on a stack of cartons midway between the little room and the base of the stairs. Bending down, she grasped Kevin's legs and began pulling him to the stairs. His body was already beginning to stiffen, and with the pain in her hip and leg increasing every moment, the job was almost more than she could accomplish.

But she had to do it, had to get him upstairs, had to get him to the ballroom. She labored on, and dust swirled up from the cellar floor, caking onto the blood that covered her clothes, settling in her hair, making her eyes sting. But at last Kevin's body lay stretched out on its back, propped against the wall.

Returning to the tiny room, Marguerite began the labor of dragging Jennifer Mayhew's corpse to the bottom of the stairs, and then Ruby's. She went back to the room then, and carefully locked the door. Satisfied that it was secure, she moved back to the bottom of the stairs and tried to lift Kevin's body up onto the stairs themselves.

It was impossible.

Marguerite whimpered in the dim light as frustration and fury welled up in her, making her whole body tremble. She kicked out at the corpse, her right foot stiffly lashing into its side, then winced as a stab of pain shot through her leg. "Damn you," she whispered. "Damn you, damn you, damn you!" Her mind churned with rage, but as an idea formed in her mind, the anger drained away.

Stepping over Kevin's body, she stumbled up the stairs and found the coil of rope on the chair lift, just where she'd left it. A few seconds later she was back in the basement.

She twisted Kevin's body around until his feet rested on the bottom step, then tied one end of the rope around his ankles, twisting it tight and tying it off as best she could.

Then, chuckling softly, she went up the stairs once more, playing out the coils of rope as she went. At the top of the stairs she had one more flash of panic: What if the rope wasn't long enough? Her heart racing, she quickened her uneven step, then sighed in relief as she reached the chair lift.

There were still two feet of rope left. Muttering quietly, she tied the end of the rope to the lift, straightened up and pressed the control button once more.

The chair began to move, and the rope, curving around the newel post, then snaking along the floor to the cellar door, grew taut.

The machinery of the lift ground in protest for a moment, then, from the cellar, there was a sharp thumping noise, then another. As the lift moved up the stairs toward the second floor, Kevin Devereaux's body moved up from the basement, his head bumping loudly on each step. As the chair reached the second-floor landing, Kevin's corpse emerged feet first from the cellar door and began dragging across the polished wood of the foyer. When it came to the bottom of the stairs, Marguerite stopped the chair lift and reversed its action. The rope went slack, and by the time the chair reached the foot of the stairs once more, the rope was free from Kevin's legs.

Grasping him under the arms, Marguerite heaved him onto the chair, then held him in place as she began wrapping coils of rope around him as she'd wrapped them around Kerry Sanders thirty minutes earlier.

At last, her brother's body tied securely to the chair, she pushed the button once more, and with her hand resting lightly on the corpse's arm, began accompanying the body on its slow ascent.

"You're going to be so proud of her," she said. "I've taught her so much while you've been gone. She dances like the wind on a meadow, Kevin. Have you ever seen the way the breeze makes the leaves dance on a beautiful fall day? It's charming, absolutely charming. And that's how she dances now. I've devoted my life to her, you know. My whole life. But it's been worth it, every minute of it. And you're going to see. You're all going to see. And you'll be so proud. So very, very proud.

"As proud as I am . . ."

The lift came to the second-floor landing, turned jerkily, then started up the last flight. And all the way Marguerite, her hand still resting on the bloody remains of her brother, kept chatting on, as if entertaining an honored guest.

Stop! Jeff commanded himself, and with an effort of sheer will made himself lie still for a moment. Then, beginning with his right arm, he began working himself free of the clinging snare in which he was entangled. He didn't know how long he'd been lying there, but it seemed like hours. The rain was still pouring down on him, but the screaming of the wind through the pine trees seemed to have eased slightly, and there was less lightning.

His right arm finally came free of the vines, and then he began stripping the clinging foliage away from his other arm and his legs. When at last he could move freely, he began methodically working his way through the tangle, gently pushing the vines apart until there was a hole through which he could crawl. At last he emerged from the collapsed wisteria, his hand sinking deep into the muddy garden that edged this side of the house.

"Jeff? Jeff!"

He barely heard his name at first, then heard it again and looked up. Above him there was nothing but blackness, but he thought he could make out his sister leaning out the window and staring down at him.

"Are you all right?" he heard.

"I'm okay," he called back. "I made it." Then, before Julie could say anything else, he dashed off into the night, using his memory more than his eyes to follow the path down past the garage and into the undergrowth beyond. If his aunt found out he'd gotten away, the first place she'd look for him was on the road. But out here, in the middle of the island, she'd never find him.

He ran as fast as he could, dodging through the clumps of vines and stands of pines, his heart pounding and his breath coming in loud, rasping gasps. Finally, his energy gone, he had to stop.

He slumped to the ground, his whole body aching, and tipped his face up so that the rain sluiced over him, washing away the sweat that had broken out all over his body. At last his panting slowed and he got back to his feet.

He took a step forward, then stopped, frowning uncertainly in the darkness.

Where was he?

There was a flash of lightning in the distance, and in the brief moment of illumination he gazed frantically around, trying to get his bearings. But nothing looked familiar, and as the lightning died and a low rumble of thunder rolled across the island, he realized he was lost.

The tendrils of panic reached out to him again, but once more he fought them down. He'd been out poking around the island every day, and he knew all the paths—every inch of them. How could he be lost?

Then, a few yards away, he thought he heard a sound—the snap of a twig, then an angry hissing—as if something were moving through the brush.

He froze, listening, trying to convince himself that it was nothing but the wind.

But the wind had suddenly died away, and the rain was pouring straight down on him.

He heard the sound again.

Whatever it was, it was moving toward him. He began running again, weaving his way through the trails, no longer caring which way he was going as he remembered the alligators that floated like logs in the ponds of the island, or lay basking in the sun, their heavy-lidded eyes half open as they waited for prey to stumble into their path. Then he was out of the tangle of brush and into a stand of pines. He broke out of the pines and hurtled out onto the road. His feet hit the mud, skidded out from under him, and he sprawled headlong into the mire.

Sobbing now, he got to his feet and tried to scrape some of the mud off his clothes, then wiped his face with a filthy arm. But he knew where he was now, and taking a deep breath, began slogging along the road toward the causeway.

*   *   *

Hal Sanders pulled his car up in front of the town hall and jumped out, slamming the door behind him even as he dashed for the front door. He was almost surprised to find it unlocked—from what Frank Weaver had said earlier, he half expected Will Hempstead to have locked up and gone home for the evening.

Hal had left his house as soon as Edith discovered Kerry was missing, sure he knew where his son had gone. But when he'd gotten to the causeway and seen the waves crashing over it, he'd been certain that Kerry wouldn't try to cross it—nobody in his right mind would. So he'd begun driving around the town, looking for his son's car, certain he would spot it at any moment, either in front of the drugstore, or parked in the driveway of one of his friend's houses.

But as the minutes had ticked by and there had been no sign of Kerry's car, his worries had slowly grown. And along with worry about his son, had come anger toward Frank Weaver and Will Hempstead. If they'd done their jobs, Kerry would be home right now.

Finally he'd decided to go to the police station. He found Hempstead and Weaver, their feet propped up on Hempstead's desk, a plate of cold french fries sitting untouched between them. Hempstead's feet dropped to the floor as Hal came into the office, water dripping from his slicker.

"What are you doing out tonight?" Hempstead asked cheerfully. "Decide to take some swimming lessons?"

"Lookin' for Kerry," Hal replied, his voice tinged with anger. "And if anything's happened to him, I guess I have you to thank, don't I?"

Hempstead rose to his feet, his genial smile fading. "Kerry?" he echoed. "What're you talking about, Hal?"

"Frank was over to the house earlier," Hal explained. "He got Kerry all riled up about what's goin' on out on the island, and I think Kerry decided to go have a look." His eyes, glaring darkly, shifted to the deputy. "Since Weaver here was too chicken to do his own job."

"Now, you just wait a minute—" Weaver began, but Hempstead cut him off.

"Now calm down, Hal," he said, "and tell me what's goin' on. You think Kerry tried to go out to the island?"

Sanders took a deep breath, then slowly exhaled. When he finally trusted himself to speak, he nodded. "It's the only thing I can figure," he explained. "I took a look at the causeway, and it's a mess out there. So I figured Kerry must've gone over to one of his friends, but now I've been all over town and I can't find his car."

"Did you go home?" Weaver asked, unconsciously echoing Hempstead's advice to Alicia Mayhew only a few hours earlier.

"No, I didn't," Sanders spat. "I came here to tell you I'm damned mad that you guys left a sixteen-year-old kid to do your jobs, and that I'm goin' back out to the causeway. And as soon as I can, I'm goin' out to the island to have a look around."

"Now wait a minute—" Hempstead began, but Sanders shook his head.

"You guys find Jennifer Mayhew?" he demanded. The two policemen glanced at each other, and Sanders knew the answer before either of them spoke. "So you're just sittin' around here waiting for the storm to stop. Well, I'm not. Now it's my kid that's out there somewhere, and you guys can help me look for him or not. But don't forget," he added, "there's an election coming up next year, and this time you might have someone running against you, Will."

Hempstead eyed Sanders warily for a moment, then made up his mind. But it wasn't the threat of a fight at election time that decided the issue for him.

It was worry.

Now there were two kids missing, and both of them had set out for Devereaux Island. And Hal Sanders was apparently determined to follow them. "We'll go along," he said, reaching for his own slicker, then tossing another to Frank Weaver. "But when we get to the causeway, I'm the one who'll decide if we try to cross it or not. If Kerry already tried, he either made it or he didn't. But I'm not going to watch you go into the sea, too, Hal. If it's too bad, we wait for the storm to pass, and that's that.''

Hal Sanders glared at the police chief. "If we wait for the storm to pass," he said darkly, "it'll probably be too late. For all we know, it already is.''

CHAPTER 26

Marguerite barely felt the exhaustion that permeated her body; indeed, as the night had worn on, she felt an increasing sense of well-being. At last everything was once more going to be as it should be. She was oblivious to the storm now, her entire being occupied with her preparations for what was to come.

The chair lift clattered to a halt for the final time, and she unbound Ruby's body, letting it slide to the floor in front of the doors to the ballroom. Coiling the rope neatly, she laid it carefully on the seat of the lift, then bent down, unheeding the burning pain in her right hip. She slipped her hands under Ruby's armpits and, still bent over, hobbled backward into the ballroom, where she placed Ruby's body with the others. She straightened up, smiling softly as she surveyed her work.

But something was missing. Something—some small detail—wasn't quite right.

And then she remembered. She hurried down to the second floor and along the corridor to her mother's rooms. In the small parlor, still sitting on the mahogany gateleg table, she found what she was looking for.

The music box.

It was large, nearly two feet square, and there was a small crank protruding from one side of its rosewood case. She touched it lovingly for a moment, then turned the crank. At last, almost reverently, she lifted its lid.

Inside the box a large metal disk began to rotate, and a soft and gentle melody filled the air. It stirred memories in Marguerite's mind, memories of times when she had been a little girl and her mother had played the music box for her and begun teaching her how to dance.

She frowned, for something in the memory was hurtful.

And then she remembered.

Her mother had made her dance to the soft strains of the simple waltz for hours sometimes, until her legs ached, and she was afraid she might collapse from exhaustion. But when she'd complained, her mother had only rewound the box, driving her on . . . on. . . .

"I never did," Helena's rasping voice screeched from Marguerite's own lips. "You were lazy. If you'd had your way, you never would have danced at all!"

"No," Marguerite's own voice pleaded, "I wasn't lazy, Mama. I just—"

Her voice shifted again, this time in mid sentence. "Don't you dare contradict me, young lady!" Helena's voice shrieked. "After everything I've done for you! Don't you dare!"

It was Helena's hand that snaked out and slammed the music box shut, cutting off the gentle melody, but Marguerite's own voice that whimpered quietly in the silence. "But I tried, Mama," she whispered. "I just—I'm sorry, Mama. . . ."

Her mind felt fragmented now, and she stood still, holding her head with her hands, feeling as if she might explode. Her madness battled within her and her body contorted, her torso twisting painfully as she tried to writhe away from the pain inside her head. And then the pain began to numb her mind as she fought against the memory of her mother that had come alive within her as she'd stood by the crypt earlier that night.

She'd loved her mother—all her life she'd loved her mother. And if it hadn't been for the accident the night she fell down the stairs . . .

She floundered then, trying to remember that night. What had happened? What, truly, had happened?

"You want to know?" her mother's voice cackled. "I can show you, you know. I can show you all of it!"

"No!" Marguerite breathed, but even as she uttered the word, she surrendered her mind to her mother.

The pain in her head ceased, and as if in a trance, she moved out of the small parlor, crossed the bedroom into the dressing room, and pulled open a large shallow drawer, nearly five feet long and three feet wide. A ball gown lay in the drawer, its color long since faded with age, its hems frayed. But now, in the dim light of the single candle that lit the room, it looked to her as if it were brand new. It was a beautiful dress, made of emerald-green satin, with a bodice worked in pearls of the palest pink. She reached out and touched the dress, and three of the tiny pearls tore loose from their rotting threads, rolling unnoticed into the corner of the drawer.

Slowly, her eyes never leaving the ball gown, Marguerite began stripping off her bloodstained clothes until she stood in only her bra and panties.

She began searching then, searching for the petticoat that would hold the gown's skirt out and rustle softly as she moved. She found it at last and put it on, then gently removed the gown itself from the drawer.

She stepped into it, easing her arms through the sleeves, then carefully buttoning up the high bodice. The top of the gown, made from the sheerest lace, tore in her fingers, but she didn't see the tiny rents in the fabric, didn't see the pearls that had fallen away from the scalloped pattern over her bosom.

She went to her vanity then and began repairing her makeup. She added color to her cheeks and lips, then patted a layer of powder over the heavy grease. She leaned forward, brushing mascara onto her eyelashes and covering the smudges below her eyes with heavy shadow. At last she turned her attention to her hair, braiding it into two long plaits which she coiled high on top of her head, held in place with two silver combs.

At last she stood up and moved to the tall mirror in the corner of her dressing room.

Through the mists in her mind she image that nigh long and hard at the reflection in the mirrons for her daugh Helena Devereaux, exactthe parlor then and picked years ago ox. Carrying it almost reve shat

the suite of rooms at the end of the corridor and started back
toward the staircase. She was moving easily now, and the
pain in her hip had ceased. Her limp, too, was gone, and she
walked with an even step, moving regally through the house,
the hem of her dress barely touching the floor. At last she
came to the stairs and started up.

Julie listened at the door of the nursery, her face glistening
with tears, her whole body trembling with fear and the exhaustion that the hours of terror had brought with them. It
seemed as if the sound of the chair lift would never end. Four
times it had moved back and forth between the first floor and
the third. But what could her aunt have been doing? And then,
a little while ago, she'd heard Marguerite's uneven tread
coming down the stairs and moving along the corridor toward
her grandmother's room.

She'd listened for a long time then, her fear growing as the
silence in the house dragged on.

Once, for a few short moments, she thought she heard the
faint sounds of music, but then the wind had come up again
and drowned it out. And, of course, it was impossible
anyway—the electricity was off.

But now she heard footsteps in the hall once more.

Even footsteps, not the strange, ominous sounds of her
aunt, moving stiffly, dragging her right leg behind her. She
wanted to cry out to whoever was there, scream to them for
help. But something stopped her, something held her back.

Then she heard the footsteps fade away as whoever was in
the house leaned went upstairs, and she hurried to the broken window, leaned out into the darkness.

She didn't know how long it had been since Jeff had run
off into the storm. But perhaps—seemed like hours—seemed like an
eternity. But perhaps it had slowly been minutes.

The storm seemed to ed like hours—seemed like an
and even the rain had slowly been minutes.

ker of hope. Maybe he would. The wind was dying,
y now.   rizzle. She felt a
                                 across the

And then she gasped in sudden terror as she heard the soft click of the lock on the door opening, followed by the creak of the door itself. She turned, and stifled a scream.

Jeff stumbled along the road, feeling his way in the darkness. There were only brief flashes of lightning now, and they were far in the distance, lighting only the clouds from which they sprang, to be followed long seconds later by the low rumble of thunder. The road, nothing more than a track of deep mud, sucked at his feet, and every step was an agonizing labor. To his left, the pines, groaning under the weight of rain-soaked moss, seemed to reach out to him like beggars in the night, trying to touch him, grasp him.

And to his right, the sound of the heaving sea, breakers crashing even in the channel, made him shrink back. He was crying now, half out of fear, half out of frustration and exhaustion. His eyes searched the mainland, but there was only darkness there, and finally he gave it up, keeping his head down as he trudged through the rain, his clothes clinging to his skin, his whole body shaking with a chill that seemed to have entered his bones.

The sound of the sea grew louder, and he looked up to find himself almost to the apron of the blacktop road over the causeway. He broke into a staggering run, his breath coming in raling gasps as he sucked in the night air.

And suddenly he was there—he'd made it!

But a moment later, as he stared at the causeway, his instant of elation faded away and he began sobbing once again.

Heavy waves were bearing up from the south, building high as they ran up into the shallows adjoining the causeway, then towering in great masses of black water before they crashed over the road in a maelstrom of churning foam. Then the water drained away, leaving the blacktop exp only a moment before the next wave flooded the ro

For a fleeting second Jeff considered the p dashing the length of the causeway between wa it was impossible. He couldn't even see the other end, and long before he'd made it even halfway across, the water would overwhelm him. He sank to the ground, a feeling of defeat flooding over him.

Until the waves calmed down, there was no way of getting any help at all.

"You're not ready," the angry voice of the apparition at the door of the nursery rasped. "Don't you know your guests are waiting?"

Julie shrank back against the wall. She knew who it was, recognized her aunt's face even under the thick layers of smeared makeup. And she recognized the voice too.

But it wasn't her aunt's voice; there was no trace in it anywhere of the gentle, melodious tones of Marguerite Devereaux. But still Julie recognized it.

Her grandmother's voice.

Her grandmother's face too.

She recognized it clearly, now, as the memory of her first glimpse of her grandmother came back to her: that hideous mask of lipstick and rouge, coming down the stairs on the chair lift, smiling at her.

But this face wasn't smiling at all. Lit from below by the lamp in Marguerite's hand, eerie shadows played across the grotesque visage, and Marguerite's eyes, glazed over with insanity, glittered evilly in the flickering yellow light.

A lump of fear rose in Julie's throat, and her fingers turned to ice as terror gripped her.

Marguerite moved forward, and Julie's eyes widened.

There was no trace of her limp at all.

Then there was no one else in the house—no one had come to help her after all.

Do what she says, a voice inside her whispered. *Do exactly as she says.*

Marguerite's right hand snaked out and slapped Julie across ˙ ˙ face. "I told you to be ready at eight, didn't I?" her voice
        Then it rose to a furious shriek. "Didn't I?"

She thinks she's Grandmother, Julie realized with sudden clarity. *She think's she's Grandmother and that I'm her.*

"I—I'm sorry, Mama," she murmured, instinctively mimicking the form of address her aunt had always used with her grandmother.

"Sorry?" Marguerite echoed, her voice edged now with Helena's acid sarcasm. "Come!"

Her fingers taking on the strength of talons, she grasped Julie's arm and jerked her roughly toward the door. Outside the nursery, she marched Julie down the corridor to the room that she herself had occupied until only a few days ago. Pushing the door open, she shoved Julie inside, hurling her against the bureau against the wall. Julie winced as her hip smashed into the hard oak, but managed to repress the moan that rose in her throat.

"Open it!" Marguerite snapped.

Julie tried to speak, but had to swallow hard to clear her throat before any words would come out.

"Y-Yes, Mama," she whimpered. Her fingers groping, she found the pulls and drew out the drop drawer. Inside she found a neatly folded leotard.

"Put it on," Marguerite commanded.

Her fingers trembling, Julie fumbled with the buttons of her blouse, then stripped off her blue jeans. Finally she began working her legs into the leotard, then her arms. At last, shivering in the thin garment, she turned to face Marguerite.

"Get your shoes."

Uncertainly, Julie started toward the closet, and when her aunt said nothing, opened the door wide.

In the dim light from the lamp in Marguerite's hand, she could barely make out a tall rack, each shelf of which was covered with worn toe shoes.

Numbly, she reached out and took a pair, then sank to the floor as she put them on and wrapped their satin ribbons around her ankles.

The shoes were too small, and already she could feel them pinching her toes. She looked up, but Marguerite was staring at her coldly.

"Upstairs," she said. "Our guests are waiting."

Her heart beating wildly, Julie let Marguerite guide her to the bottom of the stairs to the third floor.

What guests? she asked silently. *What is she talking about? There's no one in the house but us.*

But it wasn't true.

Her father was in the house somewhere, and so was Kerry Sanders.

And they were both dead.

Her aunt was going to kill her too. She knew it now, knew it with a calm certainty that seemed to drain the panic out of her body. Unless . . .

Unless she did exactly as Marguerite told her to do, and acted as if nothing were wrong.

She started up the stairs, her eyes fixing on the closed doors to the ballroom.

She was vaguely aware of something on the stairs, of a reddish smear on the floor of the ballroom's foyer. But she refused to look at it, refused to risk losing the strange composure—born of pure terror—that had come over her.

"Open the doors," Marguerite commanded.

Julie reached out, pushed gently, and the doors swung silently open on their heavy hinges.

Beyond the doors, the ballroom was pitch black.

"There are candles on the piano," Marguerite said. "Light them, my dear."

She handed Julie a small box of wooden matches, and Julie obediently took them and moved through the darkness, toward the piano. Keeping her back stiff and doing her best not to let her fingers shake, she began lighting the tapers in the enormous candelabra that sat on top of the piano. As she worked, she sensed Marguerite moving around the perimeter of the room, and slowly, as both of them continued to light candles, the room began to glow with light.

"Now turn around," Marguerite told her when the last candle was lit. "Turn around and greet our guests."

Steeling herself, Julie slowly turned away from the piano.

And a scream, unbidden and uncontrollable, tore from her throat. High-pitched, agonizing, it echoed through the room, bouncing off the walls to crash back into her own ears, deafening her.

Against the wall, four corpses were seated grotesquely in four red velvet chairs.

Kerry, his body pinned upright on the first chair by the knife that was still protruding from his chest, stared at her with sightless eyes. His mouth hung open, and a few drops of blood still dripped from his chin onto the crimson stain that covered his chest.

Next to him was Ruby, her eyes bulging, her flesh swollen around the red silk sash knotted around her neck. Her legs splayed out in front of her and her arms hung at her sides, her fingers curled into gnarled claws.

Jennifer Mayhew was beside Ruby. A dark bruise was spread over her forehead, and more bruises stained her cheeks. Her lower lip, half torn from her face by Marguerite's vicious kicks, had left her mouth no more than a bloody pulp, but her eyes, too, were open. They seemed to stare directly at Julie, and there was something accusing in their dull lifelessness, as if somehow what had happened to her might have been Julie's fault.

And finally she saw the body of her father. Covered with blood, his body was slumped over in the fourth chair, almost as if he were asleep. And yet there was a stillness to him, a devastating look of abject defeat, that would have told Julie he was dead even without the bloodstains on his clothing.

Her scream died away, and the icy chill in her fingers spread through her body, numbing her. Her mind seemed to close down, and when at last she heard her aunt's voice once more, it came from a great distance away.

"It's time," Marguerite told her. "Time to dance for our guests."

She heard the piano then, the first notes of a familiar melody whose title her numbed mind refused to remember, and even in her shock, she felt her legs and arms move into the first position.

It was a nightmare—it had to be. They couldn't all be dead—it was impossible. Her mind rejected what her eyes beheld, and she barely felt her body moving from one position to the next. She rose up on her toes, oblivious to the pain from the tight slippers, and spun into a pirouette.

The beat of the music picked up, and she whirled across the floor, her arms moving by pure instinct and years of training.

And she could feel the dead eyes on her, following her every move, watching her, reaching out to her.

They're not dead! the voice in her mind screamed. *I'm going to wake up, and they're going to be here, watching me, smiling at me.* She kept dancing, afraid to stop, afraid that if she stopped, she would find that the nightmare had not ended at all, that everything around her was real.

And then, as she danced close to Jennifer Mayhew, she suddenly saw her best friend move.

She froze in mid-step, her eyes watching in fascination.

And slowly Jennifer's body moved again, leaning forward as if she were trying to stand up.

The motion speeded up, and Jennifer fell face forward, sprawling out on the floor, her right arm outstretched, her finger reaching toward Julie.

Julie's shock broke then, and she screamed once more, covering her face with her hands as she staggered toward the door of the ballroom.

Abruptly, the music stopped, and an eerie silence fell over the room. Julie got to the door, jerked it open, and lurched into the foyer at the top of the stairs. She was at the stairs themselves, clutching at the banister to keep from collapsing, when she heard her aunt's voice once more, rasping with the furious anger of her grandmother.

"Do you think you can leave?" the raging voice demanded. "Do you think I'll let you throw away everything? All my life I've depended on you. I've trained you, loved you! I've driven you on—made you practice every day! I've taught you everything! And what are my thanks? You, wanting to run away with that filthy young man. Giving yourself to him, like a whore in the streets!" Her voice rose, screaming into Julie's ear. "Well, I won't have it! You'll never leave me! You'll stay with me forever, do you hear me?" And then, as she cowered away from her aunt, Julie felt

Marguerite's hand against her back and felt the violence of the shove that threw her off balance, twisting her hands loose from their grip on the banister.

She screamed once as she began the long tumble down the flight of stairs, then the pain in her body cut off the scream in her throat, and she was silent as she rolled over and over, her head striking some of the stairs, her spine twisting violently as she struck first the wall, then the posts that rose from each step to support the banister. At last she came to a stop, sprawled brokenly at the bottom of the stairs. The last thing she saw as blackness began to close around her was her aunt's face, looming above her, her lips twisted into an evil smile.

"You'll never leave me," she heard the voice mutter once again "You belong to me, and I'll never let you go."

And then, blessedly, Julie slipped away into the comforting darkness.

CHAPTER 27

Hal Sanders edged his car out onto the causeway, abruptly braking to a stop as a cresting wave broke against the rock levee, then surged across the road, draining away to the north. "Damn!" He uttered the word loudly, his fist slamming in frustration against the hub of the steering wheel. There was a sharp rapping on the side window, and he rolled it down to see Will Hempstead, a large flashlight in his hand, shaking his head.

"Not gonna be able to make it for a while yet," the police chief said. "But the storm's passing and the water should settle down pretty quick."

"Pretty quick might not be good enough," Sanders replied, his voice bitter. His eyes squinted as he peered through the windshield, straining to see through the blackness and the drizzle. His headlights glared brightly, but the rain quickly diffused their beams, and he could see no more than a few yards. But then the drizzle eased off, and Hal clicked the beams to the high position. As a blue light glowed softly on his dash, the headlights shone out the length of the causeway, and for just a moment Hal thought he saw movement at the other end. But in a second it was gone. The drizzle turned heavier, and once more the lights dissolved into a hazy brilliance. But Hal was already out of his car.

"You got a searchlight, don't you?" he demanded, striding toward the black and white hatchback Subaru parked a few yards away from his Ford.

"Sure do," Hempstead replied.

"Turn it on," Sanders said. "I saw something over there.

It was just for a second, but I'm sure there's something on the island."

Inside the small squad car Frank Weaver snapped on the powerful searchlight mounted on the roof and began playing it out over the water. Its halogen beam cut through the rain with a white brilliance, and a moment later they could see the tops of the pine trees on Devereaux Island.

"Lower, damn it," Sanders shouted, his eyes searching the opposite shore. "For Christ's sake, Frank, if anyone's out there, they aren't going to be climbing trees!"

"Give me a chance, will you?" Weaver muttered, twisting the control knob on the roof of the car. It moved jerkily for a moment, and the beam shot skyward, losing itself in the clouds, then came back down to sweep the water. Then he steadied it, and found the end of the causeway. For a split second there was nothing, then a figure appeared in the beam, waving frantically.

"That's Jeff!" Will Hempstead shouted. "What the hell—" He fell silent as the distant figure, still waving, started moving forward, out onto the causeway. Snatching at the microphone that hung from the radio, Hempstead switched on the bullhorn mounted just behind the spotlight.

"Stay where you are!" he shouted. "Don't try to come over here!"

But even as he spoke, he saw a wave flood across the causeway, and a moment later the small figure of Jeff Devereaux disappeared.

Jeff had seen the headlights pull up to the opposite end of the causeway, and began jumping up and down, waving his arms and shouting at the top of his voice. But his voice sounded like no more than a whisper even to himself, and he was almost certain he couldn't be seen in the misty glow of the headlights. Then the spotlight beam came on and a moment later found him. Shouting again, he waved frantically and instinctively ran toward the beacon of light.

The wave hit him at the same time he heard the faint sound

of a voice calling to him through the bullhorn. He lost his balance, stumbling, then went under. He felt himself being carried off the roadway, dragged over the rough rocks and hurled into the channel beyond. He thrashed wildly in the water for a moment, then his feet found the bottom and he pushed up, his head popping through the surface a second later. Treading water, he twisted his head around, searching for his bearings.

A second wave washed over the causeway, and a cascade of churning foam broke over him for a moment. But then he saw the spotlight shining on the trees beyond the road, and struck out for the shore a few yards away. Though the sea was choppy here, he was on the lee side of the causeway and the fearsome waves to the south couldn't reach him. A moment later, with both his shoes lost in the channel, he scrambled out of the water and back up to the mud of the road.

"Jeff!"

He heard his name plainly, turned to wave to the car on the opposite side, then realized they couldn't see him, for the beam of the searchlight was playing over the channel now.

"I'm here!" he screamed. "I'm on the road! Over here!" He waved frantically, but the seconds ticked by as the spotlight crisscrossed over the choppy water. Suddenly it moved up and raked along the road, passing right over him. A second later it was back, full on him, and he began waving again.

"Stay where you are!" he heard a metallically amplified voice shout. "Don't try to come across! You can't make it! We'll get to you!" There was a long pause, and then the voice came again. "Jeff, if you hear me, stop waving. Stop waving, count to three, then wave again, just once!"

Jeff hesitated, struggling to control himself. Then, in the glowing illumination of the searchlight, he stopped waving.

"One . . . two . . . three . . ." he said out loud.

Almost tentatively, he held up one hand and waved. A moment later his hand dropped back to his side, and, sobbing, he collapsed into the mud of the road.

*　　*　　*

"All right," Hempstead said as they watched Jeff drop to the ground. "Let's get going. Hal, move your car out of the way." As Sanders hurried back to his car and began backing it away from the end of the causeway, Will Hempstead slid into the driver's seat of the squad car and jammed the transmission into low gear. He was just starting to move forward when the back door was jerked open and Hal Sanders scrambled in.

"Don't even try to argue with me, Will," Sanders said. "My son's out there somewhere, and I'm going with you."

Hempstead said nothing as he moved the car into position at the end of the causeway. "Play the light out to the south," he finally told Frank Weaver. "I want to see what's coming."

They watched the water for five long minutes, gauging the force of the waves, searching for a pattern.

"Looks like the fifth one's the worst," Weaver finally said. Hempstead nodded in silent agreement, then waited for the next large wave to break.

"Let's go!" he declared, his right foot pressing down on the accelerator. Even as the water from the wave began draining away, the car was moving onto the causeway.

They had gone only twenty yards when the first wave hit them. Hempstead slowed the car to a crawl as water surged over the wheels. The car shuddered slightly but held the road, and as the water drained away, he pressed the gas pedal once again. They made another twenty yards before the second wave struck, and thirty more before the third.

When the fourth wave struck, Hempstead felt the squad car slew to the left, and for a moment thought he was going to lose control entirely. But then the wheels found purchase on the wet pavement again and the vehicle steadied. But already they could see the fifth wave building.

Hempstead veered the car around to the right, threw it in reverse, and spun the wheel the other way.

"What the hell are you doing?" Hal Sanders yelled from the backseat.

"Shut up and hang on!" Hempstead shouted. He slammed the transmission into the park position, and jerked hard on the emergency brake. Dead ahead of them the wave rose up out of the night, an angry mass of green water glowing in the headlights. Then it broke, smashing into the front of the car, white water churning past them, surging over the windshield.

The car shuddered once again, slid backward, and the engine died. Then, once more, the water drained away.

They were still on the road, but with thirty yards between them and the island. Hempstead twisted the key in the ignition and the starter motor ground noisily.

But the engine didn't catch.

The next wave broke, passing harmlessly beneath them as Hempstead tried the engine again.

"Grab the radio, Frank. Hal, there's a rope behind you. Let me have it!"

As Frank Weaver took a portable VHS radio out of the glove compartment and slid it into a plastic bag, Hal Sanders groped in the space behind the backseat and found the coil of rope.

As the series of waves built up, each one stronger than the last, Hempstead tied one end of the rope around the steering column and threw a bowline into the other end. "I'm gonna try to make it across right after the next big one," he said. "I'll tie the rope to a tree, and you guys can use it as a safety line."

The fifth wave of the series built in front of them, then crashed over the car, and once more they felt the light sedan slide backward toward the edge of the road. As the water receded, Hempstead leaped out of the car, shoved the coil of rope through the open window, and dropped the loop formed by the bowline over his head and shoulders. Ducking his head against the wind, he scuttled along the blacktop, then braced himself as the next wave struck. For a moment he lost his footing, but his toes found a rock at the edge of the road, and a moment later he was back on his feet. By the time the next wave broke, he'd made it to the island, where he jerked the rope free from his waist and tied it to a tree. Waving frantically, he signaled the two men. "Now, goddammit!" he yelled. "The next big one will take the car!"

As he watched, the back door of the squad car flew open and Hal Sanders emerged. Just as Hal grabbed the rope and started stumbling along the road, Frank Weaver dashed around the front of the car and started following Hal.

The third wave knocked Hal off his feet, but he clung to the rope as the water swirled over him, then regained his footing. Gasping and choking on the saltwater that had surged into his mouth when he fell, he collapsed onto the apron of the causeway, Weaver stumbling over him.

They pulled themselves to their feet just in time to watch the fifth wave hit the police car.

The car completely disappeared under the force of the water, and the rope, still tied to the tree, went taut, then snapped with a report as loud as a gunshot.

When the water had drained away, the causeway was empty. Nowhere was there any sign of the squad car.

"Jesus," Hempstead whispered in the darkness. But before either Frank Weaver or Hal Sanders could say anything at all, Jeff Devereaux was upon them, clinging to Hempstead with muddy arms.

"She killed them!" Jeff shouted. "She killed Dad, and Kerry, and Ruby, and everybody!"

A chill went through Hempstead, and he dropped to his knees, grasping the terrified boy by both shoulders. "Now take it easy," he said. "Calm down, and tell us exactly what's happened."

Still sobbing, Jeff began brokenly to tell them what had happened that night.

Julie drifted back into consciousness slowly. Her whole body hurt with a dull, throbbing pain that seemed to have no center at all, but spread through every bone and muscle in her being. Her mind seemed to be swimming in darkness, and for a while—she didn't know how long—she lay without moving, her eyes closed, trying to remember what had happened.

She'd been in the nursery and her aunt had come, but it hadn't really been her aunt at all.

And she'd put on a leotard, then gone upstairs to the ballroom.

Her friends were there, waiting for her. Kerry and Jenny, and Ruby.

Even her father.

She'd seen them, sitting on chairs in the ballroom, watching her dance.

Except—

She struggled with her memory, knowing there was something she'd forgotten, something important.

And then it came back to her.

All of them were dead.

She whimpered as a helpless desolation engulfed her soul, then rolled over.

An explosion of agony tore through her and she screamed, then tried to stifle the sound as the scream itself produced yet another spasm of pain.

"Help me," she moaned softly, her eyes burning with tears. "Oh, God, won't someone please help me?"

Then, dimly at first, she heard a movement from above. She blinked, and struggled to keep her eyes open. Candlelight flickered around her, and far up the stairs she saw another light, a brighter one.

She gasped, shrinking painfully back as she recognized her aunt at the top of the stairs, the hurricane lamp held in her left hand.

Limping painfully, her right hand grasping the banister to steady herself, she began making her way slowly down the stairs.

"Don't," Julie moaned when Marguerite was finally on the landing, looming over her, staring down at her with vacant eyes. "Please don't hurt me any more, Aunt Marguerite."

"Hurt you?" Marguerite echoed, her voice strangely hollow, as if Julie's words had no meaning to her. "But I couldn't hurt you, my darling. I love you. But you've had a terrible accident."

Julie swallowed, wincing at the pain even that simple action caused. "I—you—"

"You fell down the stairs," Marguerite told her. She was smiling gently now, her carmine lips twisting oddly. "Just like I fell down the stairs. That's what Mama told me. She told me I was clumsy and that I tripped. She said it was an accident, and that it was my fault. But I didn't believe her." She frowned, as if trying to reach into her memory. "I thought she pushed me. I thought she was angry, because of the baby."

"B-Baby?" Julie whispered, struggling to cling to her consciousness. What was her aunt talking about?

"You didn't know, did you?" Marguerite said vaguely. She wasn't looking at Julie anymore, and her eyes had taken on a furtive look. "I didn't tell anyone. Mama said everyone would hate me if they knew what I'd done. She said it was better if I pretended none of it ever happened. But I couldn't pretend. I wasn't good at it." A tiny laugh emerged from her throat. "That's why she locked me up. She kept me downstairs until I learned to pretend. And I pretended that none of it ever happened. I pretended that I was never pregnant, and that Mama never pushed me down the stairs at all. And I loved Mama. All my life I loved Mama, and did everything she wanted me to do."

Julie tried to listen, tried to make sense out of the words, but the agony in her body muddled her mind.

"But Mama left me," Marguerite went on. "They all left me. Even though I pretended, they still hated me and left me." Her eyes came back to Julie again. "You're like them, aren't you? You're going to leave me, too."

"N-No . . ." Julie breathed, suddenly certain of what was going to happen next. But it was too late. Marguerite's eyes had begun sparkling with her madness again.

"Don't lie to me," she snarled, lashing out at Julie, her foot sinking into the girl's stomach. "Don't ever lie to me!"

Julie gasped, curling up in a tight ball, struggling to breathe as the pain wrenched at her. But Marguerite's foot struck again, and Julie instinctively rolled away from it, trying to shield herself with her arms.

"Like all of them!" Marguerite screamed. "You're just like all the rest of them. I've done everything for you, but you want to leave, too, don't you? Don't you?" Her foot struck Julie again, and Julie writhed on the floor, trying to escape her aunt's wrath but unable to move because of the pain. "Well, I won't let you! You'll never leave me. Never!" She kicked Julie once more, and Julie felt herself falling again, tumbling down the main stairs this time. Knives were stabbing into her body now, but the pain was so powerful that she couldn't even scream out against it.

Let me die, she thought. *Oh, please, God, just let me die. . . .*

And then, once more, she fell into unconsciousness. She dropped down the last steps limply, like a broken doll, and finally came to rest on the floor at the foot of the stairs, in a pool of Kerry Sanders's blood.

Marguerite, still at the top of the stairs, gazed down at her, then shook her head sadly. "It's your fault," she breathed. "It's all your fault, my dear. But I can't help you now. I have my guests to think of, don't I?" She was silent for a moment, then nodded her head vaguely. "Yes. I have my guests."

Turning away, humming softly to herself, she started back up to the ballroom. By the time she reached it, Julie, still lying at the bottom of the stairs, was forgotten. Once more Marguerite was lost in the eddying whirlpool of her memories and her madness.

Will Hempstead stopped short.

Ahead of him the mansion loomed at the top of the rise upon which it had been built. The windows of the third floor sparkled brightly with candlelight.

A memory stirred in him, a memory from his youth, when he'd been no more than eighteen years old.

There had been a ball at Sea Oaks that night, and Marguerite had wanted him to come. But Helena had forbidden it, telling Marguerite that he would never be welcome here and forbidding her ever to see him again. But he'd come anyway, and stood outside, in the deep shadows of the moss-draped pines.

It had been a hot night—hot and humid—and on the third floor the French doors had been thrown wide. He'd stood hidden in the trees and watched the dancers through the open doors, heard the gentle strains of the orchestra, heard the laughter of Helena's guests as they drifted out on the balcony high up above the house's great portico. At last, as the hour grew late, he'd left, knowing deep inside him that in the end this house—and Helena—would defeat the love that was all he had to offer Marguerite.

The rain had stopped now, and as Will Hempstead stood looking up at the great house, that evening came back to him. It was that night, he remembered, when Marguerite had fallen down the stairs. It had happened late, after all the guests had left. She'd been tired, Ruby told him later, and missed her footing.

Missed her footing and plunged down the stairs, smashing not only her hip, but every dream she'd ever had.

They were going to go away together, or so they'd planned. But even before the accident, Will had decided that was never going to happen. Helena would see to that. And then, ironically, she hadn't had to, for the fall had put a stop to all Marguerite's dreams. Not only the dreams of dancing, but the dreams that included Will Hempstead, as well.

Tonight, as the storm moved north and stars began to peep through the thinning clouds, the house looked much as it did then.

Except that tonight, as he gazed up at the softly glowing ballroom, only one figure danced.

The figure of Marguerite Devereaux, her arms held up as if she were holding an invisible partner, her body moving with the strange jerkiness of a marionette as she tried to dip and sway in time to whatever music she might be hearing.

"Better let me have the radio," Hempstead said quietly, his eyes still on the ballroom windows.

"Wh-What's she doing?" Jeff quavered, clutching tightly to the police chief's hand.

"It's all right, son," Hempstead told the terrified boy. "She can't hurt you now. You're going to be okay."

He took the radio out of the plastic bag and switched it on, tuning it to the channel that was constantly monitored by one or another of the town's volunteer firemen. His voice heavy, he began calling out the codes for an emergency.

"And I'm going to need an ambulance," he said after he'd told the fire chief where he was. "Maybe two. I lost my car coming across, so be careful. Don't even try it until you're sure it's safe!"

He snapped the radio off, and then, with Hal Sanders and Frank Weaver a couple of paces behind him, started up the hill.

CHAPTER 28

Will Hempstead stared at the front door of the mansion for several long seconds. He felt a deep reluctance to take the final step of pushing it open, for already he was certain that a tragedy had taken place within the house that night and that it would be years before anyone in Devereaux would ever forget it. At last he reached out and twisted the knob. The door was not locked, and with a gentle push it swung back to reveal the entry hall, dimly aglow with the light of a single sputtering stub of a candle on the newel post.

Then he saw the crumpled form of Julie's body, curled at the bottom of the stairs, and his heart sank. Already they were far too late.

"Julie!" Jeff cried out. Dropping his grip on Hempstead's hand, he ran to his sister, dropping down on the floor beside her. "Julie!" he sobbed again. Then he looked up, his eyes—large and glistening with tears—fixing on the police chief. "She's dead," he wailed. "Aunt Marguerite killed her!"

Hempstead hurried across to the sobbing child and knelt beside him, his fingers gently touching Julie's neck. Almost immediately he found her pulse.

"She's not dead," he told Jeff, and as if to affirm his words, a low moan drifted from Julie's lips, and the fingers of her left hand twitched spasmodically. "Find a blanket," Hempstead told Hal Sanders. "And a pillow. Quick!"

Sanders disappeared into the living room and a moment later was back, carrying an afghan that had been draped over the back of the sofa and a small pillow he'd found on one of the wing chairs. Hempstead, working as carefully as he knew how, eased Julie's right arm out from under her body and gently straightened her legs. For a moment he considered moving her into the living room, but then rejected the idea, afraid that her back might already be broken. If he risked moving her, he might only compound her injuries.

"Kerry—" Hal Sanders said, his eyes fixed on the dark bruises that covered Julie's face. "He's got to be here."

Hempstead stood up, and when he spoke again, his voice took on a note of authority. "I want you to stay here, Hal. Take care of Jeff, and if Julie wakes up, don't let her move." Then he turned to Frank Weaver, a nod of his head directing the deputy's attention to the smears of blood that led from the foot of the stairs toward the door to the cellar. "Take a look down there," he said. "I'll go upstairs."

Frank Weaver stared down the steep flight of stairs that led to the basement, the bright beam of his flashlight playing over the smears of drying blood that seemed to be everywhere. The steps were sticky with blood, and even the wall adjacent to the steps was stained a brownish red. Placing his feet carefully, avoiding the worst of the mess, he started down into the basement, stopping when he reached the bottom of the stairs. Ahead of him, its door standing wide open, was a small room, and Weaver frowned in the gloom as a thought drifted through his mind.

Looks like a cell.

Steeling himself, he strode toward the little room.

It was empty, but as Weaver played his light over it, he felt a wave of nausea. There seemed to be blood everywhere—on the floor, on the wooden cot against the wall, even on the door itself. What the hell had gone on here? And where were the people whose bodies had to be the source of the carnage around him?

He turned away and hurried back up the stairs, but as he started up the main staircase, Hal Sanders stopped him, his face ashen and his hand trembling on Weaver's arm.

"Kerry," he asked shakily. "Is—Is he down there?"

Weaver said nothing, only shaking his head. Then he

hurried on up the stairs.

On the second floor he saw the glimmer of Will Hempstead's flashlight flickering through an open door at the end of the hall. Quickening his step, he moved along the length of the corridor and stepped into the bedroom.

"The basement's a mess," Weaver told the police chief. "Blood all over the place, but no bodies."

Hempstead nodded grimly, then played the flashlight over a heap of clothes on the dressing room floor. "Same thing up here," the police chief said. "There's bloody clothes all over the place. The window in the nursery's smashed, just like Jeff said," he added. Taking a deep breath, he started toward the door. "We better go up there and see what she's done. But from what I've seen so far, it's going to be one hell of a mess."

Together the two men started down the corridor, but on the stairs to the third floor Weaver stopped abruptly, listening.

Drifting down from the open doors to the ballroom above, he heard the faint sound of music. The melody was one he'd never heard before, a strangely haunting tune that tinkled softly in the otherwise silent house.

"You hear that, Will?" Weaver whispered. For a moment he wasn't sure the police chief had heard his question, but then Hempstead nodded.

" 'The Last Good Night,' " he whispered softly. "It was always her favorite song."

A great melancholy settling over him, the police chief slowly climbed the remaining steps to the ballroom.

Will Hempstead stepped through the double doors of the ballroom. It was stiflingly hot, for the windows were closed tight, but all the candles still burned brightly. A layer of pale smoke floated near the ceiling, swirling gently as Marguerite, her eyes closed, her head thrown back, slowly danced to the eerie melody of the music box. For several long moments Hempstead's eyes fixed on her uncomprehendingly. Then, as Frank Weaver swore softly, he tore his eyes from Marguerite and saw the four corpses, all of them except Jenny Mayhew still upright on their chairs.

"Jesus," he breathed. The word seemed to grow in volume as it echoed in the large room, and Marguerite's eyes snapped open.

Turning, she looked directly at Will Hempstead, the scarlet slash of her mouth spreading into a welcoming smile.

"Will," she said. "How nice of you to come. I've missed you so much, you know."

With a tiny curtsey she closed her eyes once more and resumed her dance.

"Crazy," Weaver muttered. "She's just gone completely wacko!" He started toward Marguerite, but Will reached out, his fingers clamping tight on his deputy's arm.

"No," he said, his voice quiet but his tone leaving no room for argument. "It's all over now, Frank. There's nothing more she can do. Let her finish."

Weaver froze, staring at Marguerite for a moment, then stepped back.

As the music went on, weaving a mournful spell in the candlelight, Hempstead's vision blurred and his eyes began to sting with tears. In his mind the grotesque, twisted vision before him—the strange, hobbling figure in the ill-fitting and faded dress, with its bizarre, distorted mask of Helena's evil face—faded away, and in its place came a memory of the Marguerite Devereaux he had fallen in love with so many years ago.

The Marguerite he saw then moved gracefully, her body swaying with the rhythm of the music, her fingers trailing in the air with a perfect symmetry that reminded him of a flower dancing on the breeze. Soft and perfect, her smile was gentle and her eyes sparkled with a happiness that reached out to Will, gladdening his heart.

Hempstead could even see himself, waiting as Marguerite spun toward him, reaching out to him as he had once reached out to her—

And then, as the music box abruptly stopped and a silence fell over the ballroom, the vision faded away, and Will Hempstead's eyes cleared. Before him, a few yards away,

Marguerite was curtseying low, her head bent demurely, her right hand on her skirt, her left daintily touching her bosom.

At last she rose to her feet, and her head came up so that her eyes met Will's. For a moment Will wasn't certain she even saw him, for there was an empty hollowness in her eyes that he'd never seen before. And then, once more, her mouth twisted into a parody of the sweet smile of her youth.

"Was I all right, Will?" she asked, her voice childlike and trembling with anxiety.

Will swallowed the lump that rose in his throat, then walked toward her, his hand outstretched. "You were fine, Miss Marguerite," he said, his voice breaking. "You were just fine. But I think it's time to go now."

Marguerite's smile faded, but then she nodded vaguely and took the arm that Will offered her. Pressing close to him, leaning her weight against the strength of his body, she started toward the door, then stopped and turned toward the row of chairs against the wall.

"Thank you," she said softly. "Thank you all for coming to watch me dance. But it's late now, and I have to go." Once more she curtseyed low. "Good night," she breathed, then turned away, and with Will Hempstead at her side, drifted out of the candlelit ballroom.

CHAPTER 29

The first gray light was streaking the horizon over the sea when at last the ambulances, followed by a long cortege of the townspeople's cars, crept slowly across the causeway and along the road toward Sea Oaks. Hours earlier a helicopter—its rotor clattering loudly in the night—had swept low over the channel, put down on the lawn in front of the mansion, and then, a few minutes later, had risen once more into the night sky. As it moved back across the channel, a murmur had rippled through the gathered crowd as word was passed along that Julie Devereaux had been taken off the island. A few people were certain she was dead, but most of them knew that whatever had happened, Julie must have survived. If she hadn't, there would have been no need for the helicopter. But when the helicopter didn't return, a numb silence had fallen over the crowd as they realized that the other children who had gone out to the island that day must have perished.

Alicia Mayhew was one of the first to arrive at the mansion, but as she brought her car to a halt on the lawn, she found herself strangely reluctant to go inside, for as long as she remained outside, she could still hold onto a tiny, fraying thread of hope that perhaps Jennifer was all right after all. But at last, steeling herself, she walked up the steps and crossed the veranda.

The front door stood open, almost as if to welcome expected guests into the house, but as Alicia stepped into the entry hall, she froze, her eyes fixed on the bloodstained floor, now lit by a floodlight that had been plugged into the generator beneath the stairs.

A thick, orange extension cord snaked up the staircase, and

Alicia, a strange detachment spreading through her mind, found herself following it.

She came to the third floor and paused outside the open double doors. Another floodlight stood in the center of the ballroom, its garish brilliance filling the room with a cold and shadowless light. As Alicia blinked in the glaring brightness, she heard a low moan and a muffled sob.

Holding her emotions in check, she stepped into the ballroom.

Even while two state troopers worked taking pictures of the macabre scene in the ballroom, Edith Sanders, her face streaked with tears, was already kneeling on the floor next to Kerry, her arms around her son as if she were trying to lend her own warmth to his cold body. Hal Sanders, his eyes vacant, his expression slack with shock and grief, stood next to his wife, one hand resting gently on her shoulder.

Alicia had started to turn away, uncomfortable at intruding upon their grief, when her eyes found Jennifer, sprawled out on the floor, her eyes wide as she gazed sightlessly up at the ceiling. Alicia felt her blood chill as she looked at her daughter, and then her knees buckled beneath her. She would have collapsed to the floor if Will Hempstead's arms hadn't reached out to her, supporting her as he eased her into a chair.

"I'm sorry," he breathed. "I wish you hadn't come here. There's no reason why any of you had to see this."

"Sorry?" Alicia echoed, her voice bleak. "If you'd listened to me this afternoon—" But then she fell silent, unable to go on.

"I know," Hempstead finally said as the silence in the room grew heavy. "But I couldn't imagine that Marguerite could do anything like this."

Alicia, whose eyes had remained fixed on her daughter's corpse, slowly turned to face the police chief. "Why?" she asked. "Why did it happen?"

Hempstead shook his head. "I don't know," he said at last. "And I'm not sure any of us will ever know."

Alicia's eyes hardened, and when she spoke again, her voice was bitter. "Where is she?" she asked.

Hempstead licked his lips nervously. "In her room," he said. "Frank Weaver's with her. She's been sitting there most of the night. She hasn't spoken at all since I took her out of here. She's just sitting there, staring off into space. I—well, I'm not sure she even knows what happened."

"Doesn't know?" Alicia asked hollowly, her suddenly dull eyes scanning the carnage in the room. "How can someone do this and not know they've done it?"

Once again Hempstead shook his head. "I can't tell you, Alicia," he replied. Then he drew her to her feet. "I'm taking you downstairs," he said. "I'll find someone to take you home—"

"No," Alicia interrupted. "I want to stay here with Jennifer. I can't stand her being here like this, all by herself. Please?" she asked, her eyes pleading with Hempstead. "Let me stay with her."

Hempstead hesitated, then nodded, and a moment later Alicia Mayhew, her eyes glistening with tears, eased herself onto the floor and silently took her daughter's cold hand in her own.

An hour later the ambulances were gone, one of them carrying the bodies of Kevin Devereaux and Ruby Carr, the other bearing Kerry Sanders and Jennifer Mayhew. The crowd on the lawn in front of the mansion had fallen silent as each of the bodies was borne out of the mansion. A few minutes later a ripple of whispered words passed from one pair of lips to another.

Marguerite Devereaux was being brought out of the house.

No one was certain what to expect, and once more a silence fell over them. And then the front door to Sea Oaks opened one more time, and Will Hempstead stepped out onto the veranda.

On his arm was Marguerite.

She stood still on the veranda for a moment, the rays of the rising sun falling full on her face.

Her hair, pulled back and coiled perfectly into the elegant French twist that she had worn for years, glistened brightly in the sunlight, and her face, free of any trace of a wrinkle, seemed far younger than her nearly fifty years. She was wearing a formal gown of pure white, with a cascade of sparkling rhinestones swirling over its bodice. The full skirt, overlaid with a cloud of tulle, dropped to her ankles, and from beneath the skirt the toes of white silk shoes peeped out.

But as she gazed out over the crowd of people she had known all her life, her eyes were vacant and empty.

"It's time to go, Miss Marguerite," Hempstead whispered so softly that nobody but she could hear him. She hesitated only a split second, then took his arm and, her step even and graceful, moved serenely across the veranda.

She paused, curtseyed low, and with Will Hempstead at her side, moved down the steps and across the lawn to the waiting police car.

Emmaline Carr closed the door of her tiny cabin in the clearing behind Wither's Pond and began making her way along the path to the road that would take her into the village. She, like most of the people in Devereaux, had been up all night long. She'd first walked into the village several hours ago, when the wailing of sirens had rent the peace that followed the storm.

She'd known what it meant at once, for all that day—ever since Jeff Devereaux and Toby Martin had come to visit her—she'd had a certain feeling that at last the evil seeds that Helena Devereaux had sown so many years ago had finally borne fruit. She'd known that her sister was dead, but even in her own mind she didn't blame Marguerite. As far as Emmaline was concerned, Marguerite was just as much a victim as Ruby, and as she'd walked toward the village, all she felt for Marguerite was pity.

She'd moved silently through the crowd gathered at the mainland end of the causeway, listening quietly as bits and pieces of news filtered through—coming over the radio from the island to the state police car, then spreading through the crowd. As dawn began to break, and the stream of automobiles moved out to the island, she had turned away, returning to her cabin to sit alone and think.

Finally she'd made up her mind.

She'd changed her clothes, putting on her best dress—the black one with the white collar and the mother-of-pearl buttons—tucked her good shoes into her large handbag, and slipped her feet into a pair of rubber boots. Then, as the sun came up and the heat of the morning began, she started toward town again.

Water dripped from the moss that covered the trees, and everywhere wisps of steam rose from the sodden ground. Emmaline could hear the brush moving as small animals abandoned the protection of their burrows to forage in the undergrowth, and occasionally she saw a snake slithering out of her path. She moved stolidly onward, ignoring the aching of her legs and the tiredness in her bones.

At last she came to the tiny clinic—only five rooms carved out of what had once been the plantation offices, but which had long since been divided into small stores, most of which lay vacant. She paused on the sidewalk for a moment, taking off her muddy boots and putting on the sturdy black shoes she wore only to church on Sunday. Leaving her boots outside, she stepped into the waiting room of the clinic.

Jeff Devereaux, his clothes filthy and his face smudged with dirt and tears, sat alone on a sagging vinyl-covered sofa, his eyes fixed on the floor. Emmaline watched him for a moment, then moved across the room and settled herself on the sofa, slipping her arm around the boy.

Jeff looked up, but there was no surprise in his eyes when he saw Emmaline. "She killed them," he said, his voice desolate. "She killed my dad, and Ruby, and Kerry, and Jennifer."

"I know," Emmaline crooned, drawing him closer. "But it warn't her, not really. It was your grandmother that did it, and you mustn't hate your auntie."

Jeff's chin trembled. "But she did kill them," he said. "And she almost killed Julie too. I hate her. I hate her, and I hope they kill her for what she did."

"There, there," Emmaline murmured, hiding her own anger in an effort to comfort him. "You mustn't say that. You have to forgive people for their sins, because sometimes they just can't help themselves. And that was the way your auntie was. She just couldn't help herself."

Jeff bit his lip, but then gave in to his tears once more, burying his face in Emmaline's bosom. She sat silently, holding him and gently patting his back until his sobs eased, then hugged him tight for a moment. "You stay here," she said. "I'm gonna find out how your sister is and then I'll be back. And don't you worry, you hear me? 'Cause from now on I'm gonna take care of you."

She rose to her feet, and Jeff, nodding mutely, stayed where he was. Emmaline went to the partition that separated the waiting room from the office and rapped sharply on the glass. A harried-looking nurse glanced up from a typewriter, then slid the partition open. "Unless it's an emergency—" she began, but Emmaline shook her head.

"I need to know about Julie Devereaux," she said.

The nurse looked at Emmaline uncertainly, her brows gathering into a doubtful frown. "I'm sorry, Emmaline, but since you're not a relative . . ." Her voice trailed off, and she shrugged helplessly.

Emmaline's eyes narrowed. "I'm her nanny," she said, her tone almost daring the nurse to challenge her. "She and the boy ain't got nobody else but me, and I mean to find out what's goin' on with her."

The nurse still hesitated. Emmaline's tone softened. "Please, miss," she said. "You know who I am, and you know my sister did for Miss Marguerite all her life. And she raised Mr. Kevin up, too, till Miz Helena sent him away. But Ruby's dead now, and there ain't anybody else to do for the little ones. Please?"

Still the nurse hesitated, then seemed to come to a decision. "Of course," she said, getting up from the desk and coming around to open the door for Emmaline. "She's in here," she went on, leading Emmaline down the hall. "Try not to disturb her. She woke up a few minutes ago, but I think she went back to sleep." Then, for the first time, she smiled at Emmaline. "You're the only one who's come, you know," she said. "Everyone else in town—"

"Everyone else has their own worries right now," Emmaline

finished for her. "And they going to blame the children, just because their name be Devereaux. I mean to see to it these children aren't hurt any more than they already been. Ain't much, but it's what Ruby would have wanted me to do."

The nurse held the door open, and Emmaline stepped through. "I'll speak to the doctor," she said as she closed the door. "I'm sure he'll understand." But as the nurse moved away from the little room where Julie lay, she wasn't sure Emmaline had even heard her words. The old woman was already bent over Julie's sleeping form, her fingers gently stroking the unconscious girl's forehead.

The doctor came in a few minutes later. Emmaline, sitting close by the bed, her gnarled old hand covering Julie's smooth young fingers, looked up, her eyes silently asking her question.

"She's going to be all right," the doctor said softly. "Both her hips are broken, but we can fix that. She'll take a long time to recover and need a lot of help."

"I can give her that," Emmaline replied. "You just let me know what needs to be done and—" She fell silent as she felt a tiny motion beneath her fingers. The doctor immediately forgotten, she looked down at Julie's face just as the girl's eyes blinked, then came open. Julie looked up at Emmaline, her eyes twin pools of dark terror.

"It's all right," Emmaline whispered, bending her head low to whisper in Julie's ear. "It's all over now. You gonna be all right. Emmaline's here to see to that."

Julie's jaw worked for a moment, and she managed to speak, her voice croaking softly out of her dry throat. "But who . . . who are you?"

"I'm Emmaline," the old woman replied. "Didn't Ruby ever tell you about me?" Julie was still for a moment, then her head moved a fraction of an inch. "Well, don't you worry 'bout that. Alls that matters now is that I'm here."

There was a sound in the hall outside the room then, and Emmaline looked up. Her dark eyes narrowed to slits as she recognized Marguerite Devereaux sitting in a wheelchair, Will Hempstead behind her. "What she doin' here?" Emmaline demanded, her voice low, but heavy with indignation. "After what she done, why ain't she in jail?"

"She doesn't know what happened," Hempstead replied. His attention shifted to the doctor next to Julie's bed. "She doesn't know anything anymore. We have to keep her here until they can send a team down from the hospital in Beaufort."

Bitter words formed on Emmaline's lips, but before she could speak them, Marguerite's empty eyes suddenly seemed to focus. As her gaze narrowed, a hard glint of anger flashed briefly.

"Ruby!" she said, her mother's voice rasping from her throat, her head jerking angrily toward the doctor. "Who is this man? What is he doing here? How many times have I told you that Marguerite mustn't have any visitors?"

Emmaline said nothing, for Julie's hand had tightened on her own, and when she looked down, Julie had twisted her head so that she was staring at her aunt. Her face was ashen, but the terror in her eyes was suddenly gone.

As Julie's eyes locked with her aunt's, her expression slowly began to change. She frowned, as if something were happening inside her that she didn't understand. And then, so quickly that Emmaline wasn't sure she'd seen it at all, Julie's eyes flashed with a hatred so pure it seemed as though the room itself had chilled. Emmaline shivered, but when she looked back at Julie, the girl's expression seemed merely puzzled.

At last Julie's head dropped back to the pillow and she stared once again up at the ceiling. "Just take her away," she whispered. "I don't want to see her anymore. Please . . ."

As Julie's eyes closed, Emmaline turned back to Marguerite. Her forehead, too, was furrowed with uncertainty, and there was an oddly curious look in her eyes, as if, deep within her, something was awakening, or a memory was stirring. But the vacant look of a moment ago was gone.

She remembers, Emmaline thought to herself as Will Hempstead wheeled Marguerite on down the hall. *She remembers it all, and she knows what she did.*

Will Hempstead pushed the wheelchair into the next room, where the nurse stood waiting. But as he started to ease the chair through the door, Marguerite put out her hand to stop him, her eyes searching his beseechingly. "No," she said, her voice once more her own. "I—I can't stay here. I have to go home. There's so much I have to do. Mama needs me, and there are my girls to think of. I can't leave my girls, you know. I just can't!"

Will Hempstead said nothing, a hard knot of sorrow constricting his throat.

"It's all right, Miss Devereaux," the nurse said. "We have a lovely room for you, and we're going to take such good care of you." Gently removing Marguerite's hand from the doorframe, she pushed the chair into the room and helped Marguerite out of it. Her fingers working quickly, she unzipped the back of Marguerite's dress, and as the gown crumpled to the floor, slipped a robe over her shoulders. "Now, let's get into bed," she crooned, easing Marguerite onto the metal hospital bed, and pulling the sheet over her. "Doctor will be in in a minute, and everything will be fine." She gestured Will Hempstead back into the hall, then pulled the door closed behind her, never noticing that even as she put Marguerite into the bed, the other woman's eyes, glistening with tears, never left the ball gown lying in a shapeless mass on the floor.

Five minutes later, when the doctor slipped into Marguerite's room to administer a sedative, it was already too late.

The belt of her robe knotted tightly around her broken neck, Marguerite's body swung from the sprinkler pipe that ran across the room just below the ceiling. A few inches above the ruined dress, her feet dangled helplessly, still clad in the white silk dancing slippers.

EPILOGUE

Jeff Devereaux paused at the end of the causeway, sitting in the small convertible that had been Julie's present for him on his eighteenth birthday. He gazed in something like wonder at the mansion that still dominated the island, though now it was far from being the only residence there. In fact, there were more than a hundred condominiums dotting the shore now, clustered in low groupings that blended well into the stands of pines that still remained after the golf course had been carved out of the undergrowth. The swamp had been tamed, turned into a series of water traps on the golf course, and a small creek connected the chain of ponds, eventually draining into the sea at the south end of the island, where a marina was now in the process of being built. Even from here Jeff could hear the rumble of the dredging machinery as a cove was cut to protect the small craft that would one day be moored there from the tropical storms that swept in from the sea each year, threatening the island but never destroying it.

Indeed, it seemed to Jeff as if nothing could ever destroy the island, and now, ten years after that final night of terror when the pieces of his aunt's life had shattered forever, he was no longer even certain he wanted the island destroyed.

But it hadn't always been that way.

When Emmaline Carr had finally taken him back to Sea Oaks, he'd shrunk away from the house, his whole body shivering with fear. But Emmaline had led him inside, talking to him constantly, her low voice reassuring him as she led him from room to room, showing him that nothing of his aunt or his grandmother remained.

Even the chair lift was gone.

Finally, his heart thumping wildly, Emmaline had taken him up to the ballroom. He hadn't wanted to go, not after the stories he had heard about what Will Hempstead found there, but Emmaline had shown him that it was just a room. The floor had been scrubbed clean, and the furniture—even the piano—removed. In the bright daylight it had been nothing more than a large and empty room.

"It's only a house," Emmaline explained to him that evening as they sat in the kitchen eating the supper she'd cooked. "Ain't nothin' here for you to be afraid of. Ain't no ghosts—"

"But Ruby said—" Jeff protested, and Emmaline had cut him off.

"Ruby always had stories," Emmaline said firmly. "But that's all they was—just stories. All you saw out there was your auntie, and now she's been buried." Then she'd looked directly at him, her dark eyes deep and holding a warmth Jeff hadn't felt since his mother died. "This is your house now, Jeff. Yours and Julie's. Bad things happen in lots of houses, but that don't mean we can just tear them down. We got to go on livin' in them and try to make 'em better, that's all. And that's what we're goin' to do here. In a little while we're goin' to bring your sister home and you and me are gonna make things all right for her again. And everything else, we're gonna put behind us."

Jeff hadn't quite understood at the time. And for a while—for more than a year—he'd had terrible nightmares in the house, dark dreams in which he heard his aunt's limping footsteps prowling the hall outside his door, and saw her feverish eyes glaring at him out of the blackness. But always Emmaline had been there. Eventually the dreams had stopped.

And the house had changed, for Sam Waterman had gone ahead with all of Kevin's plans, acting as trustee for the Devereaux estate. By the end of the first year the mansion had been remodeled and a manager hired, along with a chef and a small staff.

Devereaux Inn was an instant success, and by the third year the development of the rest of the island had begun.

In the fourth year, when he was twelve and Julie was nineteen, he'd gone away to private school.

"Don't believe in that," Emmaline had protested when he and Julie had first talked to her about it. "Seems to me a boy your age ought to be at home, where someone can look after him. And your grandma sent your papa away to school," she added darkly.

"It's not the same," Julie argued. "Daddy didn't want to go away, and nobody's sending Jeff away. It was his idea. He wants to go."

Emmaline's eyes had shifted suspiciously to Jeff. He was tall for his age, and looked closer to fifteen than twelve. Nor was his maturity only on the surface. Emmaline had long suspected that Jeff had grown up on that night he'd had to escape from the house to save his sister's life.

"It's true," he'd said. "When I'm twenty-one I'm going to have to take care of this whole place. Mr. Waterman can't go on taking care of us for the rest of our lives, and if I'm going to know what I'm doing, I need a good education." When Emmaline's expression hadn't changed, he'd pushed harder. "I've already skipped a whole grade. And there's a school in Charleston I can go to. I can come home on weekends and Christmas and summer vacation and—"

"And so you'd better go," Emmaline had agreed, at last convinced that it had, indeed, been Jeff's own idea. But she'd made him promise that if he didn't like it, he'd come home again. He'd promised, but, as all three of them had known when he made it, had never felt like invoking it.

Now he'd graduated, and in the fall would be starting at the University of Texas to study hotel management. But for this summer he was back once more at Sea Oaks. He drove slowly up the paved road that now wound along the edge of the golf course, giving up the car to one of the parking attendants at the entrance to the mansion itself. Julie, her eyes glistening with happiness, was waiting for him on the veranda, Emmaline at her side.

Julie hurried down the steps, her limp barely perceptible, and threw herself into her brother's arms. He was six inches taller than she now, and her arms barely reached around his broad chest, but she squeezed him tight, then looked mischievously up at him.

"You didn't drive too fast, did you?" she asked. "I didn't get you that car to kill yourself in."

"You shouldn't have gotten it at all," Jeff replied, his brows arching in mock severity. "I can think of a hundred things we need to spend money on around here—"

"And we are!" Julie exclaimed. "Everything that needs to be done gets done, and you know it. And if you don't think we can afford a nice car for you, you can go over the books yourself."

"All right, all right," Jeff protested, knowing as well as she did that the resort was making everyone in town as rich as they wanted to be. "Let go of me so I can kiss Emmaline, and then I want to know everything that's happening."

The three of them had gone through the entire mansion, and only Emmaline had found anything to criticize. But both Jeff and Julie had long since realized that no matter what they did, the housekeeping staff would never come up to Emmaline's standards. Finally, when her sharp eyes found a single smudge on one of the brass sconces in the new dining room in the east wing that had been completed the winter before, Jeff had had enough. "Why don't we all go out and inspect *your* house?" he suggested, and Emmaline glared at him as if he were still eight years old.

"This ain't no shack behind Wither's Pond," she observed. "And you ain't so grown up I can't give you a good spanking, either!"

Finally the three of them had retreated to the third floor of the original house, where an apartment had been built in the space that had once been the ballroom. They settled themselves on the balcony outside the open French doors and gazed out over the island, silently taking in all the changes that had occurred over the last decade.

"It's not like it was when we first came here, is it?" Julie finally asked after Emmaline had gone inside to leave them alone. Her voice was quiet, and trembling slightly as she remembered those first weeks on the island.

Jeff shuddered as the old memories stirred in him, then

shook his head. "And the more it changes, the better I like it." He turned to face his sister. "Are you sorry we stayed?"

Julie was silent for a moment. For her, coming back to the house had been even worse than for Jeff. She hadn't been able to walk at all for the first few months, and the only thing that had made it even slightly bearable was that Emmaline had set up a bed for her in the little room off the kitchen, so that even at night she was never alone.

Whenever she awoke at night from the dreams, Emmaline was always there, already awake, willing to stay up with her all night if necessary, often bringing Jeff down, too, the three of them sitting up as she and Jeff fought the fears the darkness always seemed to bring. But slowly her wounds had healed, and as she began to learn to walk again—Emmaline spending endless hours exercising and massaging her legs— the scars in her mind began to heal over too. "No," she said at last. "Emmaline was right. If we hadn't come back, we probably wouldn't ever have gotten over what happened."

"Have you gotten over it?" Jeff asked pointedly.

Julie's eyes clouded for a moment and she bit her lip. "I—I don't know," she confessed. "Can anyone really ever get over something like that?" Then she brightened. "I've started dancing again. Did I tell you?"

Jeff shook his head.

"Oh, it's not much. But there's an exercise bar in the gym in the golf club, and one day when I was down there, I just couldn't resist." She grinned ruefully. "I'm never going to play Lincoln Center, but I enjoy it." Then her eyes met Jeff's. "I'm even thinking of starting to teach."

A cold finger reached out of the warm evening and touched Jeff's spine.

Jeff woke up in the darkness of the warm spring night, uncertain about what had disturbed his sleep. He lay in bed for a few minutes, listening to the quiet of the house. It had to be after two, for there was no music drifting up from the lounge and no laughter from the garden around the swimming pool that now lay behind the building. And yet, very dimly, barely audible above the chirpings of the frogs and insects, he could hear something.

A tinkling sound, like a music box.

He got out of bed, slipping his arms into the sleeves of a light robe, and stepped out onto the balcony.

Moonlight glimmered on the smooth surface of the sea, and he could hear the gentle wash of waves against the beach.

And the melody of the music box was louder.

Almost against his will he turned to gaze down into the family cemetery, surrounded now by a low wrought-iron fence, protected by a locked gate from the wanderings of the hotel's guests. For a moment he saw nothing, but then his eyes adjusted to the darkness and he saw once more the pale, ghostly figure he hadn't seen in more than a decade.

But this time, he knew, it was not the ghostly image of his grandmother, or even of his aunt.

He watched sadly, his eyes filling with tears, as his sister moved stiffly around the marble crypt in which her ancestors were interred.

ENTER THE TERRIFYING
WORLD OF
JOHN SAUL

A scream shatters the peaceful night of a sleepy town, a mysterious stranger awakens to seek vengeance. . . . Once again, with expert, chillingly demonic skill, John Saul draws the reader into his world of utter fear. The author of twelve novels of psychological and supernatural suspense—all million copy *New York Times* bestsellers—John Saul is unequaled in his power to weave the haunted past and the troubled present into a web of pure, cold terror.

THE GOD PROJECT

Something is happening to the children of Eastbury, Mas-
sachusetts . . . something that strikes at the heart of every parent's
darkest fears. For Sally Montgomery, the grief over the sudden
death of her infant daughter is only the beginning. For Lucy Cor-
liss, her son Randy is her life. Then one day, Randy doesn't come
home. And the terror begins . . .

A horn honked, pulling Randy out of his reverie, and he realized he was alone on the block. He looked at the watch his father
had given him for his ninth birthday. It was nearly eight thirty. If he
didn't hurry, he was going to be late for school. Then he heard a
voice calling to him.

"Randy! Randy Corliss!"

A blue car, a car he didn't recognize, was standing by the curb.
A woman was smiling at him from the driver's seat. He approached
the car hesitantly, clutching his lunch box.

"Hi, Randy," the woman said.

"Who are you?" Randy stood back from the car, remembering
his mother's warnings about never talking to strangers.

"My name's Miss Bowen. Louise Bowen. I came to get you."

"Get me?" Randy asked. "Why?"

"For your father," the woman said. Randy's heart beat faster.
His father? His father had sent this woman? Was it really going to
happen, finally? "He wanted me to pick you up at home," he heard
the woman say, "but I was late. I'm sorry."

"That's all right," Randy said. He moved closer to the car.
"Are you taking me to Daddy's house?"

The woman reached across and pushed the passenger door
open. "In a little while," she promised. "Get in."

Randy knew he shouldn't get in the car, knew he should turn
around and run to the nearest house, looking for help. It was things
like this—strangers offering to give you a ride—that his mother had
talked to him about ever since he was a little boy.

But this was different. This was a friend of his father's. She had to be, because she seemed to know all about his plans to go live with his father, and his father's plans to take him away from his mother. Besides, it was always men his mother warned him about, never women. He looked at the woman once more. Her brown eyes were twinkling at him, and her smile made him feel like she was sharing an adventure with him. He made up his mind and got into the car, pulling the door closed behind him. The car moved away from the curb.

"Where are we going?" Randy asked.

Louise Bowen glanced over at the boy sitting expectantly on the seat beside her. He was every bit as attractive as the pictures she had been shown, his eyes almost green, with dark, wavy hair framing his pugnacious, snub-nosed face. His body was sturdy, and though she was a stranger to him, he didn't seem to be the least bit frightened of her. Instinctively, Louise liked Randy Corliss.

"We're going to your new school."

Randy frowned. New school? If he was going to a new school, why wasn't his father taking him? The woman seemed to hear him, even though he hadn't spoken out loud.

"You'll see your father very soon. But for a few days, until he gets everything worked out with your mother, you'll be staying at the school. You'll like it there," she promised. "It's a special school, just for little boys like you, and you'll have lots of new friends. Doesn't that sound exciting?"

Randy nodded uncertainly, no longer sure he should have gotten in the car. Still, when he thought about it, it made sense. His father had told him there would be lots of problems when the time came for him to move away from his mother's. And his father had told him he would be going to a new school. And today was the day.

Randy settled down in the seat and glanced out the window. They were heading out of Eastbury on the road toward Langston. That was where his father lived, so everything was all right.

Except that it didn't quite *feel* all right. Deep inside, Randy had a strange sense of something being very wrong.

For two very different families haunted by very similar fears, THE GOD PROJECT has only just begun to work its lethal conspiracy of silence and fear. And for the reader, John Saul has produced a mind-numbing tale of evil unchecked.

NATHANIEL

Prairie Bend: brilliant summers amid golden fields, killing winters of razorlike cold. A peaceful, neighborly village, darkened by legends of death . . . legends of Nathaniel. Some residents say he is simply a folk tale, others swear he is a terrifying spirit. And soon—very soon—some will come to believe that Nathaniel lives . . .

Shivering, Michael set himself a destination now and began walking along the edges of the pastures, the woods on his right, climbing each fence as he came to it. Sooner than he would have expected, the woods curved away to the right, following the course of the river as it deviated from its southeastern flow to curl around the village. Ahead of him he could see the scattered twinkling lights of Prairie Bend. For a moment, he considered going into the village, but then, as he looked off to the southeast, he changed his mind, for there, seeming almost to glow in the moonlight, was the hulking shape of Findley's barn.

That, Michael knew, was where he was going.

He cut diagonally across the field, then darted across the deserted highway and into another field. He moved quickly now, feeling exposed in the emptiness with the full moon shining down on him. Ten minutes later he had crossed the field and come once more to the highway, this time as it emerged from the village. Across the street, he could see Ben Findley's driveway and, at its end, the little house, and the barn.

He considered trying to go down the driveway and around the house, but quickly abandoned the idea. A light showed dimly from behind a curtained window, and he had a sudden vision of old man Findley, his gun cradled in his arms, standing in silhouette at the front door.

Staying on the north side of the road, he continued moving eastward until he came abreast of his own driveway. He waited a few minutes, wondering whether perhaps he shouldn't go back to his grandparents'. In the end, though, he crossed the road and started down the drive to the abandoned house that was about to become his home. As he came into the overgrown yard, he stopped to stare at the house. Even had he not known that it was empty, he could have sensed that it was. In contrast to the other houses he had passed that night, which all seemed to radiate life from within, this house—his house—gave off only a sense of loneliness that made Michael shiver again in the night and hurry quickly past it.

His progress slowed as he plunged into the weed-choked pastures that lay between the house and the river, but he was determined to stay away from the fence separating Findley's property from their own until the old man's barn could conceal him from the same man's prying eyes. It wasn't until he was near the river that he finally felt safe enough to slip between the strands of barbed wire that fenced off the Findley property and begin doubling back toward the barn that had become his goal.

He could feel it now, feel the strange sense of familiarity he had felt that afternoon, only it was stronger here, pulling him forward through the night. He didn't try to resist it, though there was something vaguely frightening about it. Frightening but exciting. There was a sense of discovery, almost a sense of memory. And his headache, the throbbing pain that had been with him all evening, was gone.

He came up to the barn and paused. There should be a door just around the corner, a door with a bar on it. He didn't understand how he knew it was there, for he'd never seen that side of the barn, but he *knew*. He started toward the corner of the barn, his steps sure, the uncertainty he'd felt a few minutes ago erased.

Around the corner, just as he knew it would be, he found the door, held securely shut by a heavy wooden beam resting in a pair of wrought-iron brackets. Without hesitation, Michael lifted the bar out of its brackets and propped it carefully against the wall. As he pulled the door open, no squeaking hinges betrayed his presence. Though the barn was nearly pitch dark inside, it wasn't the kind of eerie darkness the woods by the river had held, at least not for Michael. For Michael, it was an inviting darkness.

He stepped into the barn.

He waited, half expectantly, as the darkness seeped into him, enveloping him within its folds. And then something reached out of the darkness and touched him.

Nathaniel's call to Michael Hall, who has just lost his father in a tragic accident, draws the boy further into the barn and under his spell. There—and beyond—Michael will faithfully follow Nathaniel's voice to the edge of terror.

BRAINCHILD

One hundred years ago in La Paloma a terrible deed was done, and a cry for vengeance pierced the night. Now, that evil still lives, and that vengeance waits . . . waits for Alex Lonsdale, one of the most popular boys in La Paloma. Because horrible things can happen— even to nice kids like Alex. . . .

Alex jockeyed the Mustang around Bob Carey's Porsche, then put it in drive and gunned the engine. The rear wheels spun on the loose gravel for a moment, then caught, and the car shot forward, down the Evanses' driveway and into Hacienda Drive.

Alex wasn't sure how long Lisa had been walking—it seemed as though it had taken him forever to get dressed and search the house. She could be almost home by now.

He pressed the accelerator, and the car picked up speed. He hugged the wall of the ravine on the first curve, but the car fishtailed slightly, and he had to steer into the skid to regain control. Then he hit a straight stretch and pushed his speed up to seventy. Coming up fast was an S curve that was posted at thirty miles an hour, but he knew they always left a big margin for safety. He slowed to sixty as he started into the first turn.

And then he saw her.

She was standing on the side of the road, her green dress glowing brightly in his headlights, staring at him with terrified eyes.

Or did he just imagine that? Was he already that close to her?

Time suddenly slowed down, and he slammed his foot on the brake.

Too late. He was going to hit her.

It would have been all right if she'd been on the inside of the curve. He'd have swept around her, and she'd have been safe. But now he was skidding right toward her . . .

Turn into it. He had to turn into it!

Taking his foot off the brake, he steered to the right, and suddenly felt the tires grab the pavement.

Lisa was only a few yards away.

And beyond Lisa, almost lost in the darkness, something else.

A face, old and wrinkled, framed with white hair. And the eyes in the face were glaring at him with an intensity he could almost feel.

It was the face that finally made him lose all control of the car.

An ancient, weathered face, a face filled with an unspeakable loathing, looming in the darkness.

At the last possible moment, he wrenched the wheel to the left, and the Mustang responded, slewing around Lisa, charging across the pavement, leading for the ditch and the wall of the ravine beyond.

Straighten it out!

He spun the wheel the other way.

Too far.

The car burst through the guardrail and hurtled over the edge of the ravine.

"Lisaaaa . . ."

Now Alex needs a miracle and thanks to a brilliant doctor, Alex comes back from the brink of death. He seems the same, but in his heart there is a coldness. And if his friends and family could see inside his brain, they would be terrified. . . .

HELLFIRE

Pity the dead . . . one hundred years ago eleven innocent lives were taken in a fire that raged through the mill. That day the iron doors slammed shut—forever. Now, the powerful Sturgiss family of the sleepy town of Westover, Massachusetts is about to unlock those doors to the past. Now comes the time to pray for the living.

The silence of the building seemed to gather around her, and slowly Beth felt the beginnings of fear.

And then she began to feel something else.

Once again, she felt that strange certainty that the mill was not empty.

"D-Daddy?" she called softly, stepping through the door. "Are you here?"

She felt a slight trickle of sweat begin to slide down her spine, and fought a sudden trembling in her knees.

Then, as she listened to the silence, she heard something.

A rustling sound, from up above.

Beth froze, her heart pounding.

And then she heard it again.

She looked up.

With a sudden burst of flapping wings, a pigeon took off from one of the rafters, circled, then soared out through a gap between the boards over one of the windows.

Beth stood still, waiting for her heartbeat to calm. As she looked around, her eyes fixed on the top of a stairwell at the far end of the building.

He was downstairs. That's why he hasn't heard her. He was down in the basement.

Resolutely, she started across the vast emptiness of the building. As she reached the middle of the floor, she felt suddenly exposed, and had an urge to run.

But there was nothing to be afraid of. There was nothing in the mill except herself, and some birds.

And downstairs, her father.

After what seemed like an eternity, she reached the top of the stairs, and peered uncertainly into the darkness below.

Her own shadow preceded her down the steep flight of steps, and only a little spilled over the staircase to illuminate the nearer parts of the vast basement.

"Daddy?" Beth whispered. But the sound was so quiet, even she could barely hear it.

And then there was something else, coming on the heels of her own voice.

Another sound, fainter than the one her own voice had made, coming from below.

Something was moving in the darkness.

Once again Beth's heart began to pound, but she remained where she was, forcing back the panic that threatened to overcome her.

Finally, when she heard nothing more, she moved slowly down the steps, until she could place a foot on the basement floor.

She listened, and after a moment, as the darkness began closing in on her, the sound repeated itself.

Panic surged through her. All her instincts told her to run, to flee back up the stairs and out into the daylight. But when she tried to move, her legs refused to obey her, and she remained where she was, paralyzed.

Once again the sound came. This time, though it was almost inaudible, Beth thought she recognized a word.

"Beeetthh . . ."

Her name. It was as if someone had called her name.

"D-Daddy?" she whispered again. "Daddy, is that you?"

There was another silence, and Beth strained once more to see into the darkness surrounding her.

In the distance, barely visible, she thought she could see a flickering of light.

And then she froze, her voice strangling as the sound came again, like a winter wind sighing in the trees.

"Aaaammmyyyy . . ."

Beth gazed fearfully into the blackness for several long seconds. Then, when the sound was not repeated, her panic began to subside. At last she was able to speak again, though her voice still trembled. "Is someone there?"

In the far distance, the light flickered again, and she heard something else.

Footsteps, approaching out of the darkness.

The seconds crept by, and the light bobbed nearer.

And once more, the whispering voice, barely audible, danced around her.

"Aaaammmyy . . ."

For Beth Rogers, the voice seems like a nightmare, yet not even a little girl's fears can imagine the unearthly fury that awaits her in the old, deserted mill. Soon all of Westover will be prey to the forces of darkness that wait beyond those padlocked doors.

THE UNWANTED

Cassie Winslow, lonely and frightened, has come to False Harbor, Cape Cod to live with her father—whom she barely knows—and his family. For Cassie, the strange, unsettling dreams that come to her suddenly are merely the beginning . . . for very soon, Cassie will come to know the terrifying powers that are her gift.

Cassie awoke in the blackness of the hours before dawn, her heart thumping, her skin damp with a cold sweat that made her shiver. For a moment she didn't know where she was. Then, as she listened to the unfamiliar sound of surf pounding in the distance, the dream began to fade away, and she remembered where she was.

She was in False Harbor, and this was where she lived now. In the room next to her, her stepsister was asleep, and down the hall her father was in bed with her stepmother.

Then why did she feel so alone?

It was the dream, of course.

It had come to her again in the night. Again she had seen the strange woman who should have been her mother but was not.

Again, as Cassie watched in horror, the car burst into flames, and Cassie, vaguely aware that she was in a dream, had expected to wake up, as she had each time the nightmare had come to her.

This time, though she wanted to turn and run, she stood where she was, watching the car burn.

This time there had been no laughter shrieking from the woman's lips, no sound of screams, no noise at all. The flames had risen from the car in an eerie silence, and then, just as Cassie was about to turn away, the stranger had suddenly emerged from the car.

Clad in black, the figure had stood perfectly still, untouched by the flames that raged around her. Slowly, she raised one hand. Her lips moved and a single word drifted over the crowded freeway, came directly to Cassie's ears over the faceless mass of people streaming by in their cars.

"Cassandra . . ."

The word hung in the air for a moment. Then the woman

turned, and as soundlessly as she had emerged, stepped back into the flames.

Instinctively Cassie had started toward her, wanting to pull her back from the flames, wanting to save her.

The silence of the dream was shattered then by the blaring of a horn and the screaming of tires skidding on pavement.

Cassie looked up just in time to see a truck bearing down on her, the enormous grill of its radiator only inches from her face.

As the truck smashed into her she woke up, her own scream of terror choked in her throat.

Her heartbeat began to slow, and her shivering stopped. Now the room seemed to close in on her, and she found it hard to breathe. Slipping out of bed, she crossed to the window at the far end of the narrow room and lifted it open. As she was about to go back to bed, a movement in the darkness outside caught her eye.

She looked down into the cemetery on the other side of the back fence. At first she saw nothing. Then she sensed the movement again, and a dark figure came into view. Clad in black, perfectly silent, a woman stood in the shadows cast by the headstones.

Time seemed to suspend itself.

And then the figure raised one hand. Once more Cassie heard a single word drift almost inaudibly above the pounding of the surf from the beach a few blocks away.

"Cassandra . . ."

Cassie remained where she was, her eyes closed as she strained to recapture the sound of her name, but now there was only the pulsing drone of the surf. And when she reopened her eyes a few seconds later and looked once more into the graveyard, she saw nothing.

The strange figure that had stepped out of the shadows was gone.

She went back to her bed and pulled the covers close around her. For a long time she lay still, wondering if perhaps she'd only imagined it all.

Perhaps she hadn't even left the bed, and had only dreamed that she'd seen the woman in the graveyard.

But the woman in the graveyard had been the woman in her dream. But she didn't really exist.

Did she?

Cassie's dreams will alienate her from the other kids, as will her strange bond with crazy old Miranda Sikes—for both feel un-wanted. And in the village of False Harbor, nothing will ever be the same as John Saul spins his supernatural spell.

THE UNLOVED

The splendid isolation of a picturesque island off the South Carolina coast seems like paradise, but for Kevin Devereaux—who returns with his family to help care for his aged and ailing mother, Helena—homecoming will mean a frightening descent into his darkest nightmares . . .

"Why are you here?" he heard her demand. "You know I don't want you here!"

He tried to think, tried to remember where he was. He looked around furtively, hoping the woman wouldn't see his eyes flickering about as if he might be searching for a means to escape.

The room around him looked strange—unfinished—the rough wood of its framing exposed under the tattered remains of crumbling tarpaper. He'd been in this place before—he knew that now. Still, he didn't know where the room was, or what it might be.

But he knew the woman was angry with him again, and in the deepest recesses of his mind, he knew what was going to happen next.

The woman was going to kill him.

He wanted to cry out for help, but when he opened his mouth, no scream emerged. His throat constricted, cutting off his breath, and he knew if he couldn't fight the panic growing within him, he would strangle on his own fear.

The woman took a step toward him, and he cowered, huddling back against the wall. A slick sheen of icy sweat chilled his back, then he felt cold droplets creeping down his arms. A shiver passed over him, and a small whimper escaped his lips.

His sister.

Maybe his sister would come and rescue him.

But she was gone—something had happened to her, and he was alone now.

Alone with his mother.

He looked fearfully up.

She seemed to tower above him, her skirt held back as if she were afraid it might brush against him and be soiled. Her hands were hidden in the folds of the skirt, but he knew what they held.

The axe. The axe she would kill him with.

He could see it then—its curved blades glinting in the light from the doorway, its long wooden handle clutched in his mother's hands. She wasn't speaking to him now, only staring at him. But she didn't need to speak, for he knew what she wanted, knew what she'd always wanted.

"Love me," he whispered, his voice so tremulous that he could hear the words wither away as quickly as they left his lips. "Please love me . . ."

His mother didn't hear. She never heard, no matter how many times he begged her, no matter how often he tried to tell her he was sorry for what he'd done. He would apologize for anything—he knew that. If only she would hear him, he'd tell her whatever she wanted to hear. But even as he tried once more, he knew she wasn't hearing, didn't want to hear.

She only wanted to be rid of him.

The axe began to move now, rising above him, quivering slightly, as if the blade itself could anticipate the splitting of his skull, the crushing of his bones as they gave way beneath the weapon's weight. He could see the steel begin its slow descent, and time seemed to stand still.

He had to do something—had to move away, had to ward off the blow. He tried to raise his arms, but even the air around him seemed thick and unyielding now, and the blade was moving much faster than he was.

Then the axe crashed into his skull, and suddenly nothing made sense anymore. Everything had turned upside down.

It was his mother who cowered on the floor, gazing fearfully up at him as he brought the blade slashing down upon her.

It was he who felt the small jar of resistance as the axe struck her skull, then moved on, splitting her head like a melon. A haze of red rose up before him, and he felt fragments of her brains splatter against his face.

He opened his mouth and, finally, screamed—

The horror is a dream, only a dream. Or so Kevin thinks. Until Helena, suddenly, horribly, dies inside the locked nursery. And now there is no escape, as tortured spirits from the sinister past rise up to tell the true terror of the unloved.

CREATURE

A terrible secret lurks beneath the wholesome surface of Silverdale, Colorado, where well-behaved students make their parents and teachers proud, and the football team never—ever—loses. But soon, some of the parents in Silverdale will begin to uncover the unimaginable secret that can turn a loving child murderous . . .

"It's two in the morning, Chuck. And Jeff isn't home yet."

Chuck groaned. "And for that you woke me up? Jeez, Char, when I was his age, I was out all night half the time."

"Maybe you were," Charlotte replied tightly. "And maybe your parents didn't care. But I do, and I'm about to call the police."

At that, Chuck came completely awake. "What the hell do you want to do a thing like that for?" he demanded, switching on the light and staring at Charlotte as if he thought she'd lost her mind.

"Because I'm worried about him," Charlotte flared, concern for her son overcoming her fear of her husband's tongue. "Because I don't like what's been happening with him and I don't like the way he's been acting. And I certainly don't like not knowing where he is at night!"

Clutching the robe protectively to her throat, she turned and hurried out of the bedroom. She was already downstairs when Chuck, shoving his own arms into the sleeves of an ancient woolen robe he'd insisted on keeping despite its frayed edges and honeycomb of moth holes, caught up with her.

"Now just hold on," he said, taking the phone from her hands and putting it back on the small desk in the den. "I'm not going to have you getting Jeff into trouble with the police just because you want to mother-hen him."

"Mother-hen him!" Charlotte repeated. "For God's sake, Chuck! He's only seventeen years old! And it's the middle of the night, and there's nowhere in Silverdale he could be! Everything's closed. So unless he's already in trouble, where is he?"

"Maybe he stayed overnight with a friend," Chuck began, but Charlotte shook her head.

"He hasn't done that since he was a little boy. And if he had, he would have called." Even as she uttered the words, she knew she didn't believe them. A year ago—a few months ago; even a few weeks ago—she would have trusted Jeff to keep her informed of where he was and what he was doing. But now? She didn't know.

Nor could she explain her worries to Chuck, since he insisted on believing there was nothing wrong; that Jeff was simply growing up and testing his wings.

As she was searching for the right words, the words to express her fears without further rousing her husband's anger, the front door opened and Jeff came in.

He'd already closed the door behind him and started up the stairs when he caught sight of his parents standing in the den in their bathrobes, their eyes fixed on him. He gazed at them stupidly for a second, almost as if he didn't recognize them, and for a split-second Charlotte thought he looked stoned.

"Jeff?" she said. Then, when he seemed to pay no attention to her, she called out again, louder this time. "Jeff!"

His eyes hooded, her son turned to gaze at her. "What?" he asked, his voice taking on the same sullen tone that had become so familiar to her lately.

"I want an explanation," Charlotte went on. "It's after two A.M., and I want to know where you've been."

"Out," Jeff said, and started to turn away.

"Stop right there, young man!" Charlotte commanded. She marched into the foyer and stood at the bottom of the stairs, then reached out and switched on the chandelier that hung in the stair-well. A bright flood of light bathed Jeff's face, and Charlotte gasped. His face was streaked with dirt, and on his cheeks there were smears of blood. There were black circles under Jeff's eyes—as if he hadn't slept in days—and he was breathing hard, his chest heaving as he panted.

Then he lifted his right hand to his mouth, and before he began sucking on his wounds, Charlotte could see that the skin was torn away from his knuckles.

"My God," she breathed, her anger suddenly draining away. "Jeff, what's happened to you?"

His eyes narrowed. "Nothing," he mumbled, and once more started to mount the stairs.

"Nothing?" Charlotte repeated. She turned to Chuck, now standing in the door to the den, his eyes, too, fixed on their son. "Chuck, look at him. Just look at him!"

"You'd better tell us what happened, son," Chuck said. "If you're in some kind of trouble—"

Jeff whirled to face them, his eyes now blazing with the same anger that had frightened Linda Harris earlier that evening. "I don't know what's wrong!" he shouted. "Linda broke up with me tonight, okay? And it pissed me off! Okay? So I tried to smash up a tree and I went for a walk. *Okay?* Is that okay with you, Mom?"

"Jeff—" Charlotte began, shrinking away from her son's sudden fury. "I didn't mean . . . we only wanted to—"

But it was too late.

"Can't you just leave me alone?" Jeff shouted.

He came off the bottom of the stairs, towering over the much smaller form of his mother. Then, with an abrupt movement, he reached out and roughly shoved Charlotte aside, as if swatting a fly. She felt a sharp pain in her shoulder as her body struck the wall, and then she collapsed to the floor. For a split-second Jeff stared blankly at his mother, as if he was puzzled about what had happened to her, and then, an anguished wail boiling up from somewhere deep within him, he turned and slammed out the front door.

Secret rituals masked in science . . . hidden cellars where steel cages gleam coldly against the dark . . . a cry of unfathomable rage and pain . . . In Silverdale no one is safe from . . . Creature.

John Saul is "a writer with the touch for raising gooseflesh," says the *Detroit News,* **and bestseller after bestseller has proved over and over his mastery for storytelling and his genius at creating heart-stopping suspense. Enter his chilling world, and prepare to realize your own hidden fears . . .**

Available wherever Bantam paperbacks are sold!

(And now, turn the page
for an exciting preview of John Saul's new
masterpiece of terror, SECOND CHILD.)

An isolated enclave on the coast of
provides the eerie backdrop
to this terrifying tale . . .

SECOND CHILD
by John Saul

Secret Cove. Here, ruggedly beautiful and remote, bordered by dark woods and deserted beaches, a postcard-perfect village harbors the mansions of the wealthy—families who have summered in splendid seclusion at Secret Cove for generations.

Secret Cove. Here, one hundred years ago, on the night of the annual August Moon Ball, a shy and lovely servant girl committed a single, unspeakable act of violence. An act so shocking its legacy lives still in Secret Cove.

And now, long after the horror of that night has faded to shuddery legend, a tale whispered by children around summer campfires, an unholy terror is about to be reborn. Now, in Secret Cove, one family is about to feel the icy hand of supernatural fear . . . as Melissa Holloway, shy and troubled and just thirteen years old, comes to know the blood-drenched secret that waits behind a locked attic door. . . .

...MacIver awoke just before dawn that morning, she ...e slightest presentiment that she was about to die. As her ...swam lazily in the ebbing tide of sleep, she found herself ...ggling silently at the memory of the dream that had just roused her. It had been Thanksgiving Day in the dream, and the house was filled with people. Some of them were familiar to her. Tom was sprawled out on the floor, his big frame stretched in front of the fireplace as he studied a chessboard on which Teri had apparently trapped his queen. Teri herself was sitting cross-legged on the carpet, grinning impudently at her father's predicament. There were others scattered around the living room—more, indeed, than Polly would have thought the room could hold. But the dream had had a logic of its own, and it hadn't seemed to matter how many people, strange and familiar, had come in—the room seemed magically to expand for them. It was a happy occasion filled with good cheer until Polly had gone to the kitchen to inspect the dinner. [There, disaster awaited her.] She must have turned the oven too high, for curls of smoke were drifting up from the corners of the door. But as she bent over to open the oven door, she was not concerned, for exactly the same thing had happened too many times before. For Polly, cooking was an art she had never come close to mastering. She opened the door and, sure enough, thick smoke poured out into the kitchen, engulfing her, then rolling on through the small dining room and into the living room, where the coughing of her guests and the impatient yowl of her daughter finally jarred her awake.

The memory of the dream began to fade from her mind, and Polly stretched languidly, then rolled over to snuggle against the warmth of Tom's body. Outside, a summer storm was building, and just as she was about to drift back into sleep, a bolt of lightning slashed through the faint grayness of dawn, instantly followed by a thunderclap that jerked her fully awake. She sat straight up in bed, gasping in shock at the sharp retort.

Instantly, she was seized by a fit of coughing as smoke filled her lungs.

Her eyes widened with sudden fear. The smoke was real, not a vestige of the dream.

A split second later she heard the crackling of flames.

Throwing the covers back, Polly grabbed her husband's shoulder and shook him violently. "Tom! Tom!"

With what seemed like agonizing slowness, Tom rolled over, moaned, then reached out to her. She twisted away from him, fumbling for the lamp on her nightstand before she found the switch.

Nothing happened.

"Tom!" she screamed, her voice rising with the panic building inside her. "Wake up! The house is on fire!"

Tom came awake, instantly rising and shoving his arms into the sleeves of his bathrobe.

Polly, wearing nothing but her thin nylon negligee, ran to the door and grasped the knob, only to jerk her hand reflexively away from its searing heat. "Teri!" she moaned, her voice breaking as she spoke her daughter's name. "Oh, God, Tom. We have to get Teri out."

But Tom was already pushing her aside. Wrapped in one of the wool blankets from the bed, he covered the brass doorknob with one of its corners before trying to turn it. Finally he pulled the door open an inch.

Smoke poured through the gap, a penetrating cloud of searing fog that reached toward them with angry fingers, clutching at them, trying to draw them into its suffocating grasp.

Buried in the formless body of smoke was the glowing soul of the fire itself. Polly instinctively shrank away from the monster that had engulfed her home, and when Tom spoke to her, his shouted words seemed to echo dimly from afar.

"I'll get Teri. Go out the window!"

Frozen with terror, Polly saw the door open wider; a split second later her husband disappeared into the maw of the beast that had invaded her home.

The door slammed shut.

Polly wanted to go after him, to follow Tom into the fire, to hold onto him as they went after her daughter. Without thinking, she moved toward the door, but then his words resounded in her mind.

"Go out the window!"

A helpless moan strangling in her throat, she dragged herself across the room to the window and pulled it open. She breathed the fresh air outside, then looked down.

Fifteen feet below her lay the concrete driveway that connected the street in front to the garage behind the house. There was no ledge, no tree, not even a drainpipe to hang onto. If she jumped, surely she would break her legs.

She shrank back from the window and turned to the door once

more. She had started across the smoke-filled room when her foot touched something soft.

The bedspread, lying in a heap at the foot of the bed. She snatched it up, wrapping it around her body, then, like Tom a few minutes earlier, used one of its corners to protect her fingers from the searing heat of the door. Drawing her breath in slowly, filtering the smoke through the thick padding of the spread, she filled her lungs with air.

At last, battling with the fear that threatened to overwhelm her, she pulled the door open.

The fire in the hall, instantly sucking in the fresh air from the open window, rose up in front of her, its crackle building into a vicious roar.

Time seemed to slow down, each second dragging itself out for an eternity.

Flames reached out to her, and Polly was helpless to pull herself away as panic clasped her in its paralyzing grip. She felt the burning heat against her face, even felt the blisters begin to form wherever her skin was exposed.

She heard a strange, soft sound, like the sizzling of oil in a hot skillet, and instinctively reached up to touch her hair.

Her hair was gone, devoured by the hungry fire, and she stared blankly for a moment at the ashy residue on her fingertips. What had been a thick mass of dark blond hair only a moment ago was now only an oddly greasy smudge on the blistered skin of her hand.

Her mind began closing down, rejecting what she saw, denying the searing heat that all but overwhelmed her.

She staggered backward, the bedspread tangling around her feet as if it had joined forces with the fire to destroy her.

Faintly, as if in the distance somewhere impossibly far beyond the confines of the house, she heard Tom's voice, calling out to Teri.

She heard vague thumpings, as if he might be pounding on a door somewhere.

Then nothing.

Nothing but the hiss and chatter of the flames, dancing before her, hypnotizing her.

Backing away, stumbling and tripping, she retreated from the fury of the fire.

She bumped into something, something hard and ungiving, and though her eyes remained fixed on the inferno that was already invading the bedroom, her hand groped behind her.

And felt nothing.

Panic seized her again, for suddenly the familiar space of the bedroom seemed to vanish, leaving her alone with the consuming flames.

Slowly, her mind assembling information piece by piece, she realized that she had reached the open window.

Whimpering, she sat down on the ledge and began to swing her legs through the gap between the sill and the open casement; her right leg first, then her left.

At last she was able to turn her back on the fire. Gripping the window frame, she stared out into the faintly graying dawn for a moment, then let her gaze shift downward toward the concrete below.

She steeled herself, and clinging to the bedspread, let herself slip over the ledge.

Just as she began to drop away from the window, the corner of the bedspread still inside the room caught on something. Polly felt the pull, found herself unreasonably speculating on what might have snagged it.

The handle of the radiator?

A stray nail that had worked loose from the floor molding?

Falling! Suddenly she was upside down, slipping out of the shroud of the bedspread.

Her fingers grasped at the material; it slipped away as if coated with oil.

She dropped toward the concrete headfirst, only beginning to raise her arms to break her fall as her skull crashed against the driveway.

She felt nothing; no pain at all.

There was only a momentary sense of surprise, and a small cracking sound from within her neck as her vertebrae shattered and crushed her spinal cord.

It had been no more than three minutes since she had awakened, laughing quietly, from her dream.

Now the quiet laughter was over, and Polly MacIver was dead.

Teri MacIver stood rooted on the lawn in front of the house, her right hand clutching at the lapels of her thin terry-cloth bathrobe with all the modesty of her nearly fifteen years. Her eyes were fixed on the blaze that now engulfed the small two-story house that had been her home for the last ten years. It was an old house, built fifty years earlier when San Fernando had still been a small farming town in the California valley of the same name. Built entirely of wood, the house had baked in the sun for half a century, its wood slowly turning into tinder, and tonight, when the fire had started, the flames had raced through the rooms with a speed that stunned

Teri. It was as if one moment the house had been whole; the next it had been swallowed by flames.

Teri was only vaguely aware of what was going on around her. In the distance, a siren wailed, growing steadily louder, but Teri barely heard it. Her mind was filled with the roar of the fire, and the crackling of the siding as it curled back upon itself and began to fall away from the framework of the house, venting the interior to the fresh air that only fed the raging flames.

Her parents.

Where were they? Had they gotten out? Forcing her eyes away from the oddly hypnotic inferno, she glanced around. Down the block, someone was running toward her, but the figure was no more than a shadow in the breaking dawn.

Voices began to penetrate her consciousness then, people shouting to each other, asking each other what had happened.

Then, over the roar of the fire and the babble of voices, she heard a scream. It came from the house, seemingly unmuffled by the already crumbling walls. The sharp sound released Teri from her paralysis, and she ran around to the driveway, her eyes wide as she stared up to the second floor and her parents' bedroom.

She saw her mother, a dark silhouette against the glow of the fire. She was wrapped in something—a blanket, perhaps, or the bedspread. Teri watched as her mother's legs came over the windowsill, and a second later she saw her jump . . . then turn in the air as the bedspread tightened around her legs.

Her mother seemed to hang for a moment, suspended in midair. A scream built in Teri's throat, only to be cut off a second later as her mother slid free from the swaddles and plunged headfirst to the driveway below.

Had she heard the sound as her mother's head struck the concrete, or did she imagine it?

Teri began running then, but her feet were mired in mud, it seemed to take forever before she reached the spot where her mother lay crumpled and still on the driveway, one arm flung out as if reaching out to her daughter, as if even in death she were grasping for life.

"M-Mom?" Teri stammered, her hand falling away from her robe to tentatively touch her mother. Then her voice rose to an anguished wail. *"M-o-m!"*

There was no response, and as Teri became aware of someone running up the sidewalk, she threw herself on Polly's body, cradling her mother's head in her lap, stroking the blistered cheek of the woman who only a few hours ago had stroked her own before kissing her good night. "No," she whimpered, her eyes flooding with tears. "Oh, no. Please, God, don't let Mommy die." But even as she uttered the words, Teri already knew somewhere deep inside her that it was too late, that her mother was already gone.

She felt gentle hands on her shoulders and slowly looked up to see Lucy Barrow, from across the street. "She's dead." Teri's voice broke as she spoke the words. The admission seemed to release a tide of emotion that had been locked inside her. Covering her face with her hands, she began to sob, her body shaking.

Lucy, her own mind all but numbed by the sight of Polly Mac-Iver's seared and broken body, pulled Teri to her feet and began leading her back down the driveway. "Your father . . ." she said. "Where's your father? Did he get out?"

Teri's hands dropped away from her face. For a moment her shocked eyes flickered with puzzlement. She started to speak, but before the words emerged from her mouth there was a sharp crack, followed instantly by a crash.

Lucy Barrow grasped Teri's arm tightly, pulling her down the driveway as the roof of the house collapsed into the fire and the flames shot up into the brightening sky.

Three fire trucks clogged the street in front of the MacIvers' house, and a tangle of hoses snaked along the sidewalk to the hydrant on the corner. An ambulance had taken Polly's body away more than an hour before, but as more and more neighbors arrived to gape in dazed horror at the smoldering ruins of the house, others would point with macabre fascination to the spot where Teri's mother had plunged to her death. The newcomers would stare at the driveway for a few seconds, visualizing the corpse and imagining with a shudder, the panic Polly must have felt as she died.

Did she know, at least, that her daughter had survived the fire? No, of course not.

Heads shook sadly; tongues clucked with sympathy. Then the attention of the crowd shifted back to the smoking wreckage. Most of the beams still stood, and parts of the second floor had held intact even when the roof collapsed. Now, as sunlight cast the ruins into sharp relief, the house looked like a desiccated blackened skeleton.

Teri, who had spent the last two hours sitting mutely in the Barrows' living room, unable to pull her eyes away from the spectacle of the fire, finally emerged onto the porch. Next to her, Lucy Barrow hovered protectively, her voice trembling as she tried to convince Teri to go back inside.

"I can't," whispered Teri. "I have to find my father. He—He's—" Her voice broke off, but her eyes returned to the ruins across the street.

Lucy Barrow unconsciously bit her lip in a vain attempt to take some of Teri's pain onto herself. "He might have gotten out," she ventured, her quavering voice belying her words.

Teri said nothing, but started once more across the street, still clad in the bathrobe she'd worn when she escaped the inferno. An eerie silence fell over the block, the murmurs of the bystanders dying away as she moved steadily through the crowd, which parted silently to let her pass.

At last Teri came to the front yard of what had been her home. She stood still staring at the charred wood of the house's framework and the blackened bricks of its still-standing chimney. She took a tentative step toward the remains of the front porch, then felt a firm hand on her arm.

"You can't go in there, miss."

Teri's breath caught, but she turned to look into the kindly gray eyes of one of the firemen. "M-My father—" she began.

"We're going in now," the fireman said. "If he's in there, we'll find him."

Without a word, Teri watched as two firefighters, clad in heavily padded overcoats, their hands protected by thick gloves, worked their way carefully into the wreckage. The front door had been chopped away, and inside, the base of the stairway was clearly visible. The men started up, testing each step before trusting it to hold their weight. After what seemed an eternity, they finally reached the second floor. They moved through the house, visible first through one window, then another. From one of the rooms an entire wall, along with most of the floor, had burned away. As the firemen gingerly moved from beam to beam, they appeared to be balanced on some kind of blackened scaffolding. At last they moved out of Teri's sight as they carefully worked their way toward her room at the back of the house.

Ten minutes later the fireman with the kind, gray eyes emerged from the front door and approached Teri, who stood waiting, her eyes fixed on him.

"I'm sorry," he said, his voice made gruff by the memory of the charred remains of Tom MacIver which he had found in front of the still-closed door to Teri's bedroom at the back of the house. "He was trying to get you out. He didn't know you'd already gotten away." His large hand rested reassuringly on Teri's shoulder for a moment, but then he turned away and began issuing the orders for Tom MacIver's body to be removed from the ruins.

Teri stood where she was for a few more seconds. Her eyes remained fixed on the house as if she were still uncertain of the truth of what she had just been told. Finally Lucy Barrow's voice penetrated her thoughts.

"We have to call someone for you," Lucy said. "We have to call your family."

Teri turned away from the smoldering rubble. She stared blankly at Lucy. For a moment Lucy wasn't certain Teri had heard her, but then Teri spoke.

"My father," she breathed. "Will someone please call my father?"

Dear Lord, Lucy thought. She doesn't understand. She hasn't grasped what happened. She slipped her arms around Teri and held her close. "Oh, darling," she whispered. "He didn't get out. That's what the fireman was telling you. I—I'm sorry," she finished, wondering at the helpless inadequacy of the words. "I'm just so sorry."

Teri was motionless in her arms for a second, then pulled away, shaking her head.

"N-Not him," she said. "We need to call my real father." She wrenched away from Lucy's protective embrace, her gaze returning to the house, where three men were already working to retrieve Tom MacIver's body. "He was my stepfather," Teri said. "He adopted me when I was only four. Now we have to call my real father."

As Charles Holloway gazed at the charred remains of the MacIvers' house, he knew that everything had changed. Teri, the daughter he had not seen for so many years, was about to be transported across the country and thrust into an unfamiliar environment, filled with unfamiliar people. And he suspected that Polly had never prepared her daughter for what life would be like in the East. After all, why should she have?

He turned away from the blackened pile of rubble and crossed the street to the house bearing the address he'd scrawled on a scrap of paper earlier that morning. It was no different from the rest of the houses on the block—a small frame structure, modest, but substantial-looking. As he mounted the short flight of steps to its front porch, he found himself wondering if it would burn as fast as Polly's house had.

He suspected it would.

Charles pressed the button next to the front door and heard a soft chime sound inside. A moment later the door opened and a plump woman peered out at him. "Mrs. Barrow?" he said through the screen door. "I'm Charles Holloway. Teri's father."

Instantly, the door opened wider, and Lucy Barrow pushed the screen door open, too. "Mr. Holloway," she breathed, her relief apparent in her voice. "Thank God—I just don't know what to say. It's all been so terrible, and when Teri told me to call you—" she broke off and stood almost still for a moment, her fluttering hands betraying her confusion. "I—Well, I'm afraid none of us even knew you existed. I mean, Polly and Tom never told us—" Once again she fell silent.

Charles reached out to take her arm, gently guiding her toward her own living room. "It's all right, Mrs. Barrow," he told her. "I understand what you must have thought. It's . . ." And then his own words died in his throat as they stepped over the threshold and he saw Teri, huddled in a corner of the couch, her thin robe wrapped tightly around her slender body. Her eyes, wide and uncertain, were fixed on him, and she seemed to be holding her breath, as if she had been waiting to see if he would actually come for her.

For a long moment neither of them said a word. Then Teri stirred on the couch and got uncertainly to her feet. Her mouth opened, and when at last she spoke, her voice was rough, as though she'd spent most of the day crying. "F-Father?"

Choking with emotion, Charles strode across the room in three quick steps and slipped his arms around the girl. She stiffened for a moment, but then seemed to relax, her face resting against his chest. He clumsily stroked her hair, then tipped her face up so he could look into it. "It's all right, Teri," he whispered. "I'm here, and you're not alone, and I'm going to make everything better for you." He held her close again, and though he couldn't see her face as she pressed it once more against his chest, he imagined he could feel a tiny smile breaking through her grief.

Until this moment, he knew, she must have felt totally alone in the world.

Alone and terrified.

Charles switched off the television set in his room at the Red Lion Inn and rolled over, checking the alarm clock on the night-stand. It was eleven-thirty, and the alarm was set for six. He punched at the too-hard pillow that modern hotels seem to special-ize in, then picked up the murder mystery he'd been putting him-self to sleep with for the last month. So far he'd only managed to get through a hundred pages, which meant he'd been sleeping pretty well. But tonight he suspected he'd read at least twenty-five more. Well, just a few more days and he'd be back home.

He read a couple of paragraphs, then found himself distracted by a muffled sound from the next room. He listened for a moment, put the book aside and went to the door that separated his room from Teri's. A moment later he heard the sound again. This time he recognized it.

Teri was crying.

Pulling his bathrobe on and tying the belt around his waist, he opened the door and slipped into the other room. The lights were out, but in the glow of his own table lamp he could see Teri, curled up tightly in her bed, her arms clutching at the pillow. He moved to the bedside, eased himself down onto the bed itself and laid his hand on his eldest daughter's shoulder. "Teri? Honey? Are you all right?"

Teri rolled over onto her back and stared up at him through moist eyes. "I—I'm sorry," she said. "I was just feeling sort of lonely. I didn't mean to wake you up."

"You didn't," Charles assured her. "You should have come in."

"I didn't want to bother you," Teri breathed. "I mean, you already had to come all the way out here, and—" Her voice broke and she choked back a sob.

Charles gathered her into his arms, rocking her gently. "It's not a bother at all, and I don't ever want you to think that. I'm your father, and I love you." He felt Teri stiffen slightly in his arms, and then she pulled away enough to look searchingly up into his face.

"You do?" she said, her voice tinged with uncertainty.

"Of course I do," Charles said.

"Th-That's not what Mom said."

Charles frowned in the half darkness of the room. "What do you mean, that's not what your mother said."

Teri choked back another sob. "Sh-She said you only loved Melissa now. She said that's why you never sent me letters, or presents for Christmas or my birthday."

Charles froze. Was it possible? Could Polly really have said something like that? But it wasn't true. "Honey, what are you talking about?" he asked. "I've always sent you letters, and I never forgot your birthday or Christmas at all. Every year I've sent you a package. Didn't you get them?"

Teri shook her head. "I—I wasn't even sure you'd come today."

"Oh, Lord," Charles groaned, pulling her close once again. "No wonder you were crying. You must have been terrified."

"Y-You don't have to take me home if you don't want to," Teri said. "I can stay here—I have friends, and I can get a job. . . ."

Charles gently pressed a hand over her mouth to stop the flow of words. "I don't even want to hear anything like that," he said, feeling a sudden flash of anger toward his ex-wife. It was one thing to cut herself off from her past, but to try to alienate Teri from him was unforgivable. No wonder he'd never gotten a letter from Teri— she thought he didn't want to hear from him. "Now listen to me," he said, doing his best to keep the anger out of his voice. "I don't know why your mother would tell you something like that, but it isn't true. I never stopped loving you, and I never stopped thinking about you. And there was certainly never a question about my coming for you. You're my daughter, and you always have been. I've missed you every day you've been gone, and I've hated never seeing you. As for the letters and the presents, I can't imagine why your mother kept them from you. Why, just last Christmas I sent you a pearl necklace. It was beautiful—pink pearls, perfectly matched. And there were others, too. Toys when you were little—clothes—all kinds of things. So you mustn't think you're alone. You still have a father, and now you have a stepmother, and a sister, too."

Teri sat up now, propping herself up against the headboard. Nervously, she peered at Charles. "A sister," she whispered. "What's she like?"

Charles smiled in the darkness. "You'll love her. Yesterday was her thirteenth birthday, and she's the nicest girl you'll ever meet. In fact, she wanted me to tell you how sorry she is about what happened, but that the one thing she's always wanted is a sister. Now she has one."

Teri shifted uneasily in the bed. "But—But what if she doesn't like me?"

Charles reached out and took her hand, squeezing it gently. "Of course she'll like you," he said. "She'll love you just as much as I do."

They talked for a few more minutes, and slowly Teri calmed down, her sobs dying away. At last Charles tucked her in and kissed her good night. "And remember," he said, "if you get lonely again, you come in and wake me up."

Teri nodded. When Charles left the room, closing the door behind him, she lay still in the darkness for a few minutes, thinking.

Thinking about her mother.

Her mother, and her stepfather.

And her real father.

In a way, tonight was no different from all the other nights when she'd lain awake in her bed, trying to figure out why her mother had left her real father. It seemed to her that everything had been perfect back when they had all lived together in the huge house by the sea. Of course, she couldn't remember it now—she had been so small when the divorce had come. But even though she'd been away from Secret Cove for most of her life, deep inside she still thought of it as her real home, the place where she truly belonged.

And now she was going home again.

If only her mother could be going with her. Then everything would be the way it had been when she was a baby. Everything would be perfect. . . .

She determinedly put the thought out of her mind, refusing to dwell on the impossible.

She rolled over and tried to go to sleep, but sleep would not come. Finally, she reached out and turned on the lamp on the nightstand. Leaving the bed, she padded over to the closet and reached into the pocket of her bathrobe. When she went back to bed, she was carrying the only thing she had taken with her when she'd fled the blazing house.

She held it in her hand, studying it carefully.

It was a string of perfectly matched pink pearls.

She stared at them for a long time, fingering their smooth surfaces, rubbing them gently against her face. When she finally went to sleep an hour later, the pearl necklace was still in her hand.

**Now read the complete book,
available wherever Bantam Books are sold!**

ABOUT THE AUTHOR

JOHN SAUL is the author of twelve previous novels which have been million-copy-plus national paperback bestsellers: *Suffer the Children, Punish the Sinners, Cry for the Strangers, Comes the Blind Fury, When the Wind Blows, The God Project, Nathaniel, Brainchild, Hellfire, The Unwanted, The Unloved,* and *Creature. Second Child,* published in June 1990, has been a *New York Times* bestseller in hardcover. His latest novel is *Sleepwalk.* John Saul lives in Seattle, Washington, where he is at work on his next novel.

John Saul is "a writer with the touch for raising gooseflesh."
—Detroit News

John Saul has produced one bestseller after another: masterful tales of terror and psychological suspense. Each of his works is as shocking, as intense and as stunningly real as those that preceded it.